BOOK 1 IN THE KINGDOM SERIES

KINGDOM

OF

DANA GRICKEN

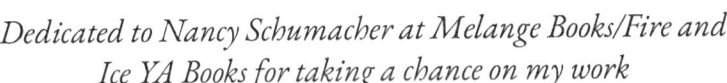

Dedicated to Nancy Schumacher at Melange Books/Fire and Ice YA Books for taking a chance on my work

1

ARRIVAL AT V CASTLE

I clutched the railing of our houseboat, trying not to vomit as we sped toward the lone island in the distance.

I always became seasick whenever we went out on the water. I first found out about that annoying little quirk when I was a kid. Dad had taken me and Mom out on a rented boat for the Fourth of July, and I hurled all over his shoes.

Dad. Oh, how I missed him.

I didn't want to reek of barf when I met a king, so I took deep breaths and tried not to glance at the water. The boat was over-crowded, carrying me, Mom, Vanessa, and our suitcases across the Indian Ocean. Russell Donahue, though he insisted we call him Russ, was our family's main bodyguard back home and for this mission. I always had a sinking suspicion he had a crush on Mom, and judging by his longing gaze on the back of her head, I felt pretty sure. Not that he'd ever admit it out loud and risk his job and friendship with her.

"How are you doing, sweetie?" Mom asked, glancing over at me.

"I've felt better," I muttered, closing my eyes. "Really regretting eating all those tacos last night."

"Well, you'd better keep them down," Vanessa said. "These are brand new shoes Daddy bought me. If you ruin them, you're paying for new ones!"

My lids snapped open to roll my eyes at Vanessa. She and I had been best friends since we were kids, growing up together at a private school back in Washington, D.C. Her mother was the one and only President Janet Bennett while her father was Dr. Derek Bennett, the First Gentleman and one of the most renowned surgeons in the United States. My mother and hers were close, with Mom working at the White House as a secretary until the president bumped her up to ambassador for this historic peace-keeping mission. It paid to have friends in high places.

Vanessa and I couldn't have been more different than night and day. Her with her bright pink dresses, and me in my ripped t-shirt and jeans, she was the only one I trusted with all my secrets. Opposites attracted. The president had sent her on this mission with us in the hopes that she might mature out of the boy-crazy, fashion-obsessed seventeen-year-old that she was. I told the president not to hold her breath.

Mom wasn't too thrilled I had spoken that way to the president of the United States.

"We're almost there," Russell said as he steered the boat, pointing at the kingdom up ahead. "Just hold on a little longer, Olivia."

"Why couldn't we have taken an airplane or something?" I asked.

Mom shook her head. "The kingdom's only accessible by boat. It's rumored they did that to deter visitors."

"Then why are they so eager to have us here now?"

Mom shrugged. "I don't know. President Bennett sent me here to find out. Their people sent us a letter, inviting us to their castle in the hopes of an alliance, so maybe they've changed their minds."

"I hope so," I muttered. "Good thing you brought Russ just in case."

As our boat reached the harbor, I breathed a sigh of relief. Solid ground, the thing I missed most since leaving Washington. I was the first one off the boat, grabbing my suitcases and backpack of art supplies. Vanessa followed with her bright pink suitcases as I fell to my knees, relishing the feel of grass on my skin. She whistled at the kingdom.

"This place is beautiful," Vanessa said. "Maybe I won't mind spending my summer vacation here after all."

I finally looked up, taking it all in. The spire of the castle was the first thing I noticed. A flock of crows circled it, then disappeared into the clear blue sky. The castle was the tallest building in the kingdom, gleaming black under the sunlight. A pathway of white brick trailed through the city, leading to hundreds of little shops and homes in the village. A string of lanterns hanging from the trees gave everything an otherworldly glow. Behind the castle, I spotted more trees that led to a lush forest. I could smell the sweet flowers and hear birds chirping.

If I believed in Heaven, I was pretty sure I'd found it. The kingdom was like something out of the 1800s, Victorian and elegant, untouched by the passage of time.

"Not bad for a first job," Mom said, helping Russell grab the rest of the suitcases. "I want this visit to go well. First contact is exciting, but tricky. Promise me you two will be on your best behavior."

"We promise," me and Vanessa said at the same time.

Mom scoffed. "I've heard that before all your shenanigans, so I hope you mean it this time. Remember, obey all their rules and be respectful..."

As Mom prattled on about etiquette, we spotted several figures walking toward us. They looked like servants with smiles on their faces, accompanied by a tall, dark-haired man in silver armor. He didn't smile. The guards in similar armor didn't, either. They wore shades of red and black which mirrored their kingdom's flag that billowed in the distance.

"King Dominic's asked me to show you the way to the castle," the dark-haired man said. "I take it you're the ambassador we were expecting?"

Mom nodded. "Yes, my name is Linda Hawthorne, and this is my daughter, Olivia. I also have the president's daughter with me, Vanessa Bennett, and our bodyguard, Russell Donahue."

"I'm General Ezra Alucard, leader of the militia," he replied. "Did the president not come with you?"

Mom shook her head. "President Bennett is very busy with other matters. She'll be here next week with her husband. She sent me in her place to begin the peace talks in the meantime."

"I see. Too bad about the president. We were looking forward to meeting her today," General Ezra replied. "We need to check your bags. Can't be too careful with security."

"Go ahead," Mom said. "Girls, open your suitcases."

Me and Vanessa both obliged—reluctantly. As one of the militia guards went through my backpack, tossing around my art supplies with the gracefulness of a bull in a China shop, I stepped forward. "Hey, be careful with that! Paint and easels don't come cheap, you know."

The guard looked up at me, hissing in anger. I crossed my arms, refusing to back down. Russell stepped forward immediately, ready to attack if the guard tried to hurt me, but Mom placed a hand on his arm to hold him back.

"Forgive my daughter's outburst," Mom said. "We're all a little on edge. The boat ride was long and stressful."

"We understand," General Ezra said, glaring at his guard. "They clearly don't have any weapons. Stop touching their things."

The guard backed off, but his gaze remained on me. I found it creepy. Vanessa's gaze briefly flitted to mine, and I knew she was thinking the same thing.

"Come," General Ezra said. "I'll show you to your rooms. After that, you can meet the king and our family in the dining hall. I'm sure you're all starving."

As General Ezra began walking away, his guards and servants in tow, we picked up our suitcases and followed. As we took the brick path to the castle, I finally noticed the people on the streets. They also wore dark colors with long dresses and jackets that seemed old-fashioned and stared at us as we passed.

"These people need a serious makeover," Vanessa whispered to me. "Looks like their closet is stuck in the medieval ages..."

"You said *our* family before," Mom said, glancing at the general. "What did you mean?"

"King Dominic is my brother," General Ezra said, without emotion.

"Well, it's an honor to meet someone in the royal family," Mom said. "Should we have bowed?"

"No. My brother is royalty, not me," General Ezra said. "I'm a fighter, always have been, always will be. My place is in the militia."

Mom didn't try to ask him any more questions after that. The general didn't seem too interested in answering them, anyway. I hoped the king would be friendlier.

General Ezra opened the chamber doors to the castle, and we walked into the foyer. It seemed much larger on the inside with dozens of hallways like mazes and black-and-white checkered flooring. The walls were a deep red and held paintings of another dark-haired man in a crown who I assumed was King Dominic. The resemblance of him and Ezra was striking, except the king was smiling.

"Inform the king our guests have arrived," General Ezra said, and the servants nodded before scurrying away. He glanced back at us. "This way."

We continued to follow the general, taking a right down a long corridor. There were a number of private rooms waiting for us. I prayed I wouldn't have to share one with Mom or Vanessa.

"Let the servants know if you need anything," General Ezra said. "Since there are only four of you, you'll have your own private quarters. Each comes with an adjoining bathroom."

"Thank God," I muttered, turning to Vanessa. "You take eight years to do your hair in the morning."

"Being *this* beautiful comes with a price, Liv. You'd know that if you weren't such a tomboy," Vanessa said, flicking her blonde hair over her shoulder. "With the right make-up and hairspray, I could make you look this fabulous, too."

I scoffed. "Never in a million years, Ness."

"Girls, stop bickering," Mom whispered, glancing nervously at the general. "It's not polite."

"In half an hour, we'll be meeting for breakfast in the dining hall," General Ezra said, ignoring us. His blank expression made it hard to read his emotions. "The king eagerly awaits your presence."

As the general walked away, his loud boots clunking down the hallway, Vanessa turned to me. "Not very friendly. And what's with that guard's weird hissing? Are they cat people or something?"

"The kingdom of V has been isolated from the world for centuries," Mom said. "You can't expect them to be completely trusting of us. For now, we'll have to earn their friendship *and* their respect. Unpack your things and get to the dining hall. And please, no more bickering, at least, not in front of our hosts."

Mom chose the room on the far left while Vanessa took the one on the right. As Russell disappeared inside his room, I sighed and entered mine, leaving the door open. It was smaller than my bedroom at home, with a single bed, an armoire, and a door that led into the bathroom. A tiny window sat above my bed, but the dark curtains kept out the sunlight.

As I unpacked my clothes and set up my easel, I realized there wasn't a television, phone, or computer. Come to think of it, I hadn't seen any kind of technology. I turned on my smartphone but couldn't get a signal and didn't see a plug anywhere.

Did they not like the sunlight? And how did they live without technology? I was right before. This kingdom *was* trapped in the 1800s. I groaned, realizing it was going to be a long vacation.

I checked my watch. I still had a few minutes to spare, and seeing the beauty of the kingdom had given me a sudden burst of inspiration, so I decided to start a new painting. Before I knew it, I was completely sucked into it and had lost all concept of time. When I heard footsteps entering my room behind me, I sighed.

"I'm coming, Mom," I muttered, putting the paintbrush down. "No need to fetch me like a child—"

As I spun around, I realized it wasn't Mom at all. A boy stood in front of me who couldn't have been any older than I was. He had dark hair like General Ezra with brown eyes and flecks of gold in them. He wore black pants with a leather jacket, and I noticed the ripple of muscles in his arms. He glanced at me and then back at the painting, his expression unreadable.

"Sorry," I muttered, trying to stay friendly for Mom's sake. "Thought you were someone else."

He glanced down at the paint on my hands. "Are you an artist?"

I shrugged. "I like to paint. Not sure if I'm good enough to be called an artist yet."

He stepped closer to the painting, admiring it. Then he smiled. "You're very good. You should have more confidence in yourself. We don't have any artists here. Their skills aren't needed."

"Uh, thanks, I guess. Too bad about your lack of artists," I said. "Who are you?"

"Christian," he replied, stepping back to look at me. "And you?"

"Olivia. Olivia Hawthorne," I replied. "I'm Linda Hawthorne's daughter. You know, the American ambassador?"

He nodded. "I know. I watched you get off the boat. I also saw your altercation with one of the guards."

"It wasn't really an altercation. I just don't like people touching my stuff, that's all," I said. "Sorry if I—"

"Don't apologize. The guards here are trained well, but sometimes, they can get out of line. If it happens again, tell me and I'll handle it," Christian said, much to my surprise. "Anyway, *I* should apologize for barging into your room uninvited. But when I walked by and saw you painting...well, I couldn't resist. As I said, we have no artists around here. You should be proud of your talent."

I didn't know what to say. I usually wasn't the one to get speechless and giddy around boys. That was more Vanessa's thing, but Christian was handsome, and no one had taken an interest in me or my art in a long time.

"You should get to the dining hall," Christian said, turning around. He looked back at me and smiled. "But it was nice to meet you, and your art. See you later, Olivia."

As he left, I quickly washed the paint off my hands and threw on a dress I had brought. Mom's idea, not mine. It was simple and black. Something that would fit in well. After I looked presentable, I stepped outside my room. Mom, Vanessa, and Russell were already waiting for me. They had changed into nicer clothes for our meeting with the king. As always, Vanessa looked like a million bucks in her pink chiffon gown.

"Nice dress. But hey, I heard voices coming from your room. Thin walls," Vanessa said. "You talking to your paintings again?"

"Come on, I only did that once," I said, my cheeks reddening in embarrassment. "I had a...guest."

"Oh, really?" Vanessa asked, wiggling her eyebrows.

"Not like that," I said, rolling my eyes. "His name was Christian. He saw me painting and wanted to introduce himself."

"Good. You two should try to make friends," Mom said. "If all goes well, the president's hoping to open a permanent embassy. That would mean we'd get to live here."

"What?" I asked. "You said this was only a summer trip!"

"I know what I said," Mom spat, "and keep your voice down, Olivia. This is my dream job and a wonderful opportunity to expand trade for the United States. If there's a chance to stay here, I'm taking it."

"But what about my friends back home? Or our house? We can't sell it—it has too many memories of Dad," I said. "We can't just move to another place, especially in my last year of high school—"

"That's enough," Mom interrupted. "We'll talk about this later."

As she stormed off down the hallway, Russell trailing behind, I turned to Vanessa. "Can you believe that? Living here, permanently?"

"I know. It sucks. Long-distance friendships just don't turn out, either," Vanessa said. "But hey, you'll be eighteen soon. Maybe you could come back to Washington, and we could get an apartment together?"

I didn't know which was worse, living with high-maintenance Vanessa or getting stranded in a foreign country. I said nothing, chasing after Mom down the hallway. Vanessa trailed behind as we followed her into the large dining hall.

As we entered, I noticed the rows of tables with red cloths. Because of the lack of windows and electricity, they had a candelabra burning to light the room. Servants stood nearby with platters of food and drinks, waiting on the King's orders to serve them. He stood next to them in his golden cape and crown. A woman stood next to him with a similar-looking crown, and I assumed she was his wife. She had blond hair, green eyes, and wore a red gown that flowed to the floor.

"Ah, the American ambassador," King Dominic said, shaking Mom's hand with a smile. "It's a pleasure to meet you, Linda. My name is King Dominic Alucard, and this is my wife, Vivienne."

"A pleasure," Vivienne said, bowing.

"This is my personal bodyguard, Dante Draven," the King added, gesturing at the man standing next to him that I hadn't noticed. He looked to be in his early twenties with blond hair, hazel eyes, and a sculpted body. He carried a sword on his belt and dressed similarly to the guards.

Dante nodded at us but didn't speak, his gaze lingering on me. Vanessa noticed and smiled, and I knew I'd get taunted for that later. Dante continued to stare at me as Mom introduced Russell.

"Our son should be here with us, too," King Dominic said, frowning, "but he likes to be fashionably late, no matter how much I insist otherwise. Teenagers can be so stubborn sometimes..."

"Oh, I understand completely," Mom said, glancing in my direction. "Introduce yourselves, girls."

I faked a smile for Mom's sake. "I'm Olivia Hawthorne, and this is my best friend, Vanessa Bennett."

"The president's daughter," King Dominic said, his eyes twinkling at her. "General Ezra told me your mother won't be joining us until next week. Disappointing, but we look forward to her arrival. Anyway, I'm sure you're starving—"

A loud tremor shook underneath our feet. I glanced at Mom, fearfully. "What was that? An earthquake?"

"We don't have earthquakes here," King Dominic said. "I don't know what that was, but I'm sure it was nothing serious—"

General Ezra rushed into the room, several guards following him. "There's been an explosion."

"Was anyone injured?" King Dominic asked.

General Ezra shook his head. "No, but you should see what's happened for yourself."

2

CARNIVOROUS CREATURES

As General Ezra and his guards fled the dining hall, King Dominic bowed at us. "Wait here. I won't be long. Help yourselves to some appetizers in the meantime."

King Dominic, Queen Vivienne, and their bodyguard, Dante Draven, rushed out of the dining hall next. Russell stayed close to us in case of an attack as one of the servants removed the lid to their platter, revealing strips of raw meat. They gestured at me to take one, but the smell of it made me nauseous.

"No thanks," I muttered. "Not hungry, and that's not my kind of food, either."

"What's going on?" Vanessa whispered. "Do you think it's serious?"

"I don't know," I said, turning toward the door, "but I'm about to find out."

Mom grabbed my arm. "You heard the king. He wanted us to wait here."

"And *I* want to find out what's going on," I said, pulling

free from her grasp. "You can stay here, but I can't just sit around while something serious might be going on."

"I'll go with her," Russell said. "Vanessa, Linda, stay here where it's safe. We'll be back soon."

Mom sighed as Russell and I left the dining hall, running down the long hallway to reach the chamber doors. As we exited the castle, I noticed a group of civilians huddled in the distance. All we had to do was follow them to the location of the explosion, and it looked like it led to the docks.

"Excuse me," I muttered, pushing through the people. Russell was hot on my heels. "Coming through."

When we had finally made it through the crowd, I spotted King Dominic, Queen Vivienne, General Ezra, and Dante again. I was right. The explosion *had* come from the docks. They stood near the boat that brought us to their kingdom, and I noticed the flames and smoke coming from it.

Someone had set it on fire.

The King and his people didn't notice us. He bent down, looking closer at the spitting flames. Several of the guards were trying to put it out using buckets of ocean water. I looked up and realized the boy I had met before, Christian, stood there, too. His eyes were as fixated on the flames as the others.

Where had Christian gone after our conversation? Who was he in the kingdom? And was it just a coincidence he had resurfaced *after* our boat erupted in flames?

"What's going on?" I asked. "Are we under attack?"

"Olivia," King Dominic said, looking up at me in surprise. "I asked you and your people to wait in the castle."

"Couldn't help it," I muttered, my eyes lingering on the boat. "Guess that explains the tremor we felt."

"Get back inside," General Ezra said to me, stepping closer. "It isn't safe for you here, and the King gave you an order."

Russell blocked him from getting to me. "She only wants to know what's going on. I do, too."

Everyone was staring at us now, including Dante and Christian. I didn't like all their gazes on me.

"Stand down, General Ezra. Olivia is our guest, not our prisoner. She has a right to know what's happened," King Dominic said, rising to his feet. "There's been a small accident, I'm afraid. It's nothing to worry about, and my guards have the blaze under control."

General Ezra stepped back reluctantly. I heard footsteps behind me and craned my neck to see Mom and Vanessa pushing through next. Mom gasped when she noticed the burning boat.

"What are you guys doing here?" I asked them. "I thought you were staying in the castle."

"Your mom was worried about you out here," Vanessa said, noticing the flaming boat. "I was, too. God, look at our boat...or what's left of it."

"Was it arson?" Mom asked. "Do some of your people not want us here?"

"No. As I told Olivia, this was a simple accident," King Dominic said. "You have nothing to fear from my people— this I promise you. We all agreed it was time to make contact with the outside world, and we're eager to work with your country."

"How are we supposed to get home now?" Vanessa asked. "Our only ride's been destroyed, and you don't look like you have any boats lying around. Why is that?"

"Never had a reason to," General Ezra muttered. "No one comes to our island."

"You said your president will be arriving next week, yes?" King Dominic asked, and Mom nodded. "Her boat can take you back home when you're ready to leave."

"Can I send a message to President Bennett?" Mom asked. "I should inform her of what's happened."

"There's no need. As I said, it was an unfortunate accident that won't happen again," King Dominic said. "Besides, we don't have any means of sending a message."

"What about a computer? Telephone?" Mom asked.

The crowd looked confused.

The King sighed. "I'm afraid we don't possess any of that technology. The only way to send a message is through carrier pigeon as we did to your president. But it could take weeks to arrive, and by then, she'll be here already."

Great. There was no way to get a message to the president or anyone else. If something else happened, would we be completely trapped?

"So that's why I couldn't find a plug for my phone," Vanessa said, holding up her dying smartphone. The people in the crowd looked at it in awe. "What's up with that?"

"Our kingdom was founded in the 1800s," King Dominic said. "Electricity and technology hadn't evolved yet."

"Oh my God," Vanessa muttered, shoving her smartphone in her pocket. "This is a nightmare."

The guards managed to put the fire out, but the boat still reeked of smoke. One side of the hull had completely burned off.

"Did anyone see what happened?" I asked.

"I saw the flames, then the boat exploded," Christian said, his eyes finally meeting mine. "I would've warned someone, but it was too late by then."

"And you didn't see anyone poking around the boat?"

"No," Christian said. "I saw no one."

I had a hard time believing that, but I let it slide, for now. Mom would've probably yelled at me if I went around accusing everyone of arson on my first day.

"Of course not. As I said, this was most likely an accident. Perhaps it was caused by a mechanical issue in your boat," King Dominic said. "Anyhow, the fire has been put out and there's no danger to anyone. I didn't want you to meet my son this way, but since he refused to show up earlier, we have no choice. Ambassador Hawthorne, meet Prince Christian, my only heir to the throne."

My mouth opened in shock. Christian was a prince? I never would've guessed. He certainly didn't look the part. He bowed at Mom and the others before his gaze rested on me.

"Why don't we return to the castle and eat? I'm starving now," King Dominic said. "Go to your room and change, Christian. That outfit simply won't do for a nice meal with our guests."

Christian glared at him but didn't argue, rushing off into the castle. After he had left, Mom and the others followed the King and his people back to the castle. As the crowd cleared out with most people returning home and the guards walking back to their posts, I hung around. I walked along the docks, looking for any signs of arson.

I spotted something near the edge of the docks. As I bent down to pick it up, I realized it was a match. And still smoking, too. I was right. Someone *had* started the fire on purpose.

As Mom suggested, maybe someone didn't want us here. Maybe the King and Christian were in on it.

I didn't know what to do with the match, so I left it where it was. I couldn't confront the king. He'd only deny it again. I could've told Russell, but what were we supposed to do about it now? Sighing, I turned around and nearly smacked into Vanessa.

"What are you doing?" she asked.

I clutched my heart. "You scared me. Why are you out here? I thought you went back inside with everyone else."

"I wanted to wait for you. And don't change the subject."

I gestured at the ocean. "I was just...admiring the water."

"Uh-huh. Sure," she muttered. I didn't want to admit the truth and freak her out. "So...when were you going to tell me your boyfriend was the prince of V?"

I scoffed, making my way back to the castle. Vanessa quickened her pace in her heels to keep up. "He's not my boyfriend. We only talked once. And I didn't know he was a prince. He didn't mention it."

"Well, he hasn't talked to me or anyone else. He must like you," Vanessa said. "And I saw the way that bodyguard looked at you, too. Dante, I think his name was. I didn't expect you to have more guys interested in you than me. Especially two of them. I have to admit, I'm a little jealous, Liv."

I rolled my eyes, opening the chamber doors to the castle. "Don't be. I barely know Christian and Dante hasn't even talked to me. But if you tell Mom or anyone else..."

"Oh, don't worry, your secrets are safe with me," Vanessa said, giggling. "Wouldn't it be great if you and Christian fell in love? You could become the princess, and eventually the queen when his parents die. Maybe then you'd finally wear more dresses, and I could do something with that bird's nest you call hair—"

"I have to go to the bathroom," I said, interrupting her nonsense. "Meet you in the dining hall."

Vanessa nodded and walked inside, but I hadn't planned on going to the bathroom. I hung around the entrance to the dining hall until I saw a figure walking my way. It was Christian wearing a black suit, and he looked like a million bucks. He seemed surprised to see me.

"Olivia, we meet again," he said. "Waiting for someone?"

"For you, actually," I replied. "You didn't mention you were a prince before."

He smiled. "Well...you never asked."

I crossed my arms, unimpressed with his answer.

He sighed. "I didn't mean to lie to you. When Father told me guests would be arriving soon, I saw it as an opportunity."

"For what?"

"To finally make friends who were interested in me and not my title," he said. "Being the prince means having certain responsibilities, and a certain reputation. Everyone treats you differently. Is it so wrong I wanted to see if someone would like me for me and not my nobility?"

"I guess I can understand that. I always thought monarchies were kind of stupid, anyway. Uh, no offense," I said. "If I promise not to treat you like a prince, does that mean you'll be honest with me?"

He smiled. "Deal. Come on. Breakfast is starting."

"One last thing," I said before he could enter the dining hall. "You're sure you didn't see anyone around the docks before the explosion? Where did you go after our conversation?"

"I went for a walk. I do that often to clear my head and get away from my father," he replied. "As I told you before, no, I didn't see anyone. It's just as Father said, probably an unfortunate accident."

"I find that hard to believe."

He frowned. "Are you implying someone set fire to the boat?"

Mom walked out of the dining hall, placing her hands on her hips. She was about to yell at me before she saw Christian. "Oh, hello, Prince Christian. I was just looking for my daughter."

"You found her," I mumbled. "I had to use the bathroom, but I'm back now."

Mom's eyes flickered between me and Christian, and I knew she had to be wondering what we were talking about. As I entered the dining hall, I noticed everyone sitting down already and eating. King Dominic sat at the head of the table next to his wife, and there was a seat for Christian. He walked past me and sat down beside his father. I took the seat next to Mom and Vanessa, across from Russell.

General Ezra was gone, but he had left a few guards in his place. I spotted Dante again, but he wasn't sitting down with us. He stood at attention next to King Dominic, keeping one hand on his sword. Did he not get to join us?

"I apologize for that unpleasantness earlier. I hope we haven't scared you away," King Dominic said. "To make up for it, I've had my chefs prepare a tasty feast for us. I hope you all enjoy it."

I glanced at the platters and felt nauseous again. Everything was meat-based, and dripping in blood. I watched in disgust as Vanessa sliced her knife through a fatty piece of liver. King Dominic, Christian, and Queen Vivienne also had similar lumps of meat on their plate and dug in ravenously.

Christian went to use his fingers, but Queen Vivienne snarled at him. He rolled his eyes and used his fork and knife instead.

"I thought it'd be totally nasty," Vanessa whispered, pointing at the liver on her plate, "but I actually like it. I don't see anything you can eat, though."

"Uh, do you not have any vegetables? Fruit?" I asked, looking at King Dominic.

King Dominic glanced at Queen Vivienne and Christian and then back at me. "Is there something wrong with the food?"

Mom glared at me. She knew where I was going with this, and she didn't want me to make a scene.

"No, not at all," I said. "It's just—"

"Olivia's a vegetarian," Vanessa interrupted. "I don't know why she'd want to give up cheeseburgers, but there's no changing her mind. Believe me. I've tried."

"I wasn't going to say anything," I said. "I normally just eat the sides my mom makes...but everything here is full of meat."

"Yes. We're carnivorous," King Dominic said. "We like our meat raw and bloody."

"Well, it's delicious," Mom said, choking down some liver.

"Dante, take Olivia out to the garden and find her something suitable to eat. Inform the chefs we'll be cooking for one vegetarian from now on," King Dominic said, glancing back at me.

"Thanks, but you don't have to go to all this trouble—"

"Nonsense. I won't have my guest starving," he said with a smile. "Go ahead. Dante will show you the way."

Vanessa gave me a smirk as Dante gestured at the door that led out of the dining hall, motioning for me to exit first. He still hadn't said anything to me. Did he even speak?

"Do you want me to come with you?" Russell asked, rising to his feet.

I glanced at King Dominic, then back at Russell. I didn't want him to think we didn't trust them. "No, I'll be fine. Stay here and eat."

Russell nodded, sitting down again but looking worried. His concerned gaze lingered on us as I walked into the corridor, waiting for Dante to catch up. He approached one of the back doors to the castle and I had to quicken my pace to keep up with him.

"We have a garden out back," he said. His voice was a lot softer than I had anticipated from someone as tall and strong as him. "We grow all kinds of plants here, from tomatoes to strawberries. I'm sure the chef could make you a salad."

"You talk," I said before I could stop myself.

He opened the door, letting me go through first. "Of course."

"It's just...well, you haven't said anything before."

"Talking is a distraction. King Dominic prefers silence from his soldiers, anyway. And I take my job very seriously in guarding his life. Please, help yourself."

As I strolled through the garden, Dante handed me a

basket. I used it to collect some of the tomatoes, lettuce, and cucumbers. "You seem really loyal to King Dominic."

"Of course, I am. He's our king."

"It's more than that. I can tell you respect him a lot."

Dante shrugged. "He saved my life when I was younger. I owe him everything."

I didn't want to press the subject and make him uncomfortable, so I busied myself in the garden. "If you only eat meat, why have a garden at all?"

"For the wildlife, mostly," he replied. "We have hunters that venture out into the forest to kill for us. We even have a holiday for it where we hunt and give thanks. Queen Vivienne maintains the garden, and she likes the beauty it brings to our kingdom."

Dante was a lot like General Ezra in terms of seriousness, but at least I could have a conversation with him. I rose to my feet and nodded at the basket. "I think I've gathered enough for now."

He took it from me before a concentrated look appeared on his face. "General Ezra teaches all the warriors here that curiosity is dangerous...but I want to know. Why are you a vegetarian?"

"When I was a kid, my dad took me on a hunting trip," I said. "It didn't feel right to me, watching a creature die. He shot the deer in the head...but it was still alive, and cried and kicked before finally bleeding to death. I became a strict vegetarian after that, and never went on a hunting trip again, much to my dad's disappointment."

"Yes, many feel killing is wrong," Dante said. "It isn't always pleasant...but sometimes, it *is* necessary."

A chill spread through my body. I wanted to believe he

was only talking about animals, but something in his tone made me think it was much more than that.

"I'll bring this to our chefs," he said, gesturing at the basket. "Make your way back to the dining hall. Your meal should be ready soon."

I followed him back into the castle before he took a right, disappearing into the large kitchen that connected to the dining hall. As I walked down the corridor, I heard someone whisper my name. It was faint, and so close to my ear, that I spun around, thinking someone was there, but I was alone in the hallway.

As I shivered, I realized the terrible truth. Someone, or something, was watching me. I could feel it.

3
THE TOUR GUIDE

Shaking off the weird feeling I'd experienced in the hallway, and the voice calling out my name. I entered the dining hall and took my seat. King Dominic and Queen Vivienne both nodded when they saw me, then returned to their conversation with Mom. Russell looked relieved to see I had returned in one piece.

Christian briefly looked up from his plate before returning to his food, and I wondered if he was upset with me for interrogating him earlier. I took a deep breath to calm myself down and fiddled with the napkin next to my plate.

Vanessa noticed, nudging me. "Hey, you feeling all right?"

I looked up at her, smiling. "I'll be fine. I think it's just the smell from the meat making me sick."

Dante entered the dining hall through the kitchen, standing at attention next to King Dominic, silent again. A moment later, a serving girl walked over to my side of the table. She opened the silver platter to reveal a giant salad with a creamy dressing. As she plated it for me, my mouth nearly watered. It smelled a lot better than the liver chunks on Vanessa's plate.

King Dominic sat forward as I took a big bite. "How is it?"

"Delicious," I said, covering my mouth with my hand. "Thanks for going to the trouble of making it."

He smiled. "It's no trouble at all. As I said, you're our guest, and hopefully our ally if the talks go well. Besides, my chefs were up for the challenge. They plan to learn a lot more vegetarian meals while you're here."

"Thank you, King Dominic. You've all been gracious hosts," Mom said. "Now, I figured I could ask you some questions to get to know you a little better. Is that all right with you?"

King Dominic grinned. "Absolutely. Please ask away, Ambassador."

"All right," Mom said, wiping her mouth with a napkin. "Your kingdom's name is very unique, only one letter. Our people sometimes use the U.S., but that's an acronym for the United States. Does V stand for anything?"

Christian glanced at his father and then back at Mom. "It stands for victory."

"Victory of what?" Vanessa asked.

Christian hesitated, so King Dominic answered for him. "We've survived for centuries and are a completely self-sustaining society. We have strong, intelligent people. I'd say that's all a victory."

"So, why not just call your island Victory, then?" Vanessa asked.

"The simple letter V is more mysterious," Queen Vivienne said. "We prefer it that way."

"Well, it's a wonderful kingdom. You should certainly be proud of it," Mom said, sipping water. "What should we call your people? The world refers to us as Americans. Should we call you Victorian's?"

"Call us Vee's," King Dominic said. "That is our kingdom name, after all."

"Understood. I'll put that in my report to the president. What are your future hopes for our two countries?"

Christian and Queen Vivienne glanced at King Dominic, waiting for him to answer. He thought for a moment before speaking. "I would say...friendship. I'm a progressive kind of king, Ambassador, and I want to see our people evolve and reintegrate into society. We've been isolated for so long, and I fear it's made my people closed-minded."

"Why *have* you been isolated?" I asked.

King Dominic sighed. "My people can be very mistrustful, especially of outsiders. I always feared the timing was never right before, but I know this is the right step for my people. Besides, our population is growing, and I would like to see us expand our reach. Perhaps one day, we may live as your neighbors."

"Does everyone share that opinion?" I asked, thinking back to the burning boat.

"As I said, my people can be very mistrustful and closed-minded," King Dominic replied. "But they've promised to behave and welcome this new change. It will be difficult at first, but my people are strong. They'll adapt and offer their full support soon enough."

"So, you've lived here your entire life? All of you?" Vanessa asked. "You've never even seen a glimpse of the outside world?"

Queen Vivienne and King Dominic hesitated, so Christian answered instead. "That's right. This kingdom is all I've ever known."

I had the strange feeling they were holding something back. What was with all the pauses and hesitations?

"Why did you contact the United States?" Mom asked. "Why not the other countries?"

"This is a small step. A test to see if it's truly a good time to branch out," King Dominic said. "Your United States is one of the most advanced first-world countries, or so I've heard. I figured your people were a good place to start."

"I see. Anyway, let's discuss our values," Mom said. "I want you to know where our people stand. We believe in equality, women's rights, and gay rights, as well as healthcare, quality education, and a judicial process. We also believe in basic respect and honesty."

"As do we," King Dominic said, smiling. "As I said, I am a progressive king. Our kingdom may look old-fashioned and conservative, but we do have modern values."

"That's good to hear. It makes my job much easier. What are your plans in the coming weeks?"

"I would like to help you set up an embassy here," King Dominic said. "As well as begin the negotiations for trade and tourism. I'm eager to see what we can offer your country. All of which I'm sure will be boring for Vanessa and Olivia, so we can speak about that in private."

"Sounds good to me. I'd also like to inquire about technology," Mom said. "With your permission, we could help you come into the twenty-first century. It would certainly make communication much easier."

Queen Vivienne leaned over, whispering something in

King Dominic's ear. He nodded and turned back to Mom. "Thank you for the offer. We'll think about it and get back to you on that. My people aren't fond of change, and I don't want to do too much at once and overwhelm them."

"Of course. No pressure," Mom said. "Is there anything else you'd like us to know about your people? President Bennett wants me to gather as much information as possible."

"We believe very strongly in hunting, spending time together, and our spirituality. We have a church in the village that we all attend privately, which is why we have no religious leader," King Dominic said. "I also believe in new beginnings. One I hope to have with your people."

"So do we. Turns out we have a lot in common," Mom said, smiling. Then it turned to a frown. "One last thing...and it's uncomfortable to bring up, but necessary. It's about the American missionary who went missing here in the 1920s. His name was Charles Browning, and we know he was planning to visit your island to convert you to Christianity based on old journals of his that we found. Do you know anything about that?"

Vanessa looked at me, equally shocked. What was Mom talking about?

King Dominic sighed. "Yes, I do. It's common knowledge around here. You see...the old king had a very bloodthirsty general. The general feared the missionary had come here to kill us, and so he attacked and killed him."

"I see. What happened to the body?"

"Unfortunately, the general dumped the body into the ocean, much to the king's disapproval," King Dominic said, shaking his head. "On behalf of my people, I apologize. I believe the missionary had good intentions, but...the old general did not want to listen."

Mom nodded. "I'm sorry to bring it up, but President Bennett wanted to know what happened to him. We had a feeling he was murdered. After his disappearance, all major countries around the world dissuaded people, even missionaries, from sailing to your kingdom. We believed you were too primitive and violent to contact."

King Dominic lifted his glass. "I assure you, my people have changed since then. Why don't we raise a toast to Mr. Browning? To forgiveness and starting over?"

"To forgiveness and starting over," Mom agreed, lifting her glass and taking a sip.

Vanessa and I did the same, wondering why Mom hadn't told us the story of the murdered missionary. I felt upset she'd leave something important like that out. Christian and Queen Vivienne both took long sips, looking uncomfortable.

"I'm glad we put that unpleasantness behind us," King Dominic said. "And regarding Olivia and Vanessa...do they still attend school?"

Mom nodded. "Yes. They're both seventeen, going into their last year of high school. Don't remind me. My daughter has grown up so fast."

"That they do," King Dominic said, glancing over at Christian. "We'd be more than happy to welcome them into St. Raven's Academy. That's our only school here. Just so you know, we have classes all year long, even during the summer months. They can start bright and early tomorrow morning."

Vanessa looked shocked. She hadn't expected coming here would mean early classes and homework, and neither had I. I would've faked sick if I'd known.

"What?" I asked. "School in the summer? But—"

Mom elbowed me under the table, shutting me up. "They'd be delighted to attend. Thank you, King Dominic."

He nodded, rising to his feet. "Well, with breakfast and our question period over, I owe you a tour of our kingdom. I can ask one of the guards to show you around—"

"I can do it," Christian said, standing up. "I've finished my work at the library, so I'm free for the day."

King Dominic looked puzzled that he volunteered, but nodded. "Very well. Change into something more casual and my son will give you a tour of V. I'll be working in the castle in the meantime, but don't hesitate to ask me for anything."

"Be careful," Queen Vivienne said, turning to Christian. "Ensure nothing happens to our guests. We've already had one...accident, and I don't want a repeat."

Christian nodded, leaving to change. King Dominic and Queen Vivienne left for the throne room as the servants began cleaning up. We thanked them for the meal and returned to our rooms.

"When were you planning on telling us they'd killed someone?" I asked Mom, my hands on my hips.

"I didn't want to scare you," Mom whispered. "Look, President Bennett and I weighed the risks before we came here. It's why we brought Russell. But you heard everything King Dominic said back there. We should still stay cautious, but I don't think they'd lure us here to kill us. And besides, that was decades ago. The United States doesn't have a squeaky-clean record, either."

"I hope you're right," I muttered, "for all our sakes."

As Mom and Russell returned to their rooms to change, Vanessa scoffed beside me. "No internet, school in the summer, *and* a shady background of killing visitors? I'm liking this country less and less by the minute. But hey, at least your cute boyfriend's giving us a tour. Maybe things *are* looking up."

"Stop calling him that," I mumbled. "I've had two conversations with him. And you know I'm not looking for anything, not this soon, anyway."

Vanessa rolled her eyes. "Look, if your mom's right and these people have changed, then I think you should go for Christian. You can't let Douchebag Dylan hold you back forever."

Dylan. Just hearing his name felt like a kick to the gut.

"We're not having this conversation," I muttered, opening the door to my room. "We both promised we wouldn't say his name here."

Vanessa followed me in as I searched through my clothes, looking for something casual. "That was only if you promised to leave your heartbreak behind, which you clearly haven't. What he did to you wasn't cool, but you have to move on at some point. Promise me you'll think about it."

"If I say yes, will you stop bugging me?"

"Maybe," she said, shrugging. "No promises."

"Fine. Now, can you get out of my room?"

She grinned, slowly sauntering to the door. "Olivia and Prince Christian, sitting in a tree..."

I rolled my eyes and slammed the door, and I could hear her humming the tune in the room adjacent to mine.

———

Ten minutes later, I had changed into my favorite blue jeans and cardigan. Me, Russell, and Mom waited out in the hallway for Vanessa to finish getting ready. As usual, she took her sweet time.

Mom knocked on her door. "Vanessa, are you coming?"

She flung open the door a second later, rolling her eyes. I glanced at her and realized she had done her hair and make-up and changed into a more casual dress. "I'm here. Happy?"

"Yes, so glad you've finally decided to join us," Mom muttered sarcastically. "We need to find Prince Christian. He's probably waiting for us—"

Christian emerged from a door behind us, scaring us all. He had changed into a black jacket and matching pants. "Sorry, I didn't mean to sneak up on you. The castle has many connecting doors and hallways. If you'll follow me, I can show you the hotspots around the kingdom."

"Where to first?" I asked.

"Let's start with St. Raven's Academy," he said. "I figured I should get you acquainted with it before your first day."

As he led us out of the castle, Vanessa turned to him. "So, Prince Christian...do you have a girlfriend?"

He gave her a funny look. "No, I don't. My work keeps me busy."

Vanessa frowned at me, disappointed with his answer. I glared at her for meddling.

"Your work?" I asked. "So, you aren't a student?"

He laughed. "I guess I look younger than my age. No, I'm not a student. I work at the library as a seeker."

"What's a seeker?" Mom asked.

Christian paused. "Right, I forgot you aren't aware of the careers around here. When students graduate from the academy, they choose from five paths: warrior, hunter, artisan, seeker, and empath."

"And what do they all mean?" I asked.

"Well, seekers concern themselves with knowledge. I work at the library, studying all sorts of things, literature, history, math. It's our job to know a little bit of everything. Warriors often end up as guards like my uncle or Dante, and hunters catch prey for us in the forest. They also preside over the Great Hunt."

"The Great Hunt?" Mom asked.

"An annual hunting contest. It's coming up soon, actually, and everyone's required to attend. We make a game out of it, then celebrate with a big feast afterward."

"And the other two?" I asked.

"Artisans run the shops in the village and make a wide variety of items," he said. "Finally, we have empaths who learn to read people's emotions. They usually end up as doctors. Our artisans also assist doctors in making healing salves, which our kingdom considers to be very important."

Christian led us down the white brick path, and more people came out to watch us. Didn't they have jobs or something better to do?

"Do you see that silver building in the distance?" Christian asked, and we nodded. "We call it the Solitude. It's our jail. Stay away from it. Our prisoners can be very dangerous, and Father doesn't want to see you get hurt. Our warden is a strong woman who keeps them in check, but accidents happen. As you've seen before."

"You have inmates, too?" Mom asked. "I'm surprised. Your kingdom just seems...so perfect."

He shook his head, leading us to a tall red building. "We're far from perfect, Ambassador."

"Any other places of interest we should know about?" Mom asked.

"A few. I'll show you when we're done here," he said, opening the building's glass door. "Welcome to St. Raven's Academy."

As we entered the building, I noticed it was much smaller than the rest of the other places in the kingdom. Unlike our schools back home, it seemed cozier with ample couches, bookshelves in the hallways, and dim lighting.

"Class is in session, so we'll have to be quiet," Christian said, "but I'm sure the professor wouldn't mind if we observed. Feel free to look around."

Christian led us to a red door down the hallway and opened it quietly. As we entered, all the kids sitting at their desks looked over at us. It was hard to pinpoint their exact ages, maybe between six and ten, but they seemed very intelligent and alert.

As Christian spoke quietly with the blonde female professor in a red robe, we took a look around the classroom. One boy with dark hair was building a small model of the castle, and it looked nearly identical to King Dominic's. I certainly wasn't making anything that good when I was their age. Scissors, chisels, and other sculpting supplies sat on his desk. He couldn't have been older than ten, his skin pale with grey bags under his eyes.

"That's amazing," I whispered. "You could be an architect when you grow up."

The boy had an odd expression on his face when he

looked up at me, his pupils blown. "You smell...different. Weird."

His brutal honesty made me turn red in embarrassment. Sniffing my shirt quickly, I hoped I didn't smell too bad. I hadn't had the chance to take a shower since we'd arrived.

"What are you working on?" I asked, changing the subject quickly.

"It's a project for our history class. I'm designing a replica of the castle," he said. "Who are you?"

"Olivia Hawthorne," I whispered. "My mom's the ambassador to the United States. We met King Dominic this morning, and now Prince Christian's giving us a tour."

The boy's eyes glossed over. I assumed he was just tired or that I was boring him, but then he did the last thing I expected him to do.

He reached over to grab the scissors on his desk and stabbed me in the thigh.

4

BAD MOJO

I groaned, staggering back from the little boy. I yanked the scissors out of my thigh and threw them on the floor, blood trickling down my leg. I looked at the boy and found him staring at my oozing blood with a hungry look in his eyes.

That was the last time I was *ever* going to talk to a child around here.

"Pavel!" Christian shouted, rushing to my side. "What did you do?"

The boy didn't reply. He only continued to stare at my dripping thigh. I placed my hand over the wound to try to stop the bleeding. Mom, Vanessa, and Russell sidestepped the other children who were staring at us and the scissors on the ground.

"Oh my God," Mom said, glancing at my thigh. "Olivia... you're bleeding!"

"Really bad," Vanessa said. "We need to get you to a doctor."

Russell hoisted the boy who had stabbed me up in the air by his collar. "All right, you little punk. Explain yourself!"

The boy's face turned into a snarl before he pushed Russell back, sending him flying into the pile of desks. He fell with a thud and a groan before Mom rushed to his side, helping him up. The rest of the schoolkids abandoned their activities, looking at me and Russell with the same hungry gaze, and swarmed us like predators.

That boy had tossed Russell. All two-hundred and fifty pounds and six feet of him—across the room like a ragdoll. The kids were either well-trained in self-defense or freakishly strong. I wasn't sure which one was worse.

"Enough," Christian said to the boy, his voice low and dangerous. "Stay back. All of you. I mean it."

The kids seemed to sober up at the tone of his voice. They moved away from us as the professor stepped forward, corralling them near the back of the classroom. Her eyes widened in shock when she realized what had happened.

"Get her out of here," the Professor said, her gaze dropping to my thigh. "Hurry!"

"Come on. We need to get you to the clinic," Christian said, turning to me. "Can you walk?"

I shook my head. "No. It really hurts."

Christian lifted me in his arms, glancing back at Mom and Russell. "Can you take him?"

Mom nodded, placing Russell's arm over her shoulder. Vanessa helped with his other arm. "Lead the way. He needs medical attention, too."

As soon as Christian carried me out of the classroom and the others followed, the Professor rushed forward and locked the door behind us. I craned my neck and watched as the children tried to claw their way out, scratching at the door and making growling noises.

They had turned into bloodthirsty animals. But why?

Christian rushed down the corridor with me in his arms, taking us out of the academy. People on the streets watched with wide eyes and murmurs as he took us to a small, white building next to the castle. He kicked open the doors and I realized it was a clinic.

Several beds were set up across the room with giant bookshelves and tables filled with potions. Some vials were green and slimy, others had black goo inside. A red-headed girl, who didn't look much older than me, stood next to one of those tables with an older woman who resembled Dante with her black hair. The other person in the room was a tall, pale man with a white lab coat, and bulging, golden-brown eyes.

The red-headed girl said nothing, but her eyes widened in shock when she saw my leg. She was busy mixing potions, so the dark-haired woman stepped forward as Christian placed me on a hospital bed. Mom led Russell over, setting him down on a bed adjacent to mine. Vanessa sat beside me and reached for my hand as Mom did the same.

"What happened to these two?" the woman asked. "They don't look familiar. Wait...aren't they our guests from America?"

Christian nodded. "They are. Olivia was stabbed with scissors, and Russell was pushed into a pile of desks. Can you help them?"

"Of course. Let me get my supplies," the woman said, rushing into a small side room.

The man in the white lab coat stepped forward, a blank expression on his face. "Blood. I can smell it..."

Christian placed a hand on his shoulder. "Why don't you go for a walk, Oscar? You've been cooped up in here for days."

"Yes, a walk," he muttered, opening the door to exit the clinic. "A walk sounds nice..."

After he had vanished, I glanced up at Christian. "Who was that?"

"Dr. Oscar Cox," Christian replied. "He's an alchemist, one of the best around here. And a good friend of my father's. He makes those healing salves I was telling you about. He's...a little mentally unstable though, so try to avoid him."

The girl walked over, glancing down at my bleeding thigh. "Ouch! That looks bad."

"It feels even worse," I muttered.

She placed a hand on my leg beside the wound, nodding. "Yes. I can feel it. Mostly pain, but some shock, too. Disbelief."

I glanced at her as she removed her hand. "How did you know that?"

"I'm an empath," she replied. "We all are who work here. It helps us cure a patient better if we can feel their pain."

"Handy skill to have."

"It is, and don't worry. Dr. Draven will patch you up," she said, her eyes flickering to Russell's. "She can help him, too. We have all kinds of concoctions that can take the pain away."

"Dr. Draven? Is she related to Dante?"

The girl nodded. "Yes, Letitia's his mother. My name's Anastasia Banes, by the way. I work as an alchemist here alongside Oscar. We're always working on new elixirs that can help our people, healing potions, sleep aids, you name it. Some of them are drinkable, others applied topically."

Dr. Draven came out of the small room, carrying ointment and bandages. She kneeled beside me. "I have to disinfect the wound first, so this might hurt a bit."

I winced as she poured the strange ointment over my cut. When the burning sensation had faded, it started to feel much better. I could move my leg again as she wrapped the white bandage around it.

"Wow," I murmured. "The pain's already going away."

She gestured at Anastasia, smiling. "Ana's the best. This ointment is her creation. Now for your friend."

She turned to Russell who pointed at his back. "I fell hard. Not sure if I broke my back or not, but it's killing me."

Dr. Draven touched his shoulder lightly, concentrating. "No, I don't sense that you fractured anything, but there is great pain. Ana, can you help?"

Anastasia nodded, rushing over to her long table of vials. She returned with something squishy and yellow. "Here, try this on him."

Dr. Draven took the vial and removed the yellow substance, rubbing it on Russell's back. He looked hesitant at first, but after a few seconds, sat up straighter and smiled. "Hey, I'm starting to feel much better."

"That's just the painkiller part of the ointment," Dr. Draven said. "But you two should still take it easy. That wound and your back should heal within a day, but you don't want to aggravate it before that."

"Well, I'm glad you'll both be all right," Mom said, rising to her feet. "But we need to talk about what happened back there. Why did that boy stab you?"

"I don't know," I said. "I was just talking to him, then he grabbed the scissors and stabbed me in the thigh. I didn't do anything to him!"

"I'm so sorry, Lin," Russell said. "I was supposed to protect all of you. And I failed."

"It wasn't your fault, Russ," I said. "You had no way of knowing that kid would stab me."

"Yeah." Vanessa nodded. "No one did. I mean, he didn't look like a troublemaker. But I guess looks are deceiving."

"Olivia and Vanessa are right. I don't blame you and you shouldn't either, Russell," Mom said, turning to Christian. "I blame the boy. This falls on him, and his apparent lack of knowing right from wrong."

The doors to the clinic opened before Christian had a chance to reply. King Dominic, Queen Vivienne, and General Ezra walked inside, their gazes falling on me and Russell.

"I'm glad you two are all right," King Dominic said. "Professor Amara told us everything. Rest assured, Pavel will be punished for this. General Ezra will see to it himself."

"You won't hurt the boy, will you?" I asked.

"No," General Ezra grunted, "but he must learn from his mistakes."

"Do all your children behave like that, King Dominic?" Mom asked. "Because after that boy stabbed my daughter, the others swarmed us. If Prince Christian hadn't intervened, I shudder to think what would've happened to us."

"I apologize for their behavior. There's something you must know about our children," King Dominic said. "When they're young, they have...difficulty controlling themselves. Most are rebellious, some even deranged."

Queen Vivienne nodded. "They usually grow out of it as

they age, like our son, Christian, did. We use firm discipline to mold them into better adults. Those who fail are locked away in our prison called the Solitude where they can't hurt anyone."

I had a hard time picturing Christian once as aggressive as that little boy, but Vanessa was right before. Looks are deceiving. Just what else were they hiding?

"That boy was incredibly strong for a small child," Russell said. "What are you feeding these kids?"

"Their diet consists of raw meat," General Ezra said. "All our people are strong, powerful, but our young don't know their own strength. It takes time to learn what is expected of them."

"Well, they'd better learn if you want us to stay. First there was the boat explosion and now this," Mom said. "Tell me honestly, King Dominic, are we safe here? Are we really welcome?"

He smiled. "Of course you are. Believe me, this isn't how I wanted our first day to play out. But in time, I think you'll come to like our kingdom, Ambassador."

"And the boy won't hurt you again," Christian said, turning to me, "either of you. I promise you that."

"I hope not," Mom said. "But I'll have to include this in my report to the president."

"Of course," King Dominic said. "I pray this will be our last accident."

My thigh was feeling much better so I swung my leg over the side of the bed. "Well, I guess we should get back to the tour now."

"I think the tour is over," Queen Vivienne said. "You've all had enough excitement for one day."

"Please," I said. "I'm feeling better already, and I really want to see the rest of your kingdom."

"Don't worry, Mother," Christian said, turning to her. "I'll be more careful this time."

King Dominic gestured over his shoulder. "Christian, a word?"

Christian nodded, walking over to his parents and General Ezra. They spoke in hushed tones as me, Mom, Vanessa, and Russell glanced at each other. Anastasia and Dr. Draven stood nearby, awkwardly.

"We should've brought more bodyguards," Vanessa muttered. "No offense to Russ, but why'd my mom only send us with one?"

"It was an act of faith, of goodwill," Mom whispered. "Bringing an army with us would've made it seem as though we don't trust them, and that's not how we want to begin our relationship. But with more of these accidents, I fear the president made a terrible mistake."

The whispering from the corner of the room stopped. Queen Vivienne bowed before she, King Dominic, and General Ezra left the clinic. Christian held out a hand to help me to my feet as Russell stood up.

"Where to next?" I asked.

"I can show you the church and the library," he said. "It's right next to the castle, in the same building. My parents want us to stay away from the academy for now."

"Have fun," Dr. Draven said as she and Anastasia returned to their work. "Stay out of trouble."

"But feel free to come back anytime," Anastasia said. "Just not for injuries, I mean."

"I'll try," I said, turning to Christian. "What about school tomorrow? Me and Vanessa both have to go."

"Maybe we should wear knee pads just in case," Vanessa joked. "And definitely watch out for little kids with scissors."

"Pavel won't be there," Christian said, opening the door to exit the clinic. "But Dante will be. My parents have ordered him to guard you two when you're at school. It gives Russell time to rest."

Russell didn't look happy leaving us in Dante's care, but he had no choice. He was in no position to argue. Vanessa nudged me with a smile on her face at the mention of Dante's name, but I only rolled my eyes. Christian took us down the same brick path as before, but instead of heading right toward the castle, we took a left. I finally noticed the two-story steeple next to it.

As we entered the chapel, no one was inside, but there were several rows of pews set up and a stained-glass window. It blocked out most of the sun, leaving only a candle to light the room. There were no crosses or holy items anywhere which seemed strange for a church.

"As my father mentioned during breakfast, faith is important to our people," Christian said. "My uncle will take Pavel here where he can beg for forgiveness for what he did to you."

"What religion do you follow, if you don't mind telling us?" Mom asked. "We have all kinds of beliefs back home: Judaism, Islam, Christianity."

"We don't follow any official religion," Christian said, leading us toward a staircase, "but we value absolution and starting fresh. Are you religious, Olivia?"

"Not really," I said, shrugging. "Haven't been for a while."

I could tell he was curious, but dropped the subject. "Come. I'll show you the library upstairs where I work. Feel free to look around and take out any book you'd like."

As we stepped into the library, several other dark-haired men and women nodded at us, reading books on various subjects. Bookshelves lined the walls, with everything from math to English to history, but I noticed it all stopped during the mid-1800s. Vanessa, Mom, and Russell took a look around as I turned to Christian.

"You don't have any recent books?" I asked. "No *Percy Jackson*?"

Christian frowned. "What's a...*Percy Jackson*?"

"Never mind. What are you working on?"

"Shakespeare," he replied, pulling out several of the bard's plays from a section of the bookshelf. "I was studying what it means to be human."

"No art books, then?"

"Sorry. As I said before, art isn't considered a necessity among my people. Maybe you could write our first art book, or better yet, teach a class at the academy."

I laughed. "Eh, I'm not really a teacher."

"Think about it," he said, smiling. "I'd like to learn one day. Maybe with some private tutoring, I can be half the artist you are."

I blushed at the thought of spending time alone with him. As he read through his Shakespeare book, I heard my name whispered again. I thought it was Christian doing it until I saw his mouth closed and his eyes trained on the book. The whisper continued as I craned my neck, searching for its origin, and saw something strange.

A section of the library had been closed off with furniture. I walked toward it, noticing the small alcove of several tomes hidden behind. The books inside felt like they were calling out to me, whispering my name.

"The truth," a voice whispered in my ear. "Find the truth…"

As I reached out to pull the furniture away, I felt a hand on my shoulder and jumped. It was Christian. "That part of the library is closed. Sorry, but no one's allowed to go in there."

The strange voices faded. I glanced back at the tomes, hoping to hear them again, but nothing happened.

"Olivia?" Christian asked. "Are you all right?"

"Uh, yeah. I'm fine," I muttered. "Why is it closed?"

"It's under repair," he replied. "Father sealed it off in case someone got hurt, and I'd say you've been injured enough for one day. It should re-open soon."

"What's inside?"

He hesitated, his eyes glancing at the alcove and then back at me. "Boring manuals on farming and agriculture. It's nothing you'd be interested in—believe me."

I groaned, suddenly feeling light-headed. "Oh, I don't feel so good…"

"You look pale," Christian said, feeling my forehead. "You have a fever, too. Come on, you should get back to your room."

Christian held my arm to balance me so I wouldn't fall, leading us over to Mom, Vanessa, and Russell.

"Whoa," Vanessa muttered. "You look like you just saw a ghost."

More like I'd just heard one, I wanted to say, but kept my mouth shut.

Christian's grip on my arm tensed at the word ghost. "She's most likely feeling sick from the blood loss. Would you mind taking her to her room?"

"I think we could all use some rest. It's been a stressful day," Mom said, reaching for me. "Come on, sweetie. We'll help you get to bed."

As Mom, Vanessa, and Russell helped me down the staircase and back to our rooms in the castle, I knew something was strange about that section of the library. Were the voices trying to lead me there? What did they want me to find?

When Mom, Russell, and Vanessa put me in bed and closed the door to my room, I instantly fell asleep, exhausted. When I woke up again, I saw darkness outside the small window. I must've fallen asleep for the rest of the day.

Dinner waited for me on a silver platter, another salad but with more variety this time. After I dug in, I started to feel much better. Maybe the voices weren't real, I told myself. Maybe they were just the product of my exhausted, stressed-out mind. I didn't believe in ghosts or spirits.

When I finished my dinner, I left the platter by the door and turned around, intending to get into bed again. But then I saw it. The crimson letters streaking down my walls.

GET OUT WHILE YOU STILL CAN, it read, in big bloody letters.

I screamed, falling to the floor.

Mom and Vanessa rushed through the door, followed by Russell. They must've heard my scream through the walls. They wore pajamas and shared similar looks of concern.

"Olivia, what's the matter?" Mom asked, kneeling beside me.

I turned to her, pointing at the wall above my bed. "Look!"

Vanessa frowned. "At what? Nothing's there, Liv."

As I glanced back, I realized Vanessa was telling the truth. The bloody letters had vanished.

That was when I knew something was seriously wrong in the kingdom of V, and it seemed like the bad mojo was only after me.

5

THE SOLEMN VOW

Five minutes later, General Ezra, Dante, and the guards of the castle showed up outside my door to investigate the scream. Vanessa, Mom, and Russell lifted me onto my bed, helping me take deep breaths.

I glanced back at the wall above my bed, double-checking, but the bloodstains had vanished.

"What happened, Liv?" Vanessa asked. "What did you see?"

I couldn't tell them about the blood streaking down the wall or the voices I'd heard. Everyone would think I was crazy, and I didn't want them to lock me away in a foreign country. I'd have to stay calm and find out what was going on, especially now that I knew someone had deliberately set our boat on fire.

"I thought I saw a spider," I lied. "Guess I was just seeing things."

Vanessa didn't believe me, and gave me a sidelong glance. "And where did this...spider go?"

"It just disappeared. Like it was never there at all."

General Ezra looked annoyed I had wasted his time for a spider. He turned to his guards, gesturing at the door. "Come on. There's nothing here. No need to wake the royals over this."

As he left, Dante stepped forward. "Will you be all right, Olivia?"

"I'll be fine." I faked a smile. "Don't worry about me."

"Dante, let's go," General Ezra growled, poking his head back inside my room. "It's late and we have other places to patrol."

"Good night, Olivia," Dante said before he and the guards fled my room.

"Are you sure you're okay?" Vanessa asked, still looking at me funny.

"Yeah, I'm sure. I probably just hallucinated the whole thing."

I hoped I had. If not...I didn't want to think about what that meant.

Mom sighed, rising to her feet. "You're probably under a lot of stress, Olivia. To tell you the truth...so am I."

"Me, too," Russell said. "I've got a bad feeling about this kingdom, Lin."

"Why?" Vanessa asked. "You aren't implying the people of V are behind this, are you? That they set our boat on fire and told the kid to stab Olivia?"

Russell shrugged. "And why not? Their people have killed before. What if they didn't murder the missionary for trespassing? What if they killed him because he found out something? Something they didn't want anyone to see."

"Like what?" I asked.

"No idea. That's the million-dollar question. We've all

seen how strange these people act. The staring, the whispering, even that odd hissing noise they make when they're angry. I've traveled to a lot of countries for the White House, and none of them have unnerved me as much as the kingdom of V."

"Well, if that's all true, what are we supposed to do?" Vanessa asked. "Our boat burned to a crisp and there's no other way off this island. We're trapped!"

"We'll have to wait for President Bennett to arrive," Mom said. "Until then, I want everyone to be careful, especially you, Olivia. I'm not sure if you're just unlucky or if you have a knack for getting into dangerous situations."

"Probably a little bit of both," I muttered, absentmindedly plucking the edge of the blanket on my bed.

"Do you want me to stay with you tonight?" Vanessa asked. "I can pull my bed into your room. We can have a sleepover, just like the old days."

"It's okay," I said. "I'll be fine on my own."

Vanessa looked hesitant but backed off. Russell rose to his feet and turned to Mom. "No matter what happens, I promise I'll be there to protect you all. No more stabbings on my watch."

Mom smiled at him, and I swore his heart would burst from happiness. "Thanks, Russ. I'm glad we brought you along. Now, come on. We should let Olivia rest."

After they left, I locked the door behind them and blew out the candle. I checked the wall again, one last time, but found nothing. I crawled into bed, closing my eyes tight. When I couldn't fall asleep, I counted sheep in my head.

It didn't work.

Half an hour later, my heart was still pounding with anxiety, and I was wide awake. I couldn't stay in my room anymore. It was beginning to feel like a prison. I rose to my feet, throwing a t-shirt and jeans over my pajamas before I slowly opened the door to my room with a squeak.

I found nothing in the hallway. Sighing in relief, I tip-toed down the corridor, intending to step outside the castle for some fresh air before I heard voices. They sounded like they were coming from the throne room. Frowning, I decided to follow the noise. As I neared the throne room, I hid behind the wall and noticed two shadow figures in the candlelight.

It was King Dominic and General Ezra. Strange, consid-ering the General had told us the king and his family were sleeping. I tried to inch closer, craning my neck to hear better, and managed to make out a few sentences.

"...think you've lost your mind," General Ezra said, placing his hands on his hips. "We both know this was a mistake. If they found out—"

"They won't," King Dominic interrupted. "Yes, there've been a few problems, but I'm certain we'll get them sorted out."

"And if we don't?" General Ezra asked. "Look, we both know the boat fire was set on purpose, and the children might not be able to control themselves if they see Olivia and Vanessa around school. I propose we tell them school is dismissed for the summer months—"

"No," King Dominic said, turning his back. "I've already told them our academy has classes in the summer. To take it back now would look suspicious—if they aren't already. I know your feelings, brother, but mine are clear. Their pres-ence here is necessary. Our people can become more than what we are. We *can* rejoin society."

General Ezra sneered. "Are you ready to risk their lives on that theory?"

King Dominic sighed. "I don't want to discuss this any further. Ambassador Hawthorne and her people are staying, and that's final. Olivia and Vanessa will attend the academy tomorrow and nothing will happen. This change won't be easy, but it *will* be worth it."

General Ezra was quiet for a moment. "You've always thought you could change the world. Make things better for people like us. It'll be a rude awakening when you realize you can't."

When I heard the General's boots heading my way, I moved from the wall and hid behind a tall vase. I held my breath as the general passed, glad he hadn't seen me. I heard King Dominic vanish down the other hall and exhaled in relief.

Russell was right. These people *were* hiding something. Everything the General said swirled around my head. *People like us?* What did that mean? And what was he so terrified we'd find out?

With a pounding heart, I rushed back to my room, suddenly not wanting that breath of fresh air anymore.

———

When the light of dawn filtered in through the curtains, my eyes opened. I'd managed to get a few hours of sleep, but I still felt exhausted. Knowing it was my first day of school, I quickly dressed, then brushed my teeth.

When I opened my door, I found a note taped to it.

MEET ME AT THE BARRACKS BEFORE SCHOOL. COME ALONE. -DANTE

I wasn't exactly sure where the barracks were, but I did remember seeing a building next to the clinic. I decided to meet Dante first before heading to school. Alone, just like he requested.

I followed the white brick path, quietly exiting my room so Mom and the others wouldn't hear. The people of V watched me with lingering stares as I kept my head down and passed. When I had made it to the clinic, I took a right and headed for the grey building which I assumed was the barracks. It had two floors and a training field outside with exercise equipment. The patrolling guards stared, but to my relief, didn't stop me.

When I stepped inside, the scent of sweat filled my nostrils. It looked like a fighting pit with a changing room around the back. Two guards were sparring in the small ring, and it took me a moment to realize Dante was one of them, his dark hair sticking up with sweat. He wore a black tank top with grey pants, and I finally saw his large biceps in all their glory. His brow furrowed in concentration as he watched each movement his opponent made.

When he looked up and noticed me, he charged into the other guard and tackled him to the floor. I had to admit. It was kind of hot. He kept him pinned beneath him with the ripple of his muscles.

"Mercy!" the guard cried out, and Dante backed off and stood up.

He held out a hand toward the guard. "Thank you for the fight, Bartholomew. You were a worthy opponent."

After the losing guard accepted Dante's hand and bowed,

he headed for the showers. General Ezra stepped forward and I realized he was watching them from the corner. "Well done, Dante. If you keep it up, I might make you my second-in-command soon."

Dante rarely smiled, but the corners of his mouth twisted upward. "Thank you, General. It would be an honor."

When General Ezra noticed me, he crossed his arms. "What are you doing here, Miss Hawthorne? The barracks are restricted to personnel."

"I invited her," Dante said, drying his sweat with a towel.

"Have you forgotten our rules, Dante?" the general asked. "No civilians are allowed within the barracks. We don't need any interruptions—"

"I was acting on the king's orders," Dante replied, reaching for a glass of water on a nearby table. "He's asked me to train Olivia."

"Really?" I asked. "Why? I'm no fighter."

"He sees potential in you. Perhaps you could even join the militia," Dante said, and General Ezra rolled his eyes. "And no offense to your friend, but you seemed like a better student."

I almost laughed. Vanessa could never fight. She'd be too worried about breaking a nail. "Yeah, that's true."

"I figured as much. The king's worried that if another... accident occurs, you won't be able to defend yourself," Dante continued. "I'll be teaching you how to fight, as well as basic survival training. If that's all right with you."

I thought about it for a moment. Learning how to kick ass from a super hot teacher? My answer was clear.

"I'll do it," I said. "Could be fun."

"Good," Dante said, bowing. "I don't know if you're aware, but King Dominic has asked me to guard you and

Vanessa. While I'll miss guarding the royal family, it's been my sole mission for years. I look forward to a change of pace."

"Well, thanks. It's always nice to have an extra guard—"

To my surprise, Dante fell to his knees, looking up at me. "My life for yours, Olivia Hawthorne, and my life for your best friend's, Vanessa Bennett. No harm will come to you, no enemy will touch you, no weapon will pierce your skin. This I swear."

General Ezra must've noticed my confused look because he grunted. "That's our most solemn vow, Olivia. A vow of protection. Dante will die for you and Vanessa. I hope you understand how serious this is."

"I do," I said as Dante rose to his feet. "And thank you, Dante."

He shook his head. "No need to thank me. I'm only doing my job."

"Was swearing a life vow necessary?" General Ezra asked, crossing his arms.

"Yes," Dante said, turning back to me. "I brought you here to start our training early, but I don't think we'll have time. I still need to shower and change. Will you wait for me?"

I nodded as Dante turned, grabbing his towel before heading to the showers. When I noticed the General's hard gaze on me, I worked up the courage to ask him something that was bothering me. "You don't want us here, do you, General?"

He looked taken back. "I beg your pardon?"

"You always seem so...standoffish. I just get the feeling

you aren't too thrilled about my people coming here, about the king wanting to open your borders."

He sighed. "I'm only being cautious. The vow Dante swore to you was the same one I took to the kingdom, to protect it and see it prosper. I fear its corruption if we allow outsiders to invade it."

"We don't want to invade your home. Look, where I come from, we have people living there from all over the world. I grew up with friends from England, Nigeria, Canada. you name it. In my experience, different cultures make life better."

"Then we'll have to agree to disagree," General Ezra grumbled.

As he left, Dante came out of the showers, smelling of berries and sandalwood. He had fully dressed in his guard uniform, and I scoffed in disbelief. "That was fast."

He nodded. "We're taught to use our time wisely. Our jobs come first, our lives and leisure second."

I followed him to the door. "Seems like a waste of a life."

"Perhaps to you," he began, opening the door for me, "but for us, it gives us a sense of purpose. How is your wound?"

"Oh, it's fine. I barely feel it anymore," I said, pointing at the bandage on my thigh. "Anastasia's elixir really helped. You have some good doctors here."

"Yes, we do. I wanted to make sure you were feeling better before practice. Does after school work for you?"

"Sure. I was going to paint, but I could push it back."

"You...paint?" he asked, looking surprised.

I blushed, suddenly feeling self-conscious. "Just a little. Maybe I'll show you later."

"I look forward to it," he said. "But about last night...are you sure you're all right?"

I faked another smile, something I was getting better at. "Really, I'm okay. You don't have to keep worrying about me."

"As your guard, I believe that *is* my duty now," he said, gesturing at the growing sunlight outside. "Anyway, I wouldn't want you to be late for your first day of school on my behalf. Let's find Vanessa and I'll walk you two to the academy."

As we made our way to our rooms, Mom and Russell were standing out in the hallway. She sighed in relief when she noticed me. "Olivia, there you are! Do you know how worried I was when I didn't find you in your room this morning?"

"It was my fault, Ambassador Hawthorne," Dante said. "I asked Olivia to meet me in the barracks. The king has asked me to teach her how to fight."

"I see," Mom said. "Well, a little self-defense can't hurt."

Vanessa came out of her room a second later, her hair and make-up looking perfect as always. "Hey, there you are. Have I mentioned how much it sucks to be the new kid?"

I laughed. "Well, at least we have each other. You ready?"

She nodded. "Dante's coming with us, right? For safety reasons?"

"Yes. General Ezra's taken Pavel out of school for now, but I'll still accompany you to your classes," Dante said. "If anyone tries to harm you, I have authority from the king to use force."

"Well, let's hope it doesn't come to that," Mom said. "Russ and I will be in meetings with King Dominic and

Queen Vivienne all day, so you know where to find me. Good luck at school, girls."

As Vanessa and I turned to follow Dante, Russell tugged on my arm. "Be careful. Holler if you need me, okay?"

I could tell Russell didn't like leaving me and Vanessa in a stranger's protection, but he had no choice. He had to guard Mom. As I nodded and we left the castle, I noticed several young people, from children to teenagers, walking toward the academy. Some eyed us suspiciously while others paid no attention at all. Dante stayed a step behind us, his eyes scanning the crowd.

As we entered the academy, my heart started to pound. I wasn't normally nervous about school, but in a foreign country, everything was different. I remembered the pain from the boy stabbing me and felt my chest constricting.

"Breathe," Vanessa said, noticing my anxiety. "Dante's watching over us now. And I'm here for you, too."

I nodded and took her advice, pushing my way through the crowds of people. We followed the kids in our age group to a small classroom down the hallway. As me and Vanessa entered, finding desks at the back of the class, Dante followed us in and spoke to the professor.

"Fresh meat," I heard a male voice mutter as I took my seat.

I looked up and noticed two teenagers, a girl and a boy, staring back at us. They both had dirty blond hair, brown eyes, and wore chokers with black clothes and dark eyeliner. They looked like twins.

"You think they'll last long here?" the girl asked the boy, ignoring us.

"None of them will," the boy muttered.

"You know what's annoying?" Vanessa asked me, loudly. "People talking about us like we're not here."

"Oh, we know you're there," the girl said. "We could smell you as soon as you walked in."

I sniffed myself, but didn't smell anything foul. It seemed like they were just trying to rile us up.

"Who are you?" Vanessa asked.

"I'm Nicolai Sanguine. This is my sister, Petra," the boy said. "And if you know what's good for you, you'll stay away from us."

"Is that a threat?" I asked.

"Wouldn't you like to know?" Petra muttered as she and Nicolai took their seats.

Vanessa looked upset. Back home, she was the popular girl. I'd grown accustomed to fading into the background, even getting teased once in a while, but it would be a big change for her. I didn't like seeing her that way and knew I had to do something.

I tapped Petra and Nicolai on the shoulders. "Excuse me, but threatening and harassing people isn't nice. Didn't your parents ever teach you manners?"

Petra whipped around, grabbing my wrist hard enough to draw blood. "Watch how you speak about my parents. Unless you want to lose some more of that precious blood."

Dante rushed over as Petra released me. "Is there a problem here?"

"Not at all," Petra said, fluttering her eyelashes at Dante. "Just getting acquainted with our new classmates."

As she turned away, Dante leaned in. "Are you okay, Olivia?"

"I'm fine," I lied again.

"All right." He nodded as he studied my face. "I'll be in the back of the classroom if you need me, standing guard."

As he walked away, I glanced down at my painful wrist. First the boat explosion, then the scissor attack, then the weird conversation between the King and the General, and now this.

"This is going to be a long summer," Vanessa muttered.

Maybe even a deadly one, I wanted to add.

6

NEW KIDS ON THE BLOCK

The professor, tall and middle-aged with black hair like Dante, cleared his throat. "Good morning, class. I trust everyone had a good sleep?"

The students nodded. Maybe they had, but not me.

"I understand we have two new students today, Olivia Hawthorne and Vanessa Bennett," the professor said, glancing at us. "My name is Professor Claudius Draven, and I teach history and English at the academy. I believe you've met my son, Dante."

No wonder I thought he looked so much like Dante. Why hadn't he mentioned his father worked at the academy? Or that his mother was a doctor?

"I told you to stop introducing me as that," Dante warned from the back of the class.

"Right, I apologize. Our militia soldiers have no familial ties. They forgo them to focus on their careers," Professor Claudius said, sighing. "As I understand it, Dante will be watching over Vanessa and Olivia, so please, everyone must be on their best behavior. I'm sure you've all heard about the...

incident in the children's classroom, and I don't want another one. Neither does King Dominic."

Petra snorted. "They need a babysitter to protect them. How pathetic."

As she and Nicolai chuckled, I glared at them. If Professor Draven heard, he didn't say anything as he turned to write on the chalkboard. As he put the chalk down, he turned to us, and I finally saw what he had written. It read: FESTIVAL OF THE NIGHT, THE GREAT HUNT, and THE SACRED HOLIDAY.

"Since I'm sure Miss Hawthorne and Miss Bennett have questions about our kingdom, I figured we could satisfy them in our history lesson today," the professor said, wiping his chalky hands on his black robe. "Does anyone want to explain the Festival of the Night to our new students?"

A girl with long black hair raised her hand. "It's a time where we give thanks to the moon and the darkness. We dance, eat, and pray in a circle."

"Sounds like a pagan ritual to me," Vanessa whispered. "If they start sacrificing babies, I'm out of there."

I snorted.

"Very good," the professor said to the student, turning back to the chalkboard. "What about the Great Hunt?"

I remembered Dante mentioning it to me while we were in the garden. It had something to do with hunting for meat in the forest.

A boy with platinum blond hair raised his hand. "It's a hunting competition. We gather in the forest on the outskirts of the island and try to hunt wildlife."

"Indeed," Professor Draven said. "And what do you win for succeeding?"

"Bragging rights, mostly," another girl with dark hair answered. "We also get a trophy and a chance to spend time with the royal family. The animals they kill are used in a big feast after the Great Hunt is over."

"Let's not let our newest residents think it's all one big game," the Professor continued. "What does the Great Hunt mean?"

"It signifies our ability to take care of ourselves and our people," Petra said, glancing at me, "and our ability to slay our enemies."

Vanessa looked at me. Was that another threat?

The class turned silent. Professor Draven nodded, looking down. "Well...yes. It also represents how capable we are of whatever we set our minds to."

I raised my hand. "Who won the Great Hunt last year?"

"That would be Dante," the Professor said, glancing at him near the back of the class with a proud glint in his eyes. "He slaughtered a total of fifty animals."

I glanced at Dante, but he just shrugged, as modest as always. After watching him take down a fellow guard with ease, I had no difficulty imagining him wrangling wildlife.

"What kind of weapons do you use?" I asked.

"We use our bare hands," Petra said. "Sometimes, even our teeth if we're really hungry. Does that scare you?"

"Petra, stop," Professor Draven said. "Weapons are permitted, such as bows and daggers, but we consider it more of a challenge to use our hands. It's a testament to our strength."

"Do we have to participate?" Vanessa asked, raising her hand.

"Well, it *is* mandatory for all citizens," Professor Draven said. "And I'm sure the Ambassador would like to learn more about our culture. The Great Hunt is an event we all hold very dear to our hearts."

"Olivia is a vegetarian," Dante said. "I'm sure she'd wish to be left out of the celebrations."

The class murmured at that, finding it weird. What was so strange about being a vegetarian to these people?

"And although I'm a big meat-eater," Vanessa said, "the idea of killing an animal in cold blood makes me sick. I don't want to get blood on my clothes, either."

"I see," Professor Draven said, tapping his chin in deep thought. "Well, I'm sure we could arrange something. Perhaps we could have you watch on the sidelines instead of participating."

"I have a question," I said. "If you hunt that much in a single day, aren't you worried about your animals going extinct?"

"We have worried about that in the past, yes. Without animals, we'd have nothing to eat. Our bodies don't digest plants well," Professor Draven said. "But our Great Hunt only happens once a year, and then we freeze all leftover meat. We're very careful with our rations."

"If we ran out of food, I suppose we'd have to start eating *your* people," Nicolai said, and Vanessa shuddered.

As he and his sister began laughing, the entire class turned silent. As I glanced around, I noticed how disturbed they all looked. It was good to know Petra and Nicolai's crude jokes weren't only bothering me and Vanessa.

Professor Draven heard that snide comment this time, stepping forward. "We don't joke about such things, Nicolai.

And you, Petra. I warned you to stop. What would King Dominic say if he heard you?"

The mention of the king made Nicolai and Petra stop laughing. "We're sorry," they said in unison.

"Don't do it again," Professor Draven warned, turning back to the chalkboard. "And finally, the Sacred Holiday. Petra and Nicolai, why don't you two explain it to Vanessa and Olivia since you're feeling so chatty today?"

"It's our annual holiday," Nicolai said, sounding bored. "School and work are closed, and we gather in the castle to celebrate the founding of our kingdom."

"We have something similar back home," Vanessa said. "We call ours Independence Day, or the Fourth of July. We usually throw big parties and parades, but I guess we'll be missing it this year."

"Ah, then you understand," Professor Draven said. "You're more than welcome to join our celebrations. It's too bad you have to miss yours. Now, kids, can someone tell me who founded the kingdom of V in the 1800s?"

"King Dominic," Petra said, quickly.

The classroom turned and stared at her as though she had said something wrong. She slunk down in her seat, looking embarrassed.

"King...Dominic?" I asked. "As in King Dominic Alucard, Prince Christian's father?"

"Uh, no, most of the kings have shared similar names in history," Professor Draven said, glaring at Petra. "Who can tell me why he founded this kingdom? And take a moment to think about your answer."

"We...thought it would be best to isolate ourselves,"

Nicolai answered. "A bad plague had spread across the world, and King Dominic wanted to protect us from it."

Professor Draven nodded, looking relieved.

Vanessa raised her hand. "But where do your people come from?"

"We believe our people originated somewhere in Europe," Professor Draven replied. "Besides the growing concerns of the plague, our culture was very different from the rest of the world. King Dominic wanted us to live our lives in peace—to start over."

King Dominic had mentioned that to us when we first arrived, that he wanted new beginnings for his people. But why did I have a feeling everyone in the kingdom of V was holding something back?

"Anyway, I think that's enough for our history lessons," Professor Draven continued. "Let's move onto English. Last week, we began studying Agamemnon. We were doing a character study into Cassandra, the Greek woman cursed with seeing true prophecies, but never being believed..."

The clock ticked slowly as we listened to the Professor drone on about ancient literature, and I wondered if Mom was having a better time in discussions with King Dominic. Everything in the classroom, from their textbooks to reading material, was old. The way they conducted school was much different from how we learned back home, too. They took frequent breaks, switched back and forth between subjects with ease, and had no learning materials after the mid-1800s. All the students were much smarter than ours, getting the answers right with little effort.

When the bell rang, Professor Draven put his chalk down and turned to us. "Well, I hope you two enjoyed your first day of class. Next week, we'll be returning to Frankenstein, a novel about a scientist horrified by his creation. See you then, girls."

As me and Vanessa stood up to leave the classroom, Petra and Nicolai pushed through us to make it out first. They sneered at us, baring their teeth before scurrying off down the hallway.

"I can't believe how rude they are," Vanessa muttered as we left the classroom. Dante trailed behind, watching our backs. "Back home, no one would've treated the president's daughter like that!"

"We're not back home, Ness," I said. "If Mom decides to stay here, I might never see it again."

"Total bummer," Vanessa said, sighing.

"Don't let two ignorant people color your perception of our kingdom," Dante said, and I remembered he was still behind us. "Our people can do better. I know they can."

King Dominic had said the same thing to General Ezra last night, but the general hadn't believed him. I wasn't sure I did, either.

"Besides, Petra and Nicolai don't have many friends here at the academy," Dante continued. "No one trusts them."

"Why?" I asked.

"Their parents are imprisoned in the Solitude," Dante said. "Both committed terrible crimes. Petra and Nicolai have had to raise each other. Although I haven't seen them commit any criminal acts, I'd still be cautious around them. And I know they miss their parents greatly."

"No wonder they got so upset when I mentioned their parents," I muttered, glancing down at my bruised wrist. "A little heads up would've been nice, Dante."

"I apologize," he said, "but our people don't like to talk about those incarcerated in the Solitude. It brings us great shame."

"What did they do?" Vanessa asked. "I know you don't like talking about it, but if there's a chance these criminals are dangerous, we deserve to know."

"Most criminals inside belong to a cult called Havoc," Dante said. "Their philosophy is just that, they enjoy causing trouble. Their preferred method is arson, but they have resorted to kidnapping and even murder before. I'd rather not get into the specifics. As I said, it brings us great shame."

Arson. Was it possible they had something to do with the boat explosion, even from inside prison?

"And they're locked up tight, right?" Vanessa asked, nervously.

Dante nodded. "Very. Warden Corina Blanchard makes sure of it."

"Then I guess we should stay away from Petra and Nicolai, just in case," I said. "What's our next class?"

"You don't have one. It's lunchtime," Dante said. "I'll show you the way."

"Good," I said with a sigh of relief. "My favorite subject."

———

As we grabbed our lunch trays from the cafeteria, another salad prepared for me, raw liver for Vanessa. We walked around, trying to find a seat. None of the other students would even look our way, let alone offer us seats.

"God, I feel like such a loser," Vanessa whispered. "Here, I think I found a spot."

There was a small table near the garbage can that no one wanted to sit next to, so me and Vanessa took it. Dante stayed a few feet away, his eyes scanning the cafeteria. I wondered when he would get to eat.

"Well, so much for making friends," Vanessa muttered. "Do the kids not like us or something?"

"I know Petra and Nicolai don't," I said, noticing them staring at us from across the cafeteria. "But everybody else... they just seem so weird."

"Weird, how?" Vanessa asked, digging into her liver.

"Like there's something we can't trust about them."

"Look, I know you're still freaked out about the boat explosion and that kid stabbing you," Vanessa said, "but I'm sure everything's fine. You're probably just feeling this way because you're homesick. I know I am. I'd give anything to have a milkshake and a cheeseburger right now."

"Yeah, maybe," I muttered, pushing my salad around with my fork. "And the worst part is, we can't even call our friends back home. We're totally cut-off from the world."

"Maybe that's a good thing," Vanessa said, her eyes flickering to Dante. "It gives you a chance for some alone time with Dante and Christian. Some of the girls back home would've thrown themselves at them already."

"Would you hush?" I asked, glancing over my shoulder at Dante. He wasn't looking at us, his gaze still trained on the crowd, but I knew his ears were sharp. "Dante's standing right there."

"Oh, he can't hear us. It's too loud in here and he's not even looking," Vanessa said. "Come on, if you had to choose between Dante, the brooding, protective type, or Christian, the playful, sensitive type, who would it be?"

"For starters, Dante's our bodyguard, and a little older than me. It would be inappropriate," I said. "As for Christian, he's a prince with tons of responsibilities. I don't want to distract him from that. Can we drop this now?"

"Gossiping about your love life is the only exciting thing about this place, but fine, I'll let it slide."

"I don't have a love life," I said. "You know I'm not ready."

She rolled her eyes. "Is this about Dylan again? I told you—"

"It's not about Dylan," I shot back. "Just drop it."

Vanessa and I didn't talk again at lunch. I felt bad for snapping at her, but I grew tired of talking about Dylan, and her constant harassment about Dante and Christian. I didn't know either of them that well, and I had no intention of dating anyone when I thought something was wrong with the kingdom.

We only had one class after lunch, my least favorite, gym. It was bad enough the academy had to torture us with boring English and history, but now they wanted me to get all sweaty, too? It was almost a crime.

Coach Nyx was a burly woman with more muscle than some of the toughest guards in the barracks. Vanessa and I stood in the gymnasium with our classmates around us, wearing ugly, black gym uniforms. Petra and Nicolai were on the other team, grinning at us. I knew that wasn't a good sign.

Dante stood at attention off to the side. The coach had set up a row of balls in front of us in a game that reminded me of dodgeball. The coach was about to blow the whistle when General Ezra came and pulled her aside, whispering something in her ear while stealing glances at us.

"What are they whispering about?" Vanessa asked. "Are they talking about us?"

"I have no idea," I muttered.

General Ezra glanced at us one more time before leaving, and Coach Nyx walked over. "All right. Listen up, everyone. I know we usually play to the fullest of our...abilities, but I've got orders from the general to tone it down. No showboating or aggression, got it?"

"Why?" Petra asked, sneering. "Is it because you're afraid those two weaklings won't be able to keep up?"

Coach Nyx glared at her. "Another outburst from you and you'll be booted out of the game, Petra. Three...two...one...go!"

Even with the coach telling the others to take it easy, I still found the game challenging. Our classmates were strong and fast, dodging with moves I'd never seen before. They glided with gracefulness as they caught and tossed the balls. I was never good at sports to begin with. It was more Vanessa's thing as she played on the volleyball team, but even she was struggling. Petra and Nicolai targeted us, their cruel laughter getting a few glares from Coach Nyx.

And by the time the others had kicked our asses, they had barely broken a sweat. We were dripping in it and panting.

"Oh my God," Vanessa said as we entered the locker room after the game. "What were those kids on? Steroids? I've never seen anyone play *that* good."

After we took our showers and changed into a fresh set of clothes, we left the locker room and found Dante waiting for us. "You did well for your first gym class. Well done."

Vanessa laughed. "I'm not sure we were watching the same game."

73

"Our students are well-trained, and very competitive," Dante said. "Don't get discouraged. While they have some advantages, you'll learn how to deal with them."

I didn't know what he was talking about, and it was too late to ask. As we left the academy to go home, I noticed Christian walking toward us. He carried a small gift bag with him.

"Olivia, there you are," he said, smiling. "Hello to you, Vanessa. Can I steal Olivia for a few minutes? I want to talk to her privately."

"I have to stay with Olivia and Vanessa at all times," Dante said. "I'm under orders from King Dominic."

"She'll be safe with me," Christian said. "Why don't you walk Vanessa to her room? I'll make sure nothing happens to Olivia."

Dante hesitated. "But—"

"I gave you an order, soldier," Christian spat. "Follow it."

Dante nodded, leading Vanessa away as she smirked at me over her shoulder. I rolled my eyes as Christian turned to me. "Sorry about that. We have to be firm with these soldiers sometimes. Can we talk? Perhaps in the gardens?"

"Sure," I said, following him. "What's with the gift bag?"

"It's for you," he said, reaching in as we took a seat on a bench underneath a cherry tree. He pulled out a beautiful crimson scarf. "I bought it for you in the markets this morning. I wanted you to have something positive that reminded you of the kingdom of V instead of that wound on your thigh."

"It's very kind of you, but I can't accept this."

"Yes, you can," he said, draping it across my shoulders. It

was soft and warm on my skin. "There, it looks perfect on you."

"Thank you," I said, frowning, "but I can't repay you."

"Perhaps you could answer some of my questions, then. What is life like outside the kingdom?"

I thought for a moment. "Well...it's very different. It's hard to describe. Maybe one day I could show it to you."

He looked down. "I wish...but I'm not sure it's a good idea for my people to leave."

"Why not?"

"It's just as you said. We're very different from the outside world," he replied. "My father believes otherwise, but I'm afraid your people would reject us."

"I'm sure they wouldn't. I accept you. You don't seem that different to me—"

My breath hitched in my throat as I glanced over Christian's shoulder. A man stood there with a cross, his skin pale and blood smeared across his neck. It looked like someone had beaten him—severely.

"You aren't listening," he said, his voice echoing. "Get out while you still can!"

And then he vanished into thin air.

7
TRAINING DAY

I stood up, rushing over to the spot behind Christian where I had seen the man, but he was gone. What was he? A ghost? A cruel prank? And more importantly, was it his voice I had heard in the hallway and his blood on the walls of my room?

"Olivia, are you all right?" Christian asked, walking over to me. He placed a hand on my shoulder when I didn't reply. "Did you hear me?"

"Uh, yeah. I'm fine," I said, looking back at him. "Sorry I spaced out there."

"I'm worried, Olivia," he said. "You look upset. Can you please tell me what's going on?"

I sighed. "I've just been...seeing things."

He frowned. "Such as?"

"It's silly," I said. "And you'll just think I'm crazy. My mom said I've been under a lot of stress, and I'm probably hallucinating—"

"I won't think you're crazy or silly," Christian said, giving me a small smile. "Trust me, I could never think those things about you."

I blushed, clearing my throat. "Well...I've been hearing voices calling my name. Then last night, I saw blood on my walls that told me to get out while I still could. When I screamed and looked away, it vanished like it was never there at all. It was so embarrassing for Mom and Vanessa to see me like that."

He didn't make fun of me, he only nodded. "Go on. What did you see just now?"

"A man," I began, "with a cross and a bloody neck. He said I wasn't listening. That I had to get out. Or else."

Christian turned silent for a moment. "I...see."

"You think I'm crazy, don't you?" I asked, crossing my arms.

"No, not at all. I believe you."

"You do?"

"I told you before, Olivia, we're a very spiritual people," he said. "Perhaps the spirits of our ancestors disapprove of us meeting with outsiders. I hope they'll change their minds as our friendship progresses."

"Even if that's true, and I'm not even sure I believe in ghosts or spirits or whatever," I said. "Why are they only after me? Mom, Vanessa, and Russell haven't mentioned seeing anything."

Christian smiled. "Perhaps the spirits are mesmerized by your beauty?"

I rolled my eyes. "Be serious."

"All right," he said, holding up his hands defensively. "I don't have all the answers yet. These spirits haven't hurt you, have they?"

"No. They've just scared the hell out of me."

"I bet. Some people would've lost their minds after seeing apparitions like that...but you haven't. You're a strong woman, Olivia."

No one had ever called me a woman before. I didn't know how to respond to that compliment, so I changed the subject.

"Maybe it's not a spirit at all," I said, glancing toward the academy. "Maybe someone here is trying to scare me away."

"Like who?"

"Petra and Nicolai Sanguine," I said. "They were harassing me and Vanessa all day. They weren't too thrilled to have new classmates, especially ones from across the world."

Christian's face turned serious. "Stay away from the Sanguine twins, Olivia. I don't want you to get hurt, all right?"

I nodded. "Don't worry, Dante already gave me the whole speech. He mentioned their parents were in jail. They did some terrible things, apparently."

"It's more than that," Christian muttered, looking away. "Just be careful around the academy. Stay with Dante at all times and report anything out of the ordinary. Besides spirits, of course."

"Okay." Christian was starting to scare me, so I decided to change the subject. "Can you keep this a secret from my mom? She has a lot to deal with, and I don't want to stress her out."

Christian smiled. "Your secret's safe with me, Olivia."

"Great. Anyway, thanks for the scarf," I said, gesturing at it, "but I have to get going. Your father asked Dante to train me, and I'm late."

Christian raised his eyebrows. "He did?"

"Yeah. He thought I'd be a good student. Dante said the King saw something in me."

Christian's eyes twinkled. "I know he did. I see it, too. Have fun, Olivia."

As Christian walked out of the gardens, I couldn't help but blush. What was I turning into? Vanessa's influence was rubbing off on me.

As I took the pathway out of the garden, I followed it to the militia building. When I entered, I noticed the usual soldiers sparring and chatting with each other about the state of the kingdom. They cleared out when they noticed me to give me room to train. I spotted Dante standing near the front doors, leaning against the wall in his training outfit. He looked relieved when his gaze landed on me.

"There you are," he said, walking over. "After I brought Vanessa to her room, I came here to wait for our lesson. I was about to look for you."

"Sorry I'm late," I said. "Christian wanted to give me this scarf as an apology gift for the whole stabbing incident."

He glanced down at the scarf, his eyes hard. "It's...a nice gift. I wouldn't want it to get ripped while we fight, so you should take it off."

"Right," I muttered. "I'll go change and be back in a second."

After I had changed in the locker room into something more comfortable. Borrowing a sparring outfit similar to Dante's, I returned to the room and found him punching a boxing bag. Sweat dripped down his skin as he heard my footsteps and turned to me.

"Ready to begin?" he asked.

I nodded. "Ready when you are. What are we doing first?"

Dante said nothing, walking over to a locker on the far side of the room. When he returned, he had a red dagger in his hands, the blade gleaming silver under the candelabra. It had a distinct V shape carved into the handle and some writing I couldn't understand.

"The King wanted you to learn with this," he said. "We use daggers sparingly, but they're the best form of protection around here. The tip is made of pure silver and very few exist. This is our strongest one, our rarest."

"Why do you want me to have it?"

"The King is entrusting it to you," Dante said. "He thinks you're worthy. We call this dagger in particular...the Slayer."

As he passed it to me, it felt heavy in my hands. "Wow."

"Be careful with it," he said. "Around here...you could really hurt someone with that. Are you ready to learn how to wield it?"

I nodded as Dante set up a row of training dummies, pointing at the left part of the chest region. "Remember, when you're fighting, always go for the heart if you want to kill something."

"Why not the eyes or face?" I asked. "Getting stabbed in the head would have to be fatal, right?"

"No. The heart is your best option. That's what we'll focus on."

"What if I can't reach the heart?" I asked. "What if my opponent dodges or something?"

"Then you attack elsewhere to take them down before going for the heart," Dante replied, moving to stand behind me. "If you don't want to kill them, any other spot on the body will suffice. But in the interest of your safety, if you're in a fight to the death, I'd rather you aim for the heart than take any chances."

"Why does the king want me to learn this?" I asked. "Is he anticipating I'll have to kill someone?"

Dante paused, and I could feel his cool breath on the back of my neck. "In the kingdom of V, one must always be prepared. I intend to protect you with my life, but if something happens to me, you should know how to defend yourself. Now, give me your hand."

"My hand?"

He nodded. "I'm going to show you how to use the Slayer."

I held out my hand with the dagger in it, and he placed his large one over mine. Guiding my dagger, he raised my arm and thrust it into the dummy's chest. The dagger pierced through the dummy's plastic skin and left a gaping hole.

"Sharp," I muttered, pulling away. "You weren't kidding about this dagger. I can feel it. It's strong."

He nodded as he stepped back. "Yes, and that was only our first lesson. In time, you'll grow more comfortable with it."

"Sounds cool," I said, setting it down. "So, what now—"

Dante kicked his leg out, tripping me. I almost hit the floor before his arm reached out and caught me in the nick of time.

Panting, I looked up at him. "What was that for?"

"That was our second lesson," he said. "Always be prepared."

He let go of me as I huffed. "You could've warned me you were doing that."

"There won't be warnings in the real world, Olivia," he said, scolding me like a parent. "Your opponent will be counting on you to be naïve and ignorant. You can't give them the satisfaction. In the coming days, I'll teach you everything I know about self-defence."

I felt like someone was watching me. I glanced up, noticing General Ezra's harsh gaze on us from the second floor. He leaned over the handrail to watch my progress. When he noticed me looking back at him, he walked away and disappeared.

"The General was watching the show," I said, grabbing a nearby bottle of water. "Does he do that a lot?"

Dante nodded. "He likes to see how we're progressing. Despite what you think about the General, and his mistrust of outsiders, he *does* care about his recruits. He's the closest thing we have to a father."

I took a long sip, giving him a funny look. "But you have a father. Professor Draven."

"Not anymore. As he mentioned in class, we give up our families in a ceremony before we join the militia."

"I met your mother, too," I said. "She helped heal me when I got stabbed. Don't you miss her? Either of them?"

"I have an obligation to the militia," he said. "My feelings are irrelevant...no matter how strong they may be."

When he looked at me, I had the feeling he wasn't just talking about his parents.

"I...lost my dad when I was a kid," I said. "I'd give anything to see him again. Russell's been a good father figure, but no one can make up for your dad. I wouldn't throw Professor Draven away if I were you. When he dies, you'll wish you hadn't."

"I'm sorry you lost your father," Dante said, "but this is our way. Both I and my father have made peace with my decision."

"Still, I couldn't do that," I said. "Having to say goodbye to Mom and Vanessa..."

"You won't have to," Dante said, stepping forward. "Not while I'm around. Even though I'm teaching you how to fight, it doesn't mean I want you to."

I hoped Dante knew how to deal with ghosts because they seemed to be the biggest threat hanging over my head, other than the Sanguine twins.

"We still have a few hours left of daylight, so let's get back to it," he said, turning away from me. "I have a few more moves I want to show you today."

We sparred until sundown. My muscles ached, but I didn't want to tell Dante and have him think I was weak. He was a good trainer, showing me different styles and dodging techniques, and I didn't want to let him down. He walked me back to my room inside the castle, and I realized I still had the dagger with me.

"Here, you should take this back," I said, handing the Slayer to him. "Mom would freak if she saw me with it."

"It's yours," he said. "You should keep it. But be careful with it, and don't tell anyone. Some of the people might not approve if they learned the King gave you a sacred weapon. Don't forget to bring it to practice tomorrow. We'll pick up where we left off after school."

"I'll keep it safe until then, and hidden from my mom," I said, opening the door to my room. "Thanks for the lesson today, Coach."

"Coach?" he asked, puzzled.

I shrugged. "Sure. You're coaching me, aren't you? What? You don't like the nickname?"

His mouth twitched upward so slightly, I almost didn't notice it. "It's just Dante to you. Always."

And then he was gone, vanishing down the hallway. Had he flirted with me? I couldn't tell. Not from someone as serious as him. Playful felt more like Christian's style. Maybe there was more to Dante than I thought.

I stored the dagger in a small box I'd brought from home and placed it under my bed where no one would find it. Then I changed into my casual clothes, jeans, and a t-shirt as always, but I added the scarf and rushed to the dining hall. It was loud and crowded with the kingdom digging into their raw meat, and I spotted Mom waving at me from a table near the back of the room.

"There you are," Mom said, and I noticed Russell and Vanessa sitting next to her. A salad waited in front of me while the others had meat on their plates. "Where did you go after school?"

"She had two dates," Vanessa said, grinning. "I'm guessing one of them gave her that stylish scarf. Trust me, I've seen her closet. She doesn't own anything that nice."

"Gee, thanks," I muttered, digging into my salad.

Mom raised her eyebrows. "Two dates? What on Earth is Vanessa talking about?"

"It's nothing," I said. "Christian gave me a scarf as an apology present, and then Dante was training me. That's all."

Vanessa smirked, but Russell leaned forward and shook his head. "I don't think you should be spending time with any of the people here, especially alone."

"We have to trust them at some point, Russ," Mom scolded.

"Trust is earned, Lin," he said. "And from what I've seen, they're going to have to work harder to win me over."

"Well, we had meetings with King Dominic all day," she said. She reached into the bag on her chair and pulled out a binder. "He seems very trustworthy, and eager for an alliance. I'm sorry you don't see that yet, Russ."

"Did you talk about anything exciting?" I asked.

She nodded, smiling. "They're building the American embassy we talked about near the academy. I also made some notes with him on future ideas..."

As Mom flipped through the binder to show us what she had talked about, an old, faded photograph slipped out. When Mom reached out to put it back into place, I noticed the man in it. It looked like he was about to set sail as he stood next to a small rowboat.

And he looked exactly like the ghost I'd seen while talking to Christian.

"Who is that?" I asked.

"Oh, that's Charles Browning," Mom said, "the missionary who was killed here."

My heart skipped a beat.

"Murdered," Russell corrected.

"As King Dominic explained, it was all a misunderstanding," Mom said, glaring at Russell. "He reiterated how sorry he was today for Mr. Browning's death."

"Oh, that makes it much better," Russell muttered.

"You're...you're sure that's him?" I asked.

"Positive. This is the only photograph we have of him," Mom said. "It's rumored to have been taken before he left for the kingdom of V, actually. President Bennett wanted me to take it to set up a memorial for him."

My hands shook. The missionary the kingdom's general had killed centuries ago was haunting me.

"Olivia, are you all right?" Mom asked. "You look like you've seen a ghost."

I winced at her choice of words. "Yeah, yeah, I'm fine. Just tired after school. And training."

"I was meaning to ask you about that," Mom said. "How was your first day of school, girls?"

"Fine," Vanessa said, "if you don't count the mean twins and getting our asses kicked at dodgeball."

"Vanessa, language!" Mom scolded. "A new school will take some getting used to. I'm sure things will turn around for you two and you'll make friends in the coming weeks."

Vanessa scoffed. "Don't count on it."

I stood up, feeling lightheaded. "I think I'll head to bed early tonight. It was a long day at school, and I'm not that hungry, anyway."

Mom smiled, blissfully ignorant. "All right, sweetie. Sleep well and I'll see you tomorrow."

"Sweet dreams," Vanessa said as I walked away.

When I got back to my room, I collapsed onto the bed, my mind spinning. The ghost had to be a trick. Someone trying to freak me out. Eventually, my eyes grew heavy, and I fell fast asleep.

I woke up a few hours later to total darkness. Heavy rain pounded against my window. As I sat up and rubbed my eyes, I heard a noise outside my window in the distance. It sounded like something crashing against the docks. When I looked outside, I squinted to make it out and couldn't believe my eyes.

It was a boat—and it was docking.

What was it doing there so late? Had President Bennett decided to come early?

I couldn't let it go, so I got dressed and headed for the militia building. General Ezra would've known what was going on. He greeted us when we arrived, and everyone said he was the eyes and ears of the kingdom.

Covering my head with my hand to avoid getting pelted by the rain, I then snuck inside the building and tip-toed past the barracks, hearing the snoring of the soldiers. I took the staircase and walked upstairs, making my way toward General Ezra's private room. I didn't hear snoring.

When I knocked on the door, he opened it lightning-fast a second later. He looked disappointed when he noticed me. "Miss Hawthorne? What are you doing here?"

"I heard a boat, General," I said. "Do you know anything about that?"

His eyebrows furrowed in confusion. "A boat? No, I wasn't told anything about any arrivals, and the last I heard, your president wasn't due for another week."

"Well, someone's on that boat. Come on. I'll show it to you."

I rushed outside, guiding the General to the docks in the pouring rain, only to find nothing. The boat had vanished.

"I don't understand," I stammered. "I heard the boat. I even saw it when I looked out my window. I swear!"

General Ezra crossed his arms. "That's two nights in a row you've claimed you saw something. If I didn't know better, I'd say you're up to something."

"I'm not," I said, turning to him with a glare. "I know what I saw!"

"Uh-huh. Sure," he muttered. "Make up whatever story you want to entertain yourself, but try not to waste my time, all right?"

As he left, I stared out at the empty docks, getting soaked by the rain. I knew I had seen a boat tonight. The only question I had was if it was real or a hallucination?

8

THE BLACK VIAL

That incident with General Ezra was embarrassing. At that point, I was pretty sure he hated me. I returned to my room. After changing out of my sopping wet clothes, I put on a fresh set of pajamas and tried to fall asleep.

Thankfully, no ghosts decided to haunt me.

I woke up to dawn and heard the quiet patter of feet outside the window. When I looked out, I noticed crowds of people walking in the same direction. From children to teens to adults and elders, they marched in a single file and said nothing to each other.

Where was everyone going at this hour?

I had a feeling me, Mom, Vanessa, and Russell weren't supposed to know about it, but I was curious. I threw on a pair of jeans and a sweater and rushed outside my room, finding everyone else still asleep. I'd have to go alone.

I decided to take my Slayer with me, just in case I ran into trouble. Dante had told me it was a good idea to keep it with me. I joined the long line outside and tapped on the woman's shoulder in front of me. She turned around, her dark hair billowing in the breeze.

"Excuse me," I said, "but what's going on?"

She looked me up and down and shook her head. "Outsiders don't need to know. This is our business. Go back to your room and stay there, foreigner."

And then she turned away to face forward, pretending like I wasn't there. The other people in line started to stare at me, realizing I wasn't one of them. I grew tired of their glances and cut ahead of the line. That was when I realized where the line ended, at the clinic.

I reached the front doors, watching as Dr. Draven, Anastasia, and Dr. Oscar Cox handed out small vials of black liquid. The kingdom of V citizens took it one by one, choked it down, and made a disgusted face before leaving the clinic. They went about their business, heading to work, school, and the markets, as though nothing had happened.

"Sorry about the taste," Anastasia said. "But it's a small price to pay, don't you think?"

"A sip of the vial keeps the monster away for a while," Oscar muttered, his eyes still blown wide. "A sip of the vial keeps the monster away for a while..."

I didn't know whether to write Oscar off or take his mumbling as a sign that something was wrong. The others ignored him, accustomed to his ramblings.

When I pushed inside the clinic, I noticed King Dominic, Queen Vivienne, Christian, Dante, and General Ezra near the back wall. They didn't have to wait in line. They drank their vials from a private supply on a nearby table.

"Ugh," Christian said, wincing as he finished his vial. "No

matter how many times I drink it, I never get used to that bitterness..."

Dante didn't react, as stone-faced as ever. "Remember why we take it and what happens if we don't, Prince Christian. That alone justifies the taste."

Christian nodded, somberly. He didn't speak again.

"What's going on here?" I asked, my hands on my hips.

Their heads snapped up, finally noticing me. They glanced around at each other before Christian stepped forward. "Olivia, we thought you were still sleeping."

"I was," I said, crossing my arms. "Footsteps woke me up."

"She's a light-sleeper," General Ezra said, glancing at them. "She woke me up last night because she thought she heard a boat docking. When I got there, I didn't see anything."

"A boat?" Dante asked, frowning. "That's...an odd thing to claim to see."

"I don't claim I saw it," I shot back. "I *did* see it. It was there!"

"Of course it was," General Ezra mocked. "Whatever you say."

While King Dominic, Queen Vivienne, and Dante looked confused, Christian had a look of recognition on his face. He was the only one I had told about seeing ghosts, so maybe he was wondering if the boat fit in somehow. I was, too.

"Is anyone going to tell me about those vials?" I asked, balling my fists at the general's dismissal. "Why you're taking them in secret?"

"It's a tradition," Christian said. "Our people have to take our medicine every few days. It helps bring us together, too.

We didn't mean to keep it a secret. We just didn't want to worry you for nothing."

"Medicine?" I asked, frowning. "Are you sick?"

"No, not at all. In fact, we don't get diseases," King Dominic said. "We believe in preventative healthcare and require all citizens to drink from our healing elixirs every few days."

"Oh. So...it's kind of like vitamins?"

"Yes," King Dominic said, smiling. "It's exactly like that."

"I heard what Oscar said at the door, though," I continued. "He mentioned something about these vials keeping the monster away for a while. Sounded like a morbid nursery rhyme."

"Oscar is a brilliant doctor and alchemist, but I'm sure you've realized by now that he isn't entirely there," Queen Vivienne said. "He loves his fairy tales and urban legends, and sometimes, he speaks them aloud. We mostly ignore him, but I'll make sure to have a chat with him and ask him to keep his stories to himself. Before he scares someone."

I had the feeling they were hiding something, but it was clear they weren't going to admit it.

"Let's get you back to your room, Olivia," Dante said, stepping forward. "It's almost time for school—"

A nearby scream made me jump. I looked over, noticing a man with reddish hair convulsing on the floor. Anastasia had screamed. It looked like he had drunk some of the black juice she'd given him, but couldn't finish the rest. It jiggled in his small vial.

"His body's rejecting it," Dr. Draven said, grabbing the man by his shoulders. "Get the emergency kit. We need to move. Fast!"

Anastasia nodded, grabbing a nearby crate of supplies and vials filled with strange liquids. Dr. Draven dragged the man into a small corner near the back of the clinic, closing the white curtain so I couldn't see what was happening. Oscar didn't react. He only continued to hand out small vials to the people waiting in line. They all seemed unfazed.

"What's going on?" I asked.

"Sometimes our people's bodies...reject the vitamins," King Dominic said. "It isn't a pretty sight."

"Will he be okay?"

"We don't know yet," Queen Vivienne said. "But rest assured, our physicians will do all they can for him. We've dealt with this before."

"If it's happened before," I began, "why do you keep taking it?"

They didn't reply.

"Come on, Olivia," Dante said, pulling on my arm. "Let's get back to the castle."

As we walked back to my room, pushing through the long line-up, I turned to Dante. "Does the medicine have anything to do with that plague I learned about in history class? The reason your people fled here?"

"Don't worry about that, Olivia," he said. "And you don't have to worry about catching anything, either. Your people don't need the medicine."

"Were you ever going to tell us about it? If you ever decide to visit our country, we'd need to know."

"King Dominic wanted to wait. You have a lot to learn about our people, but learning everything at once might overwhelm you."

Vanessa's door flung open, her backpack on. She eyed me

and Dante suspiciously. "Oh, you two are already up. Did I miss anything?"

Just everyone drinking strange black juice and avoiding my questions, I wanted to say.

"Not really," I said. "Where's Mom?"

"Oh, she's still in her room. She's waiting for King Dominic to summon her so they can go over more boring ambassador stuff. You ready for school?"

"It's only a half-day today," Dante said. "The Festival of the Night takes place this evening. It gives us the other half of the day to set up."

"Let me grab my bag," I said. "I'll be right back."

After I had my backpack, I followed Vanessa and Dante to the dining hall for a quick breakfast before we headed to the academy. The long line veering toward the clinic had disappeared, and I noticed how much livelier everyone seemed. It was like the strange liquid had changed their personalities, giving them more energy.

Dante continued to trail behind us. It was annoying having him as our shadow, but it made me feel better, so I said nothing. The bell rang as soon as we reached the academy and me and Vanessa rushed into Professor Draven's class. He was scribbling something down on the chalkboard as we took our seats and Dante returned to his usual spot. The Sanguine twins trickled in after, sneering at us before grabbing desks far away from our seats.

"Well, since it's only a half-day today, we'd better not waste time," Professor Draven said, turning to us. "And I'd like to try something different today. We're going to be learning Bloodspeak."

My hand shot up. "What's that?"

"The language of our people," Professor Draven replied. "It's almost like a secret code of communication, something only the people of V would understand."

"Uh, excuse me, Professor?" Petra asked. "Should we really be teaching that stuff to outsiders?"

The Professor glared at her. "King Dominic made it clear that we are to welcome our guests. That includes teaching them our ways, Petra."

The Professor reached into his desk and pulled out a large hunting knife. When he rolled up his sleeve and slit his arm, crimson blood dribbling down onto the desk, I gasped.

"What are you doing?" I asked.

"Demonstrating our language," he said. "It's written in our blood."

"Gross," Vanessa muttered. "Why blood? Can't you just use a pen or something?"

"Blood is sacred," Professor Draven explained. "It's life-force, energy. Without blood, you'd die. Because of that, it's very important to our people."

He turned to the chalkboard, using his blood to smear strange symbols on it. It drizzled, making me feel nauseous, but no one else in the room flinched. He drew a lot of lines and weird shapes that looked like a bunch of nonsense to me.

"Over the next few weeks, you will all come to learn Bloodspeak and identify many of the symbols. You'll even be able to read and compose your own sentences."

"Wait a second," Vanessa said. "Are we supposed to cut ourselves, too? That sounds painful. And no offense, but I don't want to scar myself."

"Coward," Nicolai muttered, and Petra snorted.

I glared at the two of them.

"You don't need to cut deep enough to scar, and you get used to the pain after a while. This is the way of our people," Professor Draven said, drying his bleeding arm with a towel. "However, I won't force you and Olivia into something that makes you uncomfortable. If you prefer, you may watch your classmates do it, but you will still learn to identify words and patterns."

Professor Draven went over a few of the symbols with us. We learned basic words like hello, goodbye, yes and no, and please and thank you. Although I wasn't crazy about the whiff of blood in the room, that disgusting coppery stench, it was cool learning a new language, even if I wasn't sure how useful it would be. Everyone spoke and wrote in English, anyway.

After a few hours, Professor Draven glanced at the clock on the wall. "I believe that concludes our lesson for today. Class is dismissed, and you may all return home to prepare for the festival tonight."

"Do we have any homework?" Vanessa asked, raising her hand.

"No, not on the day of the Festival of the Night," Professor Draven said. "Enjoy your weekend off. Bright and early next week, we'll have a guest teacher."

"Who?" I asked.

He blinked, smiling. "You, Miss Hawthorne."

I frowned. "Me? What are you talking about?"

"Oh, you didn't know?" he asked. "Prince Christian arranged for you to teach an art class. King Dominic agreed. He thinks we could all benefit from learning something new, and no one has any expertise in it besides you."

"An art class?" Nicolai asked. "And taught by *her*? What a waste of time."

"King Dominic believes in it, and so do I," Professor Draven snapped. "The whole point of making contact with the outside world was to learn their ways. I believe Olivia will make an excellent teacher."

I admired the Professor's confidence in me, but I was still worried none of the kids would accept me. I hadn't had much time to paint since getting to V, so I hoped I still remembered the basics. And why would Christian do that without telling me first?

"Liv would never admit it, but she's really good," Vanessa said, glancing at me. "Can't wait...Professor Hawthorne."

I groaned. That new title wasn't going to earn me *any* new friends.

When the bell rang, the Professor and our classmates stood up and scurried out of the room. As me and Vanessa tried to leave, Petra and Nicolai blocked our path. I gripped the Slayer in my pocket just in case. I could feel Dante's presence behind me, so I wasn't too worried.

"You don't belong here," Petra said to me. "You shouldn't even be going to this academy, let alone teaching at it."

"And we don't care if the whole royal family thinks it's a good idea," Nicolai added. "We don't want to learn anything from an outsider like you."

Vanessa scoffed. "If we wanted your irrelevant opinions, we would've asked. But we didn't, did we?"

Petra and Nicolai stepped closer, growling. I feared they'd tackle us both in the classroom.

"Get out of their way," Dante muttered, "or you'll have to deal with me."

Petra and Nicolai both hissed at Dante before disappearing down the hallway. I turned to him, sighing. "Thanks for that. Those two just never quit."

"I apologize for their behavior," Dante said as we exited the classroom. "King Dominic held a press conference before your people arrived. He explained that he wanted everyone to do their part in making you feel welcome."

"Some haven't gotten the memo," I muttered.

"It's okay," Vanessa said. "We have mean kids like that back home, too. As long as they don't get violent, we're cool."

"Speaking of violent," I said, "do you think they'll follow in their parent's footsteps? That they'll end up in the Solitude one day, too?"

Dante shuddered. "I hope not."

After we had walked Vanessa back to her room, she turned to me. "Guess I'll see you for dinner and the festival tonight." Her eyes briefly flitted to Dante. "Don't have too much fun while I'm gone, Liv."

Dante turned to me after Vanessa had stepped inside her room. "Do you have your Slayer?"

I nodded, showing him the dagger. "You told me to keep it on me. I listened."

"Good. Since we still have a few hours before sundown, are you ready for another sparring lesson?"

I grinned. "Bring it on, Coach."

He shook his head, biting back a laugh. "You're still insistent on calling me that, aren't you?"

"I think it's fitting," I said, following him to the militia building. "You know, you can give me a nickname, too."

"Oh? And what should it be?" he asked, opening the door for me.

"How about...best student ever?"

His smile was getting harder to suppress. It looked almost painful for him to stay so serious. "I'll consider it."

After I had changed into my sparring outfit, the militia building cleared out to give me and Dante space again to train. He waited for me near the familiar training dummy as I pulled out my Slayer.

"Anyone can hit a fixed target," he said, "but it takes skill to stab a moving one. I'm eager to see you try it. Ready?"

I nodded, gripping my dagger. He began moving the dummy back and forth and side to side. I took a step back, trying to match its rhythm. When I lunged out, I realized I had stabbed the dummy in its shoulder.

"Not bad," he said. "It would subdue your opponent for a few seconds, but not enough for a killing blow. Let's try that again. Remember, keep your eyes focused on the spot you want to strike."

As he began moving the dummy again, much faster this time, I lunged forward with my dagger toward its chest. I must've moved too fast, because the next thing I knew, I had tripped and fallen to the floor. The dagger slipped out of my hands and clanged on the tile, but not before scratching the flesh of my hand hard enough to draw blood.

"Olivia, are you all right?" Dante asked, helping me to my feet.

"I think so," I muttered, glancing down at my bleeding hand. "Great, now I'm bleeding."

When I looked back up at Dante, he had the same delirious look in his eyes as the little boy had right before he stabbed me. When I backed up, afraid of the crazed expression on his face, he stepped closer to me, saying nothing.

"Dante..." I began. "What are you doing?"

The sound of his name seemed to snap him back to reality. He looked up at me, embarrassed. "I...apologize, Olivia. I was distracted there for a second. Let me help you clean up."

He rushed to the back of the militia building, entering the bathroom. I heard the water turn on before he emerged with a bandage. It looked like he had splashed water on his face judging by his wet neck and t-shirt. As he wrapped the bandage around my hand, trying to stop the bleeding, I couldn't tear my gaze off him. He, on the other hand, seemed to look everywhere but me.

"Dante," I began, "what happened back there?"

He finally glanced up at me, staring into my eyes for a moment. It looked like he wanted to tell me, but something was holding him back. As he opened his mouth to speak, the door to the militia building opened and General Ezra entered.

"I thought I'd find you two here," he said. "I have news."

"What kind of news?" I asked.

"The man you saw earlier. The one who convulsed after drinking the vial?" General Ezra asked. "We've just been informed by Dr. Draven that he died this afternoon."

9
CRIME AND PUNISHMENT

Dante didn't say anything. Maybe he was taking a moment to mourn, or maybe he just didn't know what to say. If he wasn't going to ask any questions, I would. I took a step forward as General Ezra's gaze landed on me.

"That man died because he drank the black stuff in the vial, right?" I asked.

General Ezra nodded. "That's right."

"What was in it, then? Some kind of poison?"

"No, it wasn't poison. As King Dominic explained," General Ezra began, harsher this time, "the medicine is necessary for our people. For those unlucky, it can have...unfortunate side effects. Their bodies can't handle it."

"I just don't understand," I said. "Why take it if there's a risk of death? Why does it only have deadly side effects for some of your people and not others?"

"No, you don't understand," General Ezra sneered. "Outsiders never will."

A bitter silence hung in the air. I still hadn't forgotten the general's private conversation with the king. The general didn't want us here, didn't want *me*.

Dante stepped forward, clearing his throat. "His death won't be for nothing, Olivia. King Dominic will honor his memory at the festival, and Anastasia will use his body for medical research. Perhaps one day, there won't be any risk involved with the medicine."

General Ezra rolled his eyes. It was clear he didn't think so.

"I'll be patrolling the festival tonight," General Ezra said, glaring at me. "You'd better be on your best behavior, Olivia, you *and* your people. I won't tolerate any more fabricated stories."

Fabricated stories? He still didn't believe I had seen a boat. He probably wouldn't believe me if I told him I'd seen the ghost of Charles Browning, either, so I kept that to myself.

"I'll be with Olivia all night," Dante said. "I'll ensure nothing happens to her."

"Good," General Ezra said. "I'll hold you personally responsible if she gets into any trouble."

I'm not a child, I wanted to say. *I don't need a babysitter watching over my shoulder.* But I didn't have the chance to make my feelings clear as the general spoke first, his eyes flickering to my bandaged hand.

"I tried to tell my brother that training you was a mistake," he said. "You've been practicing for barely two days, and you've already hurt yourself."

"It was an accident," I said. "I dropped the dagger on my hand."

"Your...dagger?" General Ezra asked, confused.

I picked the Slayer off the ground, holding it up. "Yeah, Dante gave it to me."

"You gave her the Slayer?" General Ezra demanded, towering over Dante.

"On the King's orders," Dante said, not backing down.

"I see," the general muttered. "I wasn't aware. Next time, be more careful with that dagger. Your clumsiness could hurt someone. Someone important."

As the general turned to leave, Dante stepped forward. "General Ezra, wait. I need to speak to you. In private."

The general's gaze flickered to me before he nodded. "We can speak later tonight. I have a few duties left to finish for the day."

As he left the militia building, I couldn't decipher the look on his face. Was he angry the king had given me the dagger? He seemed to recognize it, even knew it by name.

"What do you need to talk to the general about?" I asked Dante.

"It's nothing you need to be concerned about," Dante said. "Just guard responsibilities. I'm sure you wouldn't find it interesting."

I had a feeling it was more than that, but Dante didn't seem too eager to tell me. No one seemed eager to tell me anything.

"Well, better you than me," I said, taking a swig of water. "The general's a real asshole."

"He might seem that way to those who don't know him, yes. I apologize on behalf of the general," Dante said. "He doesn't like outsiders seeing us as weak and vulnerable. He believes many things should be kept private, but King

Dominic insists on sharing everything with your people. It irritates him."

"Well, I'm glad King Dominic's in charge and not him," I muttered, turning to Dante. "So, what's next on the training schedule?"

Dante looked away. "Our training is finished for the day."

"What? But we've barely started!"

"I think we should take a break. For a few days, at least."

"Did I do something wrong?" I asked, stepping closer to him. "Are you disappointed I dropped the dagger?"

He shook his head. "I'm not disappointed in you, Olivia. In fact, I think you've been doing well for a beginner."

"Then what?" I asked, but he stayed silent. Then it hit me. "Is it because of that weird look on your face when you saw my blood?"

He still didn't reply, but his eyes held a look of remorse.

"I knew it," I said. "Dante, what's going on?"

His gaze snapped to mine. "I don't want to talk about it. But before we change the subject...I'm very sorry. It won't happen again. That I promise you."

As he walked over to the locker room to change, I followed him. "But I don't even know what happened. You won't tell me anything!"

"Please," he said, his face scrunched in pain. "I don't want to speak of it again. Respect me enough to drop it."

I sighed, realizing he wasn't going to tell me. "All right, fine. I'll let it go."

"Thank you," he said, exhaling. "Now, if you'll get changed, I'll walk you back to your room. You still need to eat dinner before the festival tonight, and it'll be dark soon."

As curious as I was, I knew questioning him would get

me nowhere. I entered the women's locker room, changing into my casual clothes before I tucked my dagger into my belt. When I left the locker room, Dante was already waiting for me outside.

He said nothing as we walked through the streets, making our way back to the castle. I noticed some of the professors and townspeople helping set up for the festival later in the field behind the castle. They were hanging more lanterns off the trees, assembling a buffet with raw meat and drinks, and dragging over something that looked like a statue.

As we reached my room, Dante turned to me. "I'll return later tonight to take you to the festival. Enjoy your dinner."

"Dante, wait," I said, but he'd already rushed off down the hallway.

The door to Vanessa's room opened and she poked her head out. "I thought I heard voices. Whoa, what happened?"

When she pointed at my bandage, I shrugged. "Oh, that. It's nothing. Trust me."

"As long as you're okay. Anyway, was that Dante?"

I sighed. "It was."

"Well, it sounded like he couldn't get away from you fast enough," Vanessa muttered. "Did you piss him off?"

"I really don't know," I muttered, truthfully. "Ness...the people here are weird."

She snorted. "You just figure that out? Come on, I'm starving. I was waiting for you before heading to the dining hall. I let your mom and Russ go ahead without us."

I pulled my sleeve down over my bandage, not wanting anyone else to see. I knew Mom would freak out and I didn't want that. Besides, my cut was already starting to feel better, and there was no point in getting worked up about something that was an accident.

We found my mom and Russell waiting in the dining hall, gesturing for us to join them at a small table. The servants delivered our food a second later, the same old boring salad for me while Vanessa, Mom, and Russell had their share of fatty meat. I picked at my food as Mom went on and on, talking about how well her meetings had gone with King Dominic and how the embassy was almost ready to open. Russell usually hung on her every word, but even he looked bored.

"Back home, it would've taken months to build an embassy. I don't know how the architects have done it so quickly. I can't believe how well things are going," Mom said, taking a sip of her water. "But how about you, girls? How are you liking the kingdom of V?"

I glanced at Vanessa. Should we tell Mom the truth? How we were both miserable? How strange things only seemed to keep happening, like the ghosts, mysterious boat, and strange medicine?

"We're doing fine, Mom," I lied. "Everything's great."

Vanessa faked a smile. "Yeah, we love it here."

Mom grinned, placing her hand on mine. "You don't know how glad I am to hear that. This will be a wonderful new home for us, Olivia, just wait and see."

She looked so happy with her new job that I didn't have the heart to tell her how I really felt. I hadn't seen her that excited about something in years. Not since Dad had died. It didn't feel right ripping that away from her.

I took a bite of my salad to hide my frown as Russell

leaned forward. "How are things going with Dante? Does he make you feel safe?"

Again, I struggled to tell the truth. How would I explain the strange expression on his face when I started bleeding? Especially when I didn't even know what had happened?

"He's a good bodyguard," I said, which wasn't a lie. "He'll be with us at the festival tonight, too."

Russell gave me a sidelong glance. I hadn't answered his question about feeling safe around Dante. If I had to be honest, I didn't feel safe around *anyone*.

"Speaking of the festival," Vanessa said, interrupting my thoughts, "do we really have to go? It just doesn't sound like my kind of thing."

"Yes, you absolutely have to go," Mom said. "Look, we want the kingdom to feel like they can be themselves in our presence. Part of that means respecting their culture, their traditions. I for one am excited to see what they have in store for tonight. And by the way, I heard about what happened earlier."

"With what?" I asked, fearing she had seen my strange exchange with Dante in the militia building.

"You know," Mom said. "The medicine."

Vanessa frowned. "What medicine? What are you talking about?"

After Mom explained it, Russell raised his eyebrows. "And a man...died from it? Right after drinking the black stuff?"

I nodded. "It freaked me out, too."

"The King was sad to hear about his death, but he assured me it's nothing to worry about," Mom said. "It isn't our place to interfere in kingdom business, anyway. And besides, I believe him."

That makes one at this table, I wanted to say.

———

After dinner, we returned to our rooms to change. The militia guards told us to dress in all black for the festival which wasn't a problem for me. Most of my clothes were dark. As I threw on the same black dress I'd worn when we first arrived, making sure to cover up my cut again with a huge bracelet, a knock came at my door. Vanessa entered a second later before she rushed over to my closet and began looking through my clothes.

"You know, you're supposed to wait for permission after knocking," I said, turning to her. "I could've been naked."

"Can't talk, need to find a dress," she said, pulling out all the black clothes I owned. "All my dresses are pink, and apparently, that's unacceptable. Thank goodness for your lack of color."

I rolled my eyes as she took her sweet time finding something suitable to wear. As the sky darkened, she emerged from my bathroom with one of the dresses Mom had bought me before we left. It was black with silver embroidery, and I'd found it a little too girly for my taste. It fit Vanessa perfectly, and she looked much better in it than I would have.

"I never thought your fashion sense would save the day," Vanessa said, checking herself out in my mirror, "but here we are. Hey, isn't Dante supposed to be here to escort us to the festival or something?"

I opened the door, peeking down the hallway. "Yeah, but

I don't see him. He's usually on time. What do you think's taking him so long?"

"He's *your* boyfriend," Vanessa said, turning to me with a smirk. "You should know."

"For the last time, he's not my boyfriend," I said, scowling. "And Christian isn't, either, so don't even go there."

"Well, you're on a first-name basis with him, so I'd say that's a start. Do you have a cute nickname for him yet? Either of them?"

I rolled my eyes. "Come on. Let's go find Dante. I'm sick of waiting around."

We tip-toed down the hallway, sneaking past Mom's room. Most of the people in the castle had already gone outside for the festival. Their laughter and small talk echoed down the corridor.

"Where are we going?" Vanessa whispered, staying close to my side.

"To the militia building," I whispered back. "That's the only place I can think of to look for him."

We slipped outside the back of the castle, careful to avoid getting caught. If General Ezra saw me, he'd think I was up to no good again, and he might tell Mom. The last thing I wanted was another lecture. As we made our way to the militia building, it looked pitch black.

"Doesn't look like anyone's home," Vanessa whispered, glancing through the window. "You don't think Dante went to the festival without us, do you? That he decided he needed a night off?"

I shook my head. "He doesn't seem like the kind of guy to do that. He takes his responsibilities very seriously. It's all he talks about. Let's see if he's in there."

We opened the door with a quiet squeak, entering the darkened militia building. Unlike earlier, there were no signs of life.

"Well, it's just like I said," Vanessa whispered. "No one's home—"

A loud crack on the second floor made us both pause. I turned to Vanessa. "Did you hear that?"

She nodded. "I did. But what was it?"

"No idea," I whispered. "I think it came from upstairs."

As we climbed the staircase, I noticed the flicker of candlelight coming from underneath the General's office door. When we approached, the crack sounded again. This time accompanied by a quiet cry of pain. The general had told me personally he'd be on duty tonight, so who was in his office?

I opened the door slowly and gasped. Vanessa stiffened behind me, and I knew she was just as startled as I was to see Dante on his knees in front of the general. Dante had his shirt off, exposing his muscular back as the general thrashed him with an old-fashioned whip. I could see the painful welts on Dante's back which were beginning to bleed.

That was the source of the crack—the General's whip on Dante's flesh. As Vanessa and I peered into the office, both frozen in silence, the general and Dante didn't notice us. They seemed too preoccupied.

"This pains me as much as you," General Ezra said, whipping him again. Dante cried out in pain much louder this time. "I hate punishing my soldiers...but this is for the best. We can't allow moments of weakness, especially not with someone who has as much self-control as you do."

"Yes, General," Dante gritted. "I...deserve this."

I was about to intervene when General Ezra put the whip down. "You may rise, Dante. Your punishment is over now."

Dante rose to his feet, groaning. "Thank you, General. I vow to never let it happen again."

"You'd better not. King Dominic made it clear what was expected of us," General Ezra said. "Now, head to the church for absolution. The festival is about to begin, and I'm sure our guests are waiting for you. Be quick, and mention nothing about this. That's an order."

Dante nodded and bowed. I pulled Vanessa back, hiding behind the wall as Dante's loud footsteps echoed toward us. He passed us before he walked down the staircase. When the general followed and fled the militia building, I breathed a sigh of relief.

"They didn't see us," I whispered. "Good."

"None of this is good, Liv," Vanessa muttered, glancing back at the office. "What the hell was going on in there? And what were they talking about with weaknesses and stuff?"

"I don't know," I said. "But I think we should follow Dante. General Ezra told him to pray for absolution in the church, remember? Maybe we'll overhear something."

"All right," Vanessa said. "I hope we'll find some answers."

As we left the militia building, we spotted General Ezra further along the brick path giving directions to his soldiers. We hid our faces, grateful for the dark sky. As we entered the church, we found Dante praying on his hands and knees in front of the stained-glass window. He had put his shirt back on to cover his lesions and lit a candle to light the room. The moonlight trickled in through the window, shining on his black hair.

When we heard him mumbling, me and Vanessa crept closer to hear what he was saying. We ducked behind a row of pews to eavesdrop.

"...which is why I beg for forgiveness, Lord," he muttered. "I am a wicked, evil creature, and I need absolution and strength. I try so hard to suppress my desires, the thing that plagues my people, but it eats away at me every day..."

"What the hell is he talking about?" Vanessa whispered.

When Dante's voice lowered, I shook my head. "I don't know. I can barely hear him now. I need to get closer."

As I crawled on my hands and knees, trying to listen in, I banged my head into a side table and knocked over a bunch of candles. As I groaned and clutched my forehead, I heard Dante rise to his feet and step away from the window.

"Who's there?" he asked. "Come out where I can see you!"

Vanessa sighed, glaring at me before she rose to her feet. I figured there was no use in hiding now that he knew someone was there, so I joined her. Dante's eyes widened when he noticed us.

"What are you doing here?" he asked, stepping closer.

"We came to pray," I lied. "Well, Ness did. I'm not that religious. But when we saw you in here, we didn't want to disturb you. We were just about to leave."

It seemed like he believed my lie. "You didn't disturb me. I apologize for being late. I was...busy with other matters."

"That's okay," I said. "Are you ready to take us to the festival now?"

He nodded. "Let's return to your rooms and get your mother. The festival should be starting any minute now."

As we left the chapel, we pushed through the crowd to

make our way back to the castle. When Dante knocked on Mom's door, she came out in a floor-length black dress. When Russell walked out of his room, his eyes lingered on Mom, transfixed by her beauty. I hadn't seen her that dressed up since the old days when Mom and Dad would have their date nights.

"Good evening, Ambassador," Dante said, bowing at her. "I hope you're ready for the festival."

"Oh, I am," she said, grinning as she turned to me and Vanessa. "You two look great. Are we good to go?"

"Just one second," Vanessa said, giving me a mysterious look. "I need some help with my dress. Liv?"

Before I could reply, Vanessa had already yanked me inside her room and shut the door behind us. Dante and the others looked puzzled but didn't protest. Mom had to know Vanessa would never ask for help with her clothes, not from me. We lowered our voices so they wouldn't hear us through the thin walls.

"Why is he acting like the general didn't just thrash him?" Vanessa whispered. "I just...I have no words, Liv. What the hell is going on around here?"

"It's just like I told you, Ness," I said, glancing out the window at the crowd, "the people here are weird. I didn't want to admit it for Mom's sake, but...I think there's something seriously wrong with the kingdom of V."

10

FESTIVAL OF THE NIGHT

Vanessa crossed her arms. "Something wrong? Like what?"

"It's hard to explain," I said. "For starters, I've been seeing ghosts—"

"Ghosts?" Vanessa asked, her eyes wide. "Oh my God!"

A knock sounded on the door. Mom's voice came through a second later. "Girls, are you okay in there?"

"Yeah, we're fine, Mom!" I called back. "Almost done!"

"We're not going anywhere until you tell me more about these ghosts," Vanessa whispered. "When did that start? And how come you didn't say anything?"

"I didn't want you to think I was crazy," I said. "First, I started hearing my name, and then the other night, 'get out while you still can' was written on my wall in blood. When you and Mom rushed in, the words had disappeared."

"Oh, so that's why you screamed," Vanessa said. "I knew you hadn't seen a spider!"

"Shh, keep your voice down," I said, glancing at the door. "Anyway, I thought maybe it was just stress playing with my mind until I saw the ghost of a man. When Mom showed me the picture of Charles Browning, I recognized him. There's no way I'd know what he looked like, unless it really was his ghost."

Vanessa sat down on her bed, silent for a few seconds. "Okay, let me get this straight. You're telling me we're stranded on an island with ghosts and no way to get home?"

I sighed. "Yeah, I guess so."

Vanessa shook her head. "Oh, we're so screwed..."

"Have you seen any ghosts?" I asked. "Or anything suspicious?"

"No ghosts, thankfully. I'm not sure I'd be as sane as you are if I had. And other than Dante getting whipped like there was no tomorrow, nothing too weird, no," she said, rising to her feet. "If you see more ghosts, you need to come and get me, okay? You're not alone. If we want to make it out of this, we need to work together."

"All right, deal. I'll let you know if I see anything, but we have to be careful."

"Olivia, afraid of ghosts?" Vanessa teased. "I thought you didn't believe in that stuff."

"I don't, but still—"

Another knock from Mom. "Girls, I hate to rush you, but we're running late as it is. We don't want to miss the festival!"

"No, of course not," Vanessa muttered, looking back at me. "You think you'll see any ghosts tonight?"

I sighed. "I hope not, but around here? You never know."

When I opened the door, Dante gave us a strange look. "Are you two all right? I heard whispering."

"Just a little gossip between two girls," Vanessa lied, looking back at me. "We're fine. Nothing to worry about."

Dante nodded, walking down the hallway. As we followed him, I noticed that every time his black shirt rubbed up against his back, he flinched in pain. Vanessa noticed too, glancing my way. It was hard to look at him knowing I couldn't help him. Should we have stopped it? Confronted the general? The guilt ate me up inside.

As we left the castle, we made our way to the field behind it, the lanterns illuminating our path. The entire kingdom had showed up, some grabbing a bite of raw meat from the buffet, others chatting and telling jokes. General Ezra and his soldiers patrolled the field, and he glared at me once he spotted us. King Dominic walked over with Queen Vivienne and Christian trailing behind.

"Ah, glad to see our guests made it," King Dominic said. "I have people to mingle with so I'll be quite busy all night, but I hope you enjoy yourselves."

"We will, King Dominic," Mom said. "Thank you for inviting us."

As he walked away with Queen Vivienne, Christian lingered. "Olivia, can I talk to you? In private?"

"Of course," I said, glancing at the others. "Be right back."

"I was ordered by the king to watch over Olivia and Vanessa tonight," Dante said. "As I told you before, I don't think it's a good idea to separate."

"And as *I* told you before," Christian said, stepping closer to Dante, "Olivia will be safe with me."

Dante said nothing, but his jaw clenched in anger. I feared he'd strike the prince.

"Well, we'll be mingling and trying some of the food," Mom said, noticing the tension between them. "I'm sure they'll be all right, Dante."

"And have fun," Vanessa said with a devilish smirk.

As they walked away, Dante's gaze never left me. Was he jealous? I couldn't tell, but I *did* know he and Christian didn't see eye to eye on much.

Christian led me toward the garden, far from the crowd and noise. I sighed in relief when I could hear myself think again.

"So, how are you enjoying the festival?" he asked, and I became aware of how close we were.

I shrugged. "Well, we just got here, but it seems...fun."

Christian smiled. "Festivals aren't your thing, are they?"

"Not really, no," I said, shaking my head. "Is it that obvious?"

He laughed. "Yes, very much so."

"I never liked parties," I said as we walked through the garden. "Back home, Vanessa was always trying to drag me to them. She loved the loud music and all the dancing, but I just wanted to stay home and paint. Less crowded."

"I know what you mean," he said, turning to me. "I much prefer the solitude of the library. It's why I spend so much time there."

"Speaking of the library, is that closed-off section open again?"

He hesitated. "No, not yet. But don't worry, I'm sure you'll be able to see it soon enough. Anyway, have you seen any more ghosts?"

I shook my head, plucking a violet from the ground to sniff it. "No, not yet. Maybe the ghosts decided to stop. But

Christian…I figured out who the ghost man is. He's Charles Browning. My mom had a picture of him."

"The man who was murdered here by the old general?" Christian asked, and I nodded. "Oh, that's not good. Perhaps his soul is stuck here, bound to the place he died."

"And there's no way to free him?" I asked. "Help his soul move on?"

Christian shrugged. "Well, I don't know much about spirits, but I believe once he sees how much our people have changed, perhaps that will give him the peace he needs to cross over. It's strange how he's only appeared to you."

I still wasn't sure I believed in all that supernatural stuff, but I had no other way to explain what I had seen. Christian seemed to believe it, and I didn't want to insult him.

I twirled the violet in my hand, looking back at Christian. "There's something else I wanted to talk to you about."

He smiled. "Oh? And what would that be?"

"You made me a professor at the academy," I said. "Why didn't you tell me beforehand?"

"I'm sorry. I hope you don't mind," he replied. "I figured since our kingdom is lacking in the arts, you could be the one to change that. And I also figured it might take your mind off the current situation, ghosts included."

"I haven't had much time to paint since we got here. Everything's been so hectic."

"You aren't mad?"

"No, I'm not mad. Just warn a girl next time, okay?"

He smiled. "You have my word, Olivia, I won't do anything behind your back like that again. But for what it's worth, I think you'll be a great teacher."

"Thanks. Now if only the Sanguine twins thought the same..."

"Have they been giving you a hard time?"

"A little," I said. "But it's nothing I can't handle."

"Good. Tell me if it gets out of hand. I want to keep you safe. Vanessa, too, of course," he added. "Perhaps the Sanguine twins will surprise you. They might even be the next van Gogh."

"Them?" I laughed. "I doubt it. They don't seem like the creative types."

"You never know." He gestured at the violet in my hand. "May I?"

I handed it to him, confused. "Uh, sure."

I realized what he was doing when he tucked it behind my ear, smiling. "There, now you look even more beautiful under the moonlight."

I blushed before I heard someone behind us clear their throat. I looked over Christian's shoulder and noticed Dante standing there, unimpressed. "The festivities are starting. King Dominic doesn't want either of you to miss it."

Christian sighed, turning back to me. "I suppose our garden walk couldn't last forever. I had a good time with you, Olivia."

I smiled. "Me, too."

As he grinned, we made our way back to the field with Dante close behind us. Christian glanced back at him, looking annoyed. It was beginning to feel like Dante was my chaperone, which ruined any private time I could get with Christian.

When we got back to the field, King Dominic had returned to his throne. A group of citizens danced around him, and the entire crowd was clapping in tune. Mom, Vanessa, and Russell stood off to the side, clapping along with them. Me, Christian, and Dante watched from a few feet away.

"Why are they dancing around the king?" I whispered.

"They're honoring him," Christian replied. "My father is something of a hero to our people. It wouldn't be going too far to say they even worship him. Would you care to join me?"

"Join you?" I asked, frowning. "Oh, I really don't dance—"

"Then I'll show you," Christian said, extending his hand. "Don't make me dance alone, Olivia."

I laughed, taking his hand. "All right. I'll follow your lead—"

I didn't expect Christian to pull me toward the throne, twirling with me around the king. His father watched us with a smile, his eyes twinkling. Mom and Vanessa cheered as Christian and I swayed, trying to keep up with the other dancers. I'd never admit it to the others, and I knew Vanessa would make fun of me for it later, but I was having a good time. So far, being around Christian was the only thing that helped me relax.

I caught Dante's eye who stood off to the side, his arms crossed. He looked angry, clenching his fist so tight I feared he'd break his hand. Was I right before? Was he jealous of me and Christian? Or was something else bothering him?

When the clapping stopped and the dancers bowed, I turned to Christian, out of breath. "Thanks for that, partner."

"Anytime, Olivia. You did well for your first festival."

I shrugged. "I had a good dance partner, that's all."

"You flatter me," he replied, grinning.

King Dominic and Queen Vivienne stood up, and I noticed dozens of golden chalices getting passed around the crowd. They had some kind of red liquid inside. The citizens held it up to their mouths, waiting for permission.

"The first part of the festival has commenced," Queen Vivienne said. "Now we'll move onto the drinking of animal blood."

"Drinking animal blood?" I whispered to Christian as he grabbed a golden chalice. "What's that for?"

"To honor the animals we hunt and kill," Christian said. "Don't worry, you and your people don't have to drink it."

The crowd gulped down the animal's blood, some even closing their eyes in enjoyment. Once they had finished, they wiped their mouths and passed the golden chalices back to the table. I glanced over at Vanessa who seemed freaked out by their choice of beverage.

"With that, I'll ask you all to join hands in prayer," King Dominic said. "This is the most important part of our festival."

When I linked hands with Christian, his skin was cold, but I felt something stirring inside me. I hadn't felt that way about anyone since Dylan. He smiled at me before he closed his eyes, joining the rest of the crowd. I decided to keep them open and noticed Dante still staring at me.

"Being human is not easy. Temptation is everywhere," King Dominic said. "But we are strong people. We always have been. We can overcome our sins and do better. With Ambassador Hawthorne's help, we can reintegrate into society and make a difference in the world."

When the crowd muttered an "amen" in agreement,

Christian dropped my hand. As everyone opened their eyes, Christian leaned in to whisper in my ear. "This is the part where King Dominic gives his speech. I think he'll be mentioning the man who died in the clinic."

Right, I had almost forgotten about him with all the festivities. I still had a bad feeling about his death.

"Thank you, everyone, for coming to the Festival of the Night. I'd also like to thank our guests for being so gracious to attend," King Dominic said, his eyes flickering to me and Mom. "First of all, I'd like to take a moment to honor the lives we've lost. I'd also like to thank Dr. Draven, Dr. Cox, and Dr. Banes for their hard work. Without them, we'd be much worse. It's a sad thing losing one of our own, but sometimes, it's unavoidable."

The crowd hung their heads, muttering prayers.

"I'd also like to honor the memory of Charles Browning, the missionary who met a tragic end here. I vow that no other lives will be lost," King Dominic continued. "To end my speech, I'd like to say this. My people, don't forget our origins. We've come far, but we have much further to go. With open-mindedness and respect, we can overcome our dark past for a better, brighter future."

The citizens cheered, but I had no idea what the king was talking about. What kind of sins had they committed? What terrible things had happened in their past besides the murder of Charles Browning?

I noticed several people walking up to that strange statue I'd seen earlier. They bowed in front of it, then made the sign of the cross and walked away. As I stepped closer to look at it, I realized that it was a hideous animal, painted solid black, that resembled something between a bat and a goblin.

"The statue is terrifying, isn't it?" Christian asked, walking up behind me.

"Very. That'll give me nightmares tonight," I muttered. "What is it?"

"An old urban legend. Our people call it the Dark Half," Christian said. "It has no conscience, no sentience. It's a monster that kills, and its bloodlust is never satiated. Some people think it represents pure evil. The darkness inside us, even."

I shuddered. "Why were all those people walking up to it and praying?"

"They're paying respect to the image, praying the beast won't return," Christian said. "Some take urban legends seriously."

It reminded me of the monster Oscar Cox had babbled about. *A sip of the vial keeps the monster away for a while.* Did the medicine have something to do with it?

"The festival is almost over," Christian continued, breaking my line of thought. "This is the part where we sit on blankets and gaze up at the moon."

"Now that, I like. What's it signify?"

"My father says that without darkness, there can be no light. We need them both, like a duality," Christian said. "So, when we look up, we're honoring the night sky for showing us that. Would you care to join me?"

I nodded. "Sure, lead the way."

It didn't seem as odd as the animal blood drinking, so I was on board. As I followed Christian to an empty blanket on the ground, I looked over my shoulder at the statue one last time. I felt like its eyes were watching me, but that wasn't the only thing I found.

I noticed Petra and Nicolai standing next to it, caressing the creature's face. They both had smiles, their lips moving in prayer. They touched it once more before they vanished, getting more animal blood to drink from the buffet. Just what were they up to?

Mom, Vanessa, and Russell sat down on one of the blankets across the field. As Christian gestured for me to sit down, I heard footsteps approaching behind us. When I turned back, it was Dante.

"Prince Christian, may I have a word with you?" he asked.

Christian shook his head. "Actually, Olivia and I were about to sit down and look at the stars. Can't this wait until—"

"It can't," Dante said, roughly. "We need to talk. Now."

He could be as cold and demanding as General Ezra sometimes. That must be where he got it from. I hadn't seen General Ezra for most of the night, but I knew he was around somewhere, no doubt keeping an eye on me.

Christian sighed, giving me an apologetic smile. "I'll be right back, Olivia. Wait here."

As he walked away, Dante pulled him toward the buffet table. I craned my neck, struggling to read their lips, but I didn't have much luck. Whatever it was, it looked serious, and I wanted to know.

I tip-toed toward the buffet, hiding behind the big bowls of raw meat to eavesdrop.

"...shouldn't be with her, Prince," Dante said. "We both know the risks if you lose control."

"Like you did?" Christian asked. "Earlier, at the academy?"

Dante growled. "How do you know about that?"

"The General told my father about your punishment. I happened to overhear," Christian said. "If you ever lose control around Olivia like that again—"

"I won't. Believe me, I'm angry enough at myself for it," Dante muttered. "But it proves my point. We're all dangerous, Christian. Some more than others, but still. You risk her life every time you ask to meet in private."

"I'd never do anything to hurt her," Christian said. "Not Olivia. And you know I'm stronger than most of our people here."

Dante scoffed. "I'd like to believe that, but none of us are above temptation, and our people haven't always stayed true to their word. Remember that your father ordered me to protect her. If you do slip up and attack her...I'll have no choice but to kill you."

Why would Christian attack me? And why would Dante have to kill him? None of it made sense. They continued to argue, with Dante fearing Christian would hurt me, and Christian swearing he wouldn't. I decided to make my way back to the blanket underneath the stars before they caught me eavesdropping.

Every time I did, I discovered something I didn't want to hear.

Christian joined me a minute later, smiling. "Sorry about that, Olivia."

"What was that all about?" I asked.

"Dante's just over-protective about you, that's all. Don't worry about it," Christian said, pointing up at the sky. "Look at that, a full moon. Isn't it beautiful?"

I was about to agree when a loud explosion rang out behind us. Christian dove on me to protect me, and I heard

Dante's footsteps rushing over to us, too. I could already smell smoke as some of the people in the crowd screamed and took cover.

"Are you okay?" Christian asked, helping me up.

I nodded. "I think so. What happened?"

"The statue," Dante said. "It just exploded."

11

OMINOUS THREATS

The crowd screamed and shoved, pushing past us to flee the field. I fought my way through the crowd, searching for Mom, Vanessa, and Russell. Both Dante and Christian stayed close behind me.

"Olivia, it isn't safe to go back!" Dante cried, pulling on my arm.

"You vowed to protect Vanessa, too," I said, glaring at him. "I'm not leaving until we find her and the others."

Christian nodded. "I agree with Olivia. She and her people are our guests, Dante. We can't let anything happen to them."

Dante looked like he wanted to pull me to safety but decided to follow as I rushed off ahead. As the crowd parted for a moment, letting me see through the frantic people, I spotted the familiar blonde hair across the field—Vanessa's. Mom and Russell stood over her as she laid on the ground, bleeding from her forehead.

"Ness!" I yelled, falling by her side. "What happened?"

"The crowd trampled her after the explosion," Russell said. "I managed to pull her away from them, but she needed a minute to rest."

"I'll be fine," she said, wiping her blood away. "Don't worry about me."

I glanced back at Dante who was staring at the ground. Vanessa was bleeding. Just like I had when I'd sparred with Dante. The sight of blood seemed to do something to him.

"I'm so sorry this happened," Christian said. "This festival was supposed to be a night of fun for us all, and now it's ruined."

"What's going on?" Mom asked. "Do you know why the statue exploded, Prince Christian?"

He shook his head. "I have no idea. The explosion was *not* part of the festival, though. That much I'm sure of. Perhaps my father would know more."

I helped Vanessa to her feet as I turned to Christian. "Do you think your parents are okay?"

Christian nodded. "They've overcome worse in the past. My uncle and the guards most likely ushered them to safety inside the throne room."

"Why didn't they come looking for you?" I asked. "You're a prince, after all, *and* their son."

"The guards know I can handle myself," Christian said. "They don't need to worry about me as much as the others."

"The guards were smart," Dante said. "We should head to the throne room, too."

We nodded, following Dante and Christian to the castle. Me, Mom, and Russell helped Vanessa walk as she still seemed a little out of it. The kingdom looked empty as everyone rushed back home. As we passed the broken statue lying in pieces in the field, I noticed Petra and Nicolai standing nearby.

And they were laughing hysterically. Did it please them to see us scared? To watch as everyone fled for their lives? Dante had said their parents were in jail for blowing things up and causing chaos. Would they do something like this?

A glimmer in the distance caught my eye. I had to squint to see it through the darkness, but it was a ghost, the spirit of Charles Browning. He had returned. But instead of warning me again, he just shook his head in disappointment and vanished.

Could the spirits have been responsible for the explosion, for all the terrible things around here? Did they even have that kind of power? The list of suspects was piling up by the minute.

"My head hurts so bad," Vanessa muttered as we entered the castle. I felt much safer inside the dark red walls. "I don't want to die here."

"I promise you won't die, Vanessa," Christian said. "Our doctors will help you and you'll be all right."

Dante locked the doors behind us as we took a right into the throne room, hearing voices. As we looked around, we saw the kingdom's most important members, King Dominic, Queen Vivienne, and General Ezra and his guards. Anastasia, Dr. Draven, and Oscar were also there, waiting in the corner of the room as the general and his guards murmured about the situation.

"It never ends," Oscar muttered. "We can't run from our past..."

"Hush, Oscar," Queen Vivienne said. "We don't want our guests to hear that and scare them away."

Too late, I wanted to say.

"You lived," King Dominic said, noticing us. "I'm glad you made it. I was about to send a search party if I hadn't heard from you."

"I told you Dante would keep them safe," Dr. Draven said, glancing at Dante. "I'm glad to see you're all right, my son."

"Don't call me that," Dante hissed.

His mother's gaze fell, disappointed. It was the same look Professor Draven had after Dante had lashed out at him. The room turned quiet in awkward silence as Dante sighed, realizing his harshness.

"We're all fine. Dante was with me and Christian," I said, changing the subject. "Ness was trampled and hurt her head pretty bad. Have anything that can help?"

Anastasia removed a few vials from her coat pocket. "I think so. Dr. Draven can assist me."

"Wait a second," I said. "Those vials...I saw what they did to that man. Now he's dead. Will Vanessa be okay drinking them?"

"Yes, we promise," Dr. Draven said. "The adverse side effects only happen to our people. Both you and Russell took the vials, remember? How do you feel now?"

"I feel fine," I said. "No side effects. My leg doesn't hurt anymore, and the stab wound is gone. No scarring, either."

"Me, too," Russell added. "Hell, my back even feels better than it did *before* I fell. Don't know what you put in those vials, but they're like magic."

"Not magic, Mr. Donahue," Dr. Draven said, "but science. It's come in handy for the evolution of our people."

King Dominic and Queen Vivienne glanced at each other.

"See? Nothing to worry about," Anastasia said, holding out her hand for Vanessa to take. "Come, Vanessa, let's sit down."

Dr. Draven and Anastasia led Vanessa to one of the chairs, helping her get comfy. Anastasia placed a hand on Vanessa's arm, trying to read her emotions.

"I feel her pain," Anastasia said. "It's just a concussion. She'll be fine."

I sighed a breath of relief as Vanessa shook her head. "That's the last festival I'll ever go to."

You and me both, I wanted to say. Between the Sanguine twins and the ghosts, just walking outside didn't seem safe.

"The statue might be gone," Oscar mumbled, "but the real monster in all of us remains..."

"What is he talking about?" Mom asked.

"It's nothing to concern yourself with. Dr. Draven, find something that can relax Dr. Cox," Queen Vivienne said, turning to us. "Oscar's just shaken from the explosion tonight, as are we. He isn't very stable to begin with, and traumatic events can trigger his episodes."

Dr. Draven nodded, pulling Oscar toward Anastasia and Vanessa. She searched through her pockets, pulling out different vials. Real monster? It never ends? Just what was Oscar talking about? The others always tried to brush him off, but the more he spoke, the more I felt like he knew something. Maybe something the others didn't want us to know.

Dante walked over to talk with the general as the king bowed at us. "I didn't want the festival to end that way, Ambassador. I deeply apologize for Vanessa's injuries. If I'd known what was going to happen, I would've canceled."

"You don't have to apologize," Mom said. "But we would like some answers. That's two explosions, King Dominic, first the boat, and now the statue. Is someone trying to drive us away?"

"No, Ambassador. My people would *never* do anything like that," King Dominic said, firmly. "As I mentioned before, accidents happen in a small kingdom like this."

"Things don't just randomly explode," I said. "How do you explain tonight?"

"I never said I had an explanation for it," King Dominic replied. "My guards will do some investigating. In the meantime, I promise, you have nothing to worry about here."

"Father—" Christian began.

"We will find a way to end these terrible, unfortunate accidents," King Dominic said, glaring at Christian. He turned back to us. "My guards will put out the fire and clean up the mess in the field. As for all of you, it's late and I'm sure you're exhausted. By morning, everything will be better. You'll see."

Anastasia brought Vanessa over to us who was looking a little better. "I gave her a vial to relieve the pain and another to speed up the healing process. She'll recover in a few days."

"Good," I said. "How do you feel, Ness?"

She shrugged. "A little better. I don't feel dizzy anymore. Still freaked out, though..."

I sighed in relief. At least the vials hadn't made her start convulsing like the man I'd seen. How come Anastasia was so certain only her people could suffer side effects from it? Were their genes somehow different from ours?

Dante finished whispering with the general before walking over to us. "I'll escort you back to your rooms. General Ezra's asked me to guard the hallway while you sleep tonight."

"A good idea. We must be prepared if another...accident occurs," Queen Vivienne said, turning to Vanessa. "I'm very sorry you were hurt, Miss Bennett. It never should've happened. I hate seeing anyone injured, especially an outsider."

As Vanessa thanked her and followed Dante, Mom, and Russell toward the hallway, Christian grabbed my hand. "Despite everything, I had a good time with you tonight, Olivia. I hope we can do it again soon."

I felt like people were staring at us and noticed King Dominic and Queen Vivienne watching us out of the corner of my eye. If they hadn't known Christian was spending time with me, they would now. I couldn't make out their expressions. Did they approve, or were they as afraid as Dante?

I smiled. "Me, too. Goodnight, Christian."

As I turned toward the hallway, Dante was waiting for me, his eyes narrowed at Christian. As I walked past him, Dante followed, leading me and the others back to our rooms. He stood at attention with his back pressed against the wall.

"I'll be here all night," he said. "If you need anything, don't hesitate to let me know. Goodnight, everyone, and I hope you feel better, Vanessa."

As the others walked inside their rooms and shut the door, I stayed behind to talk with Dante. "You'll be standing here all night? Don't you need rest? Food?"

He shook his head. "Soldiers are trained to go weeks without sleep. We've also been trained to go a while without food. My needs come last. Yours and your people are first. It won't affect my fighting skills or reaction time if that's what you're concerned about."

"You can't ask one of the soldiers to alternate watch with you so you can rest?"

"If the general wanted that, he would've ordered it," Dante said, standing as still as a statue. "He trusts me to get the job done, and I will do it. I don't need to be relieved."

"Still, that doesn't seem very healthy," I said. "I'd feel better if you got some shuteye."

His mouth twitched, but he fought back a smile. "Your concern is appreciated, Olivia, but I'll be fine. Sleep well."

As I nodded and entered my room, shutting the door, I sighed. I knew one thing—I hadn't planned on sleeping at all. But with Dante standing guard in the hallway, sneaking out wasn't going to be easy.

I sat down on my bed, watching the clock tick on the wall. After ten minutes, I quietly opened my window, then climbed through it. I landed in the garden with a thud, hoping I hadn't woken anyone up. When no one came looking, I sighed in relief.

I stood up and brushed myself off, glancing toward the field. Several guards were out there like King Dominic promised, extinguishing the fire from the statue and sweeping up the broken pieces. They didn't notice me. They were too preoccupied with their clean-up efforts, so I tip-toed around the castle toward the throne room.

I could hear voices through the window as I approached. I hid beneath the sill of the only window, listening in on the conversation. It sounded like General Ezra and King Dominic again. As I worked up the nerve to peek inside, I didn't see anyone else with them. Queen Vivienne, Christian, and the guards must've turned in for the night.

Did Christian and Queen Vivienne know about General Ezra and King Dominic's private conversations? They seemed to do it a lot.

"...both know it's not safe!" General Ezra said, slamming his fist into his palm. "One time could be considered an accident, but twice? Someone is clearly behind this. I fear it'll only get worse unless the Americans leave."

King Dominic winced. "To think one of our own could do this...it would ruin everything we've worked for—how far we've come."

"I know," General Ezra said. "But you need to face it. We may never be ready. We're placing the world at risk by opening communication with outsiders."

"We've already jeopardized the world. Not all of our people agreed to come with us, if you remember, brother," King Dominic said, looking down sadly. "I appreciate your stance on the issue, but mine is still clear. Our guests will remain in the kingdom for now."

"But—"

"No," King Dominic said. "No more arguing. My decision is final. And if someone is truly behind all these explosions, I want them punished severely, General."

I shuddered, thinking back to Dante's punishment.

"As do I. We still need to talk about other matters, however. Dante's informed me of Christian's budding relationship with Olivia," General Ezra said. "He has reservations about them spending time together, and I agree with him. What if he hurts her?"

"He won't," King Dominic said sharply, his head snapping up to look at the general. "My son is stronger than us. You know that. He can resist the urge better than we can. Your soldier, it seems, cannot."

General Ezra growled. "Dante had a moment of weakness, but I corrected him. He will not fall out of line again."

"I hope not," King Dominic said. "We both know how dangerous it would be if he did. Olivia and her family wouldn't stand a chance, you know."

"It only happened during the training session *you* ordered. I never would've allowed them to spend time alone together," General Ezra shot back. "I saw the dagger Olivia was given, the Slayer. Dante told me you were the one who decided to train her with it. Why do you want her to learn how to kill?"

"Just in case you're right, General," King Dominic said, looking at him sadly, "and our people give in to their urges and destroy the world."

When I felt a hand on my shoulder, I jumped back, fearing it was the person who set the explosion or another ghost. When my eyes focused on the tall figure in the darkness, I realized it was only Dante. I clutched my pounding heart in relief.

"Oh, it's you," I muttered. "Thank God..."

"What are you doing out here, Olivia?" he asked, briefly glancing inside the throne room's window. "You should be in bed."

"I couldn't sleep," I lied. "I wanted to go for a walk to clear my head, but then I heard voices."

He nodded. "I understand your restlessness, but you need to try. Let me walk you back to your room."

As he led me into the castle, I looked over my shoulder at the windowsill, wishing I could hear more of the king's conversation with his brother. What was all this cryptic language about resisting urges and the world getting destroyed?

"We're here," Dante said, nudging me out of my thoughts as we stopped in front of my room. "Are you all right, Olivia?"

I nodded. "Just shaken up after tonight. How'd you know I wasn't in my room?"

"I knocked. I...wanted to speak with you," he replied. "I saw the window half-open and went after you immediately. I had no choice but to leave my post."

"Sorry," I said. "Why'd you want to talk to me?"

He sighed. "It's probably better if we forget it. I'm not sure it's my place, and I don't want to upset you."

"Come on. Now I'm just curious," I said. "Tell me. I won't get mad."

He hesitated. "Very well. I wanted to tell you to stay away from Prince Christian."

I frowned. "Why?"

"I made a vow to keep you safe, Olivia. I take that vow seriously," he said. "I'm...not sure I can keep you safe if you continue to see him. That's all you need to know. Beyond that, you'll have to trust me."

I crossed my arms. "You're going to have to tell me more than that if you want to convince me."

His jaw clenched. "Don't be stubborn, Olivia. While usually endearing, it's irritating right now."

I stepped closer. "Look, you're my bodyguard. It's your job to protect me, sure, but you don't get to meddle in my life. If I want to see Christian again, I will, and you can't stop me."

"I see that. As I said, I knew it would be a mistake telling you," he said, stepping away so his back lined up with the wall. "Do whatever you want, Olivia, but I will *not* fail my duties."

I walked into my room with a huff, slamming the door behind me. I didn't care if I woke anyone up. As I flung off my shoes, I gasped when I saw a shadow figure sitting on my bed. I was about to call out for Dante when the person came closer.

"It's okay," Vanessa whispered, rising to her feet. "It's just me."

"Don't do that," I whispered back. "I thought you were a ghost. Why are you here?"

"I didn't want to be alone," she said. "Not after tonight. Can I bunk here?"

I nodded. "Sure. You take the bed. You're the injured one, after all. I'll sleep on the couch."

"Okay. You know, I'm kind of glad the statue blew up. That thing creeped me out," Vanessa said as I gathered some pillows for the couch. "What do you think happened?"

"Well," I said, sighing, "I saw the Sanguine twins poking around the statue before it exploded. I also saw the ghost of Charles Browning as we dragged you inside."

Vanessa gasped. "You did? What did he say?"

"Nothing. He's as tight-lipped as Dante," I muttered, lying down. "And then there's all that weird stuff Dr. Cox keeps saying about monsters. I can't help but feel like there's some truth there. As for the Sanguine twins, they could've rigged the statue to explode or something."

"So, what are we going to do about it?" Vanessa asked, getting under the covers in my bed.

"I have a three-part plan to get to the bottom of this," I said, glancing at her across the dark room, "and I'll need your help to make it work."

12

PIECES OF THE PUZZLE

After Vanessa agreed to help me, we both fell asleep. Or I tried to, at least. I couldn't stop thinking about the plan we had decided on. When I spotted sunlight outside my window, I quickly got dressed and checked on my cut. It was feeling better, though I decided to keep it hidden to avoid a panic. Then I woke Vanessa to get started. It always took her forever to get ready, so I decided to wait in the hallway for her.

As I walked out into the corridor, I noticed Mom's door open. She stood there, speaking with King Dominic, General Ezra, and Queen Vivienne. Russell was also standing with her, watching the king and queen closely. I knew he didn't trust them, not like Mom did.

I didn't see Christian, but Dante was still at his post, guarding the hallway with a stern look. I hadn't forgotten our argument about Christian. He hadn't, either, judging by the annoyed glance he gave me when he saw me standing there. Then his gaze returned to staring at the wall without even saying hello.

"Ah, Olivia, there you are," King Dominic said, walking over to me. "Did you have a good sleep?"

"Yes, I did," I said, trying to stay calm. "Knowing Dante was here all night made me feel better."

"That's what he's there for," King Dominic said, glancing at Dante with a smile. "Did you see anything out of the ordinary last night, Dante?"

Dante's eyes briefly flitted to mine, and I knew he was thinking about how he caught me eavesdropping. This was it. Dante was going to tell the king the truth. Then Mom would ground me for eternity for sneaking out of my room and the king would never trust me again.

"No," Dante lied. "I didn't see anything."

I almost gasped. Why had he lied for me? Why hadn't he told them he had to come looking for me, leaving his post?

"Good," General Ezra grunted. "Nice work, soldier."

"Yes, nice work, indeed. I knew you were the right person for the job," King Dominic said before he turned to me. "Anyway, I always give the kingdom the day off after the festival. It's the only evening they're allowed to stay up all night, and I figured they could use extra rest. What are you planning to do today, Olivia?"

Nothing much. Just searching for answers in dangerous places.

"I'll probably paint," I lied. "I haven't had much time to do that lately."

"Ah, yes. My son told me you're talented," King Dominic said, smiling. "I look forward to seeing what you teach at the academy."

"Thank you. I'll try my best, but I might be a little rusty."

"Oh, don't be so modest," Mom chastised. "Olivia is

gifted. Even her art teacher back home thought she could get into the Rhode Island School of Design, one of the best art schools in the United States."

"Mom!" I squealed, embarrassed.

King Dominic laughed. "Well, we're no prestigious art school, but if you ever need anything, let me know. Anyway, the reason I dropped by was to let you know the fire has been put out and there were no causalities from last night. Vanessa was the only injury. How is she doing?"

"She's better. She slept in my room last night," I said. "I'm glad no one got hurt."

"Me, too," Queen Vivienne said, quietly. "All of us are."

King Dominic nodded, glancing at Mom. "Come, Ambassador, we have a few things left to finalize before the embassy opens. Have a good day, Olivia."

"Yell if you need me," Russell whispered, then he and the others followed Mom and King Dominic down the hallway.

When it was just me and Dante, he didn't say anything, so I decided to break the silence. "You lied for me about last night. Why? Seems like it goes against all your training."

Dante finally looked at me, his gaze hard. "I didn't see the point. Nothing bad happened."

"Well, still," I said. "Thanks for that."

He nodded, bowing slightly. "You're welcome."

"If they found out you lied," I began, "would you get punished?"

He shifted uncomfortably. "Yes. Yes, I would."

I shuddered thinking back to the whipping. I didn't want Dante to get beaten again. Not for me. An awkward silence followed until Vanessa opened the door, fully dressed. She cocked her head, giving me the signal that she was ready. I nodded and turned back to Dante.

"Well, I'll just be painting all day," I said. "See you later."

"What do you paint?" he asked, surprising me.

"Anything that catches my eye, really," I said. "Animals, places, people. I'm really into landscape paintings right now."

"And you'll be teaching that at the academy when you return?"

A smile tugged at my lips. "Yes. Interested?"

He shrugged. "Maybe. I find it very similar to fighting."

"How so?"

"You have to refine your skill. Practice until you get better," Dante said. "In your case, the paintbrush is your tool to do that. For me, it's my body. Both take a lot of time, effort, and concentration. And sometimes, taking down a foe is a work of art. Of grace and beauty."

"Hmm. Never thought of it like that," I said. "Maybe you're right."

He bowed. "Have fun painting, Olivia."

As I walked back into my room and closed the door, Vanessa gave me a funny look. "What was that all about?"

I shrugged. "No idea. You ready?"

Vanessa nodded. "Yep. I'll distract Dante. When I yell out the magic words, you'll know it's safe."

"Good luck," I said. "Let's hope I find something."

Vanessa left the room, closing the door behind us. I could hear her talking to Dante, speaking much louder on purpose. "Hey, Dante. Think you can take me for a walk?"

"I really should remain at my post," Dante replied. "My apologies, Vanessa."

"Oh, come on. Olivia's not going anywhere, and she's got the door locked," Vanessa said. "Believe me, her painting can keep her occupied for a long time. All I'm asking for is a chance to stretch my legs."

Dante sighed. "Very well, I'll take you outside. Let's make it quick."

"I'm so glad you agreed," Vanessa said, her voice getting further away. "Can't wait to see those clear blue skies again..."

After hearing the secret phrase and knowing the hallway was clear, I snuck out my window without the fear of Dante hearing me fall. Once I was free from the castle, I hustled across the field toward the clinic and hoped the person I was looking for would be there.

When I entered, the clinic looked deserted. It wasn't until I heard a noise in the corner that I noticed the man I had snuck out for, Dr. Oscar Cox. He stood near the workbench, mixing several vials together. I almost smiled at the fact that I'd gotten him alone.

"What are you doing?" I asked.

He didn't jump or flinch, just continued working. "Mixing vials. Always mixing vials..."

"Do you have a moment to talk, Dr. Cox?"

He shook his head. "Too busy. Anastasia and Dr. Draven are off today, so I have to work harder. We have to keep making new medicine for next week. Medicine is important..."

"What would happen if everyone in the kingdom stopped taking that medicine?"

He turned to me, his eyes wide. "Chaos. Destruction. Death."

I shivered. "How so?"

"The monsters," he whispered. "They'd appear. You and your people would be in danger."

"What are these monsters, Dr. Cox?"

"Old monsters. Pure evil," he replied, returning to his workbench. "You wouldn't understand, but they'd rip you to pieces in seconds."

"And these monsters," I asked, inching closer. "Do they have anything to do with the statue I saw last night? Something called a Dark Half?"

He whirled around, looking at me with an angry expression. "What do you know about the Dark Half? Who told you?"

"I know nothing, really," I said, backing away. "Christian mentioned it. He said that was what the statue was. Queen Vivienne mentioned you liked urban legends. Can you tell me more about the Dark Half?"

"No, no, no," he mumbled, putting his head in his hands. "I can't. It's forbidden. We weren't supposed to tell!"

I frowned. "Who said you're not allowed to tell? And why not?"

"What's going on here?"

I whipped my head around and noticed Dr. Draven. She looked angry as her eyes flickered from me to Oscar, her hands resting on her hips. So much for getting answers out of him.

"I just came back to get my jacket. I didn't expect to see anyone but Oscar," she said. "Why are you here, Olivia? Are you injured?"

"No," I said. "I...actually came by to ask some questions

about Vanessa. Although she looks fine, I'm still worried. You're sure she'll be all right?"

It was a terrible lie, but it looked like she believed it. "It's sweet that you're concerned about your friend, but I promise you, she'll be fine. Now, why don't we let Oscar work, hmm? He prefers solitude."

Oscar said nothing. He just turned back to his workbench and continued mixing vials as though he hadn't yelled at me. But I hadn't forgotten what he said or how angry he became when I mentioned the statue, and how they're not allowed to tell. I wanted more out of him, but getting him alone was difficult in a small kingdom with eyes everywhere.

Dr. Draven grabbed her jacket and followed me out of the clinic, closing the door behind us. She turned to me when we were alone. "You've been spending a lot of time with my son, haven't you?"

I nodded. "Well, he *is* my bodyguard."

"Of course. That's what I meant," she said. "Does he ever...speak of me? Or his father?"

"Not really," I said. "He explained to me that he gave up his family to become a soldier. I don't agree with that, for the record."

Dr. Draven shook her head, sighing. "No, an outsider wouldn't. Although it was hard for me and my husband to cut off contact...it was necessary. The soldiers are valuable in keeping our kingdom safe, and we can't afford to distract them. Anyway, thanks for indulging me."

I wanted to ask why a small kingdom needed such aggressive security, but Dr. Draven had already walked off down the brick path. I added it to the list of weird things.

With the first half of my plan finished, I moved along to

KINGDOM OF V

the second. It was time to track down the Sanguine twins, but I had no idea where to find them. I decided to go to the markets and ask around when I spotted Christian chatting with a shopkeeper. I didn't want him to see me. I knew he'd ask what I was doing and want to join, so I slipped past him with my head down.

I approached one shopkeeper who was selling raw meat on a stick. "Excuse me? Can I ask you a question?"

The shopkeeper shrugged, wiping his bloody meat hands on a towel. "Sure. You're that outsider, right? The Ambassador's daughter?"

"I am." I nodded. "I was wondering, have you seen Petra and Nicolai Sanguine around? Do you know where they live?"

The shopkeeper gave me a funny look. "Why would you want to look for them? In case you didn't know, outsider, those kids aren't nice people. They're turning out just like their no-good parents."

"It's about school," I lied. "We're working on a project together."

The man sighed. "Then I feel sorry for you. They live in the homes a few blocks from here, but they usually spend the weekends outside the Solitude."

"Why?"

"For their parents," the shopkeeper replied. "They're not allowed to enter the jail. It's maximum-security, but it doesn't stop them from sitting out front in the field. Makes them feel closer to them or something. Ask them if you want to know more."

"Thanks for your help," I said, then turned away from the shopkeeper and ran into Christian.

"Olivia, is that you?" he asked, laughing. "Sorry, I didn't see you there. Are you finally exploring the markets?"

Crap. That was the kind of run-in I wanted to avoid.

"Uh, yeah," I lied. "Just checking out the sights."

"I see. Well, the shops have lots of things to buy, like the scarf I bought you. You'll like it," he said, glancing around. "Where's Dante? Isn't he supposed to be guarding you?"

"Yeah, he's here, too," I lied. "He's getting me some water. I'm waiting here for him to get back."

"When he does, why don't I take you to a nice boutique down the walkway?" he asked. "They have some bracelets there I think would look nice on you—"

"No!" I said, a little too eagerly. Christian looked taken aback. "I mean, I'd love to, but Dante doesn't want me going too far today. We're heading back to my room after he gets me water."

Christian's face fell. "Oh, I understand. Another time, then?"

I nodded, faking a smile. "Another time. Can't wait."

"Me, either," he said, grinning.

As he walked away, I sighed in relief. I didn't have much time left. Vanessa couldn't keep Dante outside forever. Eventually, he'd take her back to the rooms and realize I wasn't there.

I left the markets and rushed to the Solitude, and immediately, shivers went up my spine. It was a place of great evil. I could feel it. The Solitude looked like a typical jail with bars on the windows and a reinforced door. A tall, blonde warden stood outside, ensuring no one could get in or out.

I finally spotted the Sanguine twins on the lawn. It looked like they were eating lunch, something raw and bloody, in front of one of the boarded windows. I approached and cleared my throat, and they sneered when they looked back at me.

"Look, it's the outsider," Nicolai muttered. "And without her pet, Dante, to watch over her. Who knew she had the courage to leave the castle without him?"

"Dante's right over there," I lied, pointing in the distance. "If you try anything, he'll be on you both in a second."

"What do you want?" Petra asked, glaring up at me.

"To talk about the festival. The exploding part, to be exact."

"Yeah? Well, we don't want to talk to you," Nicolai said, turning his back. "Go away, outsider. No one wants you here."

"I'm not going anywhere," I said, walking around to look at them. "I saw you two at the festival, touching the statue before it blew up. When it did, you were laughing while the people ran for their lives."

"So? We thought they looked funny, like scurrying rats," Petra said, grinning. "What are you implying, outsider?"

"I think you made the statue explode. That you did something to it while you were touching it. Maybe you were behind our boat explosion, too."

Nicolai scoffed. "We had nothing to do with either of those things. We weren't anywhere near your stupid boat, and last night was just a coincidence."

"Really? I heard your parents are in jail for a reason," I said. "They led a group called Havoc, didn't they? People who liked to cause chaos for the thrill of it? Blowing things up seems right up their alley."

"You have no idea what you're talking about," Petra

sneered. "We haven't done anything, and our parents haven't, either. They've been locked up tight. Ask Warden Blanchard over there if you don't believe us."

"Fine. Let's say you're not behind any of this," I said. "Know who is?"

Nicolai shrugged. "Lots of people didn't want outsiders here. There was even a group called the Isolationists. Those who wanted our kingdom to stay separate from the world. In fact, even your little Prince Christian was against your people coming here at one point. Don't know if he's in the Isolationists or who their leader is, though."

Christian. I had seen him poking around the docks before the explosion. Were my first instincts right? Was he involved in this? Maybe he was only getting close to me to throw me off.

"But if I were you, I wouldn't worry about the Isolationists," Nicolai continued. "They aren't as deadly as some of the others. Not as...bloodthirsty."

"What are you talking about? Who are the others?" I asked.

Petra glanced at Nicolai. "We've already said too much about them. You've been warned, outsider. Watch your back."

I chortled. "I'm flattered. That almost sounded like you care about my safety."

"Don't get it twisted," Petra sneered. "If anything happened to you and your people, our parents would get blamed for it somehow. They always do. Everyone thinks the Sanguine's are untrustworthy criminals."

"And why do they think that?"

Nicolai sighed. "All right, we'll admit our parents did

some bad things, set fires, sabotaged things. But hell, it gets boring in a kingdom like this. They never hurt anybody. They were just looking for some fun. They're more like tricksters than killers."

"But King Dominic flipped out and banned them to the Solitude," Petra said. "Ensuring me and my brother would never see them again. He feared if they were let loose, they'd scare off outsiders. It's all he cares about, making contact with the outside world again."

It finally felt like I was getting through to the Sanguine twins. Maybe we could be friends after all.

"What are we doing, Petra?" Nicolai asked, glancing at his sister. "She's an outsider. She'll never understand our pain, or our way of life."

Or maybe not.

"You're right," Petra said, scowling as she looked up at me. "We let you pry into our lives long enough. Now, get lost, outsider. You're disturbing our picnic."

I turned, sighing as I rushed back to my room's window. So far, I had completed the first two parts of my plan, talking to Oscar and Petra and Nicolai in private, and yet they'd both backfired. I hadn't learned much, but maybe combining all my information, I had some pieces to the very large, very confusing puzzle.

I opened the window and climbed in just as I heard footsteps approaching from the hallway. I knew the click of those heels well. It was Vanessa, followed by the clunk of military boots. Dante.

"Thanks for taking me for a walk," Vanessa said, her voice echoing outside my door. "The fresh air definitely helped."

"You're welcome. Now, let me check on Olivia," I heard

Dante said. "I want to make sure she's all right while we were gone."

"Oh, I'm sure she's fine," Vanessa said, nervously. "You don't need to—"

When the door handle jiggled, I hurried to pick up a paintbrush and turned toward my easel. I flung the tarp off to reveal the half-ready painting I'd started of the kingdom. The door swung open, and I craned my neck to see Dante and a nervous-looking Vanessa.

Dante looked me over, relieved. "Olivia, there you are."

"Where else would I be?" I asked, trying to stay calm.

"Right," Dante muttered. "Is that what you're working on?"

I nodded. "Do you like it?"

He tilted his head, studying the painting. "Yes. Your mother wasn't exaggerating. You do have a talent. Perhaps the king will display the painting in his throne room when it's finished."

I blushed. "Well, I'm not sure about that, but...thanks."

Vanessa turned to Dante. "I'm going to change into my pajamas now. See you around, Dante."

He bowed, leaving the room to guard the hallway again as Vanessa closed the door. I sighed and put my paintbrush down. "That was too close. I almost got caught."

"Sorry. I tried to keep him out longer, but he kept insisting I needed to rest on my day off. That guy's as stubborn as a mule. Kinda like you," Vanessa said, rolling her eyes. "Anyway, how did it go?"

"Well, I talked to both Oscar and the Sanguine twins," I said. "They told me bits and pieces, but nothing concrete. And here I thought I'd actually get answers today..."

"So, what now?" Vanessa asked. "You never told me what the final act of your three-part plan is, you know."

"Simple. We kill time until Mom gets back from her meeting with the king," I said, "and then we get her picture of Charles Browning and contact him through a séance."

13
THE SÉANCE

Vanessa blinked. "I thought I just heard you say you wanted to do a séance, but I must be hearing things."

I scoffed. "Come on, we both want to know if it's the ghosts behind all these strange accidents. And if not, then maybe they'll have some insight into who the culprit is. They have to know something."

Vanessa crossed her arms. "Liv, these so-called ghosts have terrorized you enough. Now you want to summon them?"

"If that's what it takes," I said, "then yes. You said you'd help me, remember?"

Vanessa sighed, running a hand through her hair. "I picked a great time to be helpful. All right. I'm with you. But if these ghosts kill me, I'm coming back to haunt you."

"Then you'll have to get in line," I muttered, "because Charles Browning started haunting me first."

Vanessa and I waited an hour for Mom to get back from her meeting with the king. When we heard the click of her heels on the tile and the closing of her door, me and Vanessa rose to our feet and opened our door. When I poked my head out, Dante was still standing there, his eyes narrowing when he noticed us.

"Where are you two going?" he asked as me and Vanessa walked out into the hallway.

"Just to see my mom," I said. "That's not against the rules, is it?"

I could tell I was frustrating him, but he kept his composure. "No. She just returned from her meeting, and she's in her room. Go ahead in."

"So glad I have your permission," I grumbled.

If Dante heard that, he didn't react.

When I knocked on Mom's door, I heard the rustling of papers before the door opened. Mom looked exhausted but smiled when she saw us. "Girls, there you are. Enjoying your day off?"

"Yeah, sure," I lied. "Can we come in?"

"Of course," Mom said, opening the door wider. "Sorry for the mess of paperwork. I have to file daily reports for the president and get everything ready for the embassy's opening. Welcome to the glamorous life of an ambassador."

Vanessa shut the door behind us, and Dante's gaze lingered until he couldn't see us anymore. I turned to the bed, noticing the stacks of papers covering the blankets. Mom wasn't usually that messy, but she *was* under a lot of stress from work. I didn't envy her job.

"Speaking of the embassy," Mom said, beaming "It's finally opening tomorrow morning. I had a sneak peek of the building, and let me just say, it's everything I dreamed of. Cozy, quiet, homey. I'd love it if you girls could be there for the opening ceremony."

"Sure," I said. "Will there be snacks?"

"Of course," Mom said, "just like at the festival. And the chefs said they'll be preparing a special salad for you."

"Then we're there."

"Great. I only wish the president could be here for the opening ceremony," Mom said, sighing. "I intend to show it to her as soon as she arrives. I'm sure she'll be very pleased."

"Since we're on the subject of Mom," Vanessa said, "have you heard anything from her? She's supposed to get here soon, right?"

Mom nodded. "Very soon. Within the next few days. And no, she hasn't sent any correspondence. I wish this kingdom had phones. It would be nice to call her."

"I miss her," Vanessa said, looking down. "And I'm worried."

"I'm sure everything's fine," I said, turning to Vanessa. "She'll be here before you know it, and then she'll start embarrassing you like all moms do."

Vanessa laughed, though I could tell she was still nervous. I didn't want more people coming to the haunted, cursed island, especially not the president of the United States. What if we couldn't get everything under control by then? What if something bad happened to her?

"Embarrassing our children is a fun pastime," Mom said with a smile, turning back to her paperwork. "It's payback for all those sleepless nights. If you have kids, you'll understand what I mean."

I rolled my eyes. "Uh-huh. Listen, Mom, we came here to ask a favor."

She looked over her shoulder, puzzled. "Oh? If it's about giving you more freedom to explore the kingdom, I have no say in that. King Dominic was clear. He wants Dante watching over you at all times."

"No, it's not about that," I said. "It's about the photograph of Charles Browning. Can we see it again?"

"Sure," Mom said, lifting a giant stack of folders. "Oh, I know I put it here somewhere. The president will be so angry if I lost the only picture of him..."

As she searched, I turned to Vanessa and lowered my voice. "Without that picture, we can't do the séance."

"What are you girls whispering about back there?" Mom asked, still looking through her paperwork.

"Nothing," I said, innocently. "Find it yet?"

"No. Wait...a-hah!" Mom said, pulling out the photograph. "It was hiding. Here you go, sweetheart."

I took it from her, sighing in relief. "Thanks, Mom. Is it okay if we keep it for a little while?"

She narrowed her eyes. "I suppose. But why? What are you up to?"

"Nothing," I lied. "I was...just thinking of painting Charles Browning. You know, to honor him?"

Mom grinned. "That's a lovely idea, Olivia. When you're finished, I'll hang it up on the wall in the embassy for everyone to see."

Great. Now I actually had to do it.

"You can keep it for now," Mom continued, "as long as you bring it back soon. I want to display the picture in the embassy when it opens for the memorial."

"Will do," I said, reaching for the door handle. "Thanks, Mom."

As we left her room and walked back to ours, Dante's eyes followed us. But he didn't try to stop us this time or ask what the photograph was for, thankfully. As we closed the door behind us, I sat cross-legged on the floor. Vanessa copied and sat across from me. I lit a candle and placed it in a circle in the middle of us, then added the photograph of Charles Browning. When I reached into my belt to retrieve my dagger, Vanessa's eyes nearly bugged out of her head.

"Whoa, look at that knife," Vanessa said. "Where'd you get that?"

"It's a dagger called the Slayer," I corrected, "and it came from Dante—well, King Dominic wanted me to have it. Dante's been teaching me how to fight with it."

"Well, just be careful with it," Vanessa said. "That looks like it can kill anything."

Kill anything...like a monster in the old legends Dr. Cox was always muttering about? I wondered if it was related.

When I cut my hand with the dagger, drawing blood, I realized how sharp it was. Vanessa was right. It really could kill anything. I felt something inside it, like an energy pulsating. I barely felt the blood trickling down my hand as I stared at it.

"What the hell are you doing?" Vanessa asked, pulling the dagger away from me. "Have you lost your mind?"

"Relax," I said, grabbing the dagger back. "It's all for the séance. And keep your voice down, will you? If Dante bursts in here, I don't know how to explain this."

"Sorry," Vanessa whispered. "But why the blood?"

"It shows the spirits I'm serious," I said. "Once I let it drip onto the photo, I should be able to call them out. The candle was another necessary ingredient."

"How do you know so much about séances?" Vanessa

asked. "I'm not sure whether to be impressed or a little afraid of you."

I looked down. "When my dad died...I tried to contact him. I did a whole bunch of research online on how to speak to the dead. One website told me to light some candles, get something that belonged to the deceased, and drip blood onto it. I borrowed my dad's old shirt and used that."

"Did it work?"

"No," I said, sadly. "Nothing happened."

"Maybe you couldn't reach him because he'd already crossed over," Vanessa said. "That's the proper term, right? That if people lived good, happy lives, they could move on without a problem?"

"Yeah, maybe," I said, shrugging. "Still didn't stop me for trying for like, a year."

"I'm sorry, Liv," she said, placing a hand on my shoulder. "I wish he was still here. I can't imagine what it's like to lose a parent."

I cleared my throat. "Thanks, but it's in the past. We have to focus on the future now. And from what I've seen around here, the spirit of Charles Browning certainly didn't pass on. Not like Dad. Maybe it'll work this time, and we'll get some answers out of old Charles."

"I'm still a little freaked out, but I'm with you," she said, taking a deep breath. "Ready when you are, Liv."

I nodded, letting my blood drip onto the photograph. It dribbled over Charles Browning's face and streaked down the picture. Me and Vanessa waited in silence for something to happen, but the room turned silent. All I could hear was my pounding heart in my ears.

I sighed. "Damn, I really thought it would work—"

A strong wind blew through our room, knocking over the deodorant I kept on my dresser. It swirled around us, pelting our faces so hard that it almost hurt. The candle burned out immediately and shrouded the room in darkness. If it weren't for the sunshine outside, everything would've turned pitch black.

"Uh, is there a storm coming outside?" I asked.

"No, it's a perfect summer's day," Vanessa said, looking across at me with fearful eyes. "Something tells me that wasn't the weather, Liv. I...I think it's working."

When the wind picked up again, I glanced around the room. "Charles Browning, are you here? We need to talk."

I held onto the bloody photograph to keep it from blowing away. Vanessa leaned forward. "I think he's here, Liv. I can barely believe it, but...you're doing it. Keep going."

"I know who you are," I continued, hoping I could lure Charles out. "My mother told me the story of your death. How the people of V murdered you for trespassing."

A red glow shimmered in the corner of the room. Charles Browning appeared, glancing down at me. "If you know, why are you still here?"

"We can't leave," I said. "Our boat burned down. We're trapped here on the island."

"Who are you talking to?" Vanessa whispered.

"You...you can't see him?" I asked, looking back at her.

Her eyes flickered to the spot I'd stared at. "No, nothing's there."

I frowned. Why was it only me who was getting haunted? Why couldn't Vanessa see the spirit of Charles Browning in the corner of the room, too?

"A pity," Charles said, coming closer to me. "You

shouldn't have come here at all. The kingdom of V isn't to be trusted."

"Why not?" I asked. "I know what they did to you, but that was a long time ago. The people here have changed. Maybe they really want to be better."

"They can't. They'll always fall victim to the monster," Charles said. "And they haven't changed. Not in the least."

"Stop speaking in riddles," I said. "Just tell me everything, starting with the monsters."

"I...can't," Charles said, his face scrunched in pain. "I haven't been corporeal for a long time. The words...don't flow as easily as they used to."

Vanessa gave me a strange look from across the room, but I ignored her and focused on Charles. "That's okay. We'll start slow. When we first got here, our boat exploded. Last night, a statue blew up. I know someone's trying to scare us off. Is it you, Charles?"

When the wind knocked the pillows off my beds, Vanessa leaned forward again. "Sorry to interrupt, but...I'm scared, Liv."

"It's all right. He won't hurt us," I said, turning back to Charles. "Are you responsible?"

"You can't trust anyone here," he said, cryptically. "The truth is right in front of you. If you look harder, you'll see it. I found out the hard way..."

I sighed. So much for getting a straight answer.

"The crypts," he continued, "below the castle. It's where the deaths occurred. Not my death, but the newer victims."

I rose to my feet. "What are you talking about, newer victims?"

"Newer victims?" Vanessa asked, raising an eyebrow.

My eyes widened when a black mist formed in the corner behind Vanessa. She noticed my stare and turned around but didn't react. She couldn't see them, but I could. These were ghosts, a handful of them, but they weren't anything like Charles. He wasn't the only one haunting the kingdom.

These ghosts didn't speak. They just watched me with half-dead eyes. They had bloody necks and wrinkly skin. I couldn't tell if they were young or old, but I got one feeling from them. Anger.

"Who are you?" I asked them. "Why are you here?"

They didn't say anything, only continued to stare. It was like they were looking directly into my soul.

"They can't speak. They don't know how yet," Charles said, floating over to me. "They're new."

"How new?" I asked.

"Some weeks, other months," he said, "and other days. I watched them die, helpless to stop them. The pain eats away at me for the lost souls..."

"Lost souls? Days? I don't understand," I muttered. "Are you telling me...these spirits were once people, killed in the kingdom of V within the last few days?"

Charles didn't say anything. Whether he couldn't remember or just didn't want to tell me, I wasn't sure. As the other spirits floated toward me, I took a step back.

"Well, are they residents of V?" I asked. "Or are they outsiders who came here, like you?"

"Always outsiders," Charles said, turning to me. "The people here wouldn't kill their own. You've seen how loyal they are to each other."

Reeling, I turned back to the scarier spirits. "Are you guys responsible for the accidents around here?"

"I don't think they are," Charles said. "I don't know them that well...but I don't think they have the power to cause any harm. Not yet."

"What do you want, then?" I asked the ghosts. "Why linger here?"

As expected, they didn't say anything, so Charles spoke up. "They're trying to warn you. So am I. I've tried to protect you as best I could...but time is running out."

"For what?"

"The end of days. The coming apocalypse," Charles said, cryptically. "You can't trust Christian. He's stronger than the others, but they're all dangerous. None here are what they seem."

Charles wasn't the first one to tell me Christian wasn't safe. Dante had beaten him to it. What was so dangerous about him, about any of them? It seemed Dante knew somehow.

"Then tell me what they are. Stop being so damn mysterious!"

"They're evil. Pure evil," Charles said, floating closer to me. "We won't stop until you find a way off this island. It's for your own protection."

When the spirits used the wind to pick up my dresser and fling it against the wall, Vanessa screamed and rose to her feet. A mini tornado spread through the room, swirling my clothes with it. Me and Vanessa clung to the wall, desperate to hold onto something as the wind increased.

It was then I realized this séance had been a bad idea.

The doorknob jiggled. A second later, I heard pounding and Dante's voice. "Olivia? Vanessa? What's going on in there?"

"Dante, help!" Vanessa cried. "They're going to kill us!"

He began to kick at the door, cursing, but he couldn't get inside. "It won't open!"

"I didn't lock it," Vanessa said, turning to me. "I think the ghosts are keeping him out somehow!"

I tried to reach the door, but a strong wind knocked me off my feet. I fell back and hit my head on the dresser, seeing stars. I felt blood on my forehead when I reached a hand up. Vanessa screamed even louder and started to cry when she realized I'd gotten injured.

"Liv!" she said. "I...can't get to you! The wind is too strong!"

As I laid there on the floor, the spirits hovered above me. My head ached and I found myself growing very tired, barely able to keep my eyes open.

"Leave the kingdom of V," Charles said. "Leave before they kill you all!"

And then the spirits vanished. The wind faded, and all the objects in the room stopped swirling. Vanessa rushed to my side.

"Olivia!" she cried, nudging me. "Can you hear me? Are you all right?"

Dante kicked the door open. When he noticed me lying there, he fell to his knees. "Olivia, what happened?"

Me and Vanessa didn't say anything. Dante looked back at the ground, noticing the candle and the bloody photo of Charles. His eyes widened and I think he started to piece it together.

He looked at Vanessa, sternly. "What did you two do in here?"

Vanessa didn't have to say anything. Mom began walking

to our room, huffing. "What's with all the screaming and banging? Were you two fighting again? I told you to knock that off—"

Mom screamed when she noticed the disheveled room. She fell beside me, brushing my hair out of my face. "Oh my God, Olivia! What happened?"

Russell entered next with a fire in his eyes. "Who did this to you, Olivia? Was it one of them?"

"No one did anything to her," Dante sneered, looking up at Russell. "It was only the two of them in this room. I would've noticed if someone entered!"

"As if I trust you," Russell muttered.

"Stop arguing! Olivia needs a doctor," Vanessa said. "We have to get her to the infirmary. Liv, can you walk?"

I groaned, feeling weightless. "No, I don't think I can. Ness, if I die...you have to find out what's going on. I think...I think Charles was onto something. Promise me, Ness."

She gulped, nodding. "I promise."

I felt Dante lift and carry me down the hallway as my world faded to black.

14
THE CRYPTS

When I woke up, I was lying in a hard bed in the clinic. I sat up and groaned, trying to remember what had happened. The séance. The angry, bloody ghosts. Charles' warning. It all came back to me like a flash of lightning.

The white curtain divided my small section from the rest of the clinic, but I could see several shadow figures behind it. A second later, I heard whispered voices.

"What happened back there, Vanessa?" Mom asked in her 'you're-in-trouble' voice. "The room was a disaster!"

"I...I don't know," Vanessa lied. "You'd better ask Liv when she wakes up. She's better at explaining things than I am."

Mom sighed, but Vanessa didn't say anything else. I smiled. She was a good friend. One I knew wouldn't rat me out, not even to someone as scary as Mom.

"Eavesdropping on your friends and family?" a voice asked.

I twisted my head and saw Anastasia standing in the corner of the room. I hadn't even noticed she was there.

I paused. "Uh...maybe?"

She laughed. "I would've done the same thing. How are you feeling?"

"My head hurts," I said. "But I feel better than I did before. What happened?"

"Dante carried you here, unconscious and bloody," she said. "I gave you some painkiller vials and cleaned up the blood. You had a minor concussion, but nothing too serious."

I sighed in relief. Good, the ghosts hadn't killed me. If they had, would I be stuck on the island for eternity, too? I knew one thing for sure. I'd seen the inside of the clinic too much since arriving.

"That was hours ago. You needed your sleep, so I gave you a mixture that would keep you unconscious for a short while," she said, pointing at the darkness outside the tiny window. "Everyone was very worried about you, especially Prince Christian. He and the others are still waiting for you to wake up."

I blushed at the thought of him. But whatever my feelings were for Christian, I couldn't let it interfere with my investigation. My interrogation of Dr. Cox, the Sanguine twins, and the ghosts hadn't gone as planned, but at least I discovered one thing. Something secretive was going on. Something larger than the people of V wanted to admit.

"I knew the mention of his name would cheer you up," Anastasia said, smiling again. "Wait here. I'll let the others know they can come in and see you now."

Anastasia disappeared behind the curtain, whispering

about my awakening. The shadows walked around the curtain, and Mom's face was the first person I saw. She rushed to my side, reaching for my hand.as the others trickled in, Vanessa, Dante, Christian, and Dr. Draven.

"Oh, Olivia," Mom said. "I was so worried about you. Will she be okay, Doctor?"

"She'll be fine," Dr. Draven said. "Anastasia's vials will help. But try not to move too much, Olivia, you need to recuperate."

Vanessa and Christian walked over to my bed, standing on either side, but Dante kept his distance. I noticed the expression on his face, that thoughtful, brooding look. The one that suggested he knew what we had done.

"Hey," Vanessa said, drawing my attention back to her. "It's good to see you awake. You hit your head pretty hard on that dresser."

"I knew Olivia would be all right," Christian said, squeezing my hand. "She's tougher than she looks."

I smiled, then glanced at Dante. "Thanks for carrying me here."

He bowed, staying silent. Typical.

"Now that we know you're going to live," Mom said. "You owe us an explanation, Olivia. What happened in that room? Why was it turned upside down?"

I glanced at Vanessa, but she stayed quiet. I couldn't confess we'd done a séance. That would only freak Mom out. Christian knew I'd seen ghosts, and I was sure he wouldn't be happy to learn I was deliberately luring them out.

"There...must've been an earthquake," I lied. "This strong wind came in and knocked everything over."

Mom frowned. "An earthquake? I didn't feel anything."

"Me, either," Christian said. "The kingdom of V doesn't get many natural disasters, and we've never had an earthquake."

I froze. So much for my lie, which sounded pretty awful in hindsight.

"Well, I felt something beneath the floor," Vanessa said, going along with my lie. "It shook the whole room, and there was a lot of wind. Then Olivia fell and hit her head on the dresser. How else would you explain it?"

"Another strange accident," Mom muttered. "That's what the king would say. He and his wife came with the general earlier to check on you. You were still sleeping, so they left."

"I'm sorry I freaked everyone out," I said. "I'll try to be more careful next time and watch out for flying dressers."

Christian cracked a smile, but no one else found it funny.

"Oh, before I forget," Vanessa said, handing Mom something, "here's the photograph of Charles Browning back."

"Thank you," Mom said, glancing down at it. "Why is there blood on it?"

"Oh," I muttered, "I...must've gotten blood on it when I hit my head. Sorry."

"That's all right. It's just a smudge," Mom said. "Did you have a chance to start painting him yet, Olivia?"

"Uh, not yet," I said, realizing I hadn't even started it.

"Well, no worries. Focus on getting better first. And one more thing before we let you sleep," Mom said. "Before you passed out, you said something strange to Vanessa."

I gulped. "Like what?"

"You told her she had to find out what was going on, and that Charles was onto something," she said. "What were you talking about? Was it Charles Browning you were referring to?"

I didn't know how to explain it. I barely remembered saying it. Why couldn't I have just kept my mouth shut? Vanessa turned speechless as Mom waited for an answer.

"Olivia was delirious from the pain," Dante said, covering for me. "She didn't know what she was saying."

"Is that true?" Mom asked, looking back at me.

I nodded. "Yeah, it was just nonsense. I thought I was going to die."

"Well, we're all glad you didn't. Anyway, it's late," Mom said. "You need your rest, and we all need to get to bed, too. The embassy is still set to open tomorrow morning and I'd like it if you could be there, as long as you're feeling better, of course."

"I will be. Can't wait to see it," I said. "Goodnight, Mom."

After she kissed my forehead and walked away, Vanessa leaned in to give me a hug and whisper in my ear. "Get better, and then we need to talk about what happened back there. I want to know everything."

As she left, Dr. Draven and Anastasia both smiled at me before they followed. Then it was just me, Christian, and Dante left in the room. Christian looked over his shoulder, hoping Dante would take the hint and leave to give us some privacy. Dante only continued to stand there with his eyes trained on the wall.

"I'll let my parents know you're all right," Christian said, looking back at me. "In the meantime, my father ordered some of his soldiers to clean up your room. When you're ready to go back, it'll be spotless. They'll also be looking into what caused the disaster."

"Don't worry about it," I said. "It was probably just another freak accident."

"There's been too many of them. I want them stopped," Christian said, sounding like his father. "I want to make sure you're safe, Olivia. Whatever it takes. I'm still planning our second date, you know. While I *could* make it work here in the clinic, I was hoping for something a little more romantic."

I laughed. "Don't worry. I'll be up and out of here before you know it. Then you can take me on a thousand dates."

"I'll hold you to that," he said, kissing the back of my hand. "Sleep well, Olivia."

As he walked away, I watched his shadow fade. I hadn't forgotten the warning Charles had given me about Christian, that he was more dangerous than the rest. He didn't look dangerous, but it still bothered me.

The clinic turned quiet with everyone gone. It was only me and Dante now, and he was still standing tall near the curtain's opening. He said nothing, so I decided to start the conversation.

"Are you going to stand there all night?" I asked.

He nodded. "Vanessa will be safe with your mother and Russell. I intend to stay here and guard you."

"I'm sure I'll be fine," I said. "No one comes into the clinic, and everyone should be sleeping, anyway."

Dante's eyes flitted to mine. "I'd feel better if I stayed."

"Okay then. Want a chair or something?"

He looked away again. "I've been trained to stay on my feet for days. I think I'll survive one night."

"Fine," I muttered, trying to get comfortable in bed. "Be stubborn."

He looked back at me, his jaw clenched. "*I'm* stubborn? I'm not the one who decided to communicate with spirits!"

"So you *do* know," I said. "How'd you figure it out?"

He tried to compose himself, softening his voice. "It wasn't too difficult. We don't get earthquakes here, and I heard Vanessa calling out to me, saying they were going to kill you. I assume she meant the ghosts. Then I tried to open the door, but it wouldn't budge. Finally, your blood on the picture of the dead missionary confirmed my suspicions."

I sighed. "You got me. Are you going to tell?"

"I should," he said. "If it were up to me, I'd have you confined to your room with twenty-four-seven supervision."

"You sound just like General Ezra," I muttered. "I'm sure he'd feel better with your solution. He doesn't trust me, either."

"I *do* trust you," he said. "It's the ghosts that I don't trust."

"You believe in them?"

"Most people here do. The legends are taught at the academy," he said. "General Ezra is skeptical, but he keeps an open mind."

"I didn't ask for the kingdom's or General Ezra's views," I said. "I asked for yours."

"I...believe there are things in our world not easily explained," he said, moving closer. "And I believe there are fools who meddle in them."

"Gee, thanks," I mumbled.

"I also believe this kingdom is haunted by our past. By our mistakes. I wasn't sure how haunted we were until your séance," Dante continued. "If I didn't believe in them before, I would now. What were you thinking trying to communicate with dangerous ghosts? Do you have a death wish?"

"I wanted answers. I'm sure you've realized weird things are happening in this kingdom," I said. "Charles Browning's been haunting me since day one. All I did was encourage him to come out and chat."

"What did he have to say?"

"Not much. Ghosts love to talk in riddles," I said. "But he mentioned something about monsters and an apocalypse. Know anything about that?"

"No," Dante said, firmly. "Anything else?"

"He said Christian was dangerous, not to be trusted. You told me the same thing," I said. "Why?"

"He's...well-trained. Perhaps even stronger than I am," Dante said. "I wouldn't want him to accidentally hurt you."

I crossed my arms. "We both know it's more than that."

He glared at me. "Let me worry about your safety, Olivia, even though you make it difficult by invoking spirits. What else?"

"He wasn't the only ghost there. There were others with bloody necks," I said, and Dante raised an eyebrow. "Charles called them new. He said they were outsiders who were killed here recently in your kingdom."

Dante shook his head. "Impossible. We haven't had visitors here since Charles Browning. All your people are safe and accounted for."

"Well, I don't see why he'd lie to me about that."

"Perhaps he isn't lying. Perhaps he's just confused. Ghosts have difficulty telling time since it has no concept in their world," he replied. "Was that all?"

I thought for a moment. "He said the truth was right in front of me...and that I had to investigate the crypts. He mentioned they were below the castle. The other ghosts reacted when he said that. They got angrier. It makes me think there's some truth to it."

Dante turned silent, considering my words. "He's mistaken. The crypts are dark, cold, and quiet. There's nothing down there but coffins."

"Are you sure?"

He nodded. "Yes. There's nothing of interest to you down there."

I flung the blankets off me, rising to my feet. "Then you wouldn't mind if I took a quick look around to make sure?"

"You can't," he said, blocking my path. "It would be disrespectful for an outsider to see our crypts. The king would never allow it."

"Then we'll just have to keep it our little secret."

He crossed his arms. "I'm not taking you there. The crypts are sealed, and even I could get in trouble for trespassing. Besides, you're still recovering."

"I feel better. We both know Anastasia's a quick healer with those vials of hers," I said. "Look, I know I'm asking a lot, but think about it for a moment. What if Charles Browning is right and there *have* been recent outsiders? What if they really were killed, and there's an answer to it in the crypts?"

"I don't know about that," Dante said.

"But I do. The other night, I saw a boat docking," I said. "Then it just disappeared. I assumed maybe it was a ghost boat or something. If that's even possible. But what if outsiders *have* come here? And what if one of your people did something to them?"

He turned silent for a second. "Do you believe someone in our kingdom is capable of that? Of murder?"

"They were back in Charles Browning's day. As for your people now, I don't know," I said, sighing in exasperation. "That's what I'm trying to find out, but between your stubbornness and the ghost's riddles, it hasn't been easy!"

He handed me my Slayer from his holster. "I found this on the floor of your room. You should have it back."

I sighed, taking it from him. "You didn't give me an answer."

He removed his black jacket, draping it around my shoulders. "Didn't I? Keep that on. It's cold in the crypts."

As he led me out of the dark clinic, my eyes widened. "Are you serious?"

"Yes, but keep your voice down. General Ezra sometimes has guards hiding in the shadows. If he knew what I was doing for you...he'd never forgive me."

"Would he beat you again?" I asked.

Dante whipped around, stopping me. "What do you mean, *again*?"

I hadn't meant for that to slip out. As I stood there in silence, my eyes flickered to the back of his shirt, to the hidden scars I'd seen the general give him. Dante followed my eyes and put it together.

"You know," he muttered. "You were watching, weren't you?"

"Me and Ness went looking for you when you were late to take us to the festival," I said. "I thought maybe you were held up in the militia building...and then we heard something in the general's office. We didn't mean to find out."

"No wonder you were in the church. You followed me there," he said, turning his back to me. "It was my fault. I didn't think my punishment would take that long, but the general was angry. I'm sorry you had to see that."

"You have nothing to be sorry about. *I'm* sorry it ever happened. Look, I don't know what you did," I said, "but I know one thing. You didn't deserve that. The general had no right."

"He had every right," Dante said, quietly. "You don't understand, and I'm not allowed to explain it. Perhaps not ever."

"Can I...can I see them?"

He sighed, nodding. I lifted his shirt and gasped at the deep, red welts on his muscular back. It had gotten worse. My disgust turned to sadness and then anger at the general for inflicting that on Dante.

"Anastasia could help you," I said. "She's got a vial for everything—"

"No, I won't allow her to. These scars will never heal," he said, turning around and pushing his shirt down. "And they never should for what I did."

I wanted to ask what he was talking about, but he made it clear he wasn't going to explain. He turned and started walking toward the castle. Creeping around the kingdom at night felt eerie and dangerous, so I rushed to keep up with him.

As we neared the back of the castle, walking through the garden, I turned to Dante. "Won't the king be awake? Won't he see us?"

"Everyone should be asleep at this hour," Dante said. "Besides, we don't need to go inside the castle for this."

"But Charles Browning said the crypts were below the castle," I said. "Where else—"

Dante reached forward, pulling a torch on the back wall of the castle. A section of the ground opened, revealing a snug, descending staircase. It was dark inside and I shivered, but it wasn't from the chill in the air.

I could feel spirits down there, more ghosts. I didn't know how. What was happening to me? How had I suddenly become an expert in ghostly mojo since coming to the island?

"I'll lead the way," Dante whispered. "Stick close to me and keep quiet. It's a far walk through the tunnel before we get to the crypts."

"Do you...do you think Charles was telling the truth?" I asked. "Do you think outsiders were killed down there?"

"I hope not," Dante said. "But if it *is* true...it would ruin everything. Your people would have to leave, and we'd never be able to see each other again."

"I don't want that," I whispered, which surprised me.

"Me, either," Dante said, which was even more surprising.

I sighed. "Well, I guess there's only one way to find out. If there are ghosts down there, I'm sure I'll see them."

"If you do, I'm pulling you out," Dante said. "This isn't a social call. It's a scouting mission. We get in, we get out. I expect you not to be stubborn this time and listen to me."

"I promise," I said, then took a deep breath and followed Dante down the stairs into the spooky, underground crypts.

15

THE STRANGE SYMBOLS

The passage closed behind us as soon as we stepped down the stairs, and I jumped at the sudden loud noise. There was no turning back now, not until I found what I came for. Everything was dark until Dante reached for a torch on the wall and illuminated the way. All I could see was a long, narrow hallway with no end in sight.

As we walked along, I clung to Dante, grabbing his arm so we wouldn't get separated. To my surprise, he didn't pull away but slowed his pace so I could keep up. He swatted away the spider webs to clear a path for us as my heart pounded in fear.

Maybe coming down was a bad idea, almost as bad as the séance.

"Are you all right?" he whispered. "I can hear your heaving breathing."

"Yeah, sorry," I said. "This hallway's tight. Feels like I'm suffocating down here."

"Don't worry. The crypts are much bigger," he said. "The

hallway is the only enclosed space. Do you feel any ghosts yet?"

I paused for a moment. "No, not yet. But I don't think Charles would send us down here for no reason."

"You can't trust a spirit, Olivia," Dante scolded. "They aren't like they used to be."

The tunnel rumbled above our heads. Rock, dust particles, and dirt fell from the ceiling, coating my hair and clothes. I glanced around as small tremors echoed down the tunnel.

"What was that?" I asked.

"Tremors. It's normal," Dante said. "We built the tunnels deep underground so no one could access them, but the earth is more unstable down here. We need to be careful."

"You couldn't have told me that *before* we stepped inside?"

Dante shrugged. "You were adamant about coming down here. I wasn't sure anything was going to stop you."

He was right. I'd practically forced him to take me down into the crypts. I only hoped my stubbornness paid off. As Dante turned right at a dead-end, anxiety gripped me. I had to do something to take my mind off the rumbling, and then I remembered all those questions I had. They were a good way to pass the time.

"I spoke with the Sanguine twins a while ago," I said. "They were sitting outside the jail, having lunch."

He grunted. "They're deluding themselves if they think their parents will be released soon. What did they have to say?"

"They claim their parents weren't violent," I said, "and that they didn't deserve their harsh sentencing. Is that true?"

"They set bombs and played tricks on our people," Dante said. "That sounds violent to me."

"But no one was killed, were they?"

He huffed. "No, I suppose not. What's your point?"

"I'm trying to figure out who's behind the recent attacks," I said. "Is Havoc really that bad?"

"Yes. Even without murdering anyone, they still disobeyed our laws," he replied. "They claimed boredom to defend themselves, but that's no excuse. They're irritants, and I'm glad they're behind bars."

"Do you think they're involved in blowing up that statue at the festival?" I asked. "I know the Sanguine parents are in jail, but they could have people working on the outside."

"I wouldn't put it past them," Dante said. "They were very charismatic. Their little acts of mischief entertained people, and I could see them luring more in. But General Ezra hasn't mentioned any suspects."

I dodged a scurrying spider. "The Sanguine twins mentioned Isolationists. Know anything about them?"

Dante nodded. "A small group. Before your people arrived, a letter was left on the castle's doorsteps, begging the king to rethink allowing outsiders to come here. We aren't sure who's involved with the Isolationists, but they claim to have a few dozen members."

"A letter?" I asked. "And you didn't think to tell us that? King Dominic promised your kingdom wanted change."

"Most of us do," Dante said, taking another left. "The Isolationists aren't violent. They're just afraid and territorial. They've grown accustomed to our kingdom being cut off from the world. King Dominic didn't sense any danger from them, and I think once they see us getting along, they'll change their minds."

Between Havoc, the ghosts, and the Isolationists, I wasn't sure who to point the finger at. Everyone seemed to have a good motive for scaring us away.

"The Sanguine twins also mentioned others," I said, "more dangerous people. Does that mean anything to you?"

"No," Dante replied, quickly. "They're only trying to scare you. I trust the Sanguine twins as much as I trust the ghosts."

When I saw a chamber door at the end of the tunnel, I figured I'd better wrap up my questions. "One last thing. What do you know about the Dark Half?"

Dante stiffened. "How do you know that term?"

"Christian said it was the statue that blew up, an old myth," I said. "Then I talked to Dr. Cox and—"

"You did?" Dante interrupted. "What did he say?"

"A lot of nonsense," I said, "but he mentioned monsters, pure evil, and that if it got out, it could destroy the world."

Dante paused for a moment, thinking. "Dr. Cox is—"

"Unstable?" I asked. "Yeah, people keep saying that, but I don't buy it. Dr. Cox really believes in it, and when you pair it with the warnings from the ghosts, maybe there's some truth. What if monsters *are* lurking in your kingdom? There's a big forest behind the castle where they could hide."

Dante sighed. "It'll be dawn soon, Olivia. The more you interrogate me, the less time we have down here. Which one will it be?"

"Fine," I said. "Open the door. But I'm not letting this Dark Half business go."

"You should," Dante whispered, then opened the chamber door.

The crypts weren't what I was expecting. I thought they would be much scarier, but instead, it was just a large room with dozens of coffins. I walked closer and ran my hands along the wood. They all had strange designs on them, just like the symbol on my dagger. There were seven symbols in crimson, and they seemed familiar the more I looked at them.

"Sense anything?" Dante asked, breaking my thoughts.

"No," I said. "No ghosts...yet."

"I told you," Dante said. "There's nothing down here."

I walked around the crypts. "You know, for a really old kingdom, you don't have a lot of people buried here."

"We cremate our people and throw the ashes into the sea," Dante said. "There aren't any bodies in here."

"Why not?"

"Burning them is our way," Dante replied. "It's more efficient. The coffins are simply to remember them, a symbol of their lives."

"Can I look around?"

He sighed. "You won't leave here until you do, will you? Fine, but you can't tell anyone."

I opened the lid on a nearby casket. It was the man who had died after taking the vial, or what remained of him. He had sunken eyes, wrinkly skin, and animalistic hands. It was like he had transformed and turned into a monster.

"Why wasn't this one cremated?" I asked, horrified.

Dante closed the casket. "We haven't gotten around to burning his body yet. The King's been busy, but I hear the Burning will happen first thing tomorrow morning. You shouldn't see him like this, Olivia. It's disturbing."

"Yeah, maybe you're right," I said. "There's nothing here, anyway—"

That was when I felt it. A coldness crept up my body. I followed the origin of the feeling and realized it was coming from a far wall on the other side of the room. A wall with the same symbols as my dagger and the coffins. Before I could stop myself, I started walking toward it.

"Olivia?" Dante asked, following me. "Are you okay?"

I didn't respond. I ran my fingers along the wall, feeling something. There was a lot of emotion there, anger, sadness, grief, death. The strongest was pain, and if I closed my eyes, I could almost feel something prickling at my skin. It was nearly overwhelming. I clutched my stomach from the nausea, unable to tear my gaze away from the strange symbols that kept appearing everywhere.

"Olivia," Dante said, grabbing my arm. "Did you hear me?"

That pulled me out of it. I turned to Dante, my eyes wide. "I...I think we should leave."

"I couldn't agree more," he grumbled, "but why the sudden change of heart?"

"Because," I said, glancing back at the wall. "Something terrible happened down here."

I rushed out of the crypts, following the tunnels back to the staircase. This time, Dante struggled to keep up with me. I wanted out of there as fast as possible, away from all those strong emotions I'd felt. I didn't know if it was coming from the ghosts, but I didn't want to stick around and find out.

"What do you mean?" Dante asked.

"Not sure," I said. "All I know is we should get out of here, now."

When we reached the staircase, Dante pulled the lever on the wall to open the passage. He frowned when nothing happened. "The lever must be malfunctioning. Let me try again."

When he did, the staircase still wouldn't open. I turned to Dante. "What's going on?"

"I don't know," he muttered. "It won't open, just like yesterday when I tried to get inside your room."

As he fumbled with the lever, I craned my neck and noticed a haunting glow coming from behind us. It was Charles Browning again, and he had the other bloody ghosts with him. I backed up, crashing into Dante as they floated closer.

"Olivia, what's wrong?" Dante asked.

I could only point as the ghosts closed in on us. Charles Browning looked disappointed, shaking his head. "Coming here with one of them was a mistake. You need to be alone to discover the truth. They cannot be trusted."

"One of them?" I asked. "You mean Dante?"

Charles nodded. "He is one of them, no matter how much he appears to be normal. The truth was right in front of you. You almost discovered it. Innocent lives are counting on you."

"Innocent lives? The truth?" I asked. "I don't understand. Why can't you just tell me everything?"

"We cannot. You must learn for yourself," Charles said, "before the apocalypse comes and it's too late."

They vanished as a strong wind swept through the tunnels, opening the passage for us. I wasted no time, pulling Dante up the stairs. Once we'd gotten out, I collapsed onto the ground, feeling like I couldn't catch my breath. All that ghost-chasing and sneaking around wasn't good for my body.

Dante closed the passage and kneeled beside me. "Olivia, are you all right?"

I nodded. "Just having a panic attack. I'll...be fine."

"Take deep breaths," he said. "Come on, I'll help you up."

As he helped me to my feet, I looked at him. "I saw the ghosts again, Dante. Now I know there's something about the crypt. They said—"

"I know," Dante interrupted. "I saw them, too."

"You...you did?" I asked. "So I'm not crazy?"

Dante shook his head. "No, Olivia, but we still can't tell anyone. They'd know we were in the crypts."

My eyes flickered to his back. "And then you'd get punished. I won't let that happen, Dante. I'll keep quiet."

He nodded, gently grabbing my arm to lead me down the brick path to the clinic. We fumbled through the darkness, only finding our way back with the help of the lanterns on the trees. I sighed in relief after we stepped inside, and Dante locked the door behind us.

"At least they're gone," I said. "No ghosts followed us. Have you ever seen those ones before?"

"Never," he replied. "And I didn't recognize any of them, either, only Charles Browning from the picture your mother showed me. For whatever reason, they decided to let me see them, maybe to scare me, too."

"Well, thanks for taking me into the crypts. I know what kind of trouble you could've gotten into if we were caught."

"Some things are worth risking trouble for."

I smiled.

He helped me get into bed, then returned to his post near the curtain. "You should get some rest. I know it'll be difficult after what we saw tonight, but you should try."

"Oh, wait," I said, pulling his jacket off. "This is yours."

He shook his head. "Keep it. It looks better on you."

I wasn't sure if he intended to sound flirtatious, but he did. I blushed as I put it back on, relishing the extra warmth before I laid my head down. Although I couldn't get the images of the ghosts out of my head, and I didn't like someone watching me as I slept, my eyes grew too tired to resist.

When they opened again, I glanced out the window and noticed dawn. As I looked back, Dante was still standing in his guard position, not having moved an inch. He bowed when he saw my eyes open.

"You're awake," he said. "Did you have a good sleep?"

I shrugged. "I didn't have any nightmares if that's what you're asking, thankfully. I miss my bed back home, though. Miss Sparkles always knew how to cheer me up."

I wanted to hit myself for admitting it out loud. Dante wrinkled his face in confusion. "Miss Sparkles?"

"My, um, stuffed animal," I mumbled. "I forgot her at home. When I realized it, we were already on the boat here."

"I'm sorry," was all Dante said. I expected him to make fun of me, but he didn't. "I know what it's like to feel homesick."

I didn't know what he meant by that. Hadn't he lived in the kingdom his whole life? What would he be missing?

Unfortunately, that conversation died when the door to the clinic opened. Anastasia and Dr. Draven entered first, followed by Mom, Vanessa, and Christian. King Dominic, Vivienne, and General Ezra trickled in afterward.

"There she is," Mom said, walking over to my bed. "You look much better, sweetie. The cut on your forehead's gotten smaller. How are you feeling?"

"Better," I said, honestly. I left out the anxiety and ghosts. "No offense, but I'm getting sick of looking at these white walls."

Anastasia laughed. "Then it's a good thing you're getting discharged. I'm giving you a clean bill of health."

"I knew you'd make it," Vanessa said. "No flying dresser can hurt you."

General Ezra raised an eyebrow at that.

"Speaking of which," King Dominic said, "my guards cleaned your room and searched for the source of the tremors. They couldn't find anything. Although we didn't get the answers we were looking for, we're relieved you're all right."

"Me, too," Christian said, smiling as he reached for my hand. "And I'm glad I won't have to bust you out of here."

"Did you have any trouble last night, soldier?" General Ezra asked Dante. I knew what he was really asking. If I'd done anything suspicious.

"No, sir," Dante lied. "I saw nothing out of the ordinary."

General Ezra narrowed his eyes but eventually nodded. "Good."

I still couldn't look at the general after what he had done to Dante. I hated him for it. No matter how much Dante told me he deserved it. I still wished I'd done something to stop it.

Mom smiled. "It's a good thing you're feeling better. The embassy's opening in an hour!"

King Dominic shared her smile. "Yes, and you wouldn't want to miss it. We're unveiling something special, just for your people. I'm sure you'll love it."

As he and Queen Vivienne turned, leaving the infirmary, Christian kissed my hand. "See you there. Maybe after the embassy, we can spend some time together. Alone."

I smiled. "Sounds good to me."

As he left, General Ezra frowned at me, his eyes roaming my head. He took a step closer, and I wondered what he was doing as he reached over, pulling something out of my hair. My eyes widened when I noticed what it was.

A spider web from the crypts. Dante and I had both missed it. As the general inspected it, I feared he knew what we had done. Vanessa, Mom, Anastasia, and Dr. Draven stood there with looks of confusion.

"You should clean this clinic once in a while," Dante said, covering for me. "You left a spider web on Olivia's bed."

Dr. Draven frowned. "I haven't seen any spiders—"

"It doesn't mean they're not here," Dante said, quickly.

Anastasia and Dr. Draven looked bewildered, glancing at each other. I inspected my hair for more spiderwebs, but I couldn't find any. Figures, there was only one, and General Ezra happened to find it. I couldn't believe I'd slept with it all night and hadn't felt it.

He threw the spider web into the trash and turned to Dante. "Your shift is over. Go back to the barracks and rest."

Dante hesitated, looking back at me. "But you ordered me to guard Olivia and Vanessa—"

"I will watch over them," General Ezra said, firmly. "You've been up for days, Dante, and even we have our limits.

I'll personally relieve your shift while you sleep, eat, and shower. You may return to your post tomorrow."

Dante sighed, glancing at me. "Very well."

"Sorry you'll miss the opening," I said to Dante. "But I'll show you around when you're back on the clock."

Dante nodded, though he looked disappointed. "I look forward to that."

After he left, Mom reached for my arm. "Come on, let's get back to your room. Vanessa can help you pick out something nice to wear. Did you know I'm making a speech?"

As Mom rambled on, I rose from the hospital bed. I thanked Anastasia and Dr. Draven for healing and followed Mom and Vanessa back to the castle. As we walked, with General Ezra following close behind, there was only one thing on my mind.

I hope nothing happens at the embassy. For once, we need something to go right.

16

EMBASSY WOES

I wasn't thrilled about the idea of having General Ezra as our bodyguard for the rest of the day. The man didn't trust me, and I didn't trust him, either. Sure, it was only until Dante had eaten and slept, but even a minute with the general felt too long.

Why would the general volunteer for it, anyway? It sounded like menial work, and he could've asked one of the other guards to do it. I felt like the general of the army had more important things to do.

They say you never know what you have until it's gone, and boy, did I realize I missed Dante.

General Ezra's cold stare remained on me as I entered my room, impressed at how well the soldiers had cleaned it. It looked even better than it did *before* the disaster. Knowing Mom was expecting me, I rummaged through my closet for something to wear but couldn't decide. Once Vanessa had gotten dressed, in yet another pink gown she'd brought, she entered my room and closed the door on the general so he couldn't watch us. It felt good to get away from his gaze if only for a few minutes.

"Time to spill," she said. "What happened the night of the séance? We haven't had a chance to talk in private."

I told her everything. How Charles Browning had said the people of V were evil, his mention of monsters, and how the truth was right in front of us. I left out any mention of the crypts in case someone was listening in, but I *did* tell her about the new ghosts with blood on their necks. When I mentioned Charles talking about the recently killed outsiders, she gasped.

"And the wind?" Vanessa asked. "Why did that happen?"

"It was the ghosts. I'm not sure how much power they have in this world, if they can set fires or not, but they *can* control wind," I said. "They were trying to scare us away for our own safety. That's why the dresser hit me. They think we're in danger here...and not from them."

"Then who?"

"The people of V," I said. "The ghosts don't trust them. You should've seen their energy, it was red and dark like they were angry. Something terrible happened to them."

"Things are getting serious, Liv," she said. "Maybe we should tell someone. Like your mom."

I scoffed. "You think my mom will believe we saw ghosts? I know she believes in God, but I think we'd be pushing it."

"Then at the very least we should try to be more careful. Like not summoning spirits for starters," she said, glaring at me. Then she sighed. "I wish my mom was here. She'd know what to do..."

"She'll be here soon," I said, "along with another boat. Then we can get the hell out of this haunted kingdom."

"Sounds good to me. Anyway, what was up with that spider web in your hair?" Vanessa asked, looking for a dress for me to wear. "The general looked at it like it was some kind of revelation."

Dante had been clear. I couldn't tell anyone what we did. I shrugged. "Must've come from the clinic like Dante said. The general's just looking for any excuse to punish me. He always thinks I'm up to no good."

"That general creeps me out," Vanessa said, flinging some of my clothes she didn't like onto my floor. "He just stands there and stares, and not in the sexy, smoldering way that Dante does."

"Sexy? Smoldering?" I asked, grinning. "Are *you* crushing on our bodyguard?"

Vanessa scoffed. "Oh, please, I have eyeballs, don't I? And besides, he doesn't feel like *our* bodyguard. He spends most of his time with you. Good thing I have Russell looking out for me..."

I hadn't realized it until Vanessa pointed it out, but it was true. Dante and I *did* spend a lot of time together. I chalked it up to the fact that I got myself in danger more often than Vanessa and left it at that. She wasn't the one consorting with ghosts or venturing deep into crypts.

"Your closet is pathetic," Vanessa said, pulling out a blue miniskirt Mom had forced me to bring. "This is the best I can do with what you have. Pair this was that frilly, black top I lent you and you'll look great."

"It's just the embassy's opening ceremony," I said, cleaning up some of the rejected clothes she'd strewn on my floor. "I don't have to look Oscar-worthy."

She grinned. "Christian will be there, you know, and you

always have to look your best, Liv. It's like you haven't learned anything in our years of friendship. Too bad Dante isn't coming, or we could've had the opportunity to impress two of your boyfriends in one shot."

I rolled my eyes, throwing a shirt at her head. She dodged it and frowned when she looked at my dresser. "Hey, what's this?"

Vanessa picked up a teddy bear on top of the dresser. A card sat beside it as I rushed over, frowning. "I have no idea. I didn't even realize it was there."

Vanessa read the card aloud. "'It's not Miss Sparkles, but I hope it's an acceptable substitute.' No one signed their name. But hey, Miss Sparkles...isn't that your purple bear back home?"

"Yeah, that's right," I said, reaching for the brown teddy bear. It was plush and soft. "Wow, this is nice..."

"And sent by a secret admirer," Vanessa said, grinning. "It was probably Christian. He seems like the old romantic type. You're lucky, you know. All the boys I've been with haven't even listened to me, let alone bought me anything..."

But I hadn't told Christian. Dante was the only one I'd confided in about Miss Sparkles and how I'd forgotten her at home. He must've bought it from the markets after the general told him to rest and left it in my room. I didn't expect this kind of behavior from someone as stoic as him.

After Vanessa left, I changed into the mini-skirt and black top. I placed my new teddy bear on my pillow, surprised Dante could be so sentimental and walked out into the hallway. Mom, Russell, and Vanessa waited outside my room with General Ezra. Unlike Dante who usually nodded at my arrival, General Ezra glared in my direction.

"I can't believe this is happening. What a wonderful day for our cultures," Mom said, oblivious to the general's hatred of me. "The chefs have all the food prepared and waiting at the embassy."

"Thank God," Vanessa said, walking down the hallway with us. "I'm starving."

As we stepped outside the castle, I noticed the embassy along the brick path next to the academy. With the tarp off to reveal the building, I realized how modern it looked with sleek windows, a tall arch, and a small garden in the front.

"Wow," I said. "The builders did a great job."

"It's the nicest place in the whole kingdom!" Vanessa said, then remembered General Ezra was with us. "Uh, one of the nicest places, I mean."

If General Ezra felt offended, he said nothing.

"King Dominic wanted us to feel at home," Mom said. "He asked me what some of the buildings looked like back in Washington, then the builders sketched a drawing of it from my description. I'm still surprised at how little time it took to get it up and running…"

General Ezra said nothing, just continued following us closely while watching the crowd. I knew he didn't approve of us staying there or building an embassy. The people in the kingdom swarmed the embassy, eager to see what the inside looked like.

As we walked over, I noticed the red ribbon in front of the doors. King Dominic, Queen Vivienne, and Prince Christian stood nearby, waiting for us to arrive. We took our places in front of the crowd as the royal family grinned.

"This is a momentous day," King Dominic said, glancing at his people. "I know it feels like centuries since we've welcomed outsiders here, but times are changing. With this embassy opening, we begin a new page in our long history and welcome the people of America. Which brings me to my surprise..."

I almost forgot about the king mentioning a special surprise when I was in the clinic. I hoped it was a boat we could get back to safety in.

"I'm declaring this day, Friendship Day," King Dominic said, much to my disappointment. "It will be celebrated every year as the day we made contact with our first friends, Ambassador Hawthorne and her people."

"What a wonderful idea," Mom said, beaming. "We're so happy you think of us as friends already. I look forward to celebrating more Friendship Days with you."

Russell turned to me and rolled his eyes, and I felt the same. I glanced around at the reaction of the crowd. Some people looked excited, others leery and confused. While the general remained stoic as always, I noticed something strange flash across the queen's face. Was it...fear?

"It's my pleasure," the king said, stepping off to the side. "If you'd like to address the crowd, Ambassador, I'm sure they're all eager to hear from you."

Mom nodded, stepping forward while clearing her throat. "Yes, thank you. When President Bennett put my name forward as the ambassador to the kingdom of V, I was wary at first. Brokering an alliance with a new kingdom is always risky, especially when you have an...unfortunate past. But since coming here, and being treated wonderfully by our hosts, I have no doubt our alliance is growing strong. My daughter and I can't wait to make your kingdom our new home."

As the crowd clapped, I glanced over at Vanessa. She looked as nervous as I felt. If Mom knew half the stuff that was going on, would she still want to stay?

"Girls, would you help me?" Mom asked as King Dominic passed her a pair of scissors to cut the red ribbon. I shuddered when I remembered the boy stabbing me.

Me and Vanessa stepped forward, placing our hands above Mom's on the scissors. We helped her cut the ribbon, and when it broke, more clapping erupted from the crowd. I had to wonder if they were truly happy or just entertaining us for the sake of the king. Sometimes it felt like he and his family were the only ones who wanted us there.

"Let's head inside," Mom said. "I decorated it all myself..."

We were the first ones allowed inside, along with the general and the royal family. The rest of the crowd trickled in afterward as I took a long look around. Without electricity or technology, the building felt bare, but Mom had done as much with it as she could.

She'd strung lanterns around the room to illuminate it, created a living room area to entertain guests, and set up a desk to do her paperwork. I spotted a more private office in the back along with a bathroom. She'd also hung that picture of Charles Browning on the wall, which made me shudder as I remembered all the things he had warned me about. He wouldn't approve of an embassy. For the opening celebration, the chefs from the castle had set up a buffet with dozens of raw-meat dishes and some vegetable-oriented ones for me.

"With King Dominic's help, I plan to add more technology down the line," Mom said. "But until then, I think this place is cozy. What about you?"

"Looks great," I said. "Nice work."

Vanessa nodded. "Yeah, I'm sure my mom will love it, too."

Mom grinned. "Thanks, girls. I can't wait to show the president everything we've accomplished here when she arrives. It should be within the next few days."

"Well, I'm sure everyone's hungry," King Dominic said, pulling out a key from his pocket, "but I have another surprise for you. It's for the Hawthorne family this time."

As Mom took the key, she frowned in confusion. "Thank you, but...what does it open?"

"Your new home, of course," King Dominic said. "We've allocated you a home outside the markets where you and your daughter can live. We're calling it Hawthorne Lodge. After this, I'll personally take you to it."

"I helped Father pick out the place," Christian said, glancing at me. "I even helped decorate your room, Olivia."

I couldn't speak, so Mom grinned. "Thank you so much, King Dominic. We'll treat it with care."

I wanted to scream. I didn't want to stay in this kingdom for the rest of my life, and I didn't want my mother here, either – not with all the threats and explosions.

King Dominic turned to the crowd. "Please, enjoy the food and feel free to mingle. It *is* Friendship Day, after all, and I think we should get to know each other a little better."

As some of the people congratulated Mom, I headed straight for the buffet. I filled my plate with fruit, salad, and tofu fritters, a new recipe the chefs had learned. I didn't feel bad about taking most of it, no one else ate plants. Before I could eat, I spotted Anastasia heading my way with a man and a woman. They resembled her with red hair, green eyes, and freckled faces.

"Olivia, these are my parents, Gianna and Leon," Anastasia said as I shook their hands. "They're the head chefs at the castle."

"We wanted to congratulate you on the embassy," Leon said. "We think it'll make a fine addition to our kingdom."

"And we wanted to let you know we've enjoyed cooking for you," Gianna said. "Vegetarianism is...interesting, to say the least. It's been a welcome challenge. If you need anything else, don't hesitate to let us know."

As I thanked them and watched them walk away, I scanned the crowd, noticing Vanessa flirting with some of the more attractive, younger men. Typical Ness. I didn't see the Sanguine twins among the people, which didn't surprise me. They didn't want us here any more than the general did.

Speaking of him, he stood off to the side, talking to no one, but keeping an eye on me. I didn't want to give him more of a reason to hate me, so I vowed to stay on my best behavior. Before I could take a bite of my food, Christian walked over. I didn't want to seem impolite, so I put the plate down.

"There you are," he said, grinning. "Nice outfit."

I blushed. "Thanks, it's another one of Vanessa's choices."

"Well, she should dress you more often," Christian said, his eyes lingering on my legs long enough to make me blush. "After this, I was thinking we could walk the markets. Castle food is delicious, but there's a vendor I think you'll like. I asked him to make you vegetarian food. Then we could head to the fashion kiosk I got your scarf from and get you something that'll match."

I smiled. "Sounds like fun. Count me in."

Before he could reply, Vanessa walked past us, grabbing a plate and loading it with meat from the buffet. "Hey, love-birds. Did you thank him for the teddy bear yet, Liv?"

Christian frowned. "What teddy bear?"

I wanted to kill Vanessa for saying that. When I glared at her, she seemed to understand that he hadn't sent the bear at all. "Uh, my mistake. Excuse me..."

As she scurried away with her food, I hoped that would teach her not to meddle in my love life anymore. Christian looked back at me. "What was that all about?"

"Oh, nothing," I lied. "Nessa's just weird. So, what else can we do around here?"

He nodded and smiled, continuing to ramble on about what he had planned for us. As he spoke, I found Mom in the crowd. She stood at her desk, holding a piece of paper in her hands. She was speaking to King Dominic and Queen Vivienne, and it looked serious.

"Sorry to interrupt," I said, nodding over at my mom, "but what do you think they're talking about?"

Christian glanced back, noticing their tense conversation. "Let's find out."

As we walked over, I caught the tail end of what Mom was saying. "...isn't the first time we've been threatened, King Dominic. I'm concerned."

"I understand that, Ambassador," King Dominic said, "but I'm sure this is just the work of some punk kids trying to scare you away, such as the Sanguine twins, for example. Their parents are devious tricksters, don't forget. I'm sure some of that has rubbed off on them."

"What's going on?" I asked.

"It's nothing to worry about," King Dominic said, smiling at me. "Enjoy the party."

"Father," Christian said, crossing his arms. "We know something's wrong. Tell us."

Before King Dominic could speak, Mom thrust the paper at me. "Here, read it for yourself."

I looked down at the paper, reading it out loud. "'We don't want you here. We're better off alone as we have always been. Leave the kingdom or else.' Who'd send that?"

"As I said, immature children," King Dominic replied. "They must've broken into the embassy and left it on your mother's desk to ruin our party. They'll be sorry if I catch them…"

I remembered what Dante had told me, that they'd received a letter from the Isolationists begging King Dominic not to let us come before we arrived. The letter wasn't signed, but it sounded like too much of a coincidence.

"I'll take that," King Dominic said, grabbing the paper from my hands. "I'll enjoy destroying it. Please, return to the party and have a good time."

As the king walked away to dispose of the letter, Christian sighed. "There's never a dull moment around here. Wait here, Olivia. I'll grab a plate and join you."

As I waited for Christian, I started nibbling on the fruit, hoping he wouldn't mind. When he had his plate, I followed him to one of the chairs and sat beside him.

"I hope that letter hasn't ruined the party," Christian said.

I smiled. "Thanks, Christian. At least someone wants us—"

My words got interrupted by my coughing. When I realized I couldn't stop, I stood up, feeling my face turning red.

Christian sprung into action, handing me a glass of water. I took a long sip, but nothing seemed to stop the coughing. When my throat started to burn and I felt nauseous, I doubled over to catch my breath...

And noticed the dribble of blood on the floor. It was mine. I was coughing up blood. And that was when I collapsed.

17
HARSH REPRIMANDS

As soon as I hit the floor, spilling my plate, Christian sprang into action. "Someone, help! We need a doctor!"

The crowd paused the celebrations and swarmed me. General Ezra pushed through the people, his eyes widening at me. Mom, Vanessa, and Russell made it over, along with King Dominic and Queen Vivienne.

"Olivia, what's going on?" Mom asked, falling to her knees beside me.

I couldn't speak. I'd have to stop coughing for that, and my body wouldn't let me. It felt like my throat was closing up. If I were dying, I wouldn't even be able to say goodbye properly to my family and friends. I thought I saw a brief glimpse of the ghost of Charles Browning across the room, but it vanished in the blink of an eye.

"All right, everyone, give her some room!" General Ezra said, making the crowd back up. "Anastasia, Dr. Draven, we need help!"

With the crowd giving me space, Dr. Draven and Anastasia could push through. They fell beside me, checking my lungs with their stethoscopes and placing their hand on my forehead to feel for a fever. As Dr. Draven was trying to determine why I was so sick, Anastasia noticed the food on the ground beneath me.

"Did you eat that right before you fell ill?" Anastasia asked, picking up the plate.

I couldn't speak, so I just nodded.

"One minute we were talking and eating, and the next, she started coughing up blood," Christian said. "It happened so fast..."

"Sounds like food poisoning to me," Dr. Draven said. "And it would've been easy to target Olivia. No one else eats vegetarian food here."

My throat and stomach burned from whatever someone had doused my food with. And since the buffet was out in the open, anyone could've gotten to it. Maybe it was even the same person who left the threatening note on Mom's desk and begged the king to reconsider our alliance.

King Dominic hung his head in shame. He wanted the embassy's opening to go well, both he and Mom did. Tears welled in Queen Vivienne's eyes as the king pulled her closer. I glanced up at Christian, and his worried gaze made me wish I could comfort him somehow.

Anastasia pulled out vials that she kept in her doctor's coat. "Good thing I always carry these around in case of an emergency. I might have something that could help..."

She retrieved a vial with smelly grey liquid inside and brought it up to my mouth. With her help, I was able to drink it. It burned even worse going down, but after a few moments of deep breaths, I started to feel better, and my lungs cleared.

Finally, I stopped coughing. General Ezra reached out a hand, which shocked me, and helped me to my feet. The crowd kept their eyes on me, murmuring about the poison and all the other strange incidents. Mom and Vanessa pulled me into a hug as Russell placed a hand on my shoulder.

"How are you feeling, Liv?" Vanessa asked.

"Better," I said, glancing at Anastasia. "Thank you for saving my life."

"It's what I do," she said. "I'm glad the vial was able to help for now, but I'd like to take you to the clinic to run a few tests—"

"No," I said. "I've seen that clinic enough for one trip. I don't want to go back."

"I won't keep you there on bedrest," she said. "I just want to ensure the poison is completely out of your system. I have faith in my medicine, but it doesn't hurt to check."

"You should go, Olivia," Mom said. "You can never be too careful."

"Fine," I said, unable to resist my mother's pleading eyes. "But let's make it quick."

"Just one second," General Ezra said, his eyes on me. "Did you see anyone poking around the buffet table? Anyone who might've poisoned your food?"

I shrugged. "A bunch of people were there. I didn't see anyone suspicious, no."

"You couldn't have," Russell said, stepping forward, "but the general should've been paying better attention."

It was brave of Russell to stand up for me. The General was at least a foot taller, and his scowl could've scared off the fiercest animal. He looked down at Russell with a hard gaze. "Are you saying I wanted this to happen?"

"I'm saying you're supposed to be her guard," Russell said, "and you failed. Olivia almost died on your watch!"

"You were also here," General Ezra said, towering over Russell. "As I understand it, the president sent you with the ambassador to watch over her and her family. What's your excuse?"

"I have none. I failed her, too," Russell said, "but at least I can admit it. Maybe you even know who's responsible. After all, you haven't wanted us here from day one, General, and I don't trust you."

When the general growled, King Dominic lunged forward. "Enough! I will not have you brawling with my guests, brother."

"You heard what the outsider said," General Ezra said. "He's accusing me of poisoning Olivia!"

"Everyone's emotions are running high," King Dominic said. "We're all upset this has happened. Now, I order you to stand down and take Olivia to the clinic for further testing."

General Ezra grumbled but didn't protest.

Christian stepped forward. "I'm going, too. I want to make sure Olivia's okay."

I smiled at his concern. As I left with them, I heard King Dominic turn to one of the soldiers. "Investigate the buffet table. Search for anything that looks suspicious."

As we walked along the brick path to the clinic, I sighed. "Sorry for ruining the embassy's opening."

Mom shook her head. "You have nothing to apologize for, Olivia. You didn't plan on getting poisoned."

"No," I said, "but I should've been more careful."

"You shouldn't have to be," Vanessa muttered.

"It was my fault," Christian said. "Olivia might've seen the culprit if I hadn't dragged her away. I'll try not to be so distracting in the future."

I laughed. "Let's not get crazy now."

Christian smiled as he led me into the clinic, then helped me into the hard bed I never wanted to see again. Anastasia and Dr. Draven entered a minute later, taking my blood and rushing off to their workbench. King Dominic and Queen Vivienne walked through the doors as soon as the others had the test results.

"You're healthy," Dr. Draven said. "I don't see any remnants of the poison in your blood. Anastasia's vial worked."

"I don't know how you do it," I said, glancing at her, "but thanks again."

"I've had years of practice," Anastasia said. "My medicine's largely been trial and error, but I've seen a big improvement in the last...few years."

"Don't we know it," Christian said, cryptically.

"We're glad to hear you'll be all right," King Dominic said, turning to Mom. "Ambassador, I'm very sorry about today. The embassy's opening was supposed to be a turning point for our people, a happy celebration, and the saboteur spoiled it."

"So, now you're willing to admit someone's out to get us?" I asked.

"I'm willing to admit the poisoning can't be easily explained," King Dominic said. "I'll need more evidence before I make any accusations."

"Who would want to hurt you, Olivia?" Christian asked.

A bunch of people came to mind, from the Sanguine twins to the ghosts to the Isolationists. The Sanguine twins had even mentioned someone worse than all those things, but wouldn't say who. I had no leads, only theories, and I was sure no one would believe me.

I shrugged. "Beats me."

"Well, some of Anastasia's chemicals can be dangerous. I imagine the poison must've come from here," Dr. Draven said. "Someone must've snuck inside the clinic and stole some of it, then put it in the vegetarian food. We lock the doors to the clinic at night, but we don't have guards on patrol. We've never had a reason to."

"That ends now," King Dominic said, glancing at the general. "Station soldiers here night and day in case the thief returns."

General Ezra nodded. "I'll have my finest soldiers on it."

The door to the clinic opened and Anastasia's parents walked in. They sighed in relief when they noticed I was alive and rushed over to my bed. Anastasia gave them a quick hug before they turned to me.

"Olivia, you're all right. Thank goodness." Gianna pressed her hand against her chest. "We were worried, so we came by to check on you."

"You and your husband made the food for the event, correct?" King Dominic asked.

"We did. We make all the food for the castle, too," Leon said. "You aren't accusing us of anything, are you, your Majesty?"

"I'm only trying to find the truth," he replied. "Did you see anyone suspicious poking around the kitchen?"

"No, your Majesty," Gianna said. "If the food was

poisoned, it had to have been at the embassy. We would've noticed someone inside our kitchen."

"And we'd also like to say that we had nothing to do with it," Leon said. "We take our jobs seriously, and we'd never poison a guest."

"I'm sure you wouldn't," King Dominic said, eyeing them, "but someone out there did, and I intend to find them. This kind of crime is inexcusable."

"Could it have something to do with the letter?" Mom asked. "We'd just found it before Olivia was poisoned."

"I don't think it's related," Queen Vivienne said, quickly. "Believe me."

"Well, if it's not, then we have two problems on our hands," Mom said. "As much as I enjoy being an ambassador to this kingdom, my family's safety comes first. If something else should happen, I'll be asking the president to take us home when she arrives."

"I understand, Ambassador. Again, I'm truly sorry this has been your experience," King Dominic said. "You have my word that I'll find who's responsible. I already have a plan in mind. When you're feeling up to it, I'd be more than happy to show you to your new home."

Right, I'd almost forgotten about the key he'd given to Mom. I didn't want a new house. All I wanted was to go home and lie in my own bed, far away from all the ghosts and danger.

"Christian, I know you'd like to stay with Olivia, but I need your help with something," King Dominic said. "Meet me outside when you're finished."

Christian kissed my hand. "Feel better, Olivia. I know

Father will do everything in his power to find who's doing this. I'd really like you to stay with us."

"Me, too," I said as they left, even though I knew it wasn't possible.

"Well, everything looks good," Dr. Draven said. "You're free to leave the clinic, but I'd still recommend resting. You've been through quite the ordeal. And drink a lot of fluids to clean out your system, too."

Mom made me swear I'd follow all their instructions as they led me back to our room in the castle. It was only temporary as we'd all be moving into the new house behind the markets soon. It wasn't home, but at least it would get us out of the creepy castle.

When I turned the corner to my room and noticed Dante pacing in the hallway, I ran over to him. "Dante! What are you doing here?"

"Olivia, you're all right," he said, his mouth twitching upward slightly. It looked like he wanted to smile but forced it away. "I'm relieved."

"Yes, what *are* you doing here?" General Ezra asked. "I ordered you to rest. It's only been a few hours."

"I did. A few hours is all I need, General," Dante said. "News spreads fast, especially in the barracks. When I heard Olivia was poisoned, I knew I wouldn't be able to sleep without seeing for myself that she was okay."

"The doctors said I'll be fine," I replied. "Luckily, Anastasia had a vial on her that saved my life."

After I said it out loud, I thought about it. It sounded too convenient that she had the cure. Was it just a coincidence, or had she poisoned the food? Her parents were my chefs, after all, and she could've easily snuck into the kitchen. No one knew more about chemicals than she did.

But why? Was it just to scare me? And if so, why would she save my life afterward?

"You heard her," General Ezra grunted. "Olivia's fine. Now get some more rest, soldier."

"I'd like to return to duty. I think Olivia needs me more than ever," Dante said, then he must've remembered he was refusing an order from the general. His face turned apologetic. "Please, sir."

General Ezra sighed. "Very well. I have other matters to attend to, anyway. I'm sure the king will need my help in finding the culprit. Excuse me."

"So much for Friendship Day," Vanessa muttered as the general disappeared down the hallway.

Dante turned to my mother. "I'll put her in bed, Ambassador. I'm sure you're exhausted."

Mom hesitated, but I nodded at her. "It's okay. I trust Dante."

"And I hope he stays trustworthy," Russell said, glaring at him. "Protect her better than the general, Dante. I mean it."

"With my life," Dante replied, solemnly.

As he helped me into bed, I reached for the teddy bear he'd bought me and cuddled it. "Thanks for the gift, by the way."

He nodded. "I thought you'd like it. It was the least I could do to make this strange place seem more like a home to you. I imagine it hasn't been easy with everything going on."

I chortled. "That's for sure."

He sighed, turning somber. "The real reason I had to find

you was...to tell you how sorry I am that I failed you today, Olivia."

I frowned. "You didn't fail me, Dante."

"But I did," he said, kneeling beside me. "If the general hadn't ordered me away, perhaps I could've stopped someone from poisoning you."

"Hey, you needed your rest. You're not Superman," I said, then realized he probably had no idea who I was talking about. "And besides, the general was there the whole time. He didn't see anyone. What makes you think you would've?"

He paused, shrugging. "I don't know. I'd...just like to think there was more I could've done."

"There wasn't," I said. "Don't beat yourself up over it. As the general would say, that's an order."

He almost smiled. "By the way, I think our training sessions should resume. If something worse happens and I'm not around, you need to be better prepared. I'm also asking the general to station more guards around you. You won't see them, but they'll be there, watching from afar."

"Great," I huffed. "More soldiers."

"I know you don't like being watched," he said, "but it might be the only way to protect you. Perhaps more guards at the embassy could've prevented this."

"So, you *do* think someone's after me?" I asked. "It's taken King Dominic forever to admit it."

"King Dominic doesn't want to admit we have a problem. He's worked hard to get us to the point of communication with outsiders, and he's afraid we'll lose you," Dante said. "To be honest...*I'm* afraid of losing you."

I didn't know what to say. Before I could respond, Dante rose to his feet and walked across the room. He stood near the door, as still as a statue. I watched him in amusement, impressed at how good he was at that.

"What are you doing?" I asked.

"Guarding you," he said. "You should sleep."

"Again? I thought the whole watching me sleep thing was over once we left the clinic."

His eyes twinkled. "You should be used to it by now. But I have a question before you close your eyes."

I looked back at him. "What?"

"What will you name the bear?"

I thought about it for a moment. "Hmm. Maybe...Miss Glitter. She can be Miss Sparkles' sister from overseas."

Dante finally allowed himself a small smile. "It's a good name. Sweet dreams, Olivia."

I felt safe with Dante. He wasn't like the others in the kingdom, not even Christian, who the ghosts had warned me about. After a while, I drifted off to sleep, clutching Miss Glitter to my chest for comfort.

———

The next thing I knew, a hand was shaking me awake. I opened my eyes and realized it was Dante. I sprang up in bed, fearful. "What's going on?"

"Nothing. Everything's fine," he said. "King Dominic's giving an important speech, and I thought you might like to hear it. Your mother will be there."

"Oh, sure," I said, getting out of bed with a yawn. "How long was I asleep?"

"A few hours," he said, glancing at the sky outside. It had grown grey. "It's almost dinner."

I quickly combed my hair before following Dante into the courtyard. King Dominic stood on a small stage, addressing the people of V. They had gathered to hear his speech. General Ezra, Christian, and Queen Vivienne stood off to the side. Christian smiled at me when he saw me in the audience.

"Hey, you just made it, sleepyhead," Vanessa said, as she, Mom, and Russell walked over to us. "The whole kingdom was told the king was giving some big, fancy speech. Everyone had to come."

"Any trouble, Olivia?" Russell asked, his eyes flickering to Dante.

"None," I said. "Whoever poisoned me, they haven't tried anything else."

"And they won't," Dante said, "not on my watch."

Russell looked skeptical, but I wanted to believe him. The crowd's murmuring died down when the king raised a hand. "Thank you for joining me this afternoon. I'm sure you've all heard about the incident at the embassy. Before we eat dinner, I'd like to go over punishment. What I call the reprimands."

Dante shivered at the word. Punishment? What was the king talking about? The crowd looked around at each other, as uncertain as I was.

"School and work hours will be extended. I'm requesting everyone to put in more manual labor," King Dominic said. "Let this be a warning to the poisoner. I will make everyone's lives miserable in the kingdom until I find you. If anyone out there knows something, please come forward. Failure to comply will result in jail time. Thank you."

King Dominic fled the stage with Queen Vivienne and Christian, and General Ezra and his soldiers began dismantling it. As the crowd dispersed, groaning over their new punishments, I shook my head. I appreciated what the king was trying to do, but what if he only made things worse? What if he inspired the poisoner to seek revenge?

I had a feeling they wouldn't stop, no matter how many punishments the king doled out. And now that I knew for sure I was their target, I didn't think I could escape it.

18

NO PLACE LIKE HOME

As we ate supper in the dining hall, I noticed the angry looks from the people of V. The strict reprimands didn't apply to us, and I could tell that only pissed off the kingdom more. I didn't ask to get poisoned, and I didn't ask the king to react so harshly, either, but they didn't seem to care about those little facts.

The whole thing wasn't going to earn me any popularity points at St. Raven's Academy, but at least my meal didn't taste like poison. Dante had watched the chefs prepare it and then he took a bite, gagging at the bitterness of the salad, to assure me it was fine to eat. Dante vowed to taste all my meals first to avoid another incident.

"Is it just me, or is everyone staring at us?" Vanessa whispered, glancing around the dining hall.

"It's not just you," Russell said, glaring at people who were whispering about us at a table across the room. "We need to watch our backs. Don't go anywhere alone, you hear me?"

"Do you think the people here would try something?" Mom whispered. "That they'd retaliate against us for these reprimands?"

Russell scoffed. "If this kingdom has proven anything, Lin, it's that you have to prepare for the worst."

Dante never left my side. While we ate, he stood with his back to the wall, his eyes scanning the crowd. No one dared to say anything to us when he was around. After dinner, when the people went to start their new chores, Dante escorted us back to our room. We found King Dominic, Christian, General Ezra, and Queen Vivienne waiting for us. A group of soldiers stood in the hallway beside them.

"Ah, there you are, Ambassador," King Dominic said, smiling. "Did you all enjoy dinner?"

Mom nodded. "We always do, your Majesty. What brings you to our rooms? Is something wrong?"

"Not at all," King Dominic said. "Since Olivia's feeling better, I wanted to show you to your new home. If it's all right with you, our soldiers will begin packing your things."

Mom grinned. "Go right ahead. I can't wait to see what place you've decided on for us."

"You'll love it," Christian said, reaching for my hand. "It's the perfect home. More private, too."

Although I was happy for a change of pace, I feared it would only bring a new slew of problems. What if someone knew where we lived and targeted us? What if they blew up our house?

"What about Dante?" I asked. "Is he coming with us?"

"Of course. His orders still stand," King Dominic said. "He'll be staying with you in one of the guest rooms. He's already packed his things."

216

"One of?" Vanessa asked, confused. "How many rooms are there?"

"Six," King Dominic said. "I asked for nothing but the best for our guests."

With the soldiers' help and the fact that we hadn't packed much, we loaded our things into our suitcases in no time. I made sure to take Miss Glitter with me since she didn't fit into my suitcase. As I walked out into the hallway, saying goodbye to my empty room, Christian noticed the bear.

"Cute," he said. "Where'd you get that?"

Dante looked away, but Vanessa smirked. I couldn't tell Christian the truth. Something told me it wasn't guard-approved behavior, and I didn't want General Ezra to punish Dante again.

"I bought it in the Markets," I lied. "I forgot my old teddy bear back home, so I had another one made."

"Ah, so you've been to the Markets already," Christian said, sounding sad. "I wanted to be the one to show you around. What did you think of the shops?"

"Oh, um, they're great," I lied, knowing I hadn't explored all of it. "Very cozy."

"Aren't you a little old for one of those?" Christian asked as we began walking down the hallway.

I shrugged. "It helps me sleep. Around here, I definitely need it."

"I'm sorry things have been rough," Christian said, sighing. "This isn't what we had in mind when we invited you here, but I promise, things will get better. Maybe one day, you won't need your bear."

I couldn't tell him that I'd keep it, mostly because it was a gift, but also because it reminded me of Dante. I looked back at him, but he avoided my eyes as he led us along the white brick path. Christian noticed my gaze and looked away, confused. I wondered if he had put it together.

The people tending to their new chores bowed at the king as he passed. I knew they wouldn't try anything with the royal family next to us, but their glares on us said it all. As we walked through the Markets toward the row of houses behind it, I turned to the king.

"Can I ask you a question, your Majesty?"

King Dominic nodded. "Certainly, Olivia. What's on your mind?"

Mom glanced at me out of the corner of her eye. I had no intention of angering the king or accusing him of anything. I just wanted to make sure he knew what he was doing with these reprimands.

"Look, I'm glad you're doing something," I said, "but don't you think the reprimands could make people even angrier?"

King Dominic sighed. "I know my people are bitter about the new chores, but I can't let something like this go unpunished. My kingdom must understand how serious I am about an alliance with your people. And since I don't know who the culprit is, perhaps they'll come forward when they see how much their people are suffering for their misdeeds."

"And if they don't?" I asked. "If they come after me and my family instead?"

King Dominic gestured at Dante. "That's what your bodyguard is for, of course, and the additional soldiers I'm assigning for your protection. With them, I assure you, no harm will come to you and your people."

I didn't believe him.

Some of the children and elderly who hadn't gotten assigned chores watched us as we passed through the village homes. I noticed a large house near the water, with a garden out front, bright windows, and a spacious porch, and my eyes widened.

"Is this our new home?" I asked.

King Dominic nodded, smiling. "It is. My people aren't fans of sunlight, but the builders added in extra windows for you. The place should be move-in ready. Go have a look."

Although I missed home, the place put our old house to shame. Maybe living in a haunted kingdom wouldn't be so bad with a view like that. And since it was overlooking the water, we'd know when the president had arrived.

"Come on," Mom said, tugging on my arm. "If the outside is *this* beautiful, I can't wait to see what the inside looks like."

I laughed. Mom reminded me of an excited little child sometimes. But as we stepped inside, lugging our suitcases with us, the place certainly didn't look 'move-in ready'. The blue paint on the walls looked scratched, tables had gotten overturned, and someone had smashed the bay window overlooking the ocean. The destruction continued up the stairs.

This place looked like a tornado had struck it.

"Uh, I hope the king doesn't expect us to live like this," Vanessa muttered, putting her suitcase down beside mine.

King Dominic entered the house after us, his smile fading into a frown. "What happened here?"

"You mean, it looked better than this?" I asked.

King Dominic nodded. "We were just here yesterday

putting the finishing touches on everything, hauling in new furniture and ensuring the plumbing worked. It didn't look like this!"

"Father's right," Christian said, looking disappointed. "All our hard work...gone."

"Well, who could've done something like this?" Mom asked.

"I don't know," King Dominic replied. "It must've happened after we left yesterday. Perhaps after I gave my speech."

"Who knew about this house?" I asked.

"Only the royal family," King Dominic said. "I kept its location a secret to try to avoid something like this...but it seems it was no use."

Only the royal family? That was suspicious, considering I'd seen Christian around the first boat explosion. Was he involved? Was that why the ghosts were trying to warn me about him?

"Why?" Mom asked. "Why are they doing this?"

"It's obvious to me that your people don't want us here," Russell said. "And here I thought this house would be safer than the castle."

King Dominic ignored him, turning to General Ezra. "I want harsher reprimands in place. It's clear my message isn't getting through to someone, and I intend to make them listen."

General Ezra nodded. "Right away."

"What about our house?" I asked.

The King turned back to me. "Dante and the other soldiers will clean up this mess. I apologize for the inconvenience. Please, excuse me while I discuss the situation with the general."

As General Ezra, King Dominic, and Queen Vivienne left, Dante and the other soldiers got to work with the clean-up efforts. Christian helped carry our suitcases up to the second level, and it looked just as bad as the downstairs area. I stepped over the broken glass on the floor, avoiding the fallen debris.

Christian showed us to our bedrooms, and it looked like mine had gotten hit the hardest. Slashed curtains, a broken bed frame, and a stabbed dresser. It proved one thing. The target was me, and the culprit knew exactly where I'd sleep. It made me a little paranoid.

As Mom, Russell, and Vanessa went to unpack in their rooms, Christian followed me into mine. We grabbed a dustpan and a broom and began sweeping up the debris. I noticed a small section of the room Christian had set up, which gave me plenty of space to do my art. I put my easel and paint down as Christian sighed.

"I tried to make it feel like home," Christian said. "I'm so sorry, Olivia. We should've assigned a guard here just in case."

"It's okay," I said, turning to Christian. "You couldn't have known. And despite what happened, I'm grateful for what you tried to do."

He grinned. "I did it all for you, Olivia. But don't worry. The soldiers will have this place cleaned up in no time. No matter how far I have to go, I'll make this place feel homier one way or another."

"You've already done a lot for us, Christian," I said. "No need to keep—"

He reached for my hand. "You're worth it, Olivia."

I blushed as someone cleared their throat behind us. I spun around and noticed Dante standing in the doorway. Christian looked irritated by the intrusion.

"Sorry to interrupt," Dante began, "but the king says it's late and the Ambassador and her family should get some rest, Prince Christian. The soldiers will resume cleaning up tomorrow."

I nodded. "Tell them we said thanks."

Christian turned to me, sighing. "We'll speak again tomorrow, Olivia. And don't worry, I haven't forgotten about our date. Perhaps I can take you to the docks and we can watch the water together."

I smiled. "That sounds great—"

"About that," Dante began. "The king's requesting the Ambassador, and her family stay inside when possible, only leaving for school and the embassy. I'm afraid you won't be able to watch the water anytime soon. Official orders. Too bad."

If I didn't know better, I'd say Dante looked a little happy at that. Christian, on the other hand, looked miserable at our growing lack of alone time. I wasn't thrilled to have new restrictions, either.

Christian sighed. "We'll still make something work, Olivia. I have a few ideas in mind. See you then."

As he left, the room became quiet, and I could hear voices outside. I turned to my window, realizing it was King Dominic, Queen Vivienne, and General Ezra speaking outside on the porch as the sun set. It looked like they were waiting for Christian.

"...clearly doing this to taunt me," the king was saying.

"Whoever's behind this doesn't care about my orders, and they're escalating."

"Perhaps they aren't dangerous," Queen Vivienne replied. "Perhaps this is all a misunderstanding."

The king turned to her, shaking his head. "They had a chance to stop. I understand it all perfectly, Vivienne, this culprit is trying to harm our guests in protest. They're trying to force my hand, and I will *not* allow it."

"My soldiers will continue their investigation," General Ezra said. "If we find the person responsible, what are your orders?"

"Kill them," King Dominic said, "before they kill someone. If they're this dangerous before their transition, what would they be like if the monster resurfaced?"

He was going to murder them? King Dominic had said before his people didn't believe in that kind of punishment. And what was this about a monster and a transition? I didn't have the chance to hear anything else as Christian walked outside, and they hushed before heading back to the castle.

"Eavesdropping again?" Dante asked, and I'd completely forgotten he was still there.

"Can't help it," I said. "I want to know what's going on."

"That seems fair," he replied. "Look, General Ezra told me not to tell you or the Ambassador, but we found something while cleaning the house. I figured you'd want to know."

"What was it?" I asked.

"Another letter, begging the king to ask your people to leave," Dante said. "King Dominic doesn't want to scare you, but I thought you should know. We can't let these intimidators win. Forcing you to leave the island would only give them what they want."

"You're right," I said, sighing. "But I'm scared of what'll happen if we don't give in. Do you think they'll kill us?"

"You have my word that won't happen," Dante said, softly. "My life for yours, remember?"

I nodded, though I didn't feel much better. After we said goodnight, we headed to bed as Dante patrolled the hallway. He agreed to work in shifts with one of the soldiers that he trusted, and I was grateful he wasn't going to sacrifice his sleep for me.

When morning came, I woke up with a smile. Despite everything, the view of the ocean made up for it. As I nodded at Dante in the hallway and went downstairs into the kitchen, grabbing a bottle of water in the orange glow, I spotted Vanessa sitting in the window.

"Hey," I said. "What are you doing?"

"Just watching the ocean," she said. "Liv...I'm worried about my mom. When I talked to your mom, she said she should've arrived already."

"Look, I'm sure she's fine," I said. "You'll drive yourself crazy with worry if you keep looking for her. As Mom says, a watched pot never boils."

Vanessa sighed. "Yeah, I guess you're right. At least I have two things to distract me in the meantime."

"Like what?"

"School today," she said, looking back at me with a grin, "and the fact that it was Dante who bought you that teddy bear, not Christian. He's never bought me anything, you know."

I rolled my eyes, glancing at the stairs. "Dante's right up there, so keep your voice down. It wasn't romantic or anything. He was just replacing the one I'd lost. And thanks for making it awkward with Christian at the embassy, by the way."

"Sorry. I really thought it was him," she said. "I guess this kingdom's full of surprises, huh?"

"You've got that right. Anyway, what about you?" I asked. "I saw you flirting with some guys at the embassy. Find anyone special yet?"

"No." She shook her head. "Most people don't trust us. It's like...they're afraid to be around us for too long. No offense, but I'm glad I'm not staying here long-term. I miss the boys back home. Never had to work to get them to like me. A smile was all it took."

After we ate breakfast after finding the fridge stocked with raw meat and salad for me. Mom came down the stairs and yawned. "Morning, girls. Did everyone have a good sleep in our new home?"

I shrugged. "I guess. What are you up to today?"

"I'm heading back to work at the embassy. Don't worry, Russell will be there the whole time," Mom said. "Have fun at school, girls. Try to stay out of trouble, all right?"

"Only if trouble promises to stay away from me," I muttered, pulling on my backpack.

As usual, Dante followed us to the academy. All gazes were on us as we entered class, with some of the students shunning us for the number of chores they had now. Dante returned to his spot at the back of the class as me and Vanessa took our seats, and I noticed the Sanguine twins had returned.

"We heard you were poisoned at the embassy, outsider," Petra said. "That had to hurt."

"It did," I said. "But I survived. Disappointed?"

Nicolai scoffed. "We've never wanted you dead, outsider. We're bad, not evil. There's a difference."

"So, it wasn't you who poisoned me?" I asked. "Seems like it'd cause a lot of chaos. That's something your parents love if I remember right."

"You know nothing of our parents," Petra snarled. "That poison could've killed you. Even if our parents had done something from prison, it wouldn't have been deadly. They don't kill people, remember? There's no fun in that."

"How come you weren't at the embassy, anyway?" Vanessa asked. "I don't remember seeing you there."

"We had better things to do with our time," Nicolai said. "But we're touched you noticed."

"Not," Petra added, sarcastically.

Professor Draven entered the room, walking over to the board. "Well, class, good to see you all after the festival. It was...interesting, to say the least. I hope everyone had a good weekend. To ease tensions from all those new chores, I planned a surprise for the class today."

Soldiers began carrying things into the room. My mouth dropped when I realized what it was—my art supplies, like easels and paint. Christian walked into the room next, smiling at me. I didn't know why he was there. He didn't go to the academy anymore.

"The prince has arranged for an art class, led by our newest professor, Olivia Hawthorne," Professor Draven said. "Whenever you're ready, Olivia, the class is all yours."

"Knock 'em dead," Vanessa whispered, nudging me to stand up.

With ghosts around every corner and someone trying to kill me, it surprised me that public speaking gave me the worst anxiety. As I walked up to the board, reaching for my paint-brush and easel, I prayed nothing would go wrong with the one thing I loved the most in my life. My art.

I sighed, turning to the class to begin my lesson, and fainted.

19
DATE WITH A PRINCE

When I came to, I found myself lying on the floor with the entire class looking down at me. The Sanguine twins kept their distance in the back of the classroom. Dante, Vanessa, and Professor Draven stood to my left. On my right, Anastasia hovered above me, waving a foul-smelling vial under my nose. She smiled when she saw my eyes flutter open.

"Smell is the strongest sense. If you ever want to wake someone up, put something with a strong scent under their nose. Works like a charm," she said, putting the vial away. "How are you feeling?"

I sat up, blinking. "I feel fine. What happened?"

"That's what we want to know," Vanessa said. "You were fine one moment, then you just...fainted. It was pretty scary watching you drop. We sent some of the students to get Anastasia, and she said she had something that could help."

"How long was I out for?"

"Only a few minutes," Vanessa said, "but believe me, it felt like a lifetime."

"You didn't hit your head when you fell, did you?" Christian asked, searching for any bumps or bruises on me.

I shook my head. "No, I don't think so…"

"What about the poison from the embassy?" Dante asked Anastasia. "Could she still have some of it in her blood that caused the fainting spell?"

"No, the poison's gone. The blood test was clear about that," Anastasia said. "I think the cause of the fainting is simple, actually. Olivia, have you experienced a pounding heart, headaches, and nausea within the last few days?"

I shrugged. "Well…yeah. I just thought that was normal, you know, being in a new place, with everything going on…"

"It's called anxiety," Anastasia said. "I'm sure you've heard of it before. It can make you feel light-headed and faint."

"But I wasn't having anxiety before I fainted."

Anastasia shrugged. "You don't have to be. Anxiety can build up over time and then implode."

I rose to my feet, relieved. Anxiety was so simple, so common. At least it wasn't anything serious like poison. Now that I knew I'd live, I felt embarrassed for fainting in front of the entire room, especially Christian.

"Should we get Dr. Draven to examine her?" Dante asked.

Anastasia shook her head. "No, we shouldn't bother her for this. Just rest and take it easy, Olivia. Practice deep breathing. And if that doesn't work and you faint again, come to the clinic and we'll find something that can help."

"Perhaps we should skip the art lesson for today," Dante said. "Olivia should avoid anything stressful."

Then I'd have to avoid everyone and everything in the kingdom.

To my surprise, the classroom looked disappointed. Professor Draven and Christian did, too. I didn't want to let them down.

"No," I said. "Art helps me relax. And you've brought all my supplies here, so I'd hate for you to go to all that trouble for nothing."

"But Olivia—" Dante began.

"She said she's fine," Christian said, glaring at Dante. "Start whenever you're ready, Professor Hawthorne."

Professor. I wasn't used to someone calling me that. Dante looked hesitant but backed off, glaring at the prince.

"Come get me if you need anything," Anastasia said.

After she left, the class sat down in their seats. Dante, Christian, and Professor Draven returned to the back of the classroom to give me space to work. My anxiety began to ease when I approached my easel, but I took deep breaths anyway.

"All right, class," I began, picking up my paintbrush. "Let's start with the basics."

I started simple, teaching them about primary and secondary colors, how to hold a paintbrush, and how to wash and stipple their paintbrushes. They were fast learners. All except Vanessa. Next, I taught them different styles, from abstract to texture to watercolor, and demonstrated each of them on my easel.

People from the kingdom crowded in the corridor and the doorway to watch us. I smiled and waved, hoping they'd stop hating me for the reprimands and respect my painting skills instead. I'd forgotten how obsolete art was in the kingdom, and I couldn't imagine living without it. Christian watched me with a smile, looking impressed, and I blushed and tried to focus.

I asked the class to get started, giving them the freedom to paint whatever they wanted. Back home, our art classes were so regimented and strict. My art teacher always dictated what we had to paint, but I wanted to give my students the liberty of deciding for themselves.

As I walked around the classroom, I observed people's art over their shoulders. Most of them were so good at it that it was hard for me to believe they'd never done it before. Just like in gym class, all the people of V seemed naturally gifted in whatever they set their minds to. When I walked over to Vanessa, she sighed in frustration.

"I am *so* bad at this," she said, drawing colorful circles. "Maybe I'm just not cut out to do art. Not like you, anyway."

"Don't say that. I wasn't good at painting when I first started. Practice makes perfect," I said. "Right now, don't focus on being perfect, just focus on having fun."

Vanessa smiled. "You know, that's good advice. And making all these colors *is* pretty entertaining..."

As I walked over to the Sanguine twins, I noticed they hadn't painted anything. They were chatting and ignoring the lesson altogether. I frowned. "Where's your art?"

Petra sneered. "Who needs art? There's no point to it. It's not like fighting, or hunting, or even history. It's just stupid. Maybe you do it back home, but in the kingdom of V, we have other priorities."

"How can you know it's stupid?" I asked. "You haven't even tried it."

"We'll pass," Nicolai said, turning back to his sister.

I sighed. "Fine, if that's how you want to act—"

"I suggest listening to your new teacher," Professor Draven said, walking over. "You'll be graded on whether you can follow instructions or not, and I'm giving Olivia the authority to fail you."

"But this isn't even a class," Petra said. "Olivia's not a teacher, and art has no place in the kingdom of V! King Dominic banned it because—"

"And now he's unbanned it," Professor Draven interrupted. "Follow along with the lesson or fail the class. It's your choice."

Petra and Nicolai scowled but picked up their paintbrushes and started to paint. I watched them for a few seconds. "You know, art is a good way to get out your emotions. I paint when I'm sad and angry, and I always feel better. Just a suggestion."

The Sanguine twins said nothing, but it looked like they were thinking it over. Maybe if they took out their frustration in their art, they'd leave me and Vanessa alone.

"We can really paint whatever we want?" Petra asked.

I nodded. "Yeah, that's what art is all about. Let your imagination run free."

The Sanguine twins snickered before turning back to their easels. I didn't know what they were doing, but I figured it was best I leave them alone. As I walked around the rest of the classroom, giving advice and praising the students, the Sanguine twins whistled at me.

"Oh, Professor," Petra sang, and I knew she was up to no good. "Won't you come look at what we painted?"

I walked back over to them and looked down at their easels. They had both drawn the Dark Half, that strange statue I'd seen at the festival. In Petra's painting, the bat-like creature looked like it was transforming. In Nicolai's, the creature was killing people, spraying their blood everywhere.

My eyes widened. I started to feel sick, fearing I'd pass out again. Vanessa and the rest of the class noticed, murmuring and gasping.

"Well, what do you think?" Nicolai asked, grinning.

I couldn't speak, so Professor Draven rushed over, yanking the easels away from the Sanguine twins. "I think that's enough art for you two."

"But why, Professor Draven?" Petra asked, glancing back at me. "Olivia, excuse me, *Professor Hawthorne* said we could paint whatever we wanted. Didn't you?"

"I did," I stammered. "But I...didn't mean that."

"The instructions were unclear," Petra said, shrugging. "It's not our fault you didn't tell us what we couldn't paint."

"Detention. Now," Professor Draven said. "What you painted was highly inappropriate, and you both know it."

The Sanguine twins grinned before leaving the classroom. That was their plan all along, to get kicked out of art class. I hadn't gotten through to them as I hoped. But why would they paint the Dark Half?

"I'm sorry you had to see that, Olivia. Leave it to the Sanguine twins to ruin a perfectly good lesson," Professor Draven muttered, gesturing at the paintings. "Allow me to dispose of these for you. This kind of violence doesn't belong in a classroom."

After he threw the paintings in the trashcan, we returned to our lesson. A girl raised her hand, and I rushed over to her. "Yes? Is something wrong?"

"I have a suggestion," she said. "I love painting, but...I think we should tweak it to be more compatible with our kingdom. Why don't we try a blood painting?"

"A blood painting?" I asked, confused.

The girl nodded. "Like we do when we're practicing Bloodspeak. We can use our blood to make art."

"Well, as long as it's okay with Professor Draven," I said. "I don't have a problem with it."

Professor Draven shrugged. "I don't see the harm. And this way, I suppose we can practice our Bloodspeak, too."

"No offense, but I think I'll stick to regular paint," Vanessa said, looking nauseous.

I nodded. "That's fine. Remember, there's no pressure with art. Whatever feels right, do it."

All the classmates except for Vanessa retrieved their knives, cutting their arms a little to bleed onto the canvas. Then they cleaned their paintbrushes and swirled their blood around. Vanessa wrinkled her nose in disgust, but I found it creative the more I stared at it...

And familiar. As they drew their symbols onto the canvases, I pulled out my dagger and almost gasped. Those strange symbols I'd seen, on both my dagger and the wall in the crypts, were Bloodspeak. I hadn't realized it until now.

I turned to Professor Draven, showing him my dagger. "Professor, can you read these symbols?"

He looked at the dagger, frowning. "I'm afraid not. Those symbols look like ancient Bloodspeak, not the common kind we teach today. Symbols like these were used by our leaders back in the day to pass secret messages along."

I sighed. So much for translating the wall and my dagger. Now I'd never know what they meant, or if someone left them there on purpose.

"The library might have information on ancient Blood-speak," Professor Draven said, "but I believe that section is closed-off due to repairs. Sorry."

There was something strange about that restricted section, something secretive. Christian had freaked out when he saw me over there. How long did it take to make repairs to a small area of the library? The people had built a whole embassy in less time.

When class had almost finished, Professor Draven returned to his desk. "Well, I hope everyone had fun today. I hope to include an art lesson at least once a week, as long as that's all right with you, Olivia."

I nodded. "I'd like that. It's fun teaching when the kids are fast learners."

"Good. Now, don't forget," he said, turning to the room. "Tomorrow is the Great Hunt. King Dominic will go over the rules for the outsiders before the competition begins. Because of that, there won't be any school tomorrow."

Vanessa raised her hand. "With everything going on in the kingdom...aren't you worried something bad will happen at the hunt?"

"The king has taken precautions to ensure nothing will go wrong," Professor Draven said. "And more soldiers will be on duty. It's a tradition in our kingdom, and it wouldn't feel right to cancel it."

When the bell rang, the students took their paintbrushes and easels and left. Christian walked over to me, smiling. "Olivia, that was great. And did you see the crowd? The students weren't the only ones interested. I'm glad I came."

I blushed. "Thanks. Maybe making me a professor wasn't as bad as I thought it would be."

"I told you. Sorry about the Sanguine twins, though. They just can't be civil," Christian said, shaking his head. "Anyway, I ran into your mother at the embassy. She's working late tonight, so I figured we could have dinner together at your new house. My father is still adamant that you're not allowed to go anywhere."

I saw Dante's look of uncertainty before I glanced back at Christian. "I'd love that. See you then."

As Christian nodded and left, Vanessa smirked. "Don't worry. I'll stay in my room while you two eat. I think I'd like to work on my art. You're rubbing off on me, Olivia."

Dante cleared his throat. "Vanessa, let's get you back home. A soldier will be stationed outside the house while I train Olivia."

"Training? Are you sure that's a good idea right now?" I asked, following Dante and Vanessa out of the academy. "What if I faint again?"

"I'll be there to make sure you won't," Dante replied. "It's a risk, but one we'll have to take to ensure you're prepared."

"Back to training, huh? Expecting trouble?" Vanessa asked.

"Anything is possible," Dante replied, cryptically.

———

After we dropped Vanessa off, Dante took me to the militia building. But as we entered the sparring room, I noticed General Ezra leaving with several children. One of them was the boy who had stabbed me on my first day. Both the boy and the general said nothing as they left.

Was the general training those children? And why?

"Does the general usually let kids in here?" I asked Dante. "I've never seen them before."

Dante shook his head. "No, and they aren't allowed to be

trained until they turn eighteen. I don't know why the general had them here. I wouldn't worry about it, though, perhaps the king is worried they'll be targeted, too, and wants them to learn some techniques."

As I changed into my sparring outfit, Dante got to work setting up an obstacle course. I had to dodge and use my dagger to take down the targets, and Dante kept ramping up the difficulty level. He didn't mention what happened the last time we sparred, so I didn't, either.

Half an hour later, when I was doubled over and panting, Dante nodded. "Nice work. I think you're almost ready."

"For what?" I asked, chugging my water.

Dante hesitated. "For anything."

I put my water down, shaking my head. "I can't fight poison with a dagger."

"No, but that's why you have me," Dante said. "You did well handling the Sanguine twins today, too. You exhibited self-control like a soldier."

I shrugged. "I feel bad for them, really. It can't be easy having two parents in jail."

"Don't feel bad for anyone here," Dante said. "We're not worth it."

I didn't know how to respond, so I changed the subject. "Dante, about tomorrow. What if I get hurt during the Great Hunt?"

"You won't," he answered, quickly, "because I won't leave your side. If the tournament wasn't so important to our people, I'd petition the king to skip it, but he insists you need to learn about our culture. He's almost as stubborn as you."

When I laughed, Dante cracked a small smile. After I took a shower and changed, proud I hadn't fainted again, he walked me back to my new house. Christian was waiting on the porch with a large picnic basket, and he grinned when he saw us. I felt relieved I took a shower before coming home.

"Hey," he said, holding up the picnic basket. "Up for an early dinner?"

"With you? Of course," I said, unlocking the front door. "Come inside. Make yourself at home."

As we entered, Vanessa took one look at us and grinned. "Hello, Prince Christian. I was just heading upstairs. Enjoy your meal."

Christian nodded politely at her before setting the picnic basket down on our dining table. As he removed the food, salad for me, raw meat for him, he turned and noticed Dante standing there.

"Can you give us a little privacy?" Christian asked.

Dante shook his head. "I'm not allowed. General Ezra was clear that I was to watch over Olivia at all times."

"But you're supposed to be Vanessa's bodyguard, too," Christian pointed out. "And she's upstairs. Why don't you keep watch over her?"

Dante growled. "You know why—"

"It's okay," I said, not wanting a fight to break out. "Dante's quiet. Trust me, you won't even notice him."

He glared at Dante before sitting down. "So, I'm sure you heard about the Great Hunt tomorrow. If it makes you feel any better, I'll be there, too, and I won't be leaving your side."

"Thanks," I said, reaching for my salad. "You can never be too careful—"

Dante stepped forward, grabbing my fork. "Wait a second. I have to taste your food."

"Is that really necessary?" Christian huffed. "I saw them prepare it myself. It's not poisoned!"

Dante didn't listen and took a bite of the salad instead. He winced at the taste but nodded. "It's safe. Go ahead."

As Dante returned to his post, I dug into my salad. Christian leaned forward and cleared his throat. I knew Dante's presence made him nervous. I didn't exactly want his presence on a date, either, but I had no choice.

"I hope this doesn't sound too forward," Christian began, "but I enjoy spending time with you, Olivia. I haven't gone on many dates. I never found the right person, but when I saw you...I thought my luck might be changing."

I smiled. "Me, too. I...haven't dated anyone in a long time."

"Oh? Why not?" Christian asked, cutting his raw meat. "Sorry, that's too personal. You don't have to answer if—"

"No, it's okay," I said. "My ex-boyfriend, Dylan, cheated on me. He kept pressuring me into having sex, but...I wasn't ready yet. When I wouldn't give him what he wanted, he slept with the popular girl at my school to hurt me."

I looked down, embarrassed, but Christian reached for my hand. "Dylan was an idiot to cheat on you, Olivia. If you were mine, I'd never let you go."

Now I was blushing even harder, but it wasn't out of embarrassment.

"And I won't pressure you into anything, either," Christian continued. "If I make you uncomfortable at any time, please, let me know—"

He paused when Dante started making loud noises in the kitchen. I craned my head and noticed he was working on one of the broken cupboards that the culprit had smashed.

"What are you doing?" Christian asked, exasperated.

"Just some house repairs," Dante said, not looking at us. "Don't mind me."

"Do you have to be so loud?" Christian asked, annoyed.

Dante didn't reply to that, he just continued working. As irritating as it was, I found myself laughing. It almost felt like Dante was trying to ruin our date on purpose.

Christian laughed too, shaking his head. "I apologize, Olivia. Where was I? Oh, right, I was saying that I understand what it's like to be pressured. While it's different from your situation, my father's placed a lot of demands on me. I want you to feel respected and safe—"

The front door opened, and Mom and Russell walked in. They both had worried expressions on their faces, and I rose to my feet to find out what was wrong. Dante stopped his loud repairs and returned to his post. Mom and Russell paused when they noticed us eating at the table.

"Are we interrupting something?" Mom asked.

"No, it's fine," I said. "Are you two okay?"

Mom shook her head. "We need to talk, Olivia. It's about the president, and it's important."

20
LAST CHANCE

Christian rose to his feet. "Is there anything I can do to help?"

"Yeah, leave," Russell said, a little too harshly.

"If that's all right with you," Mom added, glaring at Russell for his rudeness. "It's a private matter, Prince Christian. No offense meant."

"Then no offense taken," he said, looking back at me with a smile. "Well, despite all the interruptions, I had a nice evening with you, Olivia."

"Me, too," I said. "Maybe next time we can do it without an audience."

Christian laughed. "It's a date. I already have something in mind. Good evening, everyone."

It looked like he wanted to kiss me, but decided against it with Mom, Russell, and Dante watching us. He grabbed the picnic basket and left, gently closing the front door behind him. I put the plates in the sink and waited for Mom to start speaking. She didn't.

When I turned around again, Russell was glaring at

Dante who hadn't moved. "In case you didn't hear us before, we wanted to talk in private. That means no one from the kingdom of V is allowed."

"Russell, please. No need to be rude," Mom chastised, turning to Dante. "What Russell means to say is that I need to speak with my daughter alone, please."

Dante's eyes flickered to me. "I really should stay with Olivia, Ambassador. It's for her own safety."

"I'll be fine, promise," I said, turning to Dante.

He sighed, nodding. "Fine, but I'll be waiting on the porch. Be quick."

After he left, I realized how little effort that took. There was no way I could've said anything that would've made him leave during my date with Christian.

"Okay, start talking," I said to Mom. "What's going on?"

Mom sighed, sitting down on the couch. "I'm worried about Janet."

"Why?" I asked. "Did something happen to the president?"

"It's more like nothing has happened," Russell said. "She isn't here, even though she was due two days ago. Your mother sent out a letter and hasn't heard back. Don't even get me started on communicating by crow…"

"Vanessa was worried about that, too," I said. "How do you know she's not just running late? Maybe something came up at the White House."

Mom sighed, glancing out the window at the ocean. "That's what I keep telling myself, but…a part of me knows something is wrong. Janet was excited to meet everyone from the kingdom of V. Brokering peace with an isolated nation would be a big accomplishment in her presidency, and I don't think she'd want to delay this. Besides, she's not the kind of woman who's late."

"I see," I muttered. "Why'd you need to talk in private?"

Mom turned to me, her face twisted with worry. "King Dominic keeps insisting the president is fine, and I don't want them to know we suspect them."

"So, you think the king's lying?"

"We don't know for sure," Russell mumbled, "but I damn well know I don't trust any of them here. There's been one problem after another..."

"What do you think happened to President Bennett then?" I asked. "Is she injured? Dead? Lost at sea?"

"That's the worst part," Mom said. "We know nothing. This kingdom is so isolated. So cut-off. I even sent a few letters to other world leaders and haven't heard anything back."

"Maybe your letters didn't make it," I said. "Crows aren't reliable."

"Or maybe our letters aren't leaving here at all," Russell said. "Maybe they're being intercepted."

I shrugged. "But why? If the president doesn't show up, we're stranded here. And from what I've seen, someone's pretty persistent to get us off this island. Seems like they'd want those letters to reach our people."

"Who knows how these people work?" Russell asked. "This could all be one big game they're playing with us, testing our resolve. I wouldn't put it past them..."

I snuck a peek at the staircase. "We can't tell Vanessa. She's worried enough."

"Yes, I agree, for now," Mom said. "But as the days pass, Vanessa will know something's wrong. I certainly did."

"Then let's hope things get better," I mumbled. "But let's play a worst-case scenario for a second. If the president doesn't arrive, ever. What happens?"

"Unless the United States sends someone for us," Mom said, "we'll be trapped here."

"Maybe that's why they gave us a house," Russell said. "Maybe they planned to keep us here forever. I say we confront them and get this over with."

"Let's not go pointing the finger," Mom said, reaching for Russell to stop him. "If they *are* responsible for delaying the president *and* causing all the strange incidents around here, do you really want to make them angry?"

"No," Russell said, huffing, "but I want to know what they want from us if they're keeping us here. Will they kill us? Torture us for information on the United States?"

"Let's hope not. Maybe the president will arrive soon and we're just being paranoid," Mom said, turning to me. "Anyway, I heard about the Great Hunt tomorrow. I have to say, I'm a little worried. The embassy's opening was a disaster. What if something else happens? Something deadlier?"

"I thought the same thing, but Dante will be there," I said. "Christian, too. They both said they'd stay with me. If someone's trying to hurt us, I don't think they'd risk killing the prince."

"Unless the prince is in on it," Russell muttered.

Mom nodded. "Speaking of which...did I see you two on a date when we walked in?"

I blushed. "Well...sort of. It's hardly a date when there's a crowd."

"I want you to stay away from that prince," Mom said,

"just in case he *is* responsible. Don't tell him that outright, but keep your distance, Olivia. It's for your own good."

That wouldn't be the first time someone had warned me about Christian. I liked him, but I wasn't sure what was going on. I didn't want to fall for him and end up broken-hearted again like I had with Dylan.

"And another thing," Mom continued. "I don't think you should attend their academy anymore. Seems too dangerous considering everything that's happened."

Mom had a right to be concerned, but I wanted to stay in school. If only so I could keep an eye on everything. I couldn't afford to miss anything.

"I know you're worried about me and Ness," I began, "but I'd really like to keep going to school here. I'm sure Ness will agree. Besides, there isn't much else to do on this island."

Mom frowned. "But—"

"Please, Mom," I begged, using my best puppy dog eyes. "We'll be extra careful. And Dante's got our backs."

"He'd better. Her mom studied her. "All right, you can keep attending the academy. But come get me immediately if anything's wrong." Mom yawned. "I'm tired after a long day at the embassy and I'm sure Dante would like to come inside now. Remember what we talked about, Olivia. Please be careful."

As Mom went upstairs to bed, Russell waited until she was gone before he turned to me. "I don't like Christian any more than your mother does, but...I think you should keep seeing him."

I frowned. "You do?"

"Now, don't get me wrong, I still want you to watch your back. I don't trust that prince. He's too charming. But this is a good chance to get close to him and find out if he's planning something with his father. If he is, let me know immediately."

"Won't Mom be upset?"

Russell shrugged. "Probably. I don't like keeping things from your mother...but this'll have to stay between us. And remember, if you need me, just call my name and I'll come running."

I smiled. "Thanks, Russ. I'm glad I'm not here alone."

"Me, either," he said. "I'd probably go nuts if I were alone on this island with these people."

"At least we have each other. If the president never shows up and we're trapped here, Vanessa will never see her family again," I said, sadly. "She wouldn't even know what happened to her mother. I don't know how I'd get through that."

"Vanessa's a strong girl. She'll make it," Russell said. "But God help me if they *are* involved somehow. Don't know what I'd do, but I couldn't let it go. If any violence starts, keep out of the way, Olivia."

Although I knew Russell was strong, I doubted he could win against General Ezra's army. I hoped it wouldn't come to anything that grim.

As Russell turned toward the staircase, I looked at him. "You care about my mother a lot, don't you?"

"Of course," Russell said. "She's a good friend, and you do grow close to the person you're guarding with your life."

"You know what I mean."

Russell paused. "I'm...not sure I do, Olivia."

I crossed my arms. "Don't think I haven't noticed the way you look at her. And I'd hate to sound like Vanessa; she's always playing matchmaker but you two would be good together."

Russell's eyebrows raised. "You think so?"

I nodded. "Mom hasn't said it out loud, but she's been lonely since Dad died. And since our days could be numbered here...I think you should tell her how you feel. I'm giving you my blessing here."

Russell sighed. "That's kind of you, but she's under enough stress as it is. She doesn't need me complicating things."

"Just think about it," I said. "If being on this island has taught me anything, it's that life is too short. We need to act while we still can."

"You're right about that," Russell muttered. "I'll... consider your advice. Goodnight, Olivia, and thanks for your support."

When he was gone, the entire house turned silent. I walked to the door to tell Dante he could come back in when I heard arguing. I looked out the window, noticing Christian and Dante in each other's faces. They argued almost as much as General Ezra and King Dominic. I thought Christian went home. Which meant he must've hung around, waiting to get Dante alone.

I pressed my ear against the window, trying to hear what they were saying, and caught the end of their argument.

"...ruined it on purpose. You've been trying to sabotage my relationship with her this whole time," Christian said. "If I didn't know better, I'd say you were jealous."

"That's ridiculous," Dante sneered, and it hurt how easily he rejected the idea of liking me. "I'm only trying to look out for her. You keep trying to put her in danger."

"I came back because I thought we could have a civil conversation about this. I suppose not," Christian mumbled. "I know how you feel about the Dark Half, but Olivia has nothing to fear from me. Nothing at all."

The Dark Half? What did that have to do with me and Christian?

"We'll see about that," Dante muttered. "For Olivia's sake, I hope you're right."

When Christian walked away in a huff, I moved from the window. Dante twisted the doorknob, walking into the house and locking it behind him. He seemed surprised when he noticed me.

"Everything okay?" he asked.

I nodded. "We're done talking. Mom and Russell went to bed. I was about to come get you."

"I apologize for taking so long outside. I...had something to take care of."

He didn't elaborate, so I dropped the subject and hoped nothing was wrong. I didn't want to cause a wedge between anyone.

"Prince Christian came back. It was late, so I sent him away," Dante muttered. "But he wanted to tell us that King Dominic's imposed new reprimands after your house's destruction. He's taking a harsher stance, earlier curfew, more chores, less time for leisure activities. I hear he's even taking away gym class at the academy."

Although I felt relieved, I'd never have to play their weird version of dodgeball again, I knew the kids would be angry at school. The last thing we needed was another reason for them to hate us, mostly me.

"Wow," I said. "He means business. I just hope it stops whoever's behind this." Unless they're ghosts. More chores would mean nothing to them. Could you even threaten spirits?

"Me as well," Dante replied. "You should get to bed, Olivia. The hunt will be long tomorrow. I'll keep watch in the hallway."

"I'll just say goodnight to Vanessa first," I said. "Won't take long."

As I walked up the stairs and knocked on Vanessa's door, it surprised me when she answered it, covered in paint. "Oh, Olivia, hey. I thought you were on a date?"

"I was," I said. "Now it's bedtime."

Her face dropped. "It's been that long? I must've gotten carried away. Well, don't just stand there, come in."

As I entered and closed the door behind me, I noticed all the paintings Vanessa had made. They weren't art gallery-worthy or anything, but they were a big improvement from what she was making in class. They ranged from abstract paintings to still life of fruit and sunsets.

"What *is* all of this?" I asked, looking around.

"Oh, just products of my boredom," she said. "I can't believe I never tried painting before. I saw you doing it all these years and thought it was too complicated, but I'm really getting the hang of it! You were right. It *does* take your mind off everything."

"I tried to tell you," I said, laughing. "I should give you extra credit for this. I doubt the Sanguine twins are doing any homework for art class."

"Don't listen to them. They're just trying to get a rise out of you," Vanessa said, rinsing the paint off her hands in the private bathroom that connected to her room. "How'd the date go?"

"Terrible," I said, flopping down on Vanessa's bed. "Dante kept ruining it. First, he insisted on eating my food, then he made as much noise as possible when me and Christian tried to talk. Fixing the house, my ass..."

Vanessa laughed, walking back into her bedroom. "Really?"

I nodded. "Then Mom and Russell came home, and it was pretty much over."

"That's rough," Vanessa said, sitting beside me. "Did you have one good conversation, at least?"

"Well...I told him about Dylan. It felt good to tell someone about it, other than you. He said he'd never pressure me, and that Dylan was an idiot."

"He's right, you know. Maybe he can help you get over what Douchelord Dylan did," Vanessa said. "So...do you like Christian?"

"I do," I said, "but..."

How could I tell Vanessa I suspected him of causing the sabotage? Of maybe even being the reason why the president was late? And how could I put into words that the ghosts had warned me about Christian?

"But what?" Vanessa asked.

"But we're so different," I said, which wasn't a lie. "He comes from another culture."

"So? People have made it work before. Love never fails. That's what my mom always says. She's been married to my dad for twenty years, so I'd say they're doing something right," Vanessa said. "Speaking of my mom, have you heard anything about her?"

It hurt keeping our feelings from Vanessa, but we all agreed we didn't want to stress her out. "Not yet."

Vanessa sighed, glancing out the window at the dark sky. "I hope she gets here soon. My mom can be pretty demanding sometimes, always barking orders, but now that I've been away from her for so long, I miss her yelling at me. Is that crazy?"

I shook my head. "Not crazy. But hey, if you need my mom to yell at you in the meantime, just let her know. It'd take the heat off me, that's for sure."

Vanessa laughed. "I'll keep that in mind. Goodnight, Olivia. I guess I'll see you tomorrow for the hunt."

I nodded, passing Dante in the hallway. After I bid him goodnight, I went into my room and closed the door. I changed into my pajamas and then got into bed under the covers. It was nothing like my room back home, but at least I had Miss Glitter for comfort.

Just as I began to fall asleep, I heard a bump come from my closet. I thought I was hearing things until it happened again. I got out of bed slowly, holding Miss Glitter close to me as I walked to the closet and peered in...and saw nothing.

When I turned around, Charles Browning appeared. I jumped back as he spoke. "You think you're safe, do you? In your new house?"

"Why do you keep haunting me?" I asked. "What do you want?"

"You're not safe," Charles said, avoiding my questions. "None of your people are. It's already too late for your president."

My heart pounded. "Why do you say that? What do you know about her?"

Charles Browning said nothing. Instead, a group of ghosts appeared behind him, the same ones as before with the bloody necks. But this time, there were more of them, newer victims. I recognized one of them well.

It was Derek Bennett, Vanessa's father, President Bennett's husband, the First Gentleman of the United States, and the famous surgeon. His neck looked bloody like the others, his skin bruised and beaten, and his eyes black and sunken in.

I couldn't believe it was him. When I knew him, he was always so happy, so full of life. That had gotten replaced by this long, empty stare.

"Mr. Bennett, is that you?" I asked. "What's going on?"

Derek said nothing. He only continued to stare at me, unblinking. What would Vanessa say if she could see this? A part of me was glad she couldn't. A part of me was also glad it wasn't *my* father who was haunting me.

"He can't talk to you," Charles said. "It takes a while for a ghost to learn communication. None of them have been dead as long as I have. I was the first victim."

"A ghost?" I asked, looking at Derek with tears in my eyes. "Then that means..."

"He is dead," Charles answered. "And soon, you will be, too."

"You're wrong. It can't be Vanessa's father," I said. "He wasn't even supposed to come on this trip. He should be back in D.C., working at the hospital. None of this makes sense!"

"You're the one who has it wrong," Charles said, cornering me. "Your first and last mistake was coming here. Get off this island! Get off before death comes for you, too. This is your last chance."

When the ghosts flew at me, I screamed and ducked. The door flung open and I moved out of the way, fearing more ghosts were coming. But when I opened my eyes again, the ghosts had vanished. The only one in the room with me was a very concerned-looking Dante.

"Olivia, I heard a scream," he said. "Are you all right?"

Mom, Vanessa, and Russell rushed into my room a second later, dressed in their pajamas. They rubbed their eyes and looked at me, waiting for an explanation, but I didn't have one. I couldn't find the words.

"Liv?" Vanessa asked.

How could I tell her that her father was dead? Especially when I didn't even know how, why, or when?

Dante seemed to catch on to what I had seen and turned to the others. "Another panic attack. Don't worry, I'll take care of Olivia."

Russell stepped forward, but Vanessa reached for him and pulled him back. I think she had a good idea of what I had seen tonight, too. "Come on, we can't help Olivia. She just needs time."

"We're here for you," Mom said, kissing my cheek. "Never forget that."

I wanted to tell her that she was right. That something terrible *had* happened to the president, but she turned and left. Once they were gone, closing the door behind them, Dante turned to me.

"What happened, Olivia?"

"There were more ghosts," I said. "They came back."

"And?" he asked. "What did they tell you?"

"We're all going to die," I whispered.

21

THE GREAT HUNT

Dante tried his best to reassure me that me and my people wouldn't die there, but a part of me couldn't shake the feeling. I'd already gotten stabbed, poisoned, and attacked by spirits. Dante's track record of protecting me wasn't looking too good.

I didn't tell Dante that I had seen the president's husband or that the ghosts had said he had died. I didn't want to believe it myself. But if the ghosts were telling the truth, how could it have happened? If the kingdom of V killed them, where had they stashed the bodies?

When I went to bed, Dante left the door open to my room so he could watch over me all night. I tossed and turned, wrestling with nightmares for the first time. The anxiety was getting to me, and I feared I was going to suffer a mental breakdown soon. Luckily, no more ghosts appeared. Their visits were erratic and spontaneous, and I wondered where they went when they weren't haunting me.

When I woke up the next morning, Dante was still in the hallway, observing me. I closed the door so I could get dressed and headed downstairs for breakfast. Mom, Russell, and Vanessa were already sitting at the table, looking over at me with pity in their eyes.

"How you feeling?" Russell asked.

"Yeah, you looked pretty bad last night," Vanessa said.

"I'm fine," I lied. "I guess I'm just worried about the Hunt."

Mom placed her hand on mine. "I could petition the king to let you stay home. I know he wants us to experience their way of life, but maybe he'd change his mind if I told him about your anxiety."

I thought about it for a moment. I didn't like the idea of hunting animals, anyway. I hadn't enjoyed it when I'd gone with my dad. But Mom and the others still had to go, and I wouldn't feel right sending them off alone.

"No, it's okay," I muttered, eating the vegetarian breakfast food I found in the fridge. "I can make it."

"If you're sure," Mom said. "Only you and Vanessa will be competing. Since I'm the ambassador, I'll be sitting next to the throne as one of the judges. King Dominic and the royal family only observes the hunt. Russell will be staying with me as well."

"Will you girls feel safe without me?" Russell asked, his eyes flickering to Dante.

"We'll be fine," Vanessa said. "We won't split up."

I nodded. "Dante will be with us, and there's supposed to be tons of soldiers on duty. Even Christian said he'd come with me."

Mom frowned. "But that's impossible. The royal family isn't allowed to compete. They're the ones overseeing the tournament."

I shrugged. "He didn't say anything like that to me. Maybe the king will make an exception."

"You have my word that no harm will come to either of them," Dante said, stepping forward. "I will not fail my duty."

Mom and Russell said nothing but shared a look that suggested they didn't believe him.

After breakfast, we followed Dante into town. The citizens walked along the brick pathway toward the forest situated on the outskirts of the island. I even noticed the Sanguine twins who looked excited about the tournament. As we entered, the smell of trees and moss filled my nostrils. I noticed three thrones set up for each member of the royal family, and two extra seats for Mom and Russell.

A chill ran up my spine as I looked around. The forest seemed peaceful enough, with the tall trees, the singing birds, and the sunlight reflecting off the water of the babbling brook. I could even see the edge of the ocean. But there was something unnatural about the whole place—something terrifying.

The royal family was already there with several guards, waiting for everyone to start the tournament. I spotted Christian, General Ezra, and King Dominic arguing behind the thrones as Queen Vivienne took her seat and addressed the crowd. She plastered on a wide smile, pretending as though her family wasn't fighting at all. The Sanguine twins giggled, loving the conflict. A few soldiers shot them glares and they stopped.

"Welcome, everyone, to the ninety-seventh Great Hunt," Queen Vivienne said. "This will be the first time guests are joining us. Although it was tempting to cancel the Great

Hunt as part of the reprimands, we decided it was too much of a tradition."

I felt relieved. The people in town hated me enough as it was.

As the arguing got louder behind her, Queen Vivienne cleared her throat and continued. "Since our guests are unfamiliar with the tournament, I'd like to explain a few things. Our Great Hunt is old, almost as old as our kingdom. It was implemented by the royal family shortly after the unfortunate death of Charles Browning."

That didn't make sense to me. After killing a missionary, they decided to organize a yearly hunt to kill more creatures? It seemed almost like the old king was rewarding them for their bloodthirsty behavior.

The arguing behind Queen Vivienne stopped as Christian stomped away, taking his seat next to her. He crossed his arms and wouldn't look at the crowd. General Ezra and King Dominic shared a look of disapproval before they walked over to us. The general stood tall, his glaring eyes on me as the king joined his wife.

"I apologize for the delay," King Dominic said, sitting down in his throne, "but we had some family business to discuss. Vivienne, did you explain the rules?"

"Not yet. I left that to you," she said. "I was explaining the tournament's backstory."

"I see. Well, the rules are simple," King Dominic said, looking at the crowd. "Whoever kills the most animals within the next hour wins the champion title. They might even impress the general, which could lead to an invitation to join his order. He handpicks all the recruits. It's a very high honor.

When Dante won last year, he caught the general's attention and was recruited."

"And it's been a privilege, your Majesty," Dante said, bowing.

"The general has a good eye for talent," King Dominic replied. "As we give out every year, everyone will receive a bow to hunt with. We also would like everyone to wear protective vests."

Petra groaned. "Why? We've never worn them before!"

"Yeah," Nicolai said. "Worried the outsiders will get hurt? We shouldn't change our rules just because of them!"

"Quiet down, both of you," General Ezra snarled. "Your outbursts may be tolerated at the academy, but not in front of the king. Another interruption and I'll disqualify and punish you myself."

The Sanguine twins hushed immediately. I wondered if the punishment was along the same lines as Dante's. He shifted uncomfortably, remembering the torture. I placed my hand on his arm to let him know I was there for him and his mouth twitched upward.

"Before we begin, let me first say this," King Dominic said, his tone serious. "I expect everyone to be on their best behavior. We've had too many incidents around here lately, and I'd hate to add more reprimands. Watch your targets and report anything suspicious. Remember, safety is our top priority."

The general passed around the vests, handing them to me, Vanessa, Mom, Russell, and Dante. Mom and Russell weren't participating, but the vests were for their own safety, just in case something bad happened. As I put mine on, I thought about what the king had said. Was something suspicious, something dangerous, lurking in the forest? Did he fear something was going to happen? Is that why he gave Mom and Russell vests even though they weren't participating?

"Right here, Ambassador," King Dominic said, gesturing at the empty seats. "You and your bodyguard can sit with us and judge the competition. It'll give us a chance to know each other a little better while everyone's competing. When it's finished, we'll announce the winner together."

"I look forward to it," Mom said, taking her seat. "What about the soldiers? Will they be allowed to participate?"

"No, our soldiers patrol the forest," King Dominic said. "They report back to us on what kills they've witnessed. I'm sending more of them out there today, just to ensure nothing bad happens to the girls. You may not be able to see them, but they're there."

I only hoped someone worthy would win the title. It was too bad the soldiers weren't allowed to compete. Knowing more guards were watching over us *did* make me feel better, but not by much. Anything could go wrong in the blink of an eye. As the general handed us our bows, I winced at the feel of the mighty weapon.

"On your mark, get set...go!" King Dominic shouted, and everyone fled into the forest.

"I might be a meat-eater, but I don't think I'll be able to kill any of these animals myself," Vanessa said. "I'm starting to get why you're a vegetarian, Liv."

"It's all right," Dante said. "We can walk around and explore the forest instead. King Dominic isn't expecting either of you to compete and win, especially not Olivia, who he knows is a vegetarian. He just wants you to witness the competition."

I sighed in relief. At least I didn't have to kill anything today.

"What should we do with our bows?" Vanessa asked.

"Keep them," Dante said. "I can even show you how to use them if you'd like, just on the trees, not on the animals."

"Sounds like fun," I said. "Maybe Vanessa will learn a thing or two."

"The only thing I've learned is that this bow doesn't match my shoes," Vanessa said. "And what if I ruin my manicure?"

As I laughed, Dante shook his head. "Are you two ready?"

"In a second," I said, glancing over at the thrones. "I just need to talk to Christian first."

As I walked over, I noticed King Dominic, Queen Vivienne, and Mom chatting and laughing. Mom was telling them a story of one of Dad's blunders on a hunting trip. Russell kept his eyes focused on the forest while Christian still had his arms crossed.

"...and then Isaac tripped over his own bear trap. All the animals heard it and ran out of the forest, and he came home all disappointed. There was no dinner that night," Mom said, smiling as the king and queen laughed. "He was a good hunter, but he could be a klutz sometimes. You would've liked Isaac. He was always interested in meeting new people, especially from different cultures."

"I wish we could've met him," King Dominic said. "We're very sorry to hear about his passing."

"I've had time to deal with it," Mom said, looking down. "It was a long time ago. And while I'll always love Isaac, I think it's time for me to move on. I know he wouldn't want me to be lonely for the rest of my life."

Russell perked up at that, and I hoped he'd confess his feelings to Mom. The two of them deserved to be happy.

"We're very lucky to have each other," King Dominic said, reaching for Queen's Vivienne's hand. "We've been together for...well, for a long time. I couldn't imagine losing her."

"Yes, death is a tragic thing," Mom said, sighing, "but inevitable, unfortunately."

King Dominic and Queen Vivienne shared a look, but I couldn't read their expressions. I cleared my throat. "I don't mean to interrupt, but can I talk to Christian for a second?"

"I don't know. Am I allowed to talk to her at least?" Christian snapped at his parents.

King Dominic nodded. "Go ahead, son, and try to come back with a better attitude, hmm?"

Christian sneered, pulling me off to the side. "I can't go with you, Olivia. I'm sorry."

I frowned. "Why not?"

"The general fears I'll get hurt. He thinks it's better if I stay here," Christian said, rolling his eyes. "He convinced my father, too. That's what we were arguing about. I know I said I'd go with you—"

"It's all right. I get it," I said. "I know you wanted to come and make sure I was safe, but Dante's with me. He won't let anything happen to me and Vanessa."

Christian balled his fists at the mention of him. "Watch your back anyway. I know you don't like to hunt, so I was planning on making this our second date. Until the general ruined it, of course."

I laughed, reaching for his hand. "We'll have plenty of time for that later, Christian. No need to rush things."

He nodded. "You're right. But can you really blame me for wanting more alone time with you? It's not every day a beautiful stranger comes to my island."

I blushed as Dante walked over. "Are you coming? Vanessa is growing impatient. She keeps saying her shoes hurt her feet if she stays in one place for too long."

I rolled my eyes. "I told her not to wear them. We went through this on a trip to New York City last year. See you later, Christian."

After we said goodbye, Christian returned to the throne and Mom waved at us. Russell's gaze stayed on the back of my head, and I knew he wished he could come with us. When me and Dante walked back over to Vanessa, she sighed in relief.

"Finally! You know standing around gives me blisters," she said, pointing at her expensive shoes. "Come on, I want to see this forest."

As we delved deeper past the trees, I could hear arrows zipping by in the distance. I couldn't see anyone, not with so many trees blocking my view. Vanessa walked ahead of us to pick some flowers as I chatted with Dante.

"I heard you won the competition last year," I said. "Aren't you sad you won't get to compete again?"

He shrugged, glancing at me. "I much prefer your company to the forest creatures."

I hid my blush. "The king said your winning title earned you a place in the general's army. What did you do before that?"

"I was lost, not literally, but spiritually. I had no purpose," Dante said. "I entered the competition for something to do and found my calling. I was a good hunter, a good stalker. The general saw my potential and recruited me, and I never looked back. My parents wanted me to follow in their footsteps, becoming a doctor or a teacher, but I knew that life wasn't for me."

"Well, I'm glad you found something you enjoy. That's how I feel about my art," I said. "What else can you tell me about the hunt's history?"

"I know the Havoc members used to compete, the Sanguine twins' parents, specifically," Dante said. "But instead of hunting, they used to stalk the hunters. They would lunge at them from the trees and try to scare them by sneaking up on them. It was all very immature."

"They never killed anyone, did they?"

"No, never. But their mind games did get them disqualified," Dante said, "and it was the reason they were banished to the Solitude. We should be on the lookout for the Sanguine twins, just in case."

I shuddered. The last thing I needed was someone playing a practical joke on me in a creepy forest.

"Look!" Vanessa cried, pointing into the distance. "See that?"

"What?" I asked with concern, rushing over to her. Dante was close behind me. "What's wrong?"

"There's a rabbit," Vanessa whispered, "right at the pond. Isn't he so cute?"

I looked at the pond and noticed the small, brown rabbit lapping up the water. I had to admit, the rabbit was adorable, but the pounding of my heart was not.

"Yeah, precious," I mumbled. "I thought you were in danger, Ness."

"Me, too," Dante added, glancing around. "Thankfully, no one's here."

"Sorry," Vanessa said, turning to us. "I just wanted you to see the bunny before it hopped away. You and the rabbit have a lot in common, Liv, you both eat the same food."

"Very funny," I muttered. "Let's keep moving—"

Vanessa gasped when an arrow shot through the bunny's head, killing it with a spray of blood. We both cried out in shock and disgust as Dante readied his bow. The Sanguine twins emerged from the shadows, laughing.

"Got you," Petra said.

"Yeah, you should've seen the looks on your faces," Nicolai said. "Priceless."

"You shouldn't have done that," Dante said, lowering his bow. "I could've injured you."

"Maybe," Petra said, "but we had faith in your reflexes."

"How could you do that?" Vanessa asked, eyes wide in horror as they continued laughing. "That poor creature!"

"Yeah, I thought you said you didn't kill?" I asked, angrily.

"We were talking about people," Nicolai said, rolling his eyes. He grabbed the dead bunny and swung it around. "But everyone needs to eat. We can't all survive off of vegetables like you, Olivia, our bodies need meat. The bloodier, the better."

When Nicolai sunk his teeth into the rabbit, Vanessa turned to me. "I think I'm going to be sick. If I vomit all over these shoes, Daddy will never let me hear the end of it."

The mention of her father almost made me sick, too. I remembered his bloody neck, the dead look in his eyes, how the ghosts said he was never coming back...

"Mmm," Nicolai said, glancing at us as he took another bite. "Tastes even better when it's fresh."

"Let's go," Dante said, reaching for me and Vanessa.

"What's the matter? Blondie and the little vegetarian can't handle the blood?" Nicolai yelled as we walked away. "You should get used to it. This is what we are. You'll find out sooner or later!"

"Don't listen to them. They're only trying to scare you," Dante said. "I know a secluded place in the forest. We can stay there until the competition is over."

The Sanguine twin's laughter died down as we walked further into the forest. We followed Dante, taking a left at a pine tree to a small clearing. Vanessa sat down on a log to rest as I tried not to think about her dead father or the poor rabbit.

"Those Sanguine twins are messed up," Vanessa muttered. "They should be thrown in jail..."

The dark feeling returned. The negative energy was at its strongest where we sat, causing goosebumps to rise on my skin. When I heard voices, I decided to follow them toward a big tree. Someone had carved another Bloodspeak symbol into it, but I couldn't understand it.

"Olivia?" Dante asked. "Olivia, where are you going?"

I didn't listen to him, completely focused on the voices and the energy. As I stepped onto the pile of leaves in front of the tree, intending to look at the Bloodspeak symbols a little closer, I realized the leaves were hiding a secret entrance in the ground.

A second later, I plummeted with a scream as everything faded to black.

22

THE LAIR

I landed with a groan on what felt like mud. As I looked around, it was too dark to see anything except for the faint glow of a torch in the distance. It seemed like I had fallen into some kind of underground lair.

I just *had* to look at the Bloodspeak on the tree. I cursed myself in the darkness. "Nice going, Olivia…"

"Olivia?" Dante called out, echoing down the hole. "Are you injured?"

When I looked up, I couldn't see Dante or Vanessa, but I knew they were there. I prayed they hadn't heard me talking to myself.

"Just my ankle," I said, rubbing it. "It's okay. I don't think it's broken."

"Where are you?" Vanessa called out next.

I looked around, shrugging. "Somewhere I'm not supposed to be. Did you know this was hidden here, Dante?"

"No, not at all," he replied. "Stay where you are, Olivia. Vanessa and I will return to the king and get help. I'll need something to rescue you with."

"We can't just leave her down there," Vanessa argued. "I'll stay here with her. You go get someone."

"No." Dante shook his head. "We can't split up. It's too dangerous. As much as I hate to leave Olivia on her own, we have no choice. We can't reach her like this."

"I'll be fine," I told them. "Just hurry!"

"Be careful," Vanessa said. "We'll be right back."

As their footsteps disappeared, I thought about what Dante had said. If he didn't know about it, then who had built it? And more importantly, what was it used for?

I heard footsteps behind me and turned around. "Hello? Who's there?"

"Well, well, well," a mysterious voice replied. "Looks like we have a visitor."

Three people stepped closer to me, their faces illuminated by the torch the first one carried. One was a woman and two were men, and they looked like brothers. The men had the same long, scraggy black hair, and the woman had curly red hair adorned with flowers. They wore black cloaks and looked like they were up to no good.

"Who are you?" I asked. "I've never seen you around before."

"We don't live in the city," the woman said. "We'd rather die than live under King Dominic's rule."

"Why?" I asked. "What's he done that's so wrong?"

"An outsider wouldn't get it. We don't have time to make you understand," the woman said. "My name is Alma Florentine. These are the Zev brothers, Mikhail and Roscoe Zev."

"Olivia Hawthorne," I said, shyly. "It's...nice to meet you."

"She's real pretty," Roscoe said, reaching out to stroke my

hair. I recoiled in disgust. "I hope we can keep her for a long time."

I gulped.

"Now, now, Roscoe," Mikhail said. It was his voice I had heard earlier. "We don't want to frighten the poor girl, do we?"

"Sorry," Roscoe said, looking down.

"You'll have to forgive Roscoe," Mikhail said, his voice as soft as silk. "He hasn't seen an outsider in a long time. He's forgotten how to behave around them."

"No harm done," I muttered.

Roscoe smiled at that, and I realized he wasn't all there. He was like Dr. Cox, but with Roscoe, there was a dark energy surrounding him that scared me. I could feel it everywhere in the lair. I tried to stay calm and friendly so they wouldn't hurt me.

"I take it you're with the Ambassador that came here, yeah?" Alma asked, circling me.

"Yeah, Ambassador Hawthorne's my mother."

"So she's valuable," Mikhail said. "Even better."

"My mom's working on a treaty between your kingdom and my country," I said, ignoring his comment. "King Dominic's eager to make it happen, and he likes having us here."

"That would be a mistake for both our people. King Dominic's a liar. He's fooling you all. He's holding us back, too," Alma said. "As for your people, you're all idiots not to see what's in front of you. You never should've come to the kingdom of V, you know."

The ghosts had said something similar to me. What was

in front of us? What weren't we seeing? I had a feeling they'd be just as elusive if I asked.

"What are we going to do with her?" Roscoe asked. "Can we please add her to the collection? She'd look real nice next to the others..."

My stomach twisted. "What collection? What others?"

"Never you mind. Roscoe doesn't know what he's saying," Mikhail said, glaring at him. "Those weren't our orders, and you know it."

Roscoe stepped forward, looking desperate. "But we've already lost so many—"

"Hush, Roscoe," Mikhail snarled, "or I'll cut out your tongue myself."

That shut Roscoe up. He glanced down at the ground, looking like a kicked puppy. I didn't know what kind of orders they were talking about, but it seemed serious.

"Now, back to business," Mikhail said, glancing at me. "We're doing very important work down here, you know. We should teach you a lesson for trespassing."

"Please, don't hurt me," I said. "Believe me, I didn't mean to fall down that hole."

"How did you end up down here, anyway?" Alma asked.

"I was walking around the forest with a few friends. The Great Hunt's on right now," I said. "I saw a Bloodspeak symbol on a tree, and I wanted to look at it. I didn't realize leaves were covering that hole, so I fell through. I wasn't looking for you on purpose. I swear."

Alma's face turned red. "How do you know about Bloodspeak?"

"Professor Draven taught it to me," I replied. "King

Dominic sent us to the academy. He wants us to learn everything about his people."

"I doubt that," Alma sneered. "If we truly did share everything, you'd despise us. You'd be so desperate to get away from us that you would swim home."

"And why is that?" I asked. "I've met some of your people already. I like them just fine."

Alma laughed. "Just give it time, Olivia. You'll change your mind soon enough."

"Help me drag her," Mikhail said.

"No! Wait!" I cried. "My guard, Dante, told me to stay where I was. He's going to get help. He'll be back any second."

"Dante? As in Dante Draven?" Alma asked.

I nodded. "Know the name?"

"We've heard of him. He's one of the best fighters in the kingdom. And Ezra's quite fond of him, even thinks of him as a son," Alma replied. "Or so I hear. We haven't been to the city in a long time."

"That's sad. It's a beautiful kingdom," I said. "But since you know Dante, you know he's determined. If you hurt me, he'll hunt you down, and he'll make you pay. General Ezra assigned him as my bodyguard, and he took a solemn vow to protect me."

Mikhail thought for a moment. "All right, we won't punish you, but we do have something else in mind. Something necessary for our mission."

"We should tie her up," Roscoe said, grinning. "I've gotten real good at tying knots. You'll see."

"No, that would only anger Dante," Mikhail said.

"Besides, she can't do anything to stop us. She's just one human."

I started to scream as the three of them dragged me further into the lair, and the torches on the walls lit our path. I noticed there were many crevices down there. Whoever those people were, they'd lived below for a long time.

I tried to fight back, but much like the other people in the kingdom, they were strong. I settled for screaming my head off, hoping Dante and the others would hear me and come to my rescue. With my painful ankle, I couldn't run.

"Stop your screaming!" Roscoe growled. "You're hurting my ears!"

"Then let me go!" I yelled back.

"Not yet," Mikhail said. "Just calm down, Olivia. I promised we wouldn't hurt you. It's not time for that, anyhow."

Not time for that? Did that mean they planned to hurt me and the others at one point?

They dragged me into one of the crevices, abruptly letting go of me. I groaned and looked around, realizing the room was some kind of secret headquarters. They had tables filled with books, maps, and science equipment. Alma walked over to the table and picked up an empty vial, one that reminded me of the kind Anastasia had at the clinic. They must've stolen some of her supplies and brought them down there.

"We need to take your blood," Alma said. "Boss's orders."

"Oh, yeah?" I asked. "And who's your boss?"

"You don't need to know that," Mikhail said, "not yet. Now, hold still..."

I started screaming again when he pulled out a syringe. He

stabbed it into my arm, draining some of my blood. When he had it, he deposited it into the vial, and they all swarmed around to look at my blood. They had that same deranged look in their eyes as Dante had when I'd cut myself on my dagger.

My dagger! Only then did I realize I had it. If I could pull it out without them seeing me, maybe I could threaten them into letting me go.

"It's so pretty," Roscoe said, his eyes wide in fascination at the bloody vial. "Even prettier than her..."

"That's enough," Alma said, ripping it away from him. "We need to focus. You can't have her blood, so get that thought out of your head."

Roscoe pouted. "No fair."

"What are you planning?" I asked. "Why do you need my blood?"

Alma laughed. "Did you think we'd tell you? How stupid would we have to be?"

"Then at least tell me this," I said. "Are you responsible for the strange incidents around here? The boat and statue explosions, or my poisoning?"

"Boss says all will be revealed in good time," Roscoe said. "We follow him. He's real good at this stuff."

Alma and Mikhail stayed tight-lipped. Roscoe was chattier than the rest, whether he meant to be or not, and it seemed that was the only information I was going to get. I craned my neck and noticed another table across the room. But instead of lab equipment, they had weapons, mostly bows, like the ones they used in the Great Hunt. They were planning something big.

"Are you hunters?" I asked.

"We have to be to catch our food," Mikhail said. "We

don't get ours delivered to us like those lazy fools in the kingdom. They've grown complacent, weak. They could be so much more, and it's sad they don't see it..."

"You see, it's in our instinct to hunt," Alma explained. "We're predators, and that's the way it should stay. Unfortunately, King Dominic doesn't agree with us."

"Isn't that what the Great Hunt is all about?" I asked. "Giving in to your instincts?"

Alma laughed. "Not as much as we'd like, no."

She didn't tell me anything else, but I had to keep her distracted. I quietly reached for the dagger around my belt, relieved when I still felt it. It was a good thing Dante had made me swear to keep it.

"You said you're predators?" I asked. "You hunt animals?"

Alma nodded, crouching beside me as I pulled out my dagger and kept it low. "Animals...and whatever else we desire. Feels like centuries since we've seen an outsider..."

"I'm not here for your entertainment," I snarled. "Let me go, now."

"Not until we hear from our boss," she replied. "We await his orders to restore our kingdom and embrace what we really are. Until then, sit tight."

"Then you leave me no choice," I said, and stabbed my dagger up at her.

It hit her in the shoulder, and Alma hissed and stumbled back. I rose to my feet, my ankle screaming in pain at the sudden weight. Pain or no pain, I had to run back to the hole and climb out somehow. Maybe I could find a rock to use as leverage. I didn't know when and if these people would let me go, but the longer I stayed down there, the sicker I felt.

"Outsider bitch!" Alma snarled, placing her hand on her wound to stop the bleeding.

When I looked at her wound, I noticed something strange had happened. It was like my dagger had burned her skin—disintegrating it like acid. Blood trickled down her arm, sizzling with heat. I backed away in fear.

"Are you okay?" Mikhail asked her.

"I'll be fine," Alma said, glaring back at me. "Get her!"

As they stepped forward to grab me, I limped back to the location of the hole, holding my dagger tight in my hand. As I felt around the dirt, searching for something to climb, Alma and the others followed me. She pulled me back by my shoulder and slammed me onto the ground with incredible strength. I cried out in pain.

"Roscoe was right. We should add her to the collection," Alma said. "She's feisty. I bet she'd last the longest."

"We can't," Mikhail said. "We don't know if that's what the boss wants. He obviously has another plan in mind if he wanted her blood."

"The boss knows she's a nosy bitch," Alma said, still clutching her wound. "With her around, she could warn the others and ruin everything. I say we should kill her, slowly. Make her suffer."

"Dante? Vanessa?" I called out, hoping they were up there again. "Can you hear me?"

No response came. I prayed the ghosts would return and help me if Dante couldn't.

"Shut up!" Alma yelled, towering over me. "You think you're invincible just because you're the Ambassador's daughter, don't you? I'll show you what happens to people who mess with Instinct—"

I watched in relief as another person slid into the lair. They had a rope and used it to climb down. I hoped it was Dante, but the shadow looked different. When they turned around, their face lit by the glow of the torches, I realized it was General Ezra.

General Ezra snarled as he looked at the three of them. "What did you do to her?"

"It's Ezra!" Alma cried, nudging Mikhail and Roscoe. "Run!"

When they took off running deeper into the lair, the general reached down for me. "Can you walk?"

I nodded as he helped me to my feet. "I think so. Who were those people?"

"Trouble," General Ezra muttered. "Come on, let's get you back to the surface."

"They seemed scared of you."

"Criminals usually are," General Ezra grunted.

"You don't want to go after them?"

"You're injured," General Ezra said. "Besides, this lair is vast and deep. They could be halfway below the kingdom by now."

My eyes widened in surprise. "You think their lair goes that far?"

"It's very possible. In fact, I'd stake my life on it."

"Well, do you know who they are?"

"Criminals, ones we couldn't catch and put inside the Solitude," General Ezra said. "That's all you need to know."

The General helped me climb the rope, and I sighed in relief when I saw sunlight again. Mom, Russell, and Vanessa were the first faces I saw, followed by Dante, King Dominic, Queen Vivienne, and Prince Christian. I rushed into Mom's arms as the general climbed up behind me.

"Are you okay?" Mom asked. "What happened?"

"I fell," I said, "and ran into some people living down there. They called themselves Instinct."

General Ezra and the royal family turned silent. It looked like they recognized the name, but they weren't eager to share what they knew. The general had told me they were criminals. Did they have something to do with Havoc?

"I'm so sorry, Olivia," Dante said. "I failed to protect you. Again."

I shook my head. "No, *I'm* sorry. I shouldn't have run off like that. If I hadn't been looking at the tree, I wouldn't have fallen through the leaves."

"The lair shouldn't have been there in the first place," Dante said. "If it's not my fault, then it isn't yours, either."

"It won't happen again," General Ezra said, turning to the soldiers on duty. "I want this entrance sealed. I also want patrols all over this forest and kingdom in search of any other entrances. I don't want anyone getting down there again, or anyone getting to the surface."

"Yes, sir!" the soldiers shouted in unison, then got to work on the leaf pile. Others separated to scout out the forest.

"You should get to the clinic," Vanessa said, glancing at my ankle. "I'm sure Anastasia has another vial that could help you. That girl's got the cure for everything."

"Not everything," Dante mumbled. "Here, I'll help you."

"I'll do it," Christian said, stepping forward as he reached for my arm. "I'm so glad you're okay, Olivia. If my father had let me go with you, perhaps I could've prevented this."

"Pointing the finger helps no one, my son," King

Dominic said. "Olivia, I'd like to extend my sincerest apologies to you. I hope those criminals below our kingdom haven't changed your opinion of us. I assure you we aren't like them."

But I wasn't assured. They had mentioned a boss, someone with a plan. It could've been anyone. How many more members did they have?

"What about the tournament?" I asked. "Is it over?"

Queen Vivienne sighed, nodding. "We've decided to end it. It doesn't feel right to continue, not after this. We realize now that we should've postponed it instead of hoping for the best. The people were upset, but they'll come to understand."

I hoped they would.

When they took me back to the clinic, Dr. Draven placed her hand on my ankle to feel my pain. "Only a sprain. Anastasia can help."

"Maybe I should just live at the clinic," I muttered, "seeing as I can't stop getting hurt. What if something else happens, something worse? Have a cure for death by any chance?"

"Don't talk like that," Dante said. "Those criminals down there will be cut off for good and nothing else will happen."

Anastasia walked over, giving me more foul-smelling vials to drink. Once I'd downed them, the pain in my ankle subsided a little, but the trauma of getting trapped in a lair with three odd strangers didn't. My fears for the future didn't vanish, either.

"I know you aren't fond of the clinic, but I think you should stay here for a little while to rest," Dr. Draven said, turning to the others. "You can visit her again soon."

Mom kissed my forehead. "Stay safe, sweetie."

Russell and Vanessa both squeezed my hand, and Christian gave me a quick kiss on my cheek. After they'd left, only me and Dante remained. I decided to ask him a few questions.

"Those people down there knew you by name," I said. "They seemed to think you were one of the best fighters in the kingdom."

"Strange," Dante said. "If they weren't criminals, perhaps I'd feel flattered."

"They called themselves Instinct, whatever that means," I said. "They also took my blood and told me they had a plan. But I'll tell you what's really strange. Using my Slayer, I managed to stab one of them, a woman named Alma. It burned her skin like acid."

"Your dagger is strong," Dante said. "I told you it could inflict damage, didn't I?"

"Yeah, sure, but I didn't think it could do *that*," I mumbled. "Do you know about Instinct? King Dominic looked like he did when I mentioned them."

Dante sighed. "I...know of them, yes."

"Who are they? What do they want?"

Before Dante had a chance to speak, a loud alarm blared through the clinic.

23
JAILBREAK

"What's going on?" I asked, sitting up in bed. "Is it Instinct?"

My heart pounded at the thought of getting trapped in an underground lair with those three again. My hand tightened around my Slayer, gripping it in fear. I wouldn't let them take me.

"I don't know. Stay here," Dante said. "I'll look outside and find out what's going on."

As he walked to the front door, I couldn't resist the urge. I jumped out of bed and followed him as he opened it. I didn't expect what I found, people screaming and running for a place to hide. The alarm sounded like it was coming from inside the castle.

"Olivia, I told you to wait in bed," Dante said, noticing me over his shoulder.

"We both know I wasn't going to do that," I muttered. "What's happening?"

"I believe King Dominic has sounded the emergency

alarm. He only rings it in dire circumstances," Dante said. "It's happened one other time in history."

"When?"

"After Charles Browning arrived," Dante said, "and our people murdered him. The kingdom was put on lockdown."

I gulped. "So, what? Are you saying there's been another murder?"

"I can't tell from here," Dante said. "I'll have to find the general. Stay inside the clinic and lock the doors. I'll be back soon."

"Are you crazy? I'm not staying here," I said. "Mom, Russell, and Vanessa are out there. I have to find them and make sure they're okay!"

"But your ankle—"

"Is feeling much better," I answered. "Anastasia's vial worked. Look, Dante, we're wasting time arguing. I'm going with you, and that's that."

He sighed. "Do you have your Slayer at least?"

I nodded, pulling out the dagger. "Right here. You don't think I'll have to use it, do you?"

"You might. What was the second lesson I taught you?"

"Always be prepared. I remember."

"Good. Now come on," Dante said, "and stay behind me."

As we left the clinic, I could smell smoke in the air. I continued following Dante along the white brick path until I saw the building on fire, the Solitude. Some of the soldiers were trying to extinguish it, but it was thick and spreading.

"Dante, we have to do something," I said. "There are prisoners inside!"

"We can't worry about that right now," Dante said. "We have other priorities. The soldiers will handle it."

Dante spotted General Ezra speaking with his soldiers in front of the castle. As he sprinted to him, I tried my best to keep up. Out of the corner of my eye, I saw something dark scurry through the garden. If Dante saw it, he didn't say anything, so my eyes could have been playing tricks on me.

"General, what's going on?" Dante asked.

"There you two are. I was getting worried. I planned to send a soldier after you if you hadn't showed up," General Ezra said. "There's been a fire at the Solitude. We don't know how it started, but we think some of the prisoners did it. There's been a jailbreak."

"Jailbreak?" I asked. "So, the criminals could be anywhere?"

General Ezra nodded. "King Dominic's placed the entire kingdom on lockdown. We're scrambling to put all the security measures in place and find the convicts."

"Where's my family?" I asked.

"I was just about to send a few soldiers to your home. That's where your family went after they left the clinic," General Ezra said. "But if you two could get them, that would save me from having to spare my soldiers. We're spread thin enough as it is."

"We'll do it," I said. "Do you think the escaped prisoners would try to break into the homes? Into Hawthorne Lodge?"

"They might. Stay alert and don't hesitate to call for backup," General Ezra said. "After you find your family, take them to the castle. They can hunker down with King Dominic. He, Queen Vivienne, and Prince Christian are already safe and accounted for."

"We're on it," I said. "What about all the kids from the academy? And the professors?"

"All the citizens are taken care of. They've been escorted to their homes and sealed inside," he said. "That was my first priority. Those kids mean a lot to me."

I thought back to the general training them hard. Was he preparing him for this or some other reason?

"What will you be doing in the meantime while we're gone?" I asked.

"Trying to put out that damn fire," General Ezra said, pointing at the burning jail, "and making sure those criminals get back where they belong."

"Do you think Instinct's behind this?"

"I don't think so. My soldiers believe the fire started from inside the jail," General Ezra said. "They'd just finished sealing the entrance in the forest when the fire started. We didn't see anyone from Instinct."

I sighed in relief. But if it wasn't Instinct, what other evil had gotten unleashed onto the kingdom?

"Come on, Dante," I said, tugging on his arm. "We can't let those prisoners get to my family."

"Dante, wait a moment," General Ezra said. "It's...about the escaped prisoners."

"What is it?" he asked.

General Ezra's eyes flickered to me, then back at Dante. "They...aren't themselves if you know what I mean. According to the warden, they were changed. I don't think they've been taking Anastasia's vials. Perhaps that was all a part of their escape plan."

Dante's eyes widened. "This is serious, General, far more serious than a simple jailbreak."

He nodded, sadly. "I trust you can handle it if you come across one of them."

"I will," Dante said. "Any casualties yet?"

"Several, but there will be a lot more if we can't stop these creatures. I wanted to ensure you were prepared to handle it."

"What are you talking about?" I asked, glancing between Dante and General Ezra. They both looked serious.

"Nothing," Dante mumbled. "Let's go, Olivia."

As we rushed down the path toward the markets, I looked over my shoulder and noticed the general moving out with his soldiers. We headed straight for the homes, and to my relief, none of them were on fire.

When I reached the front door of Hawthorne Lodge, I twisted the handle but found it locked. I pounded on the door and hoped someone could hear me. "Mom? Vanessa? Russell? Are you in there?"

No response.

I turned to Dante. "The general said they went home. Why aren't they answering?"

"Stand back, I'll get us inside. We'll find out soon."

As I took a step back, Dante kicked the door down. I pushed ahead of him and gasped when I noticed how disheveled the house looked. Much like the first day we had arrived, the entire house had gotten trashed. But that destruction was neat and tidy, this one looked like a wild animal had trampled through the place.

I noticed bloody pawprints on the floor that stretched up the staircase and knew this wasn't a person behind the damage. An animal was on the loose, something bleeding and ferocious. I didn't see any sign of it when I looked around and hoped it hadn't hurt my family.

"What the hell?" I muttered. "Did a bull crash through here?"

"Not a bull," Dante mumbled. "The ambassador must be here somewhere. We need to find her."

The shattered window caught my eye. I walked over, noticing more of the bloody pawprints. "Dante, look. This must be how the animal got in, whatever it is. This can't be the prisoners."

Dante said nothing in response.

When I heard a scream upstairs, my head shot up. "That sounded like Vanessa. Come on!"

After we sprinted up the stairs, we followed the bloody pawprints and destruction to Mom's room. She, Vanessa, and Russell stood trapped in the corner. Vanessa wouldn't stop screaming. Russell was trying to shield them with his body and had bad cuts on his arms.

"Stay back!" Russell cried, his eyes focused on something I couldn't see yet. I'd never seen him so terrified and angry before. "I don't know what you are, but I'll kill you just the same!"

As I stepped closer, I finally saw what had everyone so terrified. An ugly beast, matching the statue creature, had backed Mom, Russell, and Vanessa into the corner. It fluttered its black, bat-like wings, drool dripping down its chin. It had razor-sharp teeth, long talons, veiny arms, and coarse, black hair covering its body.

The thing that had darted out of the corner of my eye wasn't a shrub, but one of those creatures. There were more of them out there in the kingdom.

Before I had the chance to attack it with my dagger, Dante leaped forward, unsheathing his sword. In one clean swipe, he cut the creature's head off. It rolled over to me, and I stepped back, recoiling in disgust. The creature's red eyes were wide in surprise.

"Are you three all right?" Dante asked.

"We're fine," Mom said, "just horrified."

"Mom!" I cried, rushing into her arms. I pulled Vanessa into our hug. "What happened?"

Vanessa dried her tears. "We don't know. One second, I was in my room, the next an alarm was going off. Then that... that thing burst through the window downstairs and followed us up here. Russell took us into your mom's room to keep us safe, and that's when it cornered us."

"I tried my best, but...I'm not sure I could've stopped that thing," Russell said. "What was that ugly beast?"

Dante hesitated.

"A Dark Half," I answered.

"A dark...what?" Mom asked.

"A creature of urban legend," I said, turning to Dante. "Isn't that right?"

He sighed, nodding. "Yes, and a piece of advice. You can only kill it by chopping off its head. I'll come back later to burn the body and get rid of it. They thirst for human blood and never get enough. They're also sensitive to sunlight and holy objects if you don't have a weapon available. Too bad it's a cloudy day outside or the sun would've weakened them."

I shuddered, turning to Russell. "You're bleeding. Did it get you?"

"It scratched me a few times," Russell said, "but nothing too serious. Would've done a lot worse if you two hadn't showed up."

"It didn't bite you, did it?" Dante asked, his face serious.

"No," Russell said. "Why? Would that've been bad?"

Dante nodded. "Very, very bad. Come on, let's get you to the castle where it's safer."

"I saw another one of those creatures in the garden," I said. "I didn't say anything because I didn't know what it was."

"I suspected there might be more," Dante said, gripping his sword. "Keep your eyes peeled for any sudden movements. These creatures are fast and can sneak up on you, so tell me immediately if you see anything. Stay close to me and I'll get you to the castle."

As we left our house, Dante walked out first to scout for more Dark Halfs. He nodded when it was clear, then we followed him to the castle in the distance. Mom, Russell, and Vanessa all gasped when they saw the burning jail.

"Did those creatures do that?" Mom asked.

"Yes," Dante replied. "But don't worry. We'll get everything under control."

The soldiers continued to battle the blaze as we approached the castle. A soldier standing guard outside the door immediately let us in, then slammed the doors shut behind us. Dante led us to the throne room where I heard voices arguing, King Dominic and General Ezra again. Queen Vivienne, Prince Christian, Dr. Draven, Anastasia, and Dr. Cox stood around in silence.

"You're a part of the royal family whether you like it or not," King Dominic said to General Ezra. "Let your soldiers handle this and stay here where it's safe. I don't want anything to happen to you, brother."

"I can't do that," General Ezra said. "My soldiers have

barely gotten the fire under control, and someone needs to kill those abominations."

King Dominic sighed. "There shouldn't be any abominations in the first place! Oh, I prayed we had moved past this..."

"We can *never* get past our biology," General Ezra said. "It's what I've been trying to warn you about all this time."

"Olivia!" Christian shouted, which hushed King Dominic and General Ezra. Christian rushed to my side and reached for my hand. "Oh, I'm glad you and your family are all right. I wanted to go looking for you, but Father wouldn't let me leave."

"It's probably better that you didn't," I said. "One of those Dark Half creatures cornered my family. It scratched Russell up pretty good, but he's fine. No bitemarks."

"And?" King Dominic asked. "Is the creature dead?"

I nodded. "Dante killed it. Cut its head off. He saved my family."

"I was only doing my job," Dante said, shrugging like it was nothing.

King Dominic smiled, placing a hand on his shoulder. "You're a good soldier, Dante. One of the finest in the kingdom. We're lucky to have you. I'm sure you'll have them all dead soon enough."

"What?" I asked. "You're not going back out there, are you?"

Dante nodded. "I have to. You said you saw another one, and there could be even more hiding somewhere. If they're still out there, no one in this kingdom is safe."

"You can't go," I cried. "It's suicide! What if they bite you?"

"Then that will be my fate," Dante replied. "Stay here, Olivia."

General Ezra stepped forward. "Don't worry. I'm going with him. We'll have a better chance of stopping them if we're together."

"Ezra..." King Dominic warned.

"It's been decided," General Ezra spat. "My soldiers will stay here and keep you safe. Come on, Dante."

After they had left, Christian squeezed my hand. "Hey, I know you're worried about your bodyguard, but they'll be okay. They're trained for this, remember?"

How could anyone train to fight creatures like that? It didn't make sense to me. I took a seat with Mom, Russell, and Olivia. Christian sat next to me, holding my hand as Anastasia put some ointment on Russell's wounds.

"We've never had an issue with these creatures before," Queen Vivienne said. "Usually, our kingdom is a lot safer than this. I apologize that you've seen us this way. What a disaster..."

"Oh, please. There's been nothing but problems since we arrived," Russell shot back, wincing at the stinging ointment. "If it's not Olivia under attack, it's the whole goddamn kingdom!"

"Russell has a point," Mom said, "even if I wouldn't have used such...colorful language."

King Dominic sighed. "We understand you're angry about all of this. We are, too. Once the creatures are taken care of, I intend to make things better for you all. I do hope the president doesn't arrive right now..."

Mom and Russell glanced at each other. I knew what they were thinking. They doubted the president would ever arrive.

"Where did these animals come from, anyway?" Vanessa asked. "The forest? The sea? It's like they're right out of the blue."

King Dominic hesitated, glancing at Queen Vivienne and Christian. It surprised me when Oscar spoke up. "They've always been here...lurking in the shadows, waiting for our weakness. It was only a matter of time before they rose to the surface..."

"What are you talking about?" I asked.

"Don't listen to him," Queen Vivienne said. "You know how he loves his stories."

"It's our punishment, you know," Oscar continued, rocking back and forth. "We can never be free of what we really are, of the darkness inside us..."

Alma had said the same thing. What were they talking about?

"Oscar, please," Queen Vivienne said. "No need to scare our guests any further."

"Here, this should help calm him down," Anastasia said, handing Oscar a vial. "Go on, take it."

He tried to resist but downed it when he realized he had no choice. As the contents of the vial settled inside his stomach, he grew quiet. They always wanted to stop him when he spoke, especially when it was about the Dark Half's. Why wasn't he allowed to talk about it? If they were just stories, why did they fear them so much?

Russell shook his head in disbelief. Anastasia finished putting the ointment on him, and some of his cuts started to heal quickly. As the minutes passed, my uneasiness lingered. What if the creatures burst into the castle? Could we stop a whole army of them?

Christian rubbed soothing circles on the back of my hand. "Stay calm, Olivia. It'll be over soon."

"I just hate not knowing what's going on out there," I said. "I don't like being kept in the dark."

"I know, me too," Christian whispered. "But we have to trust that General Ezra will save us. He knows what he's doing."

As we waited in silence to receive word that it was safe again, I couldn't stop worrying, mostly for Dante's sake. I knew he had taken out that creature like it was nothing, but I couldn't help it. My stomach twisted when I thought of Dante dying or becoming one of those things...

It was settled. I knew what I had to do.

"I have to go to the bathroom," I said to Christian. "Where's the closest one?"

"Down the hall," he said. "Hang on. I'll get one of the soldiers to go with you."

"It's okay. I'm sure I can find it myself. The castle's the safest place in the kingdom right now."

He shook his head. "I know they secured the castle, but that doesn't mean we should be careless. You need protection."

I almost groaned. He just had to make it more difficult.

Christian stood up, walking over to the king. They whispered for a few seconds before the king nodded and pointed at one of the soldiers. The soldier walked over to me, gesturing at the door.

"I'll escort you to the bathroom," he said. "Stay behind me."

"Be careful, sweetie," Mom said. "Hurry back."

I said nothing, knowing I couldn't agree.

The soldier opened the door to the throne room, poking his head out. "It's clear. I don't hear anything. Let's make it quick."

He followed me down the hallway, motioning at the small bathroom. I turned to him and smiled. "Can you wait for me by the throne room? I need some privacy."

He shook his head. "No can do. The king wants me to stay as close to you as possible. I can plug my ears if that would help."

I sighed. "Look, I'm really sorry about this."

He frowned. "Sorry about what?"

I leaned forward and punched him, knocking him out. All of Dante's training had finally paid off. I caught him before he fell and set him down gently on the floor. My knuckles ached, but at least the guard was out of the way.

"I'm sure I'll get in trouble for that later," I muttered, pulling out my Slayer, "but right now, I need to find Dante."

24
THE SOLITUDE

I took a moment to consider my escape plan.

I remembered there were still soldiers standing outside the front door, so it ruled out that exit. I'd bet there were some stationed outside the back door that led into the garden, too, so I decided to jump out a window. There weren't many in the kingdom, another thing I found odd about the people of V, but there was one down the south corridor.

After jumping out, I heard a patrol of soldiers heading my way. I hid in the bushes as the leader of the platoon gave out his orders. "Spread out, search for more of those creatures. King Dominic wants this whole kingdom purged."

One of the soldiers, a woman, raised her hand. "But, sir... what if I can't kill them? What if...what if they look familiar?"

Look familiar? What was she talking about?

"There's no help for them now, soldier," the man in charge replied. "The prisoners deliberately stopped taking their medicine. Their fate is on them, not us, so don't feel guilty. Move out!"

After they scurried away to hunt more of those creatures, I sighed in relief and came out of hiding. The streets were bare with the citizens hiding at home. I took a look around and saw no creatures, but I couldn't let my guard down.

As I moved around the castle, I noticed the Solitude was still on fire. The soldiers were trying to extinguish it as fast as they could, but a blaze that large would take time. Dante hadn't said where he was going, but since I hadn't seen him and the general around the kingdom, my best guess was the jail.

As I walked closer, I noticed three figures standing in front of the Solitude. The grey smoke clouded my view of them until I pushed through it. Much to my surprise, it was the Sanguine twins, and they were arguing with the warden. The warden looked badly injured and scratched. She leaned against the side of the jail in pain, panting hard.

"You have to let us in!" Petra cried. "Our parents are in there!"

"Your parents probably caused the damn jailbreak," the warden said, huffing. "It's too dangerous. My orders were to stand here and prevent anyone from getting in, or anyone from getting out."

"Criminals or not, they still deserve to be saved," Nicolai hissed. "Step aside. We're going in to rescue them."

The warden pulled out her sword. "You're not going anywhere. If your parents are still alive, and they haven't become those horrible creatures, then General Ezra and Dante will get them out. Look, don't make me fight you. I'm too tired."

My gamble was right. Dante and the general *were* inside. Now I had to get in there.

"Warden…Corina Blanchard, right? I've heard your name before," I asked, pushing toward her. "Are you okay?"

The warden lowered her sword. "Yeah, that's me. One of those creatures attacked me on its way out. I think I'm okay, but I'll get Dr. Draven to look at my cuts when this is over."

"The creatures came from inside the jail?"

She seemed surprised I knew that. "Yeah, we think so. They're the ones that started the fire and triggered the jailbreak. Damn things slipped past me before I had a chance to react. While I was down, I think a few others got out, too, but I can't be sure."

I turned silent. How had these creatures come from inside the jail? What was going on behind those bars?

"You're Olivia Hawthorne, right?" the warden asked. "The ambassador's daughter?"

I nodded. "How'd you know my name?"

"Dante talks about you a lot," she said, and I almost blushed. "What are you doing out here? I don't believe for a second King Dominic would let you outside during all this. You're too important to him and the ambassador."

I sighed. "You're right. To tell you the truth…I escaped from the castle. I had to see for myself what was going on. I'm worried about Dante."

"Me, too," Corina said, sighing. "He found me here and helped me up, then he and the general disappeared inside. They haven't come back out yet."

"We need to go inside and look for them," I said. "They could be in danger."

Corina shook her head. "There's no way I'm letting you inside. King Dominic would have my head!"

"I have a dagger. Dante trained me with it. He calls it the

Slayer," I said, holding it up. "I'm not stupid. I know how to fight."

"The Slayer *is* the perfect weapon," Corina said, looking down at it in awe, "but I still can't let you in. Go back to the castle, Olivia. I'd escort you myself, but the general's ordered me to stand guard here."

"If Dante's talked about me, then I'm sure you know how stubborn I am," I said. "I'm not leaving until I know he's safe."

Corina sighed. "Even if I agreed to let you inside, I couldn't let you go alone. Too dangerous. Even General Ezra took back-up with him. I'd go with you, but my orders forbid it. I'm sorry, Olivia, but you'll have to have faith that Dante will be all right. He can handle himself."

"We could go with her," Petra said. "We'll be her back-up."

Nicolai nodded, pulling out the sword attached to his belt. "When we heard what happened, we grabbed our swords and came here to fight. We're ready."

Corina snorted. "Nice try, Sanguine twins. How do I know your parents haven't put you up to this? That all this wasn't a ploy just so you could break them out of jail?"

"That would be stupid," Petra said. "There's no way off this island. If we broke our parents out, where would we go?"

Corina shrugged. "Maybe you'd start swimming. Or maybe you'd go down and live with Instinct. Your parents always have a trick up their sleeves, don't they?"

Nicolai snarled. "Don't you dare talk about our parents like that, you—"

"The longer we argue, the longer Dante and the general's inside," I said, glancing back at Corina. "I know you don't trust the Sanguine twins, but I'll make sure they don't do anything. I trust them to watch my back."

The Sanguines looked at me with wide eyes, surprised I'd say that. No one trusted them. No one believed in them. They didn't even have friends. If they weren't so mean to me and Vanessa all the time, maybe I'd feel sorry for them.

Corina sighed. "Fine. But please, be careful. I don't want an outsider's death on my conscience. And if the general asks how you got in, don't mention me."

"My lips are sealed," I said, then turned to Petra and Nicolai. "Come on. Let's get going."

As we stepped into the jail, running past the flames, the stench of loneliness, despair, and entrapment overwhelmed me. It wasn't as strong as the ghost's energy, but it was enough to make me stumble. I leaned against the wall to catch my breath.

"What's wrong?" Petra asked.

"It's the energy in here," I said. "The prisoners...they've been suffering. I can sense some desperation, too."

"Well, yeah. They were prisoners," Nicolai said, rolling his eyes. "You can feel that just by walking into a room?"

I nodded. "You can't?"

"No," Nicolai said, glancing at his sister. "Interesting. Well, don't just stand there. We need to find our parents."

It wasn't hard to find out why a prisoner would hate that place. It was depressing, worse than our jails back home. The walls were dark grey and had no windows, although that wasn't unusual. The cells looked small and crowded on top of each other with barely enough room to turn around.

All the cell doors looked unlocked, and I wondered if the creatures had opened them before they started the fire. But that would mean the creatures were sentient. The warden mentioned people had turned into them, and I feared what else they were capable of. I spotted a man lying on the ground in a pool of his own blood. He had scratches and marks all over his body, just like Russell and Corina.

"Dead," I said, checking his pulse. "I'd say one of those creatures got him."

"Obviously, Sherlock. General Ezra will need to burn his body soon," Petra muttered. "Does he have any bite marks?"

I stepped away. "I don't know. What would happen if he did?"

"Trust me, outsider, you don't want to know," Nicolai said. "Come on. Our parents' cell was on the fourth floor. It's where they put the high-risk prisoners. We'll have to take the stairs."

As we rushed toward the staircase that led to the upper level, we passed more bodies. They matched the man's injuries on the first level. I felt sorry for them. Not even prisoners deserved that fate. The flames grew thicker when we climbed the staircase as if the fire had started from the highest floor.

"Corina mentioned Instinct before we came in," I said. "I met them. They took my blood after I fell into their hideout. Are your parents involved?"

Nicolai sneered. "Our parents don't kill, remember? They'd never get involved with those Instinct thugs. They're way too bloodthirsty for Havoc's liking."

I gulped. "You know them, then?"

Petra nodded. "We know *of* them. They're wannabe killers, and I'm not just talking about animals. If it weren't for King Dominic, they would've killed you and your people the second you got off your boat. There's nothing they hate more than outsiders."

"Why can't the king catch them?"

"They're too careful for that. They know a lot about our kingdom, like they have insider knowledge or something. They've managed to resist capture for years," Nicolai said. "And besides, they haven't done anything yet except talk about destroying the world. How could they? No outsiders come here."

Destroying the world? Why would they want that?

"They were the others we tried to warn you about," Petra said. "King Dominic didn't want us to tell you about Instinct. He was afraid it would scare you off. But you found them first, so we didn't break any laws. I love technicalities."

"Well, a little heads up would've been nice," I muttered, waving away smoke in my face. "Back to your parents. Did they cause the jailbreak?"

"I don't know. They like chaos as much as the next person, but this seems extreme. And I don't think they'd have anything to do with these creatures," Petra said, then her veneer of friendliness vanished. "Since you're so curious, why don't you pester them when we find them? I'm tired of answering your questions."

As we passed the third floor, I heard familiar grunts. "It's Dante. He's here!"

As I tried to turn and enter the third floor, Petra grabbed my arm. "Dante can defend himself. We need to get to our parents first. They could be trapped inside their cells with these creatures on the loose!"

While Petra had a point, as much as I hated to admit that. I shook my head. "You know I came in here to find Dante, and I'm not leaving without him. Go ahead without me. I'll meet up with you when I find him."

I rushed down the third-level corridor, hearing the grunting and animal shrieks growing louder. As I turned the corner, I found Dante battling three of those Dark Half creatures. One had scratched him in the leg, but other than that, he looked fine.

"Dante!" I cried. "Let me help!"

"Olivia, what are you doing here?" he grunted, stabbing at another creature. It dodged him, and he missed his chance to cut off its head. "It's not safe. You should be back at the castle!"

I didn't have a chance to respond. One of the Dark Half's turned from Dante and snarled at me, approaching like a predator in the wild. Dante tried to get over to me, but the other two creatures had him pinned down, snarling and clawing at his sides. I gripped my dagger in my hand, trembling at the thought of killing something.

This isn't a helpless animal, Olivia, I told myself. *This thing wants to kill you, and it's kill or be killed. Don't hesitate.*

As it leaped forward and nipped at me, I thrust my dagger into its chest. It wasn't enough to kill it, but it *was* enough to stun it. Before I could take the killing blow, Petra appeared to my right and sliced the animal's head off. It rolled down the hallway as Nicolai helped Dante kill the other two creatures he was fighting.

Panting, I looked over at Petra. "Thanks, but...why'd you help me?"

"I didn't help you. I'm trying to find my parents," she spat. "The faster you finish here, the faster we can get to them."

"I told you to go ahead without me. I thought you would."

"Well, you thought wrong," she said, flicking the blood off her sword. "Everyone around here thinks they know the Sanguine family, that we're so evil and predictable. They're wrong, too."

As I took a moment to catch my breath, I realized she was right. By killing these Dark Half's and saving our lives, the twins had surprised us both.

"I never thought I'd see the day the Sanguine twins came to my rescue, but you have my thanks," Dante said, turning to me with a growl. "Olivia, what were you thinking? I told you to wait in the castle. You gave me your word!"

Petra rolled her eyes. "She came back for you, you big idiot. You would've done the same for her, wouldn't you?"

"Of course," he said, his eyes still on me, "but that is *my* duty as her guard. I'm the one who should be risking his life, not the other way around!"

"I did what I thought was right. I couldn't just sit there and do nothing while you and the prisoners were in trouble," I said, shrugging. "I'd do it again in a heartbeat, so save your lecture."

He ran his fingers through his hair. "You're not only stubborn, but you're careless, too. You don't think before you act, do you, Olivia? You just rush off and hope everything works out? One day, you'll pay the price for your stupidity."

Ouch. I had to admit, that hurt, especially coming from him. His anger could cut as sharp as the generals sometimes. I didn't say anything, but he must've seen the expression on my face because he sighed.

"I apologize," he said. "That was harsher than I intended, but I just—"

"Hurl insults at each other on your own time," Nicolai snarled. "We have business here. Have you seen our parents?"

Dante shook his head. "No, not yet. The general said he was heading up to the fourth floor and would work his way down. I've seen a lot of dead bodies, but your parents haven't been among them."

"Then maybe they still have a chance," Petra said, glancing at her brother. "Let's hurry!"

As they rushed back to the staircase, Dante grabbed my arm. "You're heading back to the castle where it's safe. I don't know how you escaped, but the king won't be happy about this. I could get in trouble if he finds out you did it for me."

"I won't tell him why," I said, shrugging off his grip, "and I'm not going back. I came this far, and I want to make sure their parents are alive. But I'm just a stupid, careless girl, so what would I know, right?"

Dante sighed. "Olivia—"

"Are you two coming?" Nicolai called out. "In case you haven't noticed, this building is on fire."

"You can come," Dante said to me, "but stay behind me. Don't even think about doing anything heroic."

I nodded and rushed to the staircase behind Dante, following Petra and Nicolai up to the fourth floor. I was right. The fire had started up there. I coughed as soldiers outside the window continued to spray water onto the blaze.

"Mother? Father?" Petra called out. "Can you hear us?"

"Petra? Is that you?" a female voice called out. "We're down here. The cell is on the right!"

Petra and Nicolai rushed in the direction of her voice,

finding two people within their cells. They looked exactly like the Sanguine twins, the same red hair and green eyes, except they were older with wrinkles and ugly prison jumpsuits. Vanessa would've made a joke about them if she were there.

"Oh, you came for us," their mother said, smiling. "We knew you would."

"Why are you still in there?" Nicolai asked.

"Our cell doors are jammed. The warden didn't seem too interested in solving that little problem as she ran by," their father muttered. "Break them down and get us free. We saw some of the Dark Half's mulling around, so be careful."

Petra and Nicolai kicked down each of the cell doors, and their parents emerged with a smile. When they hugged their children, a warm, fuzzy feeling filled my stomach.

"At least we saved someone," I said. "I think all the prisoners are dead. Maybe staying inside your cells saved your lives."

Their father grinned. "That it did. Good thing we're always thinking one step ahead."

"Olivia, these are our parents," Petra began, "Vera and Lorenzo Sanguine, leaders of Havoc."

"You must be the ambassador's daughter. It's all anyone's been talking about," their mother said. "Nice to meet you, though, we wish it were under better circumstances."

"What's the matter?" Dante taunted. "I thought you liked chaos?"

"Only when *we're* in control," Lorenzo said. "We were not, and people died because of it."

"Do you know what happened here?" I asked.

"Some of the other prisoners went stir-crazy. They couldn't take living in such small cells," Vera said. "So, they stopped taking their medicine without the warden's knowledge, became those creatures, and started a fire to escape. Then they unlocked the cells to let us all out, but something went wrong. They couldn't control themselves like they thought they'd be able to and went on a killing rampage."

"Fools," Lorenzo muttered. "No one can resist the temptation as a Dark Half. We had no idea about the jailbreak, or we would've talked them out of it."

"But we can understand their desperation," Vera added. "Some of them are in here for minor crimes, petty theft, dreaming of leaving the island, but King Dominic sentences everyone to life. He's scared we'll find a way off the island and destroy the world."

"Go back to what you said before. Did you say they... became the creatures?" I asked. "The warden mentioned something similar, but I didn't have the chance to ask."

"Don't listen to them," Dante snarled. "They don't know what they're talking about."

"I just have one question," I said. "Are you and Havoc responsible for the incidents in the kingdom? Like the boat and statue explosions? What about when I was poisoned?"

"No. All our members were apprehended, and we have no one on the outside. Our children don't work for us, either," Vera said. "It might be hard to believe coming from a criminal, but we're innocent. On that, at least."

"It *is* hard to believe," Dante growled. "Have you seen General Ezra?"

"The last we saw, he was fighting off the remaining creatures down the hall," Lorenzo said. "He said he'd come back for us, but he hasn't returned yet."

"Wait here. I'll find him," Dante said, turning to the

Sanguine parents. "And don't even think about running away or making up more of your lies."

"Wouldn't dream of it," Vera muttered as Dante rushed down the corridor.

As soon as he left, Lorenzo cornered me. I held up my dagger in fear. "What are you doing?"

"Telling you the truth now that Dante's gone. Something the king forbid us from," Lorenzo began. "But things are escalating, and you need to know. The king will most likely blame this on us and execute us, so we have nothing left to lose. Surely, you've come to realize that things are not what they seem in the kingdom of V?"

I nodded. "Does this have something to do with those creatures?"

"You know those creatures are us, and it happens if we don't take our medicine," Vera said. "The king's been lying to us, claiming we can live together in peace with your people, but we know we can't."

"And why not?" I asked, my heart pounding. I felt so close to the truth.

Lorenzo sighed. "Because we're too different. Those Dark Half's out there? They're our true form, what we were before the medicine. But you would better understand us as—"

I gasped in horror as a sword swung their way, decapitating Vera and Lorenzo in one swipe.

25
HALF THE TRUTH

The Sanguine twins shrieked, a sound I'd never forget, as I froze in place. I noticed who had swung the killing blow. General Ezra had just murdered two people in front of me. It was nothing like killing those creatures, whatever they were, or seeing the bloody ghosts. This was much, much worse.

"Why did you do that?" Petra screamed through her tears.

General Ezra sheathed his sword. "They were escaped prisoners, and you know the price for disobedience. Besides, they had Olivia cornered. I thought she was in trouble."

"They were only talking to her," Nicolai spat. "They weren't going to hurt her *or* escape!"

The general shrugged, and I wondered how he could act so flippant after killing people. "I didn't know that. I figured it was better to be safe than sorry."

Nicolai fell beside his parents, reaching for their hands. No vial could save them from that. I couldn't bring myself to look at them, the stench of blood making me ill.

Petra held up her sword, aiming it at the general. "I should kill you for this!"

"Put the sword down," Dante said, rounding the corner with his weapon out. "General, I was looking all over for you. Are you all right?"

"I'm fine," the general said, nodding at Dante. "I was down the hall fighting Dark Half's when I heard movement coming from the cells. Thank you for coming to my rescue, Dante."

"He doesn't deserve to be rescued. He murdered our parents!" Nicolai cried, rising to his feet. "Right in front of Olivia, too!"

Dante glanced at me. "Olivia, is this true?"

I couldn't speak, so I just nodded.

"As I said, I thought Olivia was in trouble," the general explained, glancing back at the Sanguine twins. "An honest mistake."

"Really? Or were you just trying to silence what they were going to tell Olivia?" Nicolai asked. "She deserves to know!"

"Watch your accusations, Sanguine," the general spat, "or I'll lock you two up next."

Now I'd never know what they were planning to tell me before the general arrived. Maybe Nicolai was right, that General Ezra had wanted to silence them. I was beginning to think I'd never find out what was so strange about the kingdom of V.

"Any survivors?" Dante asked.

General Ezra shook his head. "None. the creatures killed them all."

"There could've been survivors," Petra muttered, "if you hadn't killed the last two."

"They were most likely responsible for the jailbreak," General Ezra snarled. "Everyone knows your parents were trouble. Now they can't hurt anyone else ever again. Everyone will thank me when they find out what I did."

"If it weren't for Olivia standing right there, I'd kill you myself," Petra snarled. "But I think she's been traumatized enough for one day."

I shuddered, unable to tear my eyes away from the decapitated bodies. Dante gently placed his arm around me. "Come on, Olivia. Let's get you back to the castle."

When a blast of fire erupted down the hallway, the general nodded. "Good idea. With everyone dead, there's no reason to stick around."

Dante guided me down the staircase, keeping one hand on his weapon in case the Sanguine twins tried to kill the general again. We rushed through the smoke and crackling flames before we reached the front door and headed outside.

I watched as the jail collapsed behind us in a heap of burning rubble. The soldiers rushed to the docks to fill their buckets with more water. Corina was still on duty but had moved away from the building to avoid the fire, and I noticed she was clutching her knee as if she were trying to hide something.

"You made it out!" she cried, rushing over to us. "Oh, I'm so relieved. What happened in there? I heard a lot of fighting."

"Everyone's dead, including the creatures," Dante said. "We did all we could."

Petra sneered. "Yeah, right. If you hadn't locked up some of those criminals in the first place, for petty crimes, I might add, they wouldn't have died!"

"That was King Dominic's decision, and you will respect it," General Ezra hissed. "No one could've foreseen this."

Petra and Nicolai hushed, but I could see the wheels turning in their heads. They wanted revenge. A part of me did, too. The general shouldn't have been able to get away with murder, whether or not they were criminals.

"They were only pretending to take the medicine to stage the jailbreak," Corina said. "When I discovered the full vials in their cells...it was too late. The fire had started."

General Ezra shook his head. "This wasn't your fault, Blanchard. You did your duty and made the militia proud."

She nodded, then turned to Dante. "Are you all right?"

"I'm fine, Corina. We both know I'm not easy to kill."

The tone he took with her was light and teasing and almost made me jealous. I saw the way she looked at him. It was more than friendly. I wondered if he knew she had feelings for him.

Corina smiled, but then it faded into a frown. "There's... something I have to tell you. You won't like it."

Dante raised an eyebrow. "What are you talking about?"

Corina lifted her hand from her knee, and I noticed the deep bite wound she tried to hide. "One of the creatures got me. I didn't notice it until I was checking my wounds."

"Anastasia's in the castle," Dante said. "I'm sure she has a vial on her that could stop it from spreading."

Corina shook her head, her hands trembling. "No, it's too late for me, Dante. I won't make it in time to the castle. I...can feel the change happening already. I tried to hold on as long as I could until I knew you were safe."

"Don't say that," Dante said, grabbing her arm. "Come with us to the castle. You know Anastasia can help. She's done it before. I'll stay with you until the medicine kicks in."

Corina's hands shook even harder now, sweat trickling down her forehead. "I'm sorry, Dante, but it's my time. I've run from what I am long enough and now it's caught up with me. You need to stop me before I turn, for good this time."

When she handed her sword to Dante, he shook his head. "No, I won't do it. I can't."

"You have no choice," Corina replied, her voice more urgent now. "I won't become one of those things, not again. It's what we've been trying so hard to avoid all these years."

"She's right, Dante," General Ezra said. "The change is coming. I can see it already. We need to stop it. She has too much of the disease in her bloodstream."

Nicolai sneered. "Always eager to kill, aren't you, General?"

"Shut up, Sanguine," General Ezra huffed. "This is neither the time nor the place."

Dante sighed, glancing at me. "Olivia...turn around."

"Why?" I asked.

"There's no time to explain," he said. "Just know that it's necessary, and I'm sorry you had to see all this tonight."

Corina nodded. "Please turn around, Olivia. And tell your mother I said good luck."

When Dante looked at me, I sighed and turned around. I heard a thud before everything turned silent.

"Don't look," Dante whispered to me. "You've seen enough death tonight."

Corina was dead, too. Just like the twin's parents had tried to warn me, *they* were the creatures. Everyone in the kingdom had the Dark Half inside them which was why the medicine was so valuable. It explained why Dr. Cox rambled on about monsters and evil things. But sometimes, the medicine didn't work, which is why I saw that man die. Maybe this is what the ghosts were trying to warn me about...

"If you'll excuse me, I need to speak with my soldiers," General Ezra said. "We'll get the warden's body recovered for her funeral and the Burning. We need to burn the Sanguines, too."

"What about us?" Petra asked as the general left. "Are you just going to leave us out here after killing our parents?"

"*I* didn't kill your parents," Dante spat. "You can come with us to the castle where it's safe, but you'd both better be on your best behavior."

"Would you have killed their parents?" I asked.

Dante thought for a moment. "Unless they had attacked you...then no, I would not have."

But the general hadn't hesitated. He wanted Petra and Nicolai's parents dead, and them cornering me was just a convenient excuse.

"We should get back to the castle now," Dante said. "The general will take care of everything out here."

Dante kept an arm around me the entire way back, and I was glad. I felt like I would've collapsed without his support. The guard at the front door gave me a funny look, wondering why I was out there again but waved us through.

As I walked through the castle's corridors toward the throne room, I noticed the guard I had punched sitting in a chair. He held a bag of ice to his bruised face and glared at me as I entered. King Dominic, Queen Vivienne, and Christian were muttering, probably about me. Mom, Vanessa, and Russell paced the throne room while looking nervous.

"Olivia!" Mom said when she noticed me. Everyone's heads shot in my direction. "The guard just returned and told us what you did to him. The king was about to send soldiers looking for you. What were you thinking?"

Dante stepped forward, ready to take the blame. "She did it for—"

"For the Sanguine twins," I lied, keeping Dante's name out of it. "I did it to find their parents. I wanted to ask them if they were responsible for poisoning me and blowing things up."

"Were they?" Vanessa asked.

I shook my head. "They said they weren't. I believe them."

"Perhaps you do, but the Sanguine's can't be trusted," Christian said, turning to Petra and Nicolai. "You're lucky the guards let you into our castle. Your family isn't wanted here."

Petra rolled her eyes. "Yeah? Well, we don't want to be here, either. Dante said it was the safest place right now, so here we are."

"Olivia, do you know how worried we were?" Russell asked, sounding a lot like Mom. "You could've gotten killed!"

"But I didn't. Dante and General Ezra were there to protect me," I said. "And the Sanguine twins saved my life, too."

"Truly?" Queen Vivienne asked, looking surprised.

"Is it *that* shocking?" Nicolai asked. "We're not killers. Our parents weren't, either. But your general didn't care about that when he cut off their heads."

"What is he talking about?" King Dominic asked, glancing at me.

The door opened behind us with a loud bang. General

Ezra and several of his soldiers entered the room, walking over to the king. Nicolai and Petra sneered at the general.

"There's the murderer now," Petra snarled. "Why don't you tell them all how you delighted in killing our parents?"

"My goodness," King Dominic said, turning to his brother. "Is that true?"

"Let's talk in private. I'll explain everything," General Ezra said, glancing at the Sanguine twins. "My soldiers will stay here and assure they don't cause trouble."

King Dominic nodded. "Very well. When I return, we need to talk, Olivia."

I gulped as the king, queen, and general disappeared into the next room and closed the door for privacy. Christian turned to me, looking upset. "You lied to me, Olivia. You told me you were going to the bathroom."

"I had to lie. No one was going to let me out," I said. "I'm sorry I hurt your feelings, but I had to do something."

"I thought I could trust you," he muttered, shaking his head. "I guess not."

When he walked to the other side of the throne room, trying to get as far away from me as possible, I sighed. I hadn't meant to hurt him, but I couldn't go back now. The entire room waited in silence for the king to return. As we did, Dante tugged on my shoulder and pulled me aside.

"You didn't tell them you snuck out to find me," he whispered. "Why not?"

I shook my head. "I didn't want the general to punish you again, not when your wounds are still healing. I wasn't about to implicate you after that."

He paused, thinking. "Thank you, Olivia, for breaking out of the castle to find me *and* for covering for me. Those things I said before...it was out of anger. I had no right to say them to you."

I shrugged. "Don't worry about it. As the Sanguine twins said, you would've come looking for me, too."

He gestured at Christian across the room. "I'm grateful, but I wish you hadn't jeopardized your relationship with Christian for me. I know how much he means to you."

I looked him dead in the eyes. "It was worth it."

His mouth twisted upward again, almost revealing a smile.

The door opened and King Dominic, Queen Vivienne, and General Ezra entered. The King was the first to speak. "The general's told me his soldiers have secured the kingdom. All those creatures are dead, and the fire's been put out. I assure you; this will not happen again."

"There's still a lot of clean-up to do, so we ask you to return to your homes and stay there," Queen Vivienne said. "We have a lot of planning to do for the upcoming anniversary."

"That's it, then?" I asked. "General Ezra gets to kill two prisoners and nothing happens to him? You just go on with your holidays?"

"While I made it clear to him that executing two prisoners without my approval was inappropriate," King Dominic said, glaring at General Ezra, "I believe my brother had your best interests at heart. He will not be punished for their deaths."

"Their murders, you mean," Petra said. "That figures. This kingdom has a history of covering up things."

"You're clear to go back to your house now," Christian said, stepping forward with a snarl, "so go."

The Sanguine twins wasted no time leaving. After they

were gone, King Dominic turned to me. "While I don't approve of you rushing into danger, I suppose I can understand your desire for answers. And I presume your mother will discipline you."

Mom nodded. "You're grounded for one week, Olivia. You're lucky it's not more, but you've been through a lot, so I'll take it easy on you."

I groaned. Getting grounded would make it harder to sneak around the castle and find answers. But it's not like there was much else to do around there, no cell phone or TV she could take away from me. That was the one perk in a small kingdom.

Dante gestured at the door. "After you, Olivia."

Christian didn't stop me, and I wondered if he was over me now. Maybe it was for the best, especially when I wasn't entirely sure I could trust him. As we walked home along the brick path, Vanessa turned to me.

"Are you okay?" she whispered.

I nodded. "As fine as I can be after that. Ness...the general didn't kill them because he was afraid they'd hurt me and escape. He killed them to shut them up. They were about to tell me what was wrong with this kingdom."

Vanessa turned silent at that. I didn't want to tell her about the medicine or that the people were the creatures, not with Dante so close behind us, but she knew something disturbing had happened.

When I spotted the Sanguine twins near the jail, watching the soldiers clear the rubble, I realized it was my only chance and turned to Mom. "I know I'm grounded and all, but can I talk to the twins for a second? Just to tell them I'm sorry about their parents?"

Mom sighed. "Fine but make it quick. Dante can escort you and we'll meet you back home."

As they walked away, I headed straight for the Sanguine twins. "Hey. How are you doing?"

Petra sneered. "How do you think?"

"Right. Sorry," I muttered. "Look, what happened back there shouldn't have happened at all. I know it doesn't mean much coming from me, but I'm sorry. I would've warned your parents if I'd seen the general coming."

"Thank you," Petra murmured, much to my surprise. "We know you didn't want them to die."

"Will there be a funeral?"

Nicolai snorted. "Criminals don't get a funeral. They just get cremated. That's the way it goes."

I leaned in, lowering my voice so Dante couldn't hear. "You were there. Your parents were going to tell me something. You know it, too, don't you?"

Nicolai hesitated. "Yes, Olivia. We all know the truth, even Dante and Christian."

"Then what is it? I know you're dying to tell me."

"We'll be really dying if we do," Petra said. "You don't understand, admitting it to your people is punishable by death. King Dominic made us swear an oath of secrecy before you arrived."

"Why? What's so serious that no one can breathe a word of it?"

"We can't tell you," Nicolai said. "Our parents tried and look what happened to them. We won't let that be our fate, not without getting our revenge first."

"But you'll figure it out," Petra said. "You know a lot

already, more than what King Dominic wanted you to. Piece it together."

After they had walked away, Dante tugged on my arm. "Come on, Olivia. We should get back home."

When we returned to Hawthorne Lodge, Mom and Russell were waiting for me in the kitchen. I sighed. "Are you going to lecture me now?"

"No. You know what you did was wrong. We have...something else to discuss," Mom said, glancing at Dante. "Can I have a moment alone with my daughter?"

He nodded. "I'll be upstairs if you need me."

After he left, Mom turned to me. "We're officially declaring the president missing. She should've been here days ago, and it's more than obvious something's wrong. We think Vanessa should know how we feel now."

"Yeah, sounds fair," I said. "Mom...was her husband coming with her?"

Mom thought for a moment. "You know, I think he was. It was never officially confirmed, but I believe Derek took time off to make the trip with his wife. He loves traveling. Why?"

My heart pounded. If it were true, I really *had* seen his ghost.

"Just wondering," I muttered. "I'll tell Vanessa."

"Tell her if there's anything we can do for her, just let us know," Russell said. "We're here for both of you."

After everything that had happened today, I knew one thing for sure. I'd grown tired of half-truths. And grounded or not, I wanted the full story. So I nodded at Russell and Mom, then walked upstairs with a plan for me and Vanessa to get to the bottom of it all for good.

26

THE ISOLATIONISTS

As I passed Dante in the hall, he reached for my arm. "Everything okay?"

"Everything's fine," I lied. "I just want to check on Vanessa."

I could tell he wanted to ask me what I had talked to Mom and Russell about, but he bit his lip and decided against it. I liked Dante, but the only people I trusted in the kingdom were Vanessa, Mom, and Russell, and I vowed to keep things between us. Dante nodded and let me go before I approached her door, knocking three times. I heard the patter of feet inside before the door swung open.

"Oh, hey, Liv," Vanessa said. "What's going on?"

"Can I talk to you?" I asked.

"Sure, come in," she said, moving aside to let me enter. She closed the door behind me. "I wasn't doing much, anyway, just looking out the window for Mom's boat. But with everything going on around here, maybe it's a good thing she's delayed."

"About that," I said, sitting down on her bed. "Can we talk?"

She frowned and joined me. "Of course. You look upset. Is something wrong?"

I nodded. "My mom's officially declaring the president missing. We didn't want to worry you in case her boat was just behind schedule or something, but...my mom has sent out a few letters, and the president never replied. No one has, actually."

She shook her head. "You told me everything would be okay, but I knew something was wrong! What does your mom think happened to her? Was it the kingdom of V?"

"We don't know," I said. "That's the worst part. But... there's something else."

She scoffed. "What now?"

"My mom thinks your dad came with her," I said. "If that's true..."

I left out the part where I had seen her dad's ghost. I didn't think it was best to tell her now, not when she was still processing their disappearance. And I didn't want to say anything until I knew for sure.

"Then they're both in trouble." Vanessa rose to her feet, running a hand through her hair. "So, what? My parents are both out there somewhere, maybe kidnapped, hurt, or dead?"

I sighed. "I'm sorry, Ness. I don't have any answers—"

Vanessa kicked over her easel, sending the painting she was working on across the room. "I hate this damn kingdom, Olivia. I hate everyone in it!"

And then she started crying. I sat there, startled. Vanessa usually acted calm and composed. If anyone was going to have a nervous breakdown, I assumed it would be me. As I stood up to comfort her, a knock sounded on the door.

"Is everything all right?" Dante asked from the other side.

"We're fine," I lied. "Don't worry."

When I heard Dante's footsteps disappear, I turned back to Vanessa as she dried her tears. "Look, I know you miss your mom and want answers. I do, too. And just like when we did the séance, I already have a plan in mind."

She sniffed, looking unconvinced. "Oh, yeah? Like what?"

"Well, there's not much we can do from this kingdom," I said, "but we're not totally helpless. I want to break into the castle and see what kind of information they have, if any."

"Break into the castle?" Vanessa whispered. "That won't be easy."

I nodded. "I know, especially now that we don't live there. It's why I'm thinking we should head there tonight when everyone's asleep. We'll have to be quiet and watch out for the guards on duty."

"If there's a chance we could find something, even a small chance, then we have to do it," Vanessa said. "I'm with you, but what about Dante? There's no way he'd let us out after dark. I'd offer to distract him again, but I'm pretty sure he's onto us after last time."

I smiled. "I have an idea on how to deal with him. Just be ready tonight. But until then, I think I should get you up to speed on what happened in the Solitude..."

I told her everything, from how those creatures we saw, Dark Half's, were actually the residents of the kingdom of V. How the Sanguine parents wanted to tell me something important before General Ezra killed them. I even told Vanessa how King Dominic made them all swear to keep secrets. Vanessa sat there silently, taking it all in.

"Now that I know what they really are, none of the boys here seem as cute anymore," she muttered. "But if those creatures *are* them, then what are the people of V? Shapeshifters? Demons? Something else completely?"

"I don't know," I said, shrugging. "That's what I'm hoping to find out tonight. If they brought us here for another reason...our lives could depend on getting answers."

When we went downstairs for dinner later, Mom pulled me aside. "Did you tell Vanessa what we talked about?"

I nodded. "Yeah, I told her everything, about her dad, too. She took it hard."

"I bet," Mom said, sighing. "Olivia...I have to apologize to you."

I frowned. "What for?"

"I was so desperate to become an ambassador that I didn't take the time to look at the risks. The president was desperate for a new alliance that she didn't stop and think, either," Mom said. "Between Charles Browning's death and all the terrible things that've happened to you...I regret ever coming here and bringing you girls with me. I should've known these people sounded too good to be true..."

"Hey, none of this is your fault," I said. "Vanessa doesn't blame you, either."

"Well, I wouldn't blame her if she did," Mom muttered. "Oh, I wish your father were here. He always had a sixth sense for danger. It's what made him such a good hunter. He'd know what to do..."

I nodded. "Yeah, I could really use his guidance right about now. I hope he's watching over us at least."

As we walked over to the table, Mom hugged Vanessa. "I'm so sorry about your parents, Vanessa. No matter what happens, you'll always have a place with us. We're in this together."

Vanessa gave my mom a sad smile, pulling away. "I appreciate that, Mrs. Hawthorne. There's no one I'd rather be stuck on an island with than you guys."

"I don't know what's going on with your parents, but I promise you one thing," Russell said, "nothing's happening to you three. We're all getting off this island, alive."

He glared at Dante across the room, still mistrustful of him. But as brave and macho as Russell tried to sound, I knew he couldn't help us. Dante couldn't, either. Only one thing could, and that was the truth.

After dinner, we returned to our rooms as Dante took his post in the hallway. I waited until sundown before I pulled out a piece of paper and pen and scribbled down my note, Dante's distraction. I prayed it would work.

Dante,

Meet me in my office at midnight. I need to discuss some security measures with you. If I'm not there right away, wait for me.

Don't worry about Olivia or Vanessa. I'll be sending another guard to cover your shift. Even if you don't see them, it doesn't mean they're

not there. It's important that I speak with
you soon.
    Signed,
    General Ezra

Gruff and straight to the point. Exactly how General Ezra spoke. I used my left hand to disguise my handwriting before I got into bed and waited for a quarter to midnight to arrive. When it did, I got dressed, then looked under the small sliver in my door. Dante's boots were still there.

After I climbed out my window, I waited for Vanessa to climb out hers. She jumped down, dressed in all black like me. I pressed a finger to my lips as I tip-toed around to the front door, then knocked roughly as one of the soldiers would. When I heard footsteps approaching on the other side, I left the note on the porch and rushed to hide in one of the bushes.

Dante opened the door carefully, looking around for a moment before he saw the note. Just when I thought he wouldn't buy it, he looked out into the distance and closed the front door. He locked it with his key before he walked past us and disappeared.

"It worked," Vanessa whispered. "Why'd we have to do all that again?"

"In case Dante walked in on us and realized we weren't there," I whispered. "We had to get him out of the way completely. I've bought us more time by luring him to the militia building. When he realizes the general's not coming, it'll be too late."

She grinned. "You're an evil genius, Liv."

"I'm taking that as a compliment. Now, come on, before we run out of time."

We avoided the patrolling guards in the kingdom by taking the long way around and hiding behind bushes and trees. Once we had made it to the castle, we climbed in through one of the windows, carefully avoiding the guard hotspots. We waited a few minutes until we heard nothing except for the snores of the royal family.

"Let's move," I whispered, gesturing for Vanessa to follow me.

"Where are we going?" she whispered back.

"Each member of the royal family has an office," I told her. "The general has his in the militia building where we saw him beating Dante."

Vanessa shuddered. "Don't remind me. I hope he doesn't do that to us if he catches us..."

"He won't. We'll be out of here soon," I said. "Anyway, let's check out the offices of the royal family. They have to have information in there."

As I took Vanessa down the hallway of offices, she glanced at me. "Which one first?"

"Let's start with Christian's," I replied. "The ghosts have been telling me he can't be trusted. Maybe we'll finally find the answer tonight."

As we entered the room that read PRINCE CHRIST-IAN, HEIR TO THE KINGDOM OF V, a small wooden desk, a chair, and books greeted us. Nothing looked out of the ordinary.

"I've never seen him come in here," Vanessa whispered. "I don't think he uses his office."

"You're probably right. He spends more time in the

library," I said, wiping dust off the desk. "Let's look around anyway."

As Vanessa checked the trash can, I opened the drawer and found a key. Vanessa noticed and looked up. "Well, I found nothing. What's that?"

"It says library on it," I told her, slipping it in my pocket. "I think I'll keep this. I want to sneak into the library, but it's too much for one night. Dante could realize the set-up any minute."

"Why the library?"

"There's a closed-off section that's been bothering me," I said. "Christian's been telling me it'll re-open soon, but it never does. He was really upset when I tried to get to it."

"Suspicious," Vanessa whispered, "but then again, everything is in this kingdom. I think we're done in here."

I nodded, opening the door a crack. When I heard no one out in the hallway, I took Vanessa to the closest office next, King Dominic's. His was the largest with a bigger table and several chairs for meetings. I searched through the drawers again as Vanessa examined the trash can. After a few minutes, I had turned up nothing but boring paperwork.

I sighed. "If there's information about the Dark Half's, I don't think it's in these offices. Maybe coming out tonight was a mistake. We should've gone to the library instead..."

"Hang on," Vanessa whispered, pulling paper out of the trash. "I think I found something, and you're not going to like this."

As I walked over, Vanessa handed the papers to me. I gasped as I searched through it, realizing these were all of Mom's letters she had written to the president and our government. No wonder we hadn't heard back from anyone. The crows hadn't left with them.

"Russell was right," I muttered. "He suggested our letters might not be getting out. I thought he was just paranoid, but...it looks like they *were* intercepted."

"And put in King Dominic's trash instead," Vanessa muttered. "Why?"

"He's trying to keep us here, trying to stop us from contacting the outside world," I said, putting the letters back in the trash. "I'm surprised. I assumed if anyone was out to get us, it would've been the general. He hates me."

"I just hope King Dominic hasn't done anything to my parents," Vanessa muttered, balling her fists. "What now?"

"Leave everything the way it is," I said. "He can't know we found out. Let's check out Queen Vivienne's office and get the hell out of this castle."

After we snuck out of King Dominic's office, we tip-toed toward Queen Vivienne's. Hers was the cleanest and had more decorations scattered around the room. Vanessa and I tried to hurry things along, knowing time was ticking and Dante would return to our house soon.

But as I opened one of her drawers, I found something much more incriminating than the trashed letters.

"Queen Vivienne's been sending us all those threatening notes," I said, and Vanessa's head cocked up. "See for yourself."

Vanessa read through the crumpled threatening notes the Queen had abandoned, her eyes wide. "So, she was the one who sent that letter to the embassy. She's been trying to scare us off! Do you think she's also responsible for the poison and explosions?"

"No idea. King Dominic doesn't want us to leave, but his wife doesn't want us to stay," I muttered. "Just great."

"Think they're working together?" Vanessa asked, slipping the letters back into the drawer.

"Hard to say," I said, looking in another drawer. "Look, she was planning to write another one. This letter's half-finished."

Vanessa shuddered. "Can we get out of here now, Liv? I know we came here looking for info on the Dark Half's, but it's clear we're not finding anything. Besides, this is creeping me out."

I nodded, reaching for the door. "Yeah, we should get going before one of the guards—"

As I opened the door, I nearly crashed into Queen Vivienne herself. We froze as she glared at us, and I looked down and realized she was carrying a pen. "What are you two doing here? And at this hour?"

I had no excuse, so I had no choice but to use her information against her. "I think the better question is, why are you sending us threatening letters?"

She hesitated. "I...don't know what you're talking about. How dare you accuse the queen of V of such a thing!"

"Drop the innocent act," Vanessa said. "We found your letters. One of them was half-finished."

"And you're carrying a pen. I bet you were going to finish that one you just started," I said. "Start talking or I'll go straight to my mother."

She sighed. "You must understand that we mean you no harm. We've only been sending letters to scare you. We haven't set the explosions or poisoned you, nor would we ever. We are non-violent."

"Who's we?" I asked.

"The Isolationists," she said. "I am their leader, and we have a handful of members from all walks of life here, chefs, teachers, and so on. Not everyone believes as the king does. That we should ally with the outside world. I believe very strongly that our people are incompatible with yours."

"Why?" Vanessa asked.

She hesitated. "I shouldn't say. All you need to know is that it would be safer if we kept a distance, a very far distance."

"Is it because all your people are really Dark Half creatures?" I asked. "Just like the ones who attacked the Solitude?"

Her mouth opened in shock. "How did you—"

"Answer the question."

She nodded. "Yes, that's exactly why. It's the secret King Dominic made us keep from your people so you wouldn't fear us. He believes we can overcome the beast inside of us and connect with humanity again, which is why we take that medicine. But as you've seen, it has...deadly side effects sometimes. If you knew our history, you'd agree with me. The Isolationists do."

"How did you become these creatures?" Vanessa asked. "It sounds impossible!"

"I...shouldn't say. If the King knew we were talking, I'd be in trouble," she replied. "He was very clear that no one was allowed to tell you any of this. You can't tell him what I've been doing, nor my son or General Ezra."

"We'll keep your secret," I said. "If you answer a few more questions. Are you sure you're not behind any of the other things going on around here?"

She shook her head. "No, as I said, the Isolationists are non-violent. We resort to threats, not murder. It's why I was so adamant that the poison and the threatening notes weren't connected. I knew they weren't because we only sent the letters."

"Then someone else is behind it," I said. "Any idea who?"

"If I did, I'd report them to General Ezra. I even had some of my Isolationists look into the matter, but none of them have seen anything suspicious, either. Odd."

"Could it be the people who held Olivia captive?" Vanessa asked. "Instinct, or whatever they were called?"

Queen Vivienne shrugged. "It could be. They're dangerous, bloodthirsty. You're lucky you escaped, Olivia."

"I was lucky the general found me and scared them off. But Instinct mentioned they had a boss," I said. "That boss could be behind all this. But in the meantime, stop sending these threatening letters, Queen Vivienne. Your message has gotten through to us."

Vanessa nodded. "Yeah, we'd leave this second if we still had our boat. Trust me."

"When your president arrives, I suggest you do," Queen Vivienne said. "It's for your own protection. King Dominic is willing to risk your lives to connect with the outside world, but I'm not. I meant what I wrote in my letters, stay away from us. You'll only get hurt, more than you already have."

"One last thing," I said. "King Dominic prevented our letters from getting out. Did you know about that?"

She looked surprised. "No, I didn't. Why would he do that?"

I shrugged. "That's what we want to know. You're closer

to him than anyone else. Do you think he's responsible for all this?"

"I'd like to think not. He truly wanted to open a dialogue with your people and venture beyond our kingdom again," Queen Vivienne said. "But I can't be sure of anything. It seems I'm not the only one hiding something. You're lucky I caught you snooping around tonight and not the general but watch yourselves. I haven't been sending you all those warning letters to let you get killed now."

27
THE RESTRICTED SECTION

After we said goodbye to Queen Vivienne, and we both promised we wouldn't tell anyone we'd seen each other tonight, Vanessa and I tip-toed back to Hawthorne Lodge. We glanced at the front porch, but I didn't see anyone, Dante or otherwise.

"Doesn't look like Dante's back yet," Vanessa whispered. "Do you think Queen Vivienne was lying? That maybe she *is* responsible for everything around here?"

"She could be," I said, "but I don't think she was lying about the king and Christian not knowing her plans. She seemed really scared about what the king would do if he found out."

"Yeah, you're right," Vanessa said, sighing. "It's hard to know who to trust. I miss our old life back in Washington..."

We climbed in through the windows again in case Dante had come home. As I peeked underneath my door, I didn't see his boots. My note had worked.

After I had changed into my pajamas and gotten into bed,

I heard the front door to the house creak open and footsteps in the hallway. I reached for my Slayer and swung the door open in case it was an intruder. I lowered the dagger when I realized it was just Dante, and he looked surprised to see me so late.

"Was that you making that noise?" I asked, trying to look like I'd just woken up.

Dante nodded. "Did I startle you?"

"A little. Why were you moving around?"

"I had to leave my post," Dante said. "General Ezra left a note on your porch. He said he had something important to talk about in his office and left another guard on duty. When I got there, he never showed up."

"Strange," I said, tucking my dagger underneath my bed. "What do you think happened to him?"

"I'll ask him about it tomorrow. Perhaps he was too busy and couldn't make it," Dante said, "or perhaps this is another trick from the saboteur to lure me away. Did anything happen while I was gone?"

Oh, we just found out the king's intercepted our letters and Queen Vivienne's writing threatening notes. No big deal.

I shook my head. "I didn't hear anything, except for you. It's why I pulled out my dagger."

"Smart," Dante said. "But come on, let's ensure everyone else is safe."

When we headed to Vanessa's room, I held my breath and hoped she was in bed. As Dante opened the door, the light was off, and Vanessa was snoring a little too loud. I sighed in relief. After we checked on Mom and Russell, both actually snoring, I felt relieved nothing had happened. After all, we'd driven our guard away and sneaked out. The saboteur could've been watching, and could've hurt Mom and Russell while we were gone.

Dante had been right. I really could be careless at times.

He nodded as we returned to the hallway. "Good, they're all fine. I didn't see evidence of anyone, but we can't be too careful. Next time, if the general wants to speak with me, he'll have to come here. I won't leave my post again."

I only nodded, said goodnight, and returned to bed, relieved Dante didn't suspect me and Vanessa. But as I climbed under the covers, I felt that familiar dark energy and glanced around the room. The ghost of Charles Browning and the other spirits appeared, still as transparent and terrifying as always.

"You've done well," Charles said, floating over to me. "All the information you learned tonight and during the Solitude fire was valuable."

"You knew the people of V were these creatures, didn't you?" I whispered, sitting up in bed. I didn't want Dante to hear me.

Charles nodded while the others said nothing. "I knew right before they killed me. Only then did I realize what a terrible mistake I had made in coming here. By then, it was too late for me, and too late to warn the world."

"Why couldn't you just tell me that in the first place?"

"There are limitations to being a spirit. The laws of interference prevent us from saying too much," he said. "But you're close, closer than you've been before. Keep fighting for the truth. The fate of your people depends on it."

My eyes flitted to Derek, Vanessa's father. He was still

silent and bloody. "My mom told me the president's husband came with her. He's really dead, isn't he?"

Charles nodded. The rest of the ghosts swayed behind him, silent.

I sighed. "What about the Sanguine parents, Vera and Lorenzo? Why aren't they ghosts?"

"They can't be," Charles replied. "They are not human. Only mortals killed by the people of V become ghosts, forever trapped in the place they died. They cannot crossover into the next life."

"I see," I muttered. "And there's no way to free them?"

"There is. You will have to discover how on your own."

I groaned. "Isn't there anything you can tell me? Any advice at all?"

"Some of your people are already lost," Charles said, "but others can still be saved. Hurry, Olivia, you're running out of time. The end draws near."

"What end? And what do you mean, others can still be saved?" I asked, rising to my feet. "If someone's in danger, you have to tell me!"

But Charles and the other ghosts vanished. I hated all the secrecy and doubletalk. As I laid back down, I thought about what Charles had said. *Others can still be saved.* What did that mean? And how did it relate to Derek's death?

For once, I didn't fear the ghosts anymore. I feared whoever was behind all this wouldn't stop.

When morning came, I joined Vanessa, Mom, and Russell at the breakfast table. Vanessa glanced at me, worried about the things we discovered last night, but we didn't breathe a word of it in front of Dante. When a knock sounded at the door, Dante answered and spoke with the soldier before walking over to us.

"The king's giving another speech," Dante said, "and it sounds important. Whenever you're finished, we should get going."

I downed the rest of my fruit salad and oatmeal, a new meal the chefs had learned. Then I followed Dante over to the castle. Now I finally knew why the people loved raw meat so much. They were animals, no different from wolves. As we waited for King Dominic to come onstage, I spotted General Ezra and his soldiers patrolling the crowd.

"There he is," Dante muttered. "Come with me, Olivia. Russell, guard the Ambassador and Vanessa."

"Where are you going?" Mom asked.

"To ask the general a few questions," Dante said, reaching for my arm. "We'll be right back."

"Going to ask him about last night?" I asked as we pushed through the crowd.

Dante nodded. "Yes, and I figured you'd like to know, too. You didn't tell your mother about the note last night, did you?"

Of course, I hadn't. I knew it wasn't serious. But Dante didn't know that, so I shook my head. "I didn't want to worry her. She has enough on her plate. Besides, I'm sure you and the general will get to the bottom of it."

When we reached General Ezra, he looked at me and then at Dante. "Good to see you, soldier. Is there something I can do for you?"

Dante handed the note to the general. "You tell me. Someone knocked on the door to Hawthorne Lodge last night and left this for me. Was it you?"

The general read it over and frowned. "I didn't send this. If I wanted to talk to you about something important, I'd come get you myself. Do you recognize the handwriting?"

"No," Dante said. "I wasn't sure if it was your handwriting or not, but it certainly doesn't look familiar. I waited around your office for half an hour before I decided to return to my post. I assumed you were busy, but now I see why you didn't show."

Good thing I had used my left hand instead of my dominant one. I felt bad for lying to Dante and the king, but then I remembered they had hidden things from me, too. It was only fair.

"The fact that you didn't send this confirms what I suspected," Dante continued. "Someone was trying to lure me out of that house. Fortunately, no one got hurt and nothing inside the home looked disturbed. I won't let myself get drawn away so easily next time. In fact, I think I might have to step up security."

I cursed in my head. With Dante breathing down my neck even harder, it was going to be a lot more difficult to sneak around the kingdom.

"Good. Let me know if you see anything out of the ordinary, even a shrub blowing in the wind," General Ezra said. "I'll inform the king after his speech. He can decide if this is worth more reprimands or not."

"Any idea what his speech will be about?" I asked.

"It doesn't concern you," General Ezra said before he turned to Dante. "Next time, don't leave your post. We'll communicate all our messages in-person to ensure something like this doesn't happen again. And as for you, Olivia...try to stay out of trouble."

After he had left, Dante glanced at me. "I'm sorry we didn't get the answers we were looking for. I imagine you're upset."

"Very," I lied. "Who knows what else the saboteur's planning?"

"After the king's speech, we should get back to training," Dante said. "It's been too long."

I shook my head. "I'm grounded, remember? I don't think my mom wants me going anywhere right now besides school and my room."

"Then I'll convince her to let you out for this," Dante said. "It could be a matter of life and death."

When we rejoined the others, Vanessa gave me a quizzical look. She couldn't ask questions because King Dominic walked up to the podium. Queen Vivienne and Christian were by his side again and I had to stifle a laugh. For a king so concerned about security, he had no idea that his wife was leading the Isolationists.

While Queen Vivienne stared at me from the stage, Christian barely looked my way. So much for our second date. But if he wanted to be that way, fine. I had bigger things to worry about.

When General Ezra joined King Dominic on stage, he nodded and began his speech. "Thank you all for joining me today. I'm sure everyone is curious about what'll happen to the Solitude now. Rest assured, we're already building another jail and allocating a temporary one in the meantime."

For what? I wanted to ask. All of the prisoners were dead. By killing the Sanguine parents, the general had erased the need for one. Did they anticipate more criminals? I spotted the twins in the crowd, shooting glares at the general. They hated him, and I wondered what they'd do in retaliation. I was just relieved they were leaving me and Vanessa alone for a change.

"We will tolerate no criminal activities. I'd also like to remind everyone that avoiding your medicine is an offense, one with serious consequences," King Dominic continued. "As for our holiday this evening to celebrate the kingdom's anniversary, set-up has already begun. As such, all stores and buildings will be closed. I intend to have more guards present tonight to ensure everything runs smoothly. Thank you for listening, and I hope you all have a fun evening."

After the speech had ended and the crowd thinned out, Dante turned to Mom. "Ambassador, I'd like to train Olivia today with your permission."

"I was clear that Olivia is grounded," Mom said. "She punched that poor guard in the face!"

"I know what she did was wrong, but think about it," Vanessa said. "She's bound to go stir crazy. Isn't that right, Liv?"

I nodded. "Yeah, a girl needs fresh air from time to time."

"And I'll ensure she doesn't get into trouble," Dante added. "I wouldn't have asked you if it wasn't important, Ambassador."

Mom sighed. "All right, you're free, but stay close to Dante and keep out of trouble. Consider your grounding postponed."

"Thanks. You won't regret it," I said, turning to Vanessa. "Can I talk to you? In private?"

"Sure," Vanessa said, looking worried.

"Stay where I can see you," Dante said.

I nodded and pulled Vanessa out of earshot. "Dante's

training me, but then I'm breaking into the library. With it closed down for the holiday, it's my only chance to get inside that restricted area. We might not be able to sneak out again."

"And I'm guessing you need my help?" Vanessa asked.

I nodded. "Here's what I need you to do…"

After I told her my plan, we went our separate ways. I followed Dante to the militia building where I noticed General Ezra training more kids. They stuck to their side of the barracks as I sparred with Dante.

"Why's the general training those kids again?" I asked.

"That's a new program. The general told me this morning he's trying to teach them obedience and discipline," Dante said, dodging my strikes. "The king was afraid of exposing them to fighting at such a young age, but the general insisted. He can be very convincing when he wants to be."

After we finished and I showered and changed, I found Dante again. "Can we stop by the library before going home? I want to check out a book."

He shook his head. "Everything's closed today, remember? It's a holiday. The library would be locked down tight."

I held up the stolen key, prepared to lie my ass off. "Christian gave me a library key a while back. He said I could go to the library anytime I want, even during a holiday. Come on, Dante, I'm sure he wouldn't mind. Being in that house without something to read gets boring."

Dante sighed. "All right, but let's make it quick. General Ezra might not approve if he sees you out and about."

The first part of my plan had worked. As we walked to the library, I looked over my shoulder to make sure no one was watching before I used the key to open the door. After we had entered, I locked it behind us and looked around.

"Hello?" I asked. "Anyone here?"

Silence. Phase two was another success. Now I just needed to get Dante away. Vanessa should arrive any second for that. When I heard the knock on the door as I browsed the shelves, I almost smiled.

"Is anyone in there?" Vanessa called out from the other side. "We need help!"

Dante swung the door open immediately. "Vanessa, what's wrong? Where's the Ambassador and Russell?"

"They're fine. I saw you two come this way," she said. "A fight broke out in the garden behind the castle."

"A fight? Between who?" Dante asked, concerned.

Vanessa shrugged. "No idea, but it's bad. You need to break it up!"

Dante turned to me. "Come with me, Olivia."

I shook my head. "I haven't even found a book yet. You go. I'll stay."

Dante frowned. "You know how I feel about leaving you alone, especially after last night. I'd feel better if you came with me."

"Dante, no one knows I'm here," I said. "I'll lock the door when you leave. Really, I'll be fine."

Vanessa nodded. "Everyone's gone home to get ready for the celebration tonight. I'm sure she'll be okay."

Dante sighed. "Fine, but stay put, Olivia. We'll be back in a few minutes."

After they had left, with Vanessa giving me a small smile, I closed and locked the door. We'd just gotten away with another lie. As for Mom and Russell, Vanessa had left them at home and snuck out, following my plan to the letter. I knew

Dante would realize there was no fight soon, so I had to move fast.

I wasted no time as I rushed toward the restricted section. It was still boarded, so I removed the wood and moved past it. One book immediately grabbed my attention, one on supernatural creatures. As I flipped through, a picture of a vampire jumped out at me. Someone had dog-eared the page.

"Vampires are immortal creatures that survive on flesh and blood," it read. "Their weaknesses include silver and sunlight. Most people doubt their existence, but some ancient textbooks insist they're real, and as old as time itself. There's even said to be a vampire-hunting organization hidden somewhere in Europe."

After I put the book down, I had an odd feeling, one that was dark and heavy. I looked over my shoulder, but no one was there. I brushed it aside and finally found the book I was looking for, one on ancient Bloodspeak. I flipped through the pages, holding up my dagger to translate it.

It had thirteen letters on the dagger, and it took me a few minutes to find all the symbols and decode them. Once I did, I gasped. My dagger spelled out VAMPIRE KILLER in ancient Bloodspeak.

I stepped back, almost dropping the book. Why had Dante trained me with a vampire-killing weapon? Why had it burned Alma's skin like acid? They couldn't have been vampires. It made no sense. I wasn't sure what those Dark Half creatures were, but they were nothing like the vampires I'd seen in movies.

But the kingdom of V…could vampires be what it really stood for?

Besides the dagger, there was one other place I had seen

ancient Bloodspeak symbols, the crypts. I knew I had to get down there again somehow and decode it. I stashed the book in my pocket and hoped no one would notice it had gone missing.

"What are you doing, Olivia?" a familiar voice asked behind me. "You know you're not supposed to be in the restricted area."

28

THE V WORD

When I whipped my head around, Christian was standing there. His eyes roamed from me to the opened restricted section and the key in my hand. He didn't seem to notice the small Bloodspeak dictionary in my back pocket that I had stolen, and I felt relieved. I'd need it to read what was on the wall in the crypts.

"Christian," I said, clutching my heart. "You scared me. What are you doing here? The library's supposed to be closed for the holiday."

He held up a book in his hand. "I needed a textbook. I figured I'd get some reading done before the celebration tonight. What are *you* doing here?"

"Same reason," I said, trying to sound calm. "Just needed a book."

He motioned toward the boards I had destroyed. "In the restricted section, which you know is off-limits?"

"I...found it open," I lied. "Someone must've left it like this. I thought it was open again."

He paused. "Does Dante know you're here?"

I nodded. "I convinced him to take me. I didn't think I'd get in trouble. I only wanted to look for a quick book before heading home."

He looked down at the key in my hand. "Where did you find that?"

"Found it on the ground outside," I lied again, hoping it sounded believable. "I was planning to turn it in after leaving the library."

"That's funny," he said, stepping forward, "because a library key of mine went missing in my office. It's a good thing I had a spare or I wouldn't have been able to get into the library today."

"Good thing," I agreed. "Maybe someone borrowed it and forgot to return it or something."

"And you just happened to find it. Lucky," Christian muttered. "So, did you find something that caught your eye?"

"Uh, no," I lied. "I just got here."

Christian shook his head. "Olivia, I think we both know that's not true."

"Christian, I really didn't—"

"And now you're going to lie to me about it? That hurts my feelings, Olivia," he said. "I think you did read the books in there. I also think you found out something you didn't want to. Isn't that right?"

"I—"

"I think you've found out a lot about this kingdom over the past week," he said, cornering me. "You're as beautiful as you are intelligent, Olivia. That's what I keep telling my father. It's why he wants you confined to your house so bad. It's partly to keep you protected...but also to keep you in the dark."

The king was onto me. He knew I was getting close to the truth. Here I thought he cared about my safety, when really, he was just trying to stop me. I should've known, and I should've been more careful.

"You said you convinced Dante to take you here, right?" he continued.

I nodded. "That's right."

"Then where is he now? It's not like him to abandon you," he said. "He takes his job, and you, very seriously. If I didn't know better, I'd say you planned something to get him out of the way."

"That's not true," I said, darting around him. "I have to go now, Christian. I'll see you at the party tonight."

When he grabbed my arm, I realized just how strong he was. "You're not going anywhere, Olivia. Not until you tell me what you know. You must have some theories by now. What do you think we are?"

I sighed, wanting to get out of there as soon as possible, so I looked back at him. "I know you're those Dark Half's, that you can transform into them. The Sanguine parents told me that. They were trying to tell me more before the general killed them."

He raised an eyebrow. "And I bet that's why you came to the library, isn't it? To find out the truth?"

I nodded.

"Then I'll ask you again," he said. "What do you think we are?"

Everything fell into place. The eating of raw meat, their love of hunting, what that crazy look in Dante's eyes meant when he saw my blood. He wanted to drink from me. The general punished him for that moment of weakness. It even explained why the ghosts had bloody necks.

"V...for vampire," I whispered. "You're vampires, all of you. Your last name, Alucard...it's Dracula spelled backward."

He released me. "I knew you'd figure it out eventually. My father thought it would be funny to change our last name to Alucard, that it would be poetic."

"You've been lying to us since we arrived," I sneered, "lying to *me*. You made me feel bad for lying to you when I snuck out of the castle, but you had your own secrets! Do you have any idea how stupid I feel right now?"

He shook his head. "I didn't mean to hurt you. I was trying to protect you, and your family. I *do* care about you, Olivia. Both General Ezra and Dante thought it was a mistake for me to fall for you. They feared I'd hurt you, but I couldn't stop."

"Yeah, right," I said, scoffing. "Were you ever going to tell us the truth?"

"Eventually. My father didn't want to tell you too soon and scare you away," Christian replied. "We thought it was in your best interests if you didn't know for a little while. He hoped one day we'd move past our animal instincts and reintegrate into society. But now, someone's sabotaging all our plans."

"How do the Dark Half's fit into all this?" I asked. "They don't look like your typical vampires."

"Real life is different from fiction. Dark Half's are a vampire's true form. It's what we turn into," Christian explained. "We take Anastasia's medicine to keep it at bay and look like humans. But if we stop taking it, it can wear off.

Some of our bodies reject it completely. It's a very complicated science."

"Warden Blanchard was bitten by one of those Dark
Half's," I said. "She asked Dante to kill her. Why couldn't she
have taken Anastasia's vials again?"

"The vials only stop us from reverting to our true form.
They can't protect us from getting bitten again," Christian
replied. "We just want to be normal, to feel like our old selves
again. Tell me, have you ever heard of the Scourge from
history?"

I shook my head.

"The Scourge spread through Europe in the early 1800s.
Everyone thought it was a plague, but it was a vampire
disease," Christian said. "It spread from contaminated bats to
humans, and soon, it had turned many people into those
Dark Half's. My father was a doctor, and his assistant, Oscar
Cox, worked on a vaccine after my uncle, General Ezra,
contracted the disease."

"The king was a doctor?"

Christian nodded. "Yes, but he doesn't practice anymore.
He says it brings back too many painful memories, that there
were so many people he couldn't save. He cured my uncle,
but apparently, my grandparents died of it."

"Then what happened?"

"They eventually found a vaccine. It's what Anastasia
uses in those vials, but not before Dr. Cox fell ill. After my
father cured him, Oscar went a little insane and hasn't been
the same," Christian said. "Once all the people were cured,
some still wanted to kill humans. My father decided they
needed a leader, someone to keep them in check, so he
became a vampire willingly and brought them here, far away

from humans. But a private island wasn't appealing to some of them."

"What do you mean?"

"Some vampires didn't come with us. They wanted freedom," Christian said. "Some stayed behind in Europe. Apparently, they've killed and drunk blood. They call themselves Instinct. They believe it's in our nature to kill, like the people who live below the forest. We don't know if they're working with the outsiders or where they are now. But we've heard rumors of a vampire hunting organization in Europe, so maybe they've eradicated them all. Maybe the people living below the forest just share a common name."

"What about you? How do you fit into all this?"

"I wasn't born until a century later to two vampires, Queen Vivienne and King Dominic. Vampires born and not turned are much stronger, faster, and smarter," he said. "As for my mother, she had the virus back in the 1800s, too. After my father cured her, he thought she was the most beautiful woman he'd ever seen. They got married shortly after and built this kingdom for vampires. It's why people here worship my father. Dante has the same story. My father saved his life from the virus, and he's been loyal to him ever since."

"Then you're all a lot older than you claim to be. Why did your father ask us to come here? To kill us?"

"No," Christian said, stepping closer. "My father truly wants us to be allies. He doesn't want to see any of you hurt, and he's angry someone keeps trying to sabotage our alliance. Even I doubted how safe it'd be making contact with the outside world again...but you've changed my mind. I realize now just how much we've been missing out for fear of destroying the world."

I crossed my arms. "What really happened to Charles Browning?"

"Well, my father was still the king at the time. Vampires are immortal," Christian said. "It was before I was born, but I know it was General Ezra who killed him, my uncle. He thought Charles Browning was coming to kill us all. He thought he was a vampire hunter, and had his soldiers drink from him. My father punished him for that and locked the kingdom down tight, ensuring no one else would get hurt, but what's done was done."

I knew General Ezra was a killer. He had decapitated the Sanguine twins' parents without blinking. Little did I know he had murdered Charles Browning, too.

"You know I can see ghosts," I said. "They warned me about you. Why?"

Christian nodded. "I already explained I'm a born vampire and not a turned one. My increased strength makes some fear me, which is why Dante wanted me to stay away from you. He cares for you a great deal, you know."

I tried not to blush. "Did you know the ghosts I've been seeing are ones that were killed recently? Ones with bloody necks?"

Christian frowned. "That's impossible. No one here has killed anyone on the outside recently since we've been cut-off for a century. We eat raw animal meat instead of drinking human blood. It's not as nutritious, but it's better than murder."

"Charles Browning wouldn't lie to me. His said their deaths were recent," I said. "And I know what I saw. The president's husband was one of the ghostly victims. He was coming with her to the kingdom, but they've gone missing. Suspicious, isn't it?"

"That's concerning. I'll speak to my father and the general about it," Christian said, pulling something out of his pocket. "But there's still the issue of what to do with you."

I took a step back, afraid. "What are you talking about?"

"My father made it clear. None of us were allowed to admit what we are," Christian said, and I realized he was holding a syringe. "You figured out the truth earlier than you were supposed to, and I told you more than I should have. This won't end well for either of us. The general will make sure of it. My uncle loves punishing people."

I shook my head. "I'll keep quiet. I won't tell anyone."

"I wish I could believe that, but you could let something slip. I care about you too much to watch you get punished by the general," Christian said. "It's why I had Anastasia create a memory loss concoction for me. I carried it around in a syringe in case you learned the truth. It was my failsafe, just in case."

"No, please," I cried. "I don't want to lose my memory. I've come too far!"

"Relax, Olivia. It won't hurt," Christian said. "It'll only erase your memory of the past few days, not your memories of your past or loved ones. We can start over. Go on a second date. When my father thinks my people are ready to tell the world the truth, you'll find out with everyone else, when you're supposed to."

As Christian lifted the vial, I realized I couldn't convince him to spare my memories. He had his mind made up. I sprinted toward the door, praying Dante would return and rescue me, but no one came. Christian darted forward, faster than I'd ever seen him move before, and blocked the exit. It was clear he had hidden his improved strength and speed all this time.

"Don't try to fight it," he said. "This is for the best. I'm sorry, Olivia, but I'm only trying to protect you."

When he grabbed me, I squirmed against him, but he was too strong. "You don't lie to and trick the people you care about. My mother was right. We should've never come here. I wish I'd never met you and your people."

He looked hurt, but then he sighed. "Forgive me, Olivia."

And then he stabbed the syringe into my arm. I thought I saw the familiar energy of ghosts in the room, but then my vision faded to black.

———

When I woke up, I was lying on the floor of the library. Three blurry faces hovered above me before everything came into focus. Dante, Vanessa, and Christian looked down at me with concern.

"She's waking up!" Vanessa cried. "Liv, can you hear me? Are you all right?"

I nodded, sitting up. "I think so."

"What happened?" Dante asked, turning to Christian.

"I came into the library to grab a book and found her unconscious," Christian lied. "I think she hit her head badly. Olivia, do you remember anything?"

As I looked at him, I realized I did. I remembered everything he had told me about the kingdom's history, why they needed the medicine, and what the Bloodspeak translation was. Most of all, I remembered they were vampires.

But how was that possible? Anastasia's vials had worked all those other times. I shouldn't have remembered. Christian seemed convinced I wouldn't.

"No," I lied, trying my best to sound convincing. "I... don't really remember much of anything from the past few days."

Christian looked relieved as he helped me up. "Well, I'm just glad you're all right. I was worried."

It took all I had not to recoil. I wanted to warn Vanessa, but I thought it would be better if she didn't know the terrible truth. Maybe I was just as bad as Christian for trying to protect her.

"I knew I shouldn't have left you alone. By the time Vanessa and I got to the garden, the two fighting had left," Dante said. "I bet the saboteur was behind this. If I would've been here, I could've prevented this!"

"Yes, perhaps you could've," Christian spat. "You're lucky she didn't die, Dante. Her death would've been on your conscience."

Dante said nothing but avoided my eyes. He already felt guilty, and Christian was only making him feel worse, over something he caused. I glanced at the restricted section, noticing Christian had put the boards back up. He was trying to cover his tracks.

"Should we take her to the clinic?" Vanessa asked.

"No," Christian said, quickly. "Just take her home and let her rest. I'm sure her memory will return soon. I'll see you tonight at the party, Olivia. Vanessa can fill you in on what's been happening around here."

After he kissed my cheek and left, Dante sighed and reached for me. "Let's get you back to Hawthorne Lodge."

As we left the library, I felt my back pocket. The dictionary was still there. Christian hadn't found it. It meant I didn't have to break into the library again and steal it. Only one question remained. How was I going to sneak away long enough to get into the crypts and read the writing on the wall?

When we returned home, Mom and Russell looked worried after Dante explained what happened. Mom sighed. "I knew I should've told you to stay home. This saboteur has put you through so much, Olivia. I feel so helpless to stop them..."

Mom was right. The kingdom *had* put me through a lot. From the kid stabbing me on the first day to the ghosts and poison, it was nothing but trouble. But I wasn't about to stand by as more people got hurt. All I needed was a plan to expose the lies.

"Head up to bed," Russell said. "If you're still sleeping later, we'll wake you for the party. I intend to be watching very carefully tonight."

"As will I," Dante said, and Russell looked like he didn't believe him. "Come on, Olivia."

Dante helped me upstairs and tucked me into bed. I put my dagger underneath my pillow, keeping it close in case Christian returned. No wonder he seemed so strong. He had pure vampire blood.

Vanessa looked like she wanted to stay and talk to me, but Dante insisted I needed rest and forced her out of the room. When I was alone, that familiar chill spread through the room. I craned my neck and noticed Charles Browning and the other ghosts.

"Now you know the truth," Charles said, "even if the prince wanted you to forget. We couldn't let that happen."

"Wait a second," I said, sitting up in bed. "Did you save my memory?"

Charles nodded. "Prince Christian tried to cheat. You figured out the truth fairly. As you know, ghosts have many restrictions on interference. We aren't allowed to tell you too much in the form of new information, but we could preserve what you already knew."

"That's why I felt your presence before I passed out," I said. "How did you do it?"

"It wasn't easy," Charles said, "but the spirits and I combined our energy to form a mental block in your mind that prevented the memory loss. It took a lot of power, so do try to avoid it again. We might not be able to do it twice."

"Thank you. I won't forget what you did for me, don't mind the pun," I said. "Someone here drank and killed the president's husband recently, didn't they?"

Charles nodded. "There is a deceiver among you, and the time has come to strike. Watch yourself. I know a little of their plans, but the worst is yet to come."

"What about the president? Is she still alive?"

A knock sounded on the door, and the ghosts vanished. "Olivia, sorry to disturb you. May I come in?"

It was Dante, so I nodded. "Of course. Couldn't sleep, anyway."

When the door opened, I noticed the soldiers by his side. "I'm sorry to do this to you, but the general wants to search the house. He's afraid the saboteur has planted something."

"Like what?" I asked, worried.

Dante shrugged. "We don't know. The king thinks he's

being paranoid, but I believe it's better to be safe than sorry, especially after the note last night and the library incident. He wants you, Vanessa, the Ambassador, and Russell to wait outside until he's finished so you don't get in the way."

I rose from my bed, nodding. "All right, I'll go with you. I hope nothing's wrong."

As I walked downstairs with Dante, I followed him out the door. Mom, Russell, and Vanessa were already waiting on the lawn. Dante stood with us as the general and his soldiers searched the house. After ten minutes, General Ezra walked outside.

"We found nothing," General Ezra said. "Sorry to intrude, but I take security precautions seriously. It's safe to go back inside now."

"It's all right, General," Mom said. "Thank you for looking out for us."

He nodded, turning to Dante. "As for you, you know today's a holiday. The library is off-limits. You had no right to take Olivia there."

Dante sighed. "I know, General, and I'm sorry—"

"It was my fault," I said. "I remember now. I forced Dante into it."

"Why am I not surprised? I'll be lenient this time, but not the next," the general said, turning to his soldiers. "Come on, we need to assist with the preparations for the party. I've grown tired of this saboteur slipping by us. I intend to catch them if they try anything tonight."

As he walked away, I thought back to what the ghosts said. *The time has come to strike.* They couldn't have been talking about the party, could they?

29

THE BACKSTABBER STRIKES

When I went back up to my room, I tried to sleep a little, but I couldn't. Not after what happened with Christian. I tossed and turned until it was dinnertime, then went downstairs to eat with Vanessa, Mom, Russell, and Dante. After we finished, we all went back upstairs to get dressed for the party.

A knock came at my door before it opened, revealing Vanessa holding a long red gown. She wore a pink mini-dress with white high heels. "I think this would look great on you. Christian won't be able to keep his hands off you, you know."

If only she knew I didn't have feelings for Christian anymore. How could I when he had lied to me and tried to erase my memory? Dante hadn't done anything like that, but he *had* agreed to the secrecy. None of them had the decency to tell us they were vampires.

"Thanks," I muttered, reaching for it. "I'll put it on."

"Are you okay? You sound upset," Vanessa said. "Did your memory come back?"

I sighed. "I never lost it."

She frowned. "What? But you told—"

"I know what I said to Christian. That's what he needs to believe," I said. "Trust me. What's going on in this kingdom is way worse than you think, Ness."

She was about to question me when another knock sounded on the door. Those rough knocks could only belong to Dante. "We're leaving in ten minutes."

"I should get dressed," I said, turning my back to her. "I'll meet you downstairs."

After she had left, I quickly put the dress on and brushed my hair. I made sure to take a purse big enough to fit the dictionary inside. I wasn't sure if I would be able to sneak away from the party to get into the crypts, but if I had an opportunity, I planned to take it.

As I turned toward the door, I realized I'd almost left without my dagger. In light of everything, I never wanted to leave without it again. I walked over to my bed and checked under my pillow where I'd put it, but it was gone.

"No, no, no," I muttered. "I know I left it here..."

As I tore up my room in search of it, someone roughly knocked on the door again. "Olivia, we're leaving now. Are you coming?"

"Dante, get in here," I said. "We have an emergency."

The door opened quickly as Dante rushed inside. "What's wrong? Are you all right?"

"My dagger's missing," I said, turning to him. "I left it under my pillow, and now it's vanished. I know I didn't lose it. I was careful with it!"

"I'll help you look," Dante said, but I stopped him.

"Don't bother. I already did," I said. "It's gone."

"Then someone stole it," he said. "But who? And when?

You had it with you this morning when we went to the library, right?"

I nodded. "Yeah, I did. I remember putting it under my pillow when we got back, and...there's only one explanation."

He raised an eyebrow. "What?"

"The general and his soldiers were just here, searching the house. They even had us step outside," I said. "Maybe one of them took it."

"But why?" Dante asked. "They know the king wanted you to have it. No one questioned that order. The General didn't approve at first, but he came around."

I sighed. "Well, it disappeared right after they came inside the house. Can't be a coincidence."

Dante shook his head. "We can't go accusing anyone in the militia. The general trusts all his soldiers. He wouldn't appreciate us pointing the finger at them."

"What should I do in the meantime?"

"There's nothing we can do. We'll just have to hope whoever has it returns it soon or gets sloppy and leaves it behind."

"I'm really sorry, Dante. I didn't mean to lose it."

"I know you didn't. This wasn't your fault," Dante said. "That Slayer dagger is one of a kind, *and* deadly. King Dominic won't be happy to hear it's missing..."

I thought about that for a second. Why would King Dominic want me to have a weapon that could kill vampires? His own people? Was it because he feared I or someone else might have to use it? That his kind might attack me and my family? Maybe he was looking out for us after all.

"Come on. I'm still your bodyguard," Dante said, "and I intend to keep you safe with or without it."

Safe? No human was safe in the kingdom. Not with vampires hanging around.

As we walked down the stairs, Mom, Vanessa, and Russell were waiting for us. Mom looked gorgeous in a violet dress, but Russell's change of apparel into a suit shocked me. I'd never seen him out of his regular clothes.

"Wow, Russell," I said. "You look like a million bucks."

"You really think so?" he asked hesitantly, looking down at his suit. "King Dominic sent it over. He wanted me to look the part tonight."

"You look very handsome," Mom said. "I'm only disappointed you took this long to wear a suit in front of us."

Russell blushed and cleared his throat. "Yes, well...thank you. It's getting late, so we should probably get going."

Vanessa smiled at me, and I knew what she was thinking, that she wanted Russell and my mother to end up together as badly as I did. But then her smile faded to a frown as she stared at me. She knew something was bothering me, but I couldn't tell her the truth, not until I had all the answers.

As we left the Lodge, I felt bare without my dagger. Dante's reassurance didn't make me feel better. I thought about who could've taken it as we walked down the brick path, pushing through the well-dressed crowd.

When we reached the castle, I noticed more security on patrol. They greeted everyone before we came in and even searched our purses and bags for weapons. The general watched everyone carefully. When we had permission to enter, Mom turned to Dante.

"Does the general anticipate trouble?" she asked.

"Not at all," Dante said. "The general just wants to be extra careful. There's nothing wrong with that."

We followed the people to the throne room where the party had already started. Some were singing and clapping, others dancing and mingling. Mom immediately got pulled into a conversation with some of the richer, upper-class people. Russell stayed with her as Vanessa and I went to the buffet, but not before Dante insisted on trying our food first. It wasn't poisoned, much to our relief.

As I ate some of the salad, I looked at the line of thrones near the front of the room. Christian and Queen Vivienne were sitting there, but King Dominic was missing. I found it odd.

"Where's King Dominic?" I asked Dante.

He frowned. "I don't know. Perhaps he's still getting ready."

I scanned the crowd. "The king's not the only one missing. I don't see the general in here, either."

"I'm sure he's still by the front doors, watching everyone," Dante said. "Don't worry, you'll see them both soon enough."

"So, what are we supposed to be celebrating tonight, anyway?" Vanessa asked. "I can't keep up with all these parties."

"It's to commemorate our kingdom's anniversary," Dante said. "It's been a hundred and eighty years of life on the island. It's a time where we reflect on our past and look to the future."

The future. And what did King Dominic and his people want that to be? A vampire revolution? One where they take over the world? Or did he seriously think there could be peace?

Russell walked over, grabbing two drinks. "I offered to

bring your mother back some refreshments. I had to get away from all that ambassador talk for a minute."

"You should ask her to dance," I said. "The other couples are."

Russell shook his head. "Oh, I couldn't do that..."

"You never know if you never ask," Vanessa said, smirking.

Russell smoothed down his tux. "All right, but if she says no, I'm never listening to you two again."

We watched as he walked over to Mom, tapping her shoulder. She excused herself from the people she was talking to and turned to Russell, confused. We couldn't hear what he said to her, but when he held out his hand, she smiled and took it.

"We did it," Vanessa said, grinning at me. "I'm not the only one who's good at playing matchmaker."

As I sipped my drink, someone cleared their throat behind me. When I turned around, it was Christian. "Sorry to interrupt, Olivia, but may I have this dance?"

When he held out his hand, I felt like I had no choice. "Of course."

I glanced back at Dante who seemed less than thrilled but didn't stop us. Christian led me out to the dance floor, and we swayed next to Mom and Russell and the other dancers. Russell winked at me as I laughed and turned back to Christian.

"You look like you're in a good mood," he said. "How are you feeling?"

"My memories are still a little hazy," I lied, "but I'm okay."

"Glad to hear it. Since you don't remember much, I was

thinking we could start over," he said. "Not sure if you recall, but our first date was a disaster thanks to Dante. I was hoping I could steal you away to—"

Queen Vivienne walked over to us. "I need to speak with Olivia in private, my son."

Christian frowned. "We're dancing, Mother."

"It's important. Go mingle," she said. "Now."

Christian sighed, turning to me. "Thank you for the dance, Olivia. We'll talk later."

After he walked away, Queen Vivienne nodded at a secluded part of the throne room. "Come, let's speak away from the crowd."

When we were far enough away, I turned to her. "What's going on?"

"I wanted to ask you if you're any closer to finding out who's responsible for the kingdom's sabotage," she said. "I hear there was an incident in the library yesterday?"

I didn't know how to tell her it was her own son, so I just nodded. "Yeah, I passed out. I don't remember what happened, but I haven't found out anything else. What's going on with the Isolationists?"

"We've stopped sending threatening letters as you requested," she said. "We have no desire to see you, or your loved ones hurt. If I discover anything, I'll let you know, and I hope you'll do the same."

"Deal."

"Good. Now, if you'll excuse me, I need to find my husband," she said. "He told me to go ahead while he got ready, but now I'm worried. It isn't like him to be gone this long."

After she walked away, I turned around and nearly

crashed into Dante. "I saw you speaking with Queen Vivienne. Everything all right?"

"Other than you giving me a heart attack?" I asked. "Yeah, I'm fine."

"My apologies," he said. "I just wanted to keep an eye on you."

Behind him, I watched as the Sanguine twins pushed through the crowd. It looked like they were leaving. I noticed the expressions on their faces, one of horror and uneasiness. I immediately had a bad feeling.

"Dante, can I get some fresh air outside?"

He hesitated. "We really should stay within the throne room—"

"Please," I said. "Just five minutes."

He sighed. "All right. I left Vanessa with Russell and your mother, so she should be safe in the meantime. Follow me."

As we took the back exit into the garden, I didn't see the Sanguine twins anywhere. Where had they gone? And why had they looked so strange? When I felt the outline of my purse, remembering the dictionary was still inside, I pushed the thought of them aside and focused on my plan.

"Feeling better?" Dante asked.

"A little," I said. "Dante...I need to ask another favor."

"What kind of favor?"

"One where we break into the crypts again," I said. "We could do it right now. No one would notice."

He looked over his shoulder, then turned back to me. "Olivia, if anyone sees us, we'd both get in trouble. We weren't supposed to be there the last time. What could you possibly hope to find down there now?"

"Well, it's about Bloodspeak—"

I stopped talking when I heard footsteps approaching. Dante pulled me behind him as three shadow figures emerged from the darkness. My mouth fell open in shock as I recognized them as Alma Florentine and Mikhail and Roscoe Zev.

"And here we thought we'd have to work to get you away from the crowd," Alma said. "Thanks for making it easy for us."

I frowned. "What are you talking about?"

"Boss wants everything to go according to plan," Roscoe said. "And we always listen to the boss."

Dante's grip tightened on me as he glared at them. "I don't know who you are, but I want you to leave us alone. Now."

"It's Instinct, Dante," I whispered. "They're the ones who took my blood after I fell down the hole."

Dante growled. "You're lucky you're still standing, Instinct. The king was clear. No violence against outsiders."

"We don't follow the king," Mikhail said. "Our allegiance is to Instinct, to embracing who we truly are."

"You're talking about being vampires," I said.

Dante frowned at me. "How did you—"

"She's smart," Mikhail said, then nodded at Alma and Roscoe. "Too smart. Get him!"

In the blink of an eye, the three of them pounced onto Dante and began punching and kicking. I screamed and tried to intervene, but Mikhail flung me away, sending me crashing into the castle wall with a groan. If I had my Slayer, I could've stopped them and saved Dante.

When I recovered, the three pulled away. I looked down at Dante and gasped, noticing how bloody and beaten he was. I glared at them. "What was the point of that?"

"Don't worry. It'll all make sense soon enough," Alma said. "We weren't trying to kill him."

"Are you going to attack me, too?"

Mikhail shook his head. "No, we just needed to get Dante. This way, you don't have an alibi. What our boss has in store for you is much, much worse."

As they sprinted away into the darkness, I leaned beside Dante. "Can you hear me?"

His breathing was labored, but he nodded. "Get...inside. It's...safer in there. Warn them about Instinct before it's too late..."

And then he fell unconscious. I stood up, his blood on my red dress as the back door to the castle opened. A soldier stepped out and I rushed over to him. "Please! You have to help. Dante's been beaten—"

The soldier sneered. "You've certainly been busy tonight, haven't you?"

"What are you talking about?" I asked.

He grabbed my wrists, tying a rope around them. "The general's placing you under arrest. We've been looking all over the castle for you."

I scoffed. "Under arrest? What for?"

"The murder of King Dominic."

I gasped. "He's...dead?"

The soldier sneered. "Don't pretend like you don't know. The general warned us you'd act innocent."

"It's not an act. I didn't kill him!"

The soldier rolled his eyes, pulling me along. "Uh-huh. We'll let the evidence determine that. Anastasia's analyzing it now."

"Wait! What about Dante?"

"I'll get Dr. Draven to come for him," the soldier replied. "As for now, you should be more concerned about *your* fate."

As the soldier pulled me back into the throne room, the music and dancing had stopped. Everyone turned and looked at me, gasping and murmuring. Mom, Russell, and Vanessa rushed over, but the soldier wouldn't let them get too close.

"Olivia, what's going on?" Mom asked.

"I don't know," I said. "But I didn't do anything. I swear!"

When the soldier pushing me along spotted Dr. Draven, he turned to her. "Olivia hurt someone else, doctor, your son. He's bleeding out in the garden."

"You think *I* beat him?" I asked. "It was Instinct. They ambushed us out there. Besides, do you really think I could overpower Dante? He's more than a foot taller than me!"

"Dante's been training you, hasn't he?" the soldier asked. "I think anything's possible with an outsider."

"If my son dies, you'll live to regret it, Olivia," Dr. Draven said, angrier than I'd ever seen her. Then she rushed out the door to find Dante.

I hoped Dante lived. Not only because I cared about him, but because he had to wake up and tell everyone about Instinct. It was clear they weren't going to believe me. The soldier pulled me through the throne room into King Dominic's office.

I found him slumped over his chair, a dagger in his back. But it wasn't any regular dagger, it was mine, the Slayer. Christian stood nearby, comforting a crying Queen Vivienne as General Ezra barked orders at his soldiers.

"Get the body out of here and burn it," General Ezra said.

"Last thing our people need is seeing their king turning into a Dark Half."

"Here she is," the soldier escorting me said. "I found the murderer."

General Ezra stepped forward, shaking his head. "I always knew you were trouble, Olivia. I didn't think you'd commit murder, but as I've been telling my people, outsiders are capable of anything. They can't be trusted."

"This is insane," I said. "First of all, what's my motive for killing King Dominic? I liked him. Christian, please. Tell them they're wrong!"

"I want to believe you, Olivia," he said. "But you were missing when my mother found him dead."

I rolled my eyes. "I stepped outside for some air. The Sanguine twins did, too. I don't hear you accusing them!"

"It wasn't their dagger we found in the king's back," General Ezra said. "This is your Slayer, isn't it?"

I nodded. "Yes, but it went missing earlier. Right after you searched my house, actually."

He sneered. "How convenient, and now you try to shift the blame. I suppose we'll only know the truth after Anastasia finishes analyzing the evidence."

"What evidence? I didn't kill King Dominic. You won't find anything—"

A soldier poked their head into the office. "General? Anastasia has the results."

"Take Olivia with us," General Ezra said. "I'm eager to hear this."

The soldier dragged me to the clinic as General Ezra, Queen Vivienne, and Christian followed. Mom, Russell, and

Vanessa caught up, and soon, the whole kingdom crowded behind us.

As we entered the clinic, I noticed a badly-beaten Dante lying in one of the beds. Dr. Draven was treating him, but he was still unconscious. I wanted to go over to him, but the soldier forced me toward Anastasia at the workbench instead.

"Well?" General Ezra asked.

"We found the king's blood on it, which isn't a surprise," Anastasia said. "But we also found Olivia's blood on it, too. I'd say there was a struggle, and she got injured when the king fought back."

"Oh, come on!" I cried. "There was no struggle because I didn't kill him. Look, I don't have any wounds! My blood could've been on the dagger from training with Dante. That doesn't mean—"

I stopped talking when I realized the truth. Instinct had taken my blood and stolen my dagger. They must've had someone within the militia do it for them as they searched our house. It was all to frame me, but I didn't understand why yet.

"I'm convinced Olivia killed my brother," General Ezra said, "and I'm sure the kingdom will feel the same way in light of the evidence. Bring the prisoner to the castle's cells."

30
THE DEPARTURE

As the soldier dragged me back to the castle, the townspeople screamed insults at me. Murderer. Saboteur. Coward. They seemed convinced I had killed King Dominic and injured Dante. General Ezra egging them on only angered them further. Mom, Russell, and Vanessa followed, trying to argue my innocence.

"You can't do this!" Mom cried. "Olivia wouldn't kill anyone. And even criminals get an attorney and a fair trial. It's the law!"

"We don't care about your laws, outsider," one of the soldiers said. "Now step back."

"The hell I will!" Russell argued, but then a soldier punched him in the face, and he collapsed.

"Don't hurt them!" I yelled over my shoulder. "I'll go with you, just leave my family out of this!"

"We'll find a way to save you, Liv," Vanessa yelled. "Don't worry!"

As Mom and Vanessa helped Russell to his feet, they

disappeared from view as I entered the castle. The soldier brought me to a small cell down the hall from the king's office, threw me inside, and locked it behind me.

"You're lucky the Solitude burned down," he muttered. "We would've put you in there instead, and you wouldn't have lasted a day."

As I sat down on the small bench and sighed, still in my party dress, I realized what would happen to me now. If they executed me, I'd never find out who really killed King Dominic and sabotaged us. I still had my purse on me and the dictionary inside. It seemed I'd never know what was on the crypt wall, either, and what the ghosts were trying to tell me. Too bad they couldn't interfere and save me.

"General Ezra will be here soon," the soldier said. "He'll decide your fate. Until then, I'll stand guard and make sure you don't escape. You never know what an outsider's planning to do."

"Can I see my family at least?" I asked.

The soldier sneered. "Why should we show you any mercy? You didn't show it to King Dominic."

"What'll happen to my family? You won't hurt them, will you?"

"Not unless we discover they had a connection to the murder," the soldier said, turning back to look at me. "We'll probably eject them from the island."

"They won't leave without me!"

The soldier scoffed. "We won't give them a choice. General Ezra warned us letting outsiders come here wasn't a good idea, but King Dominic never listened. If only we'd realized how dangerous you are—"

The soldier suddenly cried out, then fell to the floor, unconscious. I took a step back in fear as footsteps approached. When two people stepped into the light, my mouth fell open.

"Petra and Nicolai?" I asked, confused. "What are you two doing here?"

Nicolai reached for the key off the soldier's body. "Isn't it obvious? We're rescuing you. And before you ask, we just knocked the guard out. We didn't kill him."

"But...why?"

"Because we know you didn't kill King Dominic. First off, we saw your face when General Ezra killed our parents. You were traumatized, and that's not exactly killer material," Petra said. "And we know who *did* kill the king."

When Nicolai unlocked my cell, I stepped over the unconscious guard. "Who?"

"General Ezra," Nicolai said. "We saw him sneak up behind the king and stab him with your dagger. Then he went back to the party like nothing happened and waited for someone to find the body."

"I should've realized it..." I said, trailing off. "He's the boss Instinct keeps talking about. General Ezra stole my dagger when he searched my house earlier, then took my blood from Instinct and left it on the dagger. Since he's the general, no one would've questioned him for sneaking around the castle. I bet he's behind all the sabotage, too. He was there every time something bad happened."

Nicolai nodded. "We were following General Ezra around tonight, hoping to get him alone. We wanted to kill him for murdering our parents. But when we saw him kill the king, we figured something big was about to go down and got out of there."

"That's why you two looked so freaked out at the party. I wish you'd done it," I muttered. "Maybe then King Dominic would still be alive, and I wouldn't be in this mess. Why would he kill the king, his own brother?"

Petra rolled her eyes. "Don't you get it? The general's framing you to prove to our people that outsiders can't be trusted. That you're our enemy. It was his plan all along, I'm sure. He knew he couldn't control the kingdom and wage war against the outsiders with King Dominic still alive."

"I know you're all vampires. Does this have something to do with that?"

"Took you look enough," Petra muttered. "And yeah, it does. General Ezra thinks we should hunt and kill your people, just like we used to in the old days. That's Instinct's whole thing. The general's outside right now, trying to convince all our people of that. He wants us to leave the island, meet up with Instinct members over in Europe, and take over the world. Something about birthright bullshit."

"We have to stop him and warn the world," I said. "But first, I need to do something. We need to get my family and head into the crypts."

Nicolai scoffed. "What you *need* is to get off this island before General Ezra drinks your blood."

"And I will," I said, "but the crypt is important. Trust me. I'll meet you in the garden."

"Fine," Petra huffed. "We'll get your family and bring them to you. But watch your back, all right?"

I smiled. "I will. You know...that almost sounded like you care about me."

"Don't push your luck," Nicolai said before he and Petra rushed outside.

I took the back door out of the castle, relieved to find no guards. The whole kingdom was too busy listening to General Ezra's speech. As I waited in the garden, I heard footsteps approaching and hid.

"Olivia?" a familiar voice asked. "Are you here?"

I popped out. "Dante! Are you okay?"

When I saw him, I realized how beaten he still looked. He nodded. "I'll be fine. My mother wanted me to rest, but I told her I couldn't. When she told me what happened, I knew I had to find you. I was coming to get you out of the cells, but it seems you found a way. How?"

"The Sanguine twins broke me out," I said. "Good timing. But you know the general could kill you for even talking to me. You're hurt enough as it is. Maybe it's safer if you don't get involved."

His gaze didn't waver. "I said I'd protect you, and I won't fail you now."

I blushed. "Did you tell them I wasn't responsible?"

"I tried," he said, "but they weren't convinced."

"General Ezra was counting on them not believing you. It was all his fault. He was planning this from the start with Instinct. It's why they jumped you," I said. "But Dante, I think there's something big hidden in the crypts."

Before I had a chance to explain my theory, several people turned around the corner. Dante reached for his sword, but I stopped him when I realized it was Mom, Vanessa, Russell, and the Sanguine twins.

"Wasn't easy sneaking away from the crowd," Petra said, "so I suggest you hurry up."

I nodded, turning to Dante. "Open the crypts."

"Why?" Vanessa asked.

"Yes, shouldn't we be trying to get you off this island instead?" Dante asked.

I pulled out the Bloodspeak dictionary. "It's important we do this. You'll see."

After Dante pulled the lever, revealing the staircase, he handed me the Slayer. "Here, I stole this from the clinic. I'm sure you'll want it back for protection. Olivia, I never meant to lie to you about what I am. The king demanded—"

"I know," I interrupted, taking the dagger from him, "and I'm not mad. Not anymore."

He finally smiled, one that was big and beautiful.

"What are you?" Mom asked.

"They're vampires, Mom. Those Dark Half creatures you saw? Those were their true form," I said. "It might seem crazy, but the truth was all there. We just didn't want to believe it. And King Dominic tried to hide it with their medicine."

Mom, Russell, and Vanessa looked at Dante and the Sanguine twins in horror. Vanessa knew half the truth, but we'd kept Mom and Russell in the dark.

"We trusted you," Mom said to Dante. "I let you around my daughter. Little did I know how evil you really are!"

"They're not all bad," I said, glancing at Dante and the Sanguine twins. "We can talk about this later."

As we went down into the crypts, Dante closed the passage behind us. We were safe down there, for now. We followed Dante through the narrow corridors, making our way toward the crypt door. After he opened it, I rushed over to the wall with the symbols.

"This was written in ancient Bloodspeak, the kind that's

not taught in school," I said. "Someone put this here for a reason. I think it's a secret message."

"Well, what does it say?" Russell asked.

It took me a few minutes to make the ancient translation, but when I did, I looked up in shock. "It reads...Instinct Only. It must be a door!"

"Then it leads somewhere," Mom said. "But where? What could the group that took your blood be hiding?"

"We have to get inside," I said, feeling the wall. "There must be a way—"

The Sanguine twins pushed me out of the way, then kicked down the wall. Dust and rock sprayed around us until it revealed a snug entrance that we could squeeze through. It was dark and cramped but clearly hid something serious.

"That saved us time," Petra said. "You're welcome."

I nodded. "Thanks. Come on, let's see what Instinct doesn't want anyone to find."

As soon as we walked through, a dark, evil feeling consumed me. Dante caught me before I could fall. When we heard muffled cries, I realized why.

President Janet Bennett sat tied up against one of the walls, her mouth taped. There were bags under her eyes, her skin was pale, and it looked like she hadn't slept in a long time. Much like the ghosts I had seen, I found blood and bite marks on her neck.

"Mom!" Vanessa cried, rushing over to her. "Oh my God...what happened?"

After she tugged the tape off her mouth and removed the chains, she helped hold President Bennett up while she explained the situation. "Our boat arrived early one night. Then a few soldiers came to greet us..."

I realized then I *had* seen a boat arrive that night, and it was the president. General Ezra tried to make me sound crazy, but he knew all along. He was probably waiting in his office for his soldiers to report back. If only I'd decoded the message earlier...

"They brought us down here and hid our boat," she said. "Since then, they've been drinking from me slowly and keeping me alive for future feeds. It feels like I've been down here forever. God, I'm so weak..."

"They're vampires, Janet, and don't worry, we'll find a way off this island and get you to a doctor," Mom said. "Who else came with you?"

"They're all dead," she muttered. "All the bodyguards I brought. Even..."

"Even your husband," I said.

Tears welled in Vanessa's eyes. "What are you talking about? Dad can't be dead!"

"They kept me alive since I was more valuable, but they were planning to drink me to death, too. Feeding off people is different from turning them into vampires, which they said they were careful not to do," she replied. "They drank the others and stored their bodies in the next room as trophies. Your father came with me, and I...I couldn't protect him..."

Vanessa rushed off into the other room, and a moment later, I heard her cry out. When I followed her, I saw her father's dead body. Others were there, too. All of them ghosts now. They'd made sure not to turn them into Dark Half's.

"This is Instinct's fault," Dante said. "This is what they want. Why they're so dangerous. We have to get you off the island before—"

"I knew you'd find our victims soon enough," General

Ezra said, approaching behind us. He had several soldiers, Alma Florentine, and Roscoe and Mikhail Zev with him. "Bravo."

"Why, General?" I asked.

"My brother was a delusional fool who thought vampires could live with humans again. He thought if we took our medicine and resisted our natural urges, everything would be all right," General Ezra spat. "But he's wrong. We were made to drink and kill. I knew he'd never listen to me, so I had to kill him. He's kept us on this island for too long. Deprived us of too many worldly pleasures."

Dante looked at the soldiers, sneering. "Is the entire militia involved, too?"

The general nodded. "Yes, and so are the kids I was training. We've even kidnapped Dr. Cox to have him develop a vaccine that gives us our minds back in our Dark Half forms. I wanted to include you, Dante, but then you swore that pathetic vow to Olivia. I knew you cared for her too much to join Instinct."

"Even if I hadn't met her, I'd never help you," Dante snarled. "Killing and drinking is evil, and we're better than that. We've evolved."

The General laughed. "No, we haven't. Even you struggled to control your urges. At one point, you wanted to drink Olivia's blood and had me punish you for it."

"Because I knew it was wrong," he said. "Vampires aren't perfect, but if we try, we don't have to be savages. The medicine's a good starting point."

"Now you sound like King Dominic," the General muttered, shaking his head. "Everything I did, bombing the boat and statue, the poison, was to give you a preview of what's to come. We've missed so much in the real world, and now we're taking it back."

"What happens now?" I asked.

"I contact my Instinct friends over in Europe. The ones who didn't move here centuries ago like the king wanted," the general said, "and we get off this damn island and reclaim what we lost. But the people can't know I killed the king. They'd never listen to me if they did. Prince Christian and Queen Vivienne still think you're guilty, and that's the way it'll stay. You all know the truth, and you must die for it so we can conquer the world."

"Finally," Alma said, "more humans to drink from. The others just weren't enough."

Vanessa scowled. "You'll pay for killing my father, you vampire bitch!"

Alma laughed. "Oh, yeah? There's no escape—"

Dante lifted his sword, slashing it at the rocks above our heads. When the crypts foundation began to collapse, he pushed us forward. "Go, I'll cover you. Get to the docks!"

The Sanguine twins nodded, pulling out their weapons. "Us, too. It's time for payback."

I hesitated. "But Dante—"

"Now!" he growled.

Russell grabbed us, forcing us along as Dante and the Sanguine twins fought off General Ezra and Instinct. We ran through the passage until we made it back and opened the staircase, fleeing the crypts. When we spotted those kids Dante had trained, including the one boy who had stabbed me, we quickened our pace. They looked frightening as they strolled across the field toward us.

"We're almost there, Mom," Vanessa muttered, noticing

how weak she looked. She and Russell continued pulling her along. "I can't believe we left Dad back there…"

"We had no choice," I said. "He was dead, Ness, there was nothing we could do for him."

When we reached the docks, the entire town was chasing after us to kill us, Russell looked around. "How the hell are we getting off this island? We're missing an important part of our escape plan, a damn boat!"

"The general hid our boat somewhere within the docks," President Bennett said. "If we could only find the mechanism that opens the secret compartment—"

The president stopped speaking once we noticed a ship approaching through the fog.

"Is that the boat belonging to those Instinct contacts the general was talking about?" I asked.

Vanessa squinted, looking closer. "No…I think they're human!"

When the boat docked, I realized Vanessa was right. They *were* human and wore American flag pins. They looked like bodyguards. There were other people onboard with dark outfits and similar daggers to mine. One of them, a handsome boy around our age with blond hair and green eyes, looked at us in surprise.

"President Bennett, Ambassador Hawthorne!" one of the bodyguards said. "When we hadn't made contact with either of you, we feared the worst and sent a boat. We apologize it took this long, but some people from England insisted we pick them up first and bring them along."

"Good timing," Mom said. "All the people here are—"

"Vampires," the green-eyed boy answered in a British accent. "We know. We informed the United States government of that nasty little truth when the president was reported missing."

"Who are you?" Russell asked.

"We call ourselves the Assembly. We've been hunting vampires for a long time from our headquarters in Europe," the boy said. "My name's Jason Mears. Sorry to make your acquaintance like this."

"If you knew already, why didn't you warn the world about vampires?" Mom asked. "About the kingdom of V?"

"Can you imagine if we did? People would've lost their minds," Jason replied. "And secondly, we didn't know about the kingdom of V until recently. Before that, we assumed vampires were scattered in our world until we captured a vamp, one from Instinct in England. We tortured them into a confession. Apparently, they've been working with some important general of V and sending him secret human victims for years. Right under our noses, too, the bloody bastards!"

"You can explain more later," Russell said, pointing over his shoulder. "The entire kingdom wants us dead."

"Right then. Climb aboard," Jason said, making room for us. "Now that you know about vampires, we need to work out a plan. No doubt they're already plotting world domination."

We helped the president onto the boat first, then the rest of us climbed on. Jason gestured at my dagger. "Where'd you get that?"

"King Dominic gave it to me," I said. "He was a good vampire. I think he wanted me to have it in case of an attack like this."

"There are *no* good vampires, love," Jason replied, turning to the sea captain. "Get us out of here!"

When a figure approached our boat, limping and bleeding, I held up my hand. "Wait!"

Dante panted, catching up with us. "Olivia, you made it. I'm glad."

"What happened back there?" I asked.

"We fought, then the crypts caved in. Some of the soldiers died, but I think General Ezra and the Instinct vamps who took you escaped," Dante replied, wiping blood off his face. "Too bad."

"And the Sanguine twins?"

"They're fine. They're helping me form a revolution to stop the general," Dante said. "We don't know how much traction we'll make, but we have to try. I also ran into Prince Christian and quickly told him the truth."

"What did he say?"

"He's sorry he doubted you," he replied, "and he still cares. He and Queen Vivienne are going to play along with the general's plans but work for us in secret. It might be the only way to win this war."

"What'll happen to you? To all the vampires who oppose the general?"

"I don't think he'll kill us. He's trying to promote unity among the vampires, and it'd look bad," Dante replied. "But I'm sure he has a plan for us. He always does."

"You could come with us," I said. "There's room on the boat."

He shook his head. "I can't. Your people would never accept me. Besides, I need to stay here and fight. I won't let Instinct define our people. But before I forget..."

He handed me the bear he had bought me, Miss Glitter. "Dante...you went back for this?"

He nodded. "Something to remember me by. We'll see each other again, Olivia. I believe that."

And then he sprinted away, holding the crowd back from reaching the docks. I noticed Prince Christian and Queen Vivienne among the people, looking concerned for us.

"Go!" Jason yelled at the captain.

I felt seasick again as the boat sped away, but I took a deep breath and forced it down. I was leaving the kingdom of V forever, and that was enough to put a smile on my face. We had made it.

Jason glanced at me, almost disapprovingly. "You keep interesting company. Friends with a vampire?"

"You don't know everything about them," I said, clutching Miss Glitter to my chest.

He laughed. "Oh, no? You should see the body counts in Europe, love. Hasn't been easy covering it up from the media. And there's been a lot of vamp movement lately. Something big's coming. I'd bet this general git is behind it."

As the boat traveled further from the island, the people became smaller in the distance behind us. I watched the ghosts hover above them, Vanessa's father included, but no one else could see them but me. I wondered what would happen to them now and how I gained the gift of speaking to spirits.

Jason gestured at the dagger in my hands. "With the war coming, we could use more recruits. You've already got a weapon and look like you know how to fight. This way, you'll get to see up close and personal what those vamps you call friends have been doing to our people. What do you say?"

I didn't like the idea of killing anything, but when I looked at the president's beaten face and what the general had done to Vanessa's father, I wanted revenge.

I nodded. "I'm in."

He grinned. "Then welcome to the Assembly. The battle for Earth starts now."

THANK YOU FOR READING

Did you enjoy this book?

We invite you to leave a review at the website of your choice, such as Goodreads, Amazon, Barnes & Noble, etc.

DID YOU KNOW THAT LEAVING A REVIEW...

- Helps other readers find books they may enjoy.
- Gives you a chance to let your voice be heard.
- Gives authors recognition for their hard work.
- Doesn't have to be long. A sentence or two about why you liked the book will do.

ABOUT THE AUTHOR

Dana Gricken is a multi-genre author from Ottawa, Canada, writing stories since she was old enough to hold a pencil. She has been published in fantasy before with *The Dragonwitch Chronicles*  and *The Soulless War Trilogy* and has more books coming out in 2024 and beyond like the *Jessica Prince Mysteries* series.

In her spare time, she enjoys reading, playing video games, mailing letters to friends, spreading kindness, educating about mental health struggles, and watching *Star Trek* with her cats. She hopes her books bring joy and make people feel less alone. She wants to write over a hundred novels in her lifetime.

You can connect with her @DanaGricken on all social media or her website:

danagricken.com

 facebook.com/dana.gricken.7
 x.com/DanaGricken
 instagram.com/danagricken